THE DAUGHTER
OF THE DOCTOR
AND THE SAINT

Other books by Edward Swift

NOVELS

Splendora
Principia Martindale
A Place with Promise
The Christopher Park Regulars
Mother of Pearl
Miss Spellbinder's Point of View

NONFICTION

My Grandfather's Finger

FORTHCOMING BOOKS

Walking on Glory
Dreaming on a Burning Bed

THE DAUGHTER
OF THE DOCTOR
AND THE SAINT

a novel by

Edward Swift

Ravenhill Press
San Miguel de Allende
2011

Library of Congress Cataloging in Publication Data

Swift, Edward, 1943
The Daughter of the Doctor and the Saint
ISBN 978-0-615-35846-8

To the memory of my cousin

Dana Pullen

who gave me the threads to weave this story

In the city of Guanajuato there is a museum, La Alhóndiga de Granaditas, which celebrates Mexico's cultural and political history. On one of the walls you will find a poem by an indigenous poet whose name has long been forgotten.

Sólo venimos a dormir.
Sólo venimos a soñar.
No es verdad,
No es verdad,
Que venimos a vivir en la tierra.

PART I

On the Street of Merchants and Peddlers

On the day the president came to lunch Señora Josefina Esperon arose before dawn. She was eighty-two years old. Her country was celebrating two hundred years of independence, and she was determined to make the occasion a memorable one for herself as well as the nation. Wrapped in a black kimono that smelled faintly of camphor, she sat on her balcony overlooking the Street of Merchants and Peddlers, and in the first hour of dawn she bleached her face with rice powder. Before the air was too heavy to breathe, she rouged her cheeks and lips, drew black lines around her eyes, and while the capital city, which she hardly recognized anymore, slumbered in tropical heat, she smoked one filterless cigarette.

"Smoking aids the circulation," she said to her servant who was making the bed. But the old servant, who was called Contenta and whose real name was long forgotten, had spent fifty-seven years in that house, and she knew beyond a doubt that there was nothing wrong with the Señora's circulation, it was her nerves.

"At your age you should know better than to invite the president of the country to lunch," Contenta said. "What were you thinking? How many times have I told you, there isn't any food in the house?"

"All you think of is food," Señora Esperon replied. "Food is the least of our worries, especially today."

"All I think of is God," said Contenta. She fingered the many rosaries draped around her neck, wrapped around her wrists and ankles. "God will come to our aid, surely."

"As surely as not," replied Señora Esperon.

Allowing her thoughts to drift with the smoke that disappeared into the yellow sky, she gazed over tile rooftops to the remains of the harbor where her parents had arrived in the year 1901. So long ago, she thought and so many changes, almost none for the better. The capital city was once a bustling port, a gateway into a new world, where tall ships from Spain, Portugal, and Italy unloaded their cargo of wine, spices, and silks and returned with a bounty of new flavors and aromas. But after two hundred years of independence there were no ships in the harbor, no fishing boats docked to the rotting piers, and no passengers waiting for arrivals or departures. The crescent-shaped harbor had been diminished in size by the encroaching salt marsh and in place of the ships and fishing fleets, oil derricks stood like prehistoric skeletons facing the open sea where red algae floated like ribbons of blood.

"Today," she said, "the sea is the color of wine, and the sky is hiding behind sulfur smoke. Will there be a tomorrow?"

"There will always be a tomorrow," Contenta answered with assurance.

"How can you believe such a thing?" Señora Esperon replied in astonishment. On realizing what she had just said, and the various answers she was likely to receive, she quickly added, "Please don't respond to my question. Today I do not wish to cause myself unnecessary aggravation."

While Contenta swept the balcony, her rosaries jangled like raw nerves but Señora Esperon remained calm, even though she too was uncertain as to how the day would end.

"What are you thinking now, Señora?" Contenta asked.

"I am remembering what was and what may never be again," she said. Her eyes moved across the city veiled in smoke and yellow clouds. "At one time this was the most beautiful city in the Americas, a city of boulevards, palm trees, and gardens. A city with an opera house and a season, a national theatre, a museum, a symphony orchestra, and many poets. Oh, where are our beloved poets?"

"They are dead and buried, Señora," Contenta answered.

"Don't remind me," she cried. "What has happened to our city?"

Her eyes, which were once the color of water and sky, wandered over tile rooftops, into the amber colored clouds, and down to the red-streaked sea. This was the harbor of her birth, the capital city, her home, and she had never ventured beyond its boundaries. "I can imagine what is out there," she had always said. "So why go?"

On the corner of Independence Avenue and the Street of Merchants and Peddlers she had lived in a house of forty-three rooms, four balconies, and two courtyards for her entire life, a life that now seemed too long and circuitous but not without a certain order. Both of her parents were buried in the larger of the two courtyards, and she would be buried there also; she had chosen her day, just as her mother had chosen hers, and she would not change her mind when the final hour arrived. She would not turn back; she promised herself this, because now, crippled with arthritis and burdened with the upkeep of such a house, there was nothing to turn back to and no one to turn back for. And so she sat on her balcony and awaited the inevitable. While surrounded by exhaust fumes and descending clouds filled with grit, she smoked her cigarette slowly, and she thought of her mother, Eufemia Esperon y Blanco, immortalized in the minds of her countrymen. The dead poets had seen the ocean in her eyes and the sun bleached desert in her pale skin. They said that her hair was like obsidian and her cheeks and lips had been touched by the rainbow. From the day she had arrived in the capital until the day of her death, portrait painters had found their way to her door. They had gathered on the Street of Merchants and Peddlers to wait impatiently for one fleeting glimpse of the woman whose image they hoped to capture.

Like our poets, she was a citizen of another world, her daughter thought, as she faced a morning sky and the sulfur clouds. On a narrow tapestry so long it stretched three times around the large courtyard, her mother's life and death had been recorded, and on that auspicious day, the day the president was coming to lunch, the woven document would be displayed for the first time.

No, she was not of this earth, Josefina Esperon thought as clouds descended over the sea, the city of her birth and her house of two courtyards and forty-three rooms. The poets were right. She was of the sky and clouds. She belonged to the wind, not the water, not the soil, not even the mountains. And her death, although it was indeed marked with sadness, had not been a sad occasion, not as sad occasions go, for she had chosen her day, had stood before her open grave without fear, wondering aloud if her life had been a dream from which she had suddenly awakened. Had it been the life of another she had lived, or had it indeed been her own; and what was to follow the grave? "It is as if I've been away a long time," Eufemia had said to her daughter, who had already, celebrated her sixteenth year. "And now I have returned to something I cannot quite remember. Where is the ship that brought us here? Where is the harbor? The crinoline wings, the halo, and the star? What has happened to them? Where is my beautiful hair? My handsome doctor? My beloved saint? My Angel? Surely they are waiting for me somewhere."

"They are with you, Mother," her daughter said.

"Where is the day of my arrival?" Eufemia asked.

"Is it not today, Mother?"

"No. It was long ago, my daughter. Where have you been, and where is my Angel?"

Seventeen years before her celebrated death, Eufemia and her husband, Doctor Alejandro Esperon, had arrived in the capital city. It was the beginning of a new century, and the end of a long and tumultuous voyage. A dark cloud had followed them across the Atlantic Ocean, but on the last day of their crossing they sailed under a brilliant October sky into a crescent-shaped harbor of clear, green water. The port was filled with ships and music. The air was fragrant with many flowers, and the sea breeze was sweet and gentle; but the sun was too harsh on Eufemia's delicate skin so the captain of the ship presented her with a brimmed hat on which she fashioned a veil of sheer, white silk.

"This is a country of many villages and outposts," the captain told the couple shortly before they docked, "but there is only one city, and the people who live in it are very sly. In no time at all they will have you believing that this is the oldest port in the Americas. Oh, these braggarts, there is little they will not say or do. Are you sure this is the place for you, Doctor?"

"This was my first choice," Doctor Esperon said.

"Aside from the royalists you'll have the Indians to contend with," the captain continued. "If a stone can think, they can hear it thinking. They'll read your mind, Doctor. They'll tell you who you are even before you can decide for yourself. And what's more, they'll predict your future, if you let them."

"I'll predict my own future," Doctor Esperon replied. "I assure you Captain, we will be very happy here."

Relieved to be arriving, at last, Eufemia repeated her husband's words. "We will be very happy, Captain. I am sure of it. I can foresee the future as well."

For the doctor and his new bride the country represented a rare opportunity, a land waiting to be rediscovered all over again. It was his ambition to open wide the door between medicine and botany and to produce his own pharmaceuticals: tinctures, tablets, and tonics that would cure the ills of the new world, the old world, or any world for that matter. He had been offered three posts, one at home in Spain, one in the north, and one in the tropics. "The tropics," he had said, "there I can grow my plants while learning about new ones." In a small valise, he carried many packages of seeds and roots wrapped in cotton: *Digitalis purpurea*, for disorders of the heart and vital spirits, hawthorn for angina, milk thistle for ailments of the liver, and bilberry for broken veins. He carried calendula for the skin, *Lobelia inflata* for asthma, mullein for infections of the ear, and comfrey for diabetic ulcers, bites of spiders, and staph infections that he expected to encounter in the tropics. To fight tuberculosis, typhoid and scarlet fever, he carried rhizomes of *Coptis chinensis*, and for pain, sleep, and sedation: the seeds of *Papaver somniferum*, *Passiflora incarnata*, *Sanguinaria*, and *Valeriana officinalis*.

"Yes," he said, when the boat docked, "my plants will grow very well here."

At first glance the capital city appeared as the image of Paradise. It was resting on a marshy, coastal plain that climbed steadily from the blue-green ocean into rolling hills and then, cloud-covered mountains of astonishing heights. The streets, which ran parallel to the coastline were bordered with flame trees, with tamarind, jacaranda, and manchineel, while the avenues and boulevards, all heavily planted with palms, ran from the harbor to the French Park where a band shell, designed by a Parisian architect, was surrounded by towering cypresses crowned with bromeliads, orchids, and nesting egrets.

"Everything is blooming," Doctor Esperon exclaimed. "Even in October."

With his valise in one hand and two letters of introduction in the other, he led his wife across stately thoroughfares and down shady, cobbled streets in search of the Hotel Carmina where a suite of rooms had been reserved. "We must hurry," he said. "We are already a day late." His steps were quick and eager but hers were hesitant. The capital was a city of many churches, and she desired to enter each one she saw. "No," her husband said. "There will be much time for visiting churches. Right now we must find our hotel."

"You go ahead of me," she said. "I am very tired."

He rushed on, thinking she would follow close behind, but she did not hasten her steps, and at each corner he waited for her to catch up with him.

"I cannot walk any faster," she finally told him. "As you see I am carrying a load."

Under her long, white veil and white, flouncing skirts she moved slowly through the tropical heat, toward her husband who was dressed in black, and whose meticulously trimmed beard was beginning to show signs of neglect. Along the way she clung fiercely to her load: three orange trees from Andalucia, and a pet monkey her father had brought back from Africa. The orange trees, which measured half her height, had already lost their leaves as well as the damp cloth she had wrapped around their roots. Doctor Esperon was certain that the trees would never live and the monkey, cradled in his wife's arms, would never die. The monkey's name was Angel, and he was dressed in a lace gown with a pair of crinoline wings and a skull cap on which Señora Esperon had fastened a wire halo.

For a few moments she stopped at an open-air market to observe Indian women in heavily embroidered dresses. Some of them were weaving on back-strap looms, others were selling fruits, herbs, and vegetables, the likes of which Eufemia had never seen, and with names that were unknown to her: zapote, guayaba, and papaya, nopales, chayote, epazote, huazontle, mango, and the most enticing of all, mamey, arranged in pyramids, the topmost fruit sliced in half and left to bleed like a sacrificial heart in the open air.

An Indian woman with a bunch of onions balanced on her head pushed her way through the crowd. "My husband," Eufemia called, "here, at last, is something I recognize: onions."

"We have been expecting you for you a long time," said the woman with the onions. "Why did you keep us waiting?"

"Our crossing was very difficult," Eufemia replied.

Calling to her from the next street corner, the doctor urged her to hurry along, but by then she was surrounded by many Indian women who were staring into her ocean-blue eyes and touching her pale skin. "You have come to represent us," one of the women said, and Eufemia, replied: "I have come to represent God the Father, God the Son, and God the Holy Ghost."

"Your necklace," said the woman with the onions on her head, their greens trailing like ribbons down her back. "Your necklace for my onions."

Eufemia removed the crucifix from her neck and traded it for the bunch of onions, which she accepted as flowers. To her husband, who was still waiting for her on the next corner, she called out again, "These people are ready for a message, and I am ready to deliver it. I'm exactly where I need to be."

"And so am I," he said, "don't make us any later than we already are."

The Indian women hardly noticed the winged monkey clinging to Eufemia's neck. Instead, they were drawn to her fair skin, her watery eyes, and warm smile, all of which told them that she understood who they were and what they had endured. "You will never leave this place," said one of the women. "You will die three times. But you will never leave us."

Unclear as to what her response should be, Eufemia replied: "I believe in the Communion of Saints, the forgiveness of sins, the resurrection of the body, and the life everlasting. Amen."

Taking matters into his own hands, the doctor led his wife away from the curious women who followed them to the next street and would have followed them farther had he allowed it. "Go home," he said, waving his arms furiously. "Surely you have something better to do." With that, the women returned to their looms and their pyramids of fruit while Doctor Esperon guided his wife down a side street that ended at the central plaza where laurel trees had been given the shape of inverted bowls and each park bench bore the name of a poet. The tallest building on the plaza, indeed the tallest in the entire capital, was the Cathedral of Our Lady of the Sea, which occupied the eastern side of the square. Constructed over the remains of an ancient pyramid, the cathedral was conceived in the Romanesque style, but two centuries after construction had begun, a baroque facade was used to complete the structure.

"It is like the great cathedral at Santiago de Compostela," Eufemia exclaimed.

"Not exactly," the doctor replied.

"Yes," Eufemia argued. "Exactly."

Across the plaza from the cathedral was the Police Headquarters, a two-story building covered in decorative tiles, which was much too garish in color and far too close to Our Lady of the Sea to receive Eufemia's approval. The other two building were more to her liking. On the north side of the square, the National Palace, also adorned with a baroque facade, stared into the lace covered windows of the Hotel Carmina, which stood like a monument to simplicity in comparison to its neighbors. Eufemia approved of it without reservation.

The Carmina was known for elegant rooms, quiet atmosphere,

French cuisine, and many house rules stringently enforced. The management prohibited the wearing of sleeping costumes in public areas, the excessive use of cuspidors, the preparation of food by guests, and the playing of musical instruments except in the music room and only there between the p.m. hours of four and eight. The hotel took a strong position against gambling on premises, the use of invective, the blowing of one's nose in the dining room, the growing of plants and the keeping of pets, but when Eufemia Esperon glided across the lobby with her winged monkey, her bouquet of onions, and three orange trees, every house rule, fifty-three in all, was forgotten.

"Here we have an exception," the concierge announced to his assistants. He was rapidly removing a sign that prohibited the keeping of pets in the hotel, when Eufemia approached him.

"For shame," she said in a scolding voice. "Human beings often behave as animals, and you certainly allow them to overnight in your sanctuary, so why, then, will you not allow an animal who is in reality more human than the most human of beings?"

Her Castilian accent and lilting voice made the concierge tremble and stumble over his words. "Your pet is a welcomed addition to our hotel family," he said. The words dropped falteringly from his tongue for he had already fallen under the spell of the doctor's wife.

Relieved to hear those words spoken, Eufemia turned to her husband with assurance. "You see," she said. "The people here are very reasonable. We have come to the right place, after all. We have arrived, at last."

"At last," the doctor sighed.

Their arrival hardly seemed possible to either of them for they had endured a stormy crossing. The sea had been restless all the way. And many times the doctor had been certain that they would never live to see their new home. But once inside the Hotel Carmina the hardships of their crossing ceased to exist. At last they had safely arrived at their destination, and to Eufemia's great delight, there were many items on the hotel menu that appealed to her beloved Angel.

"When Angel dies he will surely go to Heaven," she told the hotel maids who were put in charge of changing his diapers and mopping the floor behind him, "because he is perfect in every way."

"Yes," the maids laughed, "he is practically a saint already."

Within a few days everyone in the Hotel Carmina was talking about the new doctor and his beautiful wife who loved a winged monkey more than she loved her husband. Oh, yes, Doctor Esperon thought, when he overheard someone saying this, I'm afraid it may be true.

The Hotel Carmina had welcomed many famous and beautiful women into its halls, among them: Pavlova, Bernhardt, and Langtry, along with Carlota Montejo, the nation's leading classical actress, who kept a suite of rooms facing the plaza. But never had the Carmina been so disrupted by a guest as it was by Eufemia Esperon. Her dark hair, light skin, and sea-blue eyes caused waiters to trip and fall in her presence. Desk clerks lost the ability to speak when she approached them, and high governmental officials stepped to one side and bowed when she crossed the lobby. Guests and hotel staff alike followed her through doorways and down corridors, into sitting rooms, dining rooms, and ballrooms just to have an opportunity to stand before her for one brief, speechless second, to listen with rapture to her melodious voice, to breathe with her, to offer her a hand, a chair, a glass of champagne, or to pet the monkey that accompanied her everywhere. "It has always been this way," the doctor told the concierge. "My wife's beauty poisons the heart. No one is safe in her presence."

The doctor himself was no exception. While still a medical student at the University in Salamanca, the first glimpse of his future wife had caused him to lose his heart to sickness and half a semester to drink before regaining his balance and academic discipline once again. On completing his hospital requirements, but still not quite on his feet, he married the lovely Eufemia Blanco in her family chapel. "A marriage made by the gods," their friends said, but within a very short time the handsome doctor suspected that the gods had led him astray.

On their wedding night Eufemia screamed at the first sight of her naked husband. "Are you man or animal?" she demanded to know.

"I'm your husband," he replied. And when he entered her she fainted in his arms.

The next morning, wracked with pain and deep bruises, she wept bitterly over her lost virginity, and for three days thereafter, she suffered chills, fever, and headaches so intense the Heavens opened up to her. She saw many worshipers with golden candlesticks and bare feet passing by her throne. She saw a courtyard filled with birds, flowers, and butterflies of every color. She saw a desperate street, a beautiful harbor, and a long cloth on which her name had been written many times.

On the third morning of her marriage, she heard a voice begging her to arise. "The journey on which I am sending you is an important one. You will be called upon to endure many trials leading to your Heavenly reward. You are my messenger, and I am your message." Hearing this, she came straightway out of bed and summoned her husband. "This is the day of our departure," she reminded him. "Why aren't you ready?"

"I have canceled our passage," he said. "We will wait until your health improves."

"There is nothing wrong with my health," she insisted. "We must leave at once. Where is my Angel?"

Two hours later, the doctor and his bride embarked upon the first leg of a long journey that would take them to the smallest country in the Americas. They had been told that medical doctors were desperately needed there, and in one week it would be possible to set up the kind of lucrative practice that would take years to establish in Spain. From Valencia they set sail; he with the desire to bring the latest medical discoveries to a new world; and she with a desperate longing to speak the word of God to people who might not otherwise have an opportunity to hear it.

On the first night of their voyage, when the doctor attempted to make love to his wife for the second time, Eufemia's screams of pain awakened the entire ship and gave the captain cause to worry for the safety of his favored passenger. A priest, who occupied a nearby cabin, was called into service, and by reciting the Twenty-third Psalm repeatedly, he was able to induce a deep sleep that lasted twenty-six hours, and was broken only by the sounds of a raging storm that followed them across the ocean.

"This voyage is a test of faith," Eufemia wrote in her journal. "Hail rains down upon our tiny ark, and the wind blows us off course, but our Blessed Mother appears in each dark cloud. And my Angel is with me. And my husband is dining alone. And we are far away."

On the fourth night of the voyage, Eufemia sacrificed her family jewels to calm the troubled sea. One after another she cast her necklaces into the water. "God does not wish me to love these priceless ornaments," she told her husband when he stopped her from throwing the last ruby necklace and diamond brooch into the waves. "These articles of vanity will please the Father who will deliver us from this storm. God does not wish me to live with riches."

"But your husband does," the doctor replied. He forced her back to their cabin where the smell of his cigars sickened her and caused Angel to vomit in her lap.

"This is our cabin," the doctor said. "You must stay here until the storm is over."

"My place is elsewhere," Eufemia argued. "I cannot stay here tonight."

"You have no choice," her husband told her.

After a light supper he called for a pot of tea into which he added tincture of *Datura stramonium* to settle her stomach and promote a restful sleep, but in the middle of the night when the drug wore off, Eufemia escaped to pace the deck and pray for deliverance. And so it was, night after night. Eufemia left their nuptial bed to make peace with the sea, and her husband followed her for fear that she would sacrifice herself to the high waves. Each night when he led her back to their cabin she begged him not to touch her, to allow her to sleep alone on a chair, on the floor, or even in the corridor outside their room.

"Why did you agree to marry me?" Doctor Esperon finally asked, and his wife answered: "Because I foolishly believed that you were created in the image of God, but now that I have seen you, I know that I was wrong."

After one week at sea, Eufemia confessed to her journal that the image of God was a deceiving one, and the human need for physical gratification had been greatly overestimated. On secretly reading the journal, the doctor discovered that his wife preferred sleeping with her dear Angel, who was much less trouble even when wretched by sea sickness. "My Angel," she wrote, "sees visions of our destiny. He stares for hours into the high waves, but his heart, like mine, does not beat with fear."

"I should have known all along," Doctor Esperon would one day confess to his only daughter, "that great beauty does not come without the price of a tragic flaw, and in your mother's case it was her overpowering desire to sleep with God."

Eufemia wore her piety like a priceless necklace for all to see, and upon arrival in the capital city, she let it be known that she was a disciple of Saint Teresa of Ávila. Although she had been born in Madrid, into lineage exceedingly high, on coming to the Americas she denounced her place of birth. Swelling with pride, she said that she had been born only a few steps from the birthplace of the woman whose love of God had made the town of Ávila famous.

"She will make our little nation and our tiny port equally famous," the hotel staff said. "Her beauty will be immortalized by our painters and poets."

One week after their arrival, and two days after assuming his post at the Hospital of the Sacred Heart, the doctor and his wife moved into a colonial house on the corner of Independence Avenue and the Street of Merchants and Peddlers. The house of two courtyards and forty-three rooms had been the nation's first convent, a refuge during the battle for independence. The Carmelite nuns had given food and shelter to the insurgents who were executed, along with the sisters, in the smaller of the two courtyards. After that the house passed into the hands of a city magistrate and had remained in the magistrate's family for five generations until Doctor Esperon bought it for his young bride and the many children he intended to sire. The decision to purchase such a large house had been his and his alone, and only after the papers had been signed did he escort his wife into their new home.

"There are four balconies, two courtyards, and a lotus pool already filled with goldfish," he told her. "I will give you a child for each bedroom in the house."

"How many bedrooms are there?" Eufemia asked. She was standing in the large courtyard and staring in bewilderment at the immense house surrounding her.

"Enough to make you very happy," came the doctor's reply.

Like an animal thrown into a cage for the first time, she hurled Angel to the ground and bounded up the marble stairs to the gallery that circled the big courtyard. "I will count them," she shouted to her husband below. "I will count them, every one." Galloping through the second-floor rooms, she tore out her hair, shredded her lace handkerchief, and clawed her face. On counting thirty-five bedrooms, she ran down the stairs and threw herself at her husband's feet. "How could you," she screamed. "Have you no respect. Please take me home."

"On the day we arrived you said that you were going to be very happy here," he reminded her.

"I was happy," she cried, "until today."

There was nothing the doctor could say that would calm her. The servants he had hired the day before stood some distance away and stared in alarm at their new mistress lying face down in the courtyard, beating the ground with her fists, and sobbing uncontrollably.

"Perhaps," they whispered among themselves, "we should

have gone to work in the insane asylum instead of here."

As a last resort, the doctor strapped his wife into bed and administered tincture of *Valeriana* at regular intervals. "Someone must stay with her at all hours," he told the servants. At that time they had not yet learned to love their mistress whose beauty disintegrated with fits of rage leaving her pale and spent like an apparition supported only by a breeze. Still they agreed to sit with her, to cool her brow with a damp cloth, and fan her face during the heat of the day. But no one cared to be alone with her, not even while she slept, so they kept watch two at a time until the third day when Eufemia's fever broke. "Why am I tied to this rack?" she screamed. "What have I done to deserve this torment? Read me my list of charges." She slipped through the straps that bound her and threw a shoe at the two attending servants who ran to the nearest balcony. "Have mercy on us," they cried to the people on the street. "The doctor's wife is possessed by a demon." While merchants and peddlers tried to understand what the servants were telling them, Eufemia accosted a housemaid who was mopping the gallery.

"Where is my Angel?" she asked the girl.

"I haven't seen an angel," she answered.

"Liar," Eufemia screamed. "I will cut out your tongue."

Frightened by her sharp voice and flashing eyes, the young girl ran for the front door, and on that day she became the first of many employees to abandon the doctor's household because his wife, even in all her beauty, had eyes that boiled water and a voice that shattered mirrors, windowpanes, and ordinary drinking glasses.

"Liars will be condemned to everlasting damnation," Eufemia cried, and another servant fled through the side entrance.

With the rest of the staff stepping lightly around her or hiding behind tables and chairs, Eufemia searched the house for her beloved Angel, and on finding him chained to a post in the small courtyard she demanded to know who was responsible for such an act of unkindness. "That person," she announced in a loud voice, "will be tortured with nails and thorns." Hearing this, two more servants abandoned their jobs without delay. They fled down the Street of Merchants and Peddlers without demanding their pay or closing the front door behind them.

"Who has mistreated my dearest Angel," Eufemia asked her pet. "Whisper the name in my ear, and I will punish the villain." Cradling the monkey in her arms, she visited every room in the house and after inspecting the entire second floor for the third time, she chose her private sitting room, bedroom, and chapel. The rooms had vaulted ceilings, thick walls and French windows giving onto the street and the large courtyard as well.

"In this courtyard I shall plant my orange trees," she told her husband. "And there" she pointed to the rooms she had chosen for herself, "is where I shall live."

"Your own sitting room and chapel, I can agree to that," the doctor said, "but your own bedroom—never."

Reluctantly, she joined her husband in their matrimonial bed, but she could not sleep. "You smell of astringents and gauze," she told him. "How can I rest here?"

Thereafter, before going to bed, Doctor Esperon scrubbed his body with strong soap and applied cologne to cover what hospital odors might still linger on his body, but even with these precautions, his wife still could not sleep. The sight of her husband repulsed her. The mere thought of sleeping with him brought on bouts of depression and dread. Before retiring for the night she paced the floor, wandering like a wraith from empty room to empty room while praying for the courage to love her husband. Before their marriage she had loved him, or she thought she had loved him because he was very handsome, brilliant, and soft spoken, and years later after his tragic death she would learn to love him again, but while he lived, and particularly when she was forced to sleep with him, love was not present.

"Perhaps," the doctor suggested, "we need a better mattress. One that's a little softer. Perhaps a larger bed is the answer."

The next day the longest and widest bed that could be found

was delivered to the house of forty-three rooms, but even that did not solve their problem. Night after night Eufemia continued to suffer from insomnia brought on, she was certain, by lack of privacy. She would lie in their new bed with her eyes open and her heart racing while her husband attempted to sleep. In the middle of the night she often prayed aloud, first to Saint Teresa, and then to the Blessed Virgin whose image hung on every wall. Awakened by his wife's desperate appeals for guidance, the doctor would gladly send her back to her own quarters where she could pray aloud as often as she pleased.

Preferring her own company, particularly during nervous bouts when she felt the need for constant supplication, Eufemia retreated, at last, and with her husband's consent, into her own corner of the house where the servants were only occasionally allowed. There in her private sitting room, bedroom, and chapel, she lived with the monkey, Angel, who clung to her for fear that someone would put him on another boat destined for a long voyage over stormy seas. In those rooms, closed off from the rest of the house, Eufemia taught Angel to sit at a table and eat with a spoon. She taught him to kneel with her before the Blessed Virgin, and scolded him for chewing his crinoline wings or admiring himself in the mirror.

"Turn away mine eyes from beholding vanity; and quicken thee me in thy way," she whispered into Angel's ears.

"Nothing must happen to the monkey," the remaining servants chattered among themselves. "If he runs away and never comes back, our mistress will surely die of a broken heart."

How long, the doctor wondered, can a monkey possibly live? If Angel were to die today, would Eufemia's heart truly be broken, and if so for how long? He remembered the first day he had seen her, a girl of sixteen, crossing the great plaza in Salamanca. She was holding her father's hand as if she were a mere child, as if she would have been completely lost without him, and every few steps she demanded to stop in order to make sure that the baby monkey she carried in a small box was still breathing. "Angel will not die,

Father," she said. "I will keep him alive forever."

How old must this monkey be? the doctor wondered. At least five years, he guessed, and if it were to die today, would he be forced to find another monkey exactly like it in order to preserve his wife's precarious balance? And what if another monkey exactly like Angel could not be found? What then? Would she accept a substitute, a singing canary perhaps? What had kept him from falling in love with a woman carrying a song bird? Or a cat? Why did it have to be a monkey?

While pondering these and other questions that he considered impertinent but occupying, the doctor came to the conclusion that his wife needed an industrious occupation to distract her from religious pursuits and the salvation of her pet. He had already established his private practice in three rooms facing the small courtyard and was ready to break ground for his garden of medicinal plants. He needed a nurse and someone to help tend the garden, but Eufemia refused to assist him. "I have work of my own," she said. "And it is very important."

She preferred keeping to her private apartment where she spent her time meditating, reading, and jotting down her passing thoughts in a thick journal, which she intended to leave to the world of true believers. Already she had filled a dozen leather bound volumes with suggestions and practices for achieving perfection, and now she was teaching herself to write with both hands simultaneously in order to record her fleeting thoughts, those that interrupted or came between the lingering ones.

In exchange for her own apartment, which she said was essential to her spiritual advancement, she dined with her husband three evenings a week, and if she were not exhausted by her labors, she sometimes agreed to pass the night in their communal bed. "Yes, I desire you," she told him, "but at odd hours of the day, and always when you're not present."

If he could persuade her to take it, a second glass of wine after dinner would sometimes make her more receptive to his desire, but even then, receiving him was never without pain. Upon penetration, she would awaken the house with screams that the servants said had nothing to do with pleasure. They were certain that their mistress was too high strung and possibly too small to receive her husband. "The Señor is made like an animal," the chambermaids said, "his pants do little to hide it."

Eufemia dreaded her husband's penis as she would a sword slicing her from the inside out. She had never seen him in a flaccid state, only when he was drawn to his full size, long, fearsome, and erect, springing from a thick bed of black hair that revolted her. And yet, she was his wife. She reminded herself that, for reasons she could no longer remember, she had agreed to marry him, and that many duties were expected of her.

Calling their union *holy* and *blessed*, because he thought those words would inspire love to return to her heart, the doctor coerced her into their common bed as often as her nerves would allow. Over and again he told her that the more they made love the more she would desire him.

"I've only one desire in my heart," Eufemia said, "and it's not an earthly one."

Eventually Doctor Esperon came to realize that his own pleasure was not worth the agony his wife endured both during and after their union. The nights they spent together depleted her energy and left her desperate for solitude and burning with fever. For days, thereafter, she would linger on the brink of nervous collapse, and only the sight of Angel kneeling at the altar could restore her strength.

"Angel," she told the servants, "gives me hope for the good of mankind."

There was among the staff at that time, a servant whose mother was a curandera known for love potions guaranteed to restore vitality to the most obstinate of men and cause the coldest wife to burn with desire. The doctor, who was then willing to try any method available, slipped a potion into his wife's drinking water and waited for her to come to him. But Eufemia did not respond, and the curandera was put to question.

"Allow me to examine your wife," she said, and the next afternoon Eufemia received her.

After the examination, the curandera told the doctor that his wife had the vagina of a ten year old girl. "This is something you, her husband, a doctor of medicine, should have already realized," she said. "Love potions will not work on her. She is made for other things. Hair has not yet appeared on her body, and now, it never will."

What the curandera did not know, and what the doctor could not easily explain, was that his wife had plucked herself smooth. From puberty on, she had harbored the desire to remain innocent in appearance and with skin unspoiled by the growth of hair. "Hair is a woman's crowning glory," she said, "its place is on the head; only the head." By the time she married the doctor she had removed all body hair with tweezers and salves, leaving behind her thick eyebrows, eyelashes, and her crown of glory, a long, dark mane that fell below her shoulders to frame a face as luminous as the white moon. It was said that she powdered herself with crushed pearls in order to achieve such a complexion, but Eufemia had never powdered her face or colored her cheeks and lips.

"You glow," the doctor had said when they first met.

"Because God has touched me," she had replied.

And the curandera said the same. "She has surely been touched by God."

Hearing this, Doctor Esperon shook his fists acrimoniously while the curandera fled through the side door and onto the street. "Who asked for your opinion?" he demanded to know. "In this house we do not need to hear what you have to say."

"You do not *wish* to hear what I have to say," the curandera replied from the other side of the street, "but I will say it anyway. Your wife will never be a wife."

Having heard it said, the doctor retreated into his office where he drank a bottle of brandy, and before the night was over, he admitted that which he had known for a long time: his marriage had been a mistake, a terrible mistake, one that could never be easily rectified. On realizing this, he chose five rooms across the courtyard from his office. "This," he said, "will be *my* private apartment." And from that hour on, he forced himself to look with admiration upon other women and to relinquish all desire he felt for the woman he had married. He refused to go near her wing of the house; he refused to look her in the eye, or speak her name, and he even abandoned their evening meals because sitting across the table from such untouchable beauty gave him a nervous stomach, heartburn, and bad dreams. From then on they lived private lives under the same roof. Their spare rooms were empty, and there was no promise of ever filling them, or so the doctor thought. Little did he know that his wife was already carrying his child.

Complaining of dizziness and weakness of stomach, Eufemia showed up unexpectedly at his office and demanded to be treated at once. That day every chair in the waiting room was occupied and patients were lined up across the small courtyard, but Doctor Esperon, apologizing for the delay, ushered his wife into the examination room and prescribed an anodyne to soothe her nerves. Once she regained her composure, he made a preliminary exam and discovered a second heartbeat. "A child," he said, "you are carrying my child."

"God's child," Eufemia replied.

For two weeks thereafter, she remained amazingly calm and sweet of countenance. She smiled at the servants each morning and addressed them affectionately by name, but during the afternoon when the blazing sun, shining directly into the large courtyard, drew every breath of energy from the house and all its inhabitants, Eufemia retreated inside herself. During that hour when the shadows were short, and all the fish were hiding at the bottom of the lotus pool, she was seen on her hands and knees beneath her beloved orange trees.

"She's eating the earth," the servants whispered among themselves. "This is a sure sign of pregnancy."

When the doctor asked them what secrets they were whispering, they told him of a chapel only a short distance from the city.

It had been built over red clay rich in minerals and was visited by expectant mothers. "If your wife is pregnant," said one of the servants, "a small amount of this clay eaten every day will help the baby develop. It will also diminish the pain of childbirth."

"Yes, my wife is pregnant," Doctor Esperon told his servants, "and I forbid you to tell her about this chapel."

The servants refused to listen to him, and on afternoons when the waiting rooms were filled to capacity, and the doctor was too busy caring for his patients to pay close attention to the activities of his household, the servants tried to persuade Eufemia to visit the Church of the Holy Earth. "You will feel so much better if you visit this place," they said. "The earth there is holy." But Eufemia refused to leave the house with servants she did not trust, and as a last resort, the servants brought the holy earth to her. Every morning a bowl of the red clay was left outside her door, and by afternoon the bowl was empty. She consumed the dry, red powder by mixing it with water or milk, and when she asked for more, the servants supplied it. "Pregnancy agrees with her," they said. "She glows like an angel. And she behaves like one also."

They said that she was carrying a special child of God that expelled the demon from her body and left her radiant. They said that she was, at last, content; surrounded by Heavenly music and sweet fragrance that visited her from above. They said that she had been touched by something divine that had released her wrath and replaced it with a constant smile. "She's become a saint," they told the merchants and peddlers, and it was then that they adopted her as their patroness. She waved to them each morning from her balcony, and she spoke to them with a smile in her voice. "When she graces us with her presence," they said, "our customers do not complain so much, and the day is more profitable as well."

Soon the doctor realized that his wife had become the heartbeat of his house and street, that his servants were showing more concern for her than for him, and although their allegiance to Eufemia offended him at first, he came to realize that it also afforded him a certain freedom. He no longer needed to worry about his wife's well-being. The servants would take care of her in their own way, and he would take a mistress to satisfy his need for a woman.

The first mistress came to him for the removal of a mole between her upper lip and right nostril, a mole that so enhanced her beauty the doctor refused to remove it. The public recognized her as Carlota Montejo, the leading actress at the National Theatre, *a rare and startling treasure*, she was called by her devoted fans, who waited for her at the stage door with flowers in their arms, and carried her on their shoulders back to the Hotel Carmina where she often delivered a late-night recitation from her balcony. When she graced the stage of the National Theatre the galleries were packed to overflowing, and on the day she first visited the doctor in her trailing capes and bright dresses, all activity on the Street of Merchants and Peddlers ceased until she had entered the house of two courtyards.

After the first consultation Carlota announced to a waiting room filled with patients that she could live with her mole because it was her only imperfection, but she could not live without her new doctor. From that day forth, she visited him every afternoon. When she performed at the National Theatre he sat in her private box, and when she solicited money for the local orphanage that bore her name the doctor was the first to contribute. "I was an orphan," she said. "And therefore, I support all orphans. I believe in all orphans. And I love all orphans. My orphanage is my greatest achievement."

Although she was nearly twice the doctor's age—was said to have given birth to dozens of children out of wedlock, and would sleep with anyone to secure a donation for her orphanage—the servants found no reason to criticize the doctor's choice of a mistress, for Carlota was a woman much experienced in the world and only she would be able to receive him.

"She has given herself to some of the wealthiest men in this nation," the chambermaids gossiped among themselves.

"She keeps their names in a little red book."

"And she's never met a man she could not satisfy."

Within a few months, however, they were amused to learn that the actress did not succeed in satisfying the doctor's voracious desire. On coming to learn that he had taken a much younger mistress, one who visited him after Carlota had left for the theatre, they bragged to the merchants and peddlers that their doctor, although he was small of stature, was a man of great strength and virility. They said that he had the penis of a horse and the sexual drive of a rabbit, and that he had practically killed his angelic wife trying to penetrate her. "How she became pregnant," they said, "only God can say."

The servants approved of the doctor's mistresses because they occupied most of his free time, giving them the opportunity to care for Eufemia without his interference. By then they had grown to love her to the point of worship. Under their care, she was permitted to sustain, without interruption, her meditative life, which brought a great tranquility into the house. Often she invited one or two of them to kneel with her in the private chapel and always they accepted her invitation not because they wanted to pray, or needed to rest, but because they wanted to be near her, to breathe the same air she breathed, and to hear her begging the Heavenly Father to bless them. They were convinced that she was a holy person because no one that beautiful could come from any place except Heaven. "The child she is carrying," they said, "will surely be blessed with beauty and purity of heart."

Doctor Esperon was certain that his wife was too fragile to live through the strain of childbirth, and that it was better for his reputation to allow the servants to care for her. Relinquishing his desire to deliver his own child, he asked the household staff to find an experienced midwife, a responsibility the servants were all too happy to assume, for by then Eufemia belonged to them, and they promised themselves, and God as well, that they would care for her through the birth of the child and for the rest of her life.

"The baby will arrive early," they said.

"How do you know this?" the doctor asked.

"Because her skin has become transparent," they replied. "And because she talks to the child constantly."

Eight months after Eufemia Esperon had eaten the courtyard dirt, the first labor pain arrived, and twelve hours later at five o'clock in the afternoon, a daughter entered the world on a March wind that blew lamp shades and window curtains through the house and into the sandy courtyards where whirlwinds of dust ripped leaves off the orange trees and tore bougainvillea from walls and arches. The child was born with a full head of thick, black hair and a strawberry birthmark as round as the full moon on the back of her neck. "Perhaps we have been led astray," the servants whispered among themselves. "This child has the temperament of a windstorm, and there's nothing to stop her."

She was named Josefina Pilar in memory of her grandmothers, and two hours after her birth, when the servants were still chasing curtains through the windy house, Señora Eufemia cried out in delirium for her mother, her father, her brothers and cousins. She called for her grandmothers, her childhood nurse, and her family priest.

"They're not here, Señora," a servant said.

"Then bring me my Angel," Eufemia pleaded. "I don't want to die alone."

Quickly the servants dressed the monkey in its crinoline wings and brought it to Eufemia's bedside, and while holding him in a tight embrace she closed her eyes and hemorrhaged in the bed that her daughter would sleep on for the rest of her life.

According to her last request, she was bathed in lavender water and dressed in a simple white robe. Her face was neither powdered nor painted, and her feet were covered with the blue silk slippers her mother's mother had worn to her last confession. A coffin, blacker than ebony, was immediately sent for, and in one night craftsmen carved the family crest on the lid and lilies on the sides. After hibiscus and rose petals were sprinkled throughout the house, Eufemia's body was carried into the large courtyard for public viewing. The entire city, or so it seemed to the stricken servants, filed past the casket. At last the archbishop arrived, followed by the Carmelites, the Franciscans, the Capuchins and a choir of children dressed as angels. Some of the mourners stayed much longer than others. They lingered near the casket, or gathered on the second-floor galleries for the pleasure of beholding Eufemia's beauty a little longer.

"In death," the servants agreed, "she is far more beautiful than in life."

Soon the noonday sun fell into the courtyard, but in spite of the rising temperature the mourners lingered on in small groups standing inside what little shade could be found. It was then that the doctor noticed beads of moisture on his wife's forehead. He removed the droplets with a white handkerchief, and when he touched her lips with the back of his hand, she opened her mouth and then her eyes. A wave of excitement roiled through the crowd of mourners.

"Did you see that?" came a voice from the gallery. "She opened her eyes."

"Yes," Doctor Esperon said. "I saw it too. It happens so many times. When the body relaxes the eyes and the mouth will often open."

He closed her eyelids with his fingers, placed coins on each of them, and when he turned his back to walk away, Eufemia sat up in her coffin.

The servants, the merchants, and the peddlers fell to their knees while the archbishop, the Carmelites and the Franciscans moved in to form a circle around the coffin. Everyone else screamed with fright and trampled every vine in the courtyard trying to escape. "Do not leave me," Eufemia begged, but the sound of her voice sent them running with fear out the door and down the street. Those who remained in the courtyard were not afraid. For them, the doctor's wife was living proof of God's goodness and mercy, and while the archbishop sprinkled holy water on her tired body, the servants lifted her from her coffin and carried her back to her bedroom where they fed her rich broth to build her strength.

"We have seen a miracle," the archbishop said.

"Things like this happen more often than you think," the doctor argued. "There's a plausible explanation."

But the archbishop refused to listen. "My people," he said, "are in desperate need of a miracle. Do not try to deprive them of something the medical profession refuses to understand."

Childbirth left Eufemia weak and impatient. "I have no nourishment to spare," she said, each time the baby was brought to her for nursing. "This child will suck the last drop of blood from my body."

When it became apparent to the doctor that his wife had no milk, he hired an Indian woman with a smiling face and tearing amber eyes to bathe and nurse his daughter, to chew her first bites of solid food, and to rub her gums with camphor when her baby teeth appeared. The Indian, who had milk but no children, and whose name was too difficult even for the doctor to pronounce, was called Fuerte because she never seemed to tire even though her feet were flat, her spine was weak, and her eyesight was diminished by an incurable infection that caused constant tearing. With a backstrap loom under one arm, and a rolled tapestry of 142 panels under the other, Fuerte entered the house on large paddle-like feet, but she walked in astonishing silence, floating on a smile through the many rooms of the doctor's house.

In spite of her perpetual smile nothing about Fuerte's physical appearance spoke of contentment. Her nose, which seemed to begin in the center of her forehead, extended downward beyond her upper lip. Her hands were red and swollen from years of weaving and cleaning, and her feet were unusually flat and broad. Fuerte's hair was thin, her ears were large, and her infected amber-colored eyes were laced with bulging veins, permitting her to see very little beyond an extended arm. But in spite of these imperfections Fuerte was touched with a vision that penetrated the future with shattering accuracy and a memory that reached back to the beginning of time.

"I am a weaver," she told the doctor on the day she entered

his house. "But that will not interfere with what you want me to do." Her only request was a room of her own and someone to arrange her threads for she was unable to distinguish one color from another. "I can see colors in my mind," she said, "but not on my loom."

"And what are you weaving?" the doctor asked.

"I am weaving the past, the present, and the future all at the same time."

"And how do you know?"

"Because everything is the same."

"And when will you finish?"

"That's not for me to say."

On the long dress, which she wore every day, she had woven the history of her village and her family. "So we will never forget," she said. "So when you see me you will be reminded. And you will never forget either."

"And what does your dress say?" the doctor asked.

And Fuerte answered as if reciting a poem:

Three times we were invaded.
Three times we were burned.
And three times our temples were destroyed.
And after the third time,
    new temples were built on top of old temples.
And the conquerors said:
This is very good.
The old gods will be forgotten.
The new gods will be remembered.
And only the saved will go to Heaven.
But the people said:
Heaven is for all.
And the old gods did not vanish with the new,
And the new gods did not vanish with the old.
This has been repeated many times over,
And will be repeated again in many ways yet to come.

For nothing is new and nothing is old.
Everything is the same.

"And here," she said, pointing to a border of designs that circled her neck, "this is the name of my village, The Place Where Clouds Gather. And here are the names of my mother and grandmothers who were also weavers. After the third invasion their looms were taken from them, and without their looms they could not live. And here, this explains our method of working. We embroider as we weave, and that is why my short threads must be arranged by color."

Then she turned around to show him the story of the sacred spider embroidered on the back of her dress. "The spider taught us to weave our language," she said. "Without her we would forget everything."

"Where I come from we're trained to forget everything," the doctor replied. He agreed to arrange her threads by color according to her instructions, and on hearing this she smiled; tears trickled down her face and fell onto the stone floor.

And so Fuerte entered the house on her paddle-like feet, walking in astonishing silence with the child strapped to her broad stomach. She was given a room on the gallery level, because the light there was good, but light she did not need, and to the doctor's astonishment, she often wove in the dark; her hands traveling the loom like a pair of spiders dancing on water.

When she told the doctor that too much light was painful to her eyes, he offered a cure for her infection, but Fuerte refused to take it. "I am the way I am," she said. "Nothing can be done about that."

For quite some time Doctor Esperon was uncertain as to how much she understood, so he issued instructions slowly and precisely for he was convinced that the perpetual smile conveyed a certain weakness of mind. He always expected her to forget everything that he said, but to his surprise, Fuerte forgot nothing; even when one ear was turned to voices speaking to her from faraway places, she heard, understood, and remembered everything the doctor said. She also took it upon herself to issue words of advice she felt he needed to hear.

One day she showed up at his crowded office with an urgent message. "I have just been told to warn you: never run for public office," she said.

"Who asked you to warn me?" Doctor Esperon inquired.

"I don't know. Only a few minutes ago someone whispered this into my left ear."

"Was it a member of the household?"

"No, Señor. For I was alone in my room at the time."

"But were you doing anything?"

"Oh yes, Doctor," Fuerte replied. "I was weaving."

"And my daughter?"

"She was sleeping at my side."

In due time he understood that the whisperings came to her when she was preoccupied with the past, present, and future of her ongoing tapestry. "I have now woven one hundred and forty-five panels," she said. "When my fingers are busy, I can hear things. What I hear is the future."

"What about the past?"

"The past is what I remember."

"I don't understand?"

"Everything in the future happened yesterday."

Repeating everything she had heard, Fuerte advised the doctor to bury his pistol, never make friends with presidents of any nation, and relinquish his seat at the opera before his daughter came of age.

"I don't have a seat at the opera," the doctor laughed.

"But one day you will," Fuerte said, "and when you do you must give it up or else your daughter will suffer too much embarrassment."

Her advice, which was always spoken as prophesy, was not directed solely at the doctor. To the servants she said that Eufemia was a smoking mountain that would one day explode in their faces. But to the servants Eufemia was still a living saint, and they were unwilling to listen to the paddle-footed nursemaid who lived in some blissful state of insanity that allowed her to weep and smile at the same time.

"Do not allow a politician inside this house." With a grin that betrayed her serious intention Fuerte delivered her message:

"A politician will be very bad for the doctor, and so will night visitors."

"Do not answer the door after nine in the evening, and do not allow Eufemia to touch the child; her malcontent is infectious."

"And one thing more, do not allow our lady to sleep on her side for her body will produce a sour odor that nothing, not even the juice of sea grass, will eliminate."

"Sea grass indeed," the servants laughed. "Politicians, night visitors, and infectious malcontent. Who in their right mind could believe such babblings?" And when they were told that the infant Josefina would one day become more famous than any president or poet the nation had yet produced, they became angry with the old nursemaid who had taken over the entire household.

"How can anyone become more famous than our beloved poets?" they cried. "Poets live forever and their fame increases, even after they are dead."

"Remember what I say," Fuerte replied, "it will come true."

"We will remember nothing," the servants answered. "We will not even listen to you."

Leaving her with all the housework, the servants devoted themselves to caring for their saint, whose recovery was prolonged by a sharp pain that traveled to the extremities of her body. Gradually, the pain vanished and with it her angelic countenance. "Where is my pain?" she asked the servants. "I require it. It draws me closer to God." Deprived of her suffering, she was unable to meditate, and without meditation she grew restless. Fire returned to her eyes and voice, and her discontent surfaced with flashes of bad temper. She cursed her servants for walking with heavy footsteps, which shook the house and disturbed her meditation. She railed at them for talking behind her back, for serving food that was not fit to eat and for placing the infant in her arms. "I'm not the mother of this child," she cried. "This child is dark like the night and I am fair. Can't you see that she does not belong to me?"

For staring at her too long and with eyes that held no respect, Eufemia slapped a chambermaid and pushed her helper down the stairs. For entertaining lascivious thoughts in her presence she beat another servant with a crucifix and threw a chamber pot filled with her own excrement across the bedroom floor. She demanded that the staff cease praying to the saints, even to the Blessed Mother. "I am a living saint," she announced from her balcony to the Street of Merchants and Peddlers. "I will gladly hear your prayers and carry them directly to the Heavenly Father." Several times a day the servants, who were beginning to doubt the validity of their own devotion, fell upon their knees in Eufemia's presence, but each time they prayed to her she became suspicious of their motives and attacked them for confusing veneration with malevolence.

In a very short time, the servants became disillusioned, and one by one they walked out and did not return. "She's no saint after all," they said. "She's the Devil in disguise." In every corner of the capital city, they defiled her reputation, but those of secure faith who had never worked in the doctor's house, and had never visited it for any length of time, refused to listen to what the ex-servants were saying.

"Now they will know," Fuerte said, "what it is like to be ignored."

After the staff had abandoned him, Doctor Esperon came to realize that Fuerte's capacity for work surpassed that of an army of servants, so he put her in full charge of the daily running and maintenance of the house. With the infant Josefina strapped to her broad stomach, she did the washing and ironing, the cooking and cleaning, all the marketing, the sewing, the watering of the plants. She whitewashed the walls when they needed it, pruned the orange trees by touch, and every morning at dawn she scrubbed the sidewalk and street in front of the doctor's house. In spite of her failing eyesight Fuerte did not neglect a single task, except caring for the monkey. She was convinced, for reasons the doctor could never quite understand, that the monkey was a dog, and dogs, according to her thinking, were capable of taking care of themselves.

There was no dissuading her of this: the monkey was a dog, and dogs, as everyone knew, needed nothing more than an occasional bone on which to sharpen their teeth. Firmly convinced that reason was on her side, Fuerte ignored the dog, which was a monkey, and the doctor ignored the monkey, which was no angel, and in turn Eufemia ignored not only her husband but Fuerte as well, for such a blithe spirit in one so large and intruding made her saintly heart dwell on evil deeds.

Being ignored by the resident saint was of no consequence to Fuerte. She had grown to expect such dismissals, particularly from those who searched for the surest path through the Christian Heavens. "I have never believed in saints," she told the doctor, "only in myself and the gods."

Against the doctor's orders she turned her back on Eufemia by disregarding her comings and goings, allowing her at all hours of the day or night to roam the streets alone, marching like a soldier into battle. Armed with dozens of rosaries she had strung herself she walked barefoot or on sandals pierced with sharp tacks that bit deeply into the soles of her feet. Along the way she recited the Beatitudes, the Sermon on the Mount, the Ten Commandments, and from *The Way of Perfection* she delivered the words of her beloved Saint Teresa:

"Remember I consider it quite certain that those who attain perfection do not ask the Lord to deliver them from trials, temptations, persecutions, and conflicts. Perfect souls are in no way repelled by trials, but rather desire them and pray for them and love them. They are like soldiers: the more wars there are the better they are pleased, because they hope to emerge from them with the greater riches."

Cradling Angel in her arms she made her good will tours into the most desperate parts of the city to distribute rosaries, milagros, and copies of *The Way of Perfection*. She was careful to explain, particularly to the Indians, who had no formal education, that *The Way of Perfection* was a book of beautiful thoughts not firewood and that one day she would return to teach them how to read the thoughts from each page. "Our blessed Teresa of Ávila has given us the foundation on which to build the contemplative life," she said. "Her words will always comfort us."

For speaking out in praise of their suffering, the poor people of the capital grew to love Eufemia as much as she loved the saint of Ávila, and the more she walked among them, the more they demanded her presence. They waited impatiently for the first word of her arrival on their dark and narrow streets paved with mud, sprinkled with animal excrement, and lined with open sewers. After these holy walks she broke out in rashes, boils, and sties that she welcomed into her body. She returned to her chapel with mud-splattered clothing, with scabies, fever, and eyes inflamed with visions of the crucified Christ. Without ceasing she thanked God for visiting her with pestilence from which she promised to emerge with a greater love than ever. "All of life," she said, "is a test of faith. O Lord! Send me a battle to fight and I will win it for you."

She spent Christmas Eve of her twenty-third year wading through mud and backwaters, to find the true celebrants of Christ among the impoverished and homeless who loved her. Before midnight she collapsed with fever and was carried home by seven beggars who had followed her the entire day. By dawn she was swollen with infection; by noon she was covered with sores; and by evening she was singing deliriously with saints and angels. The fever persisted, and within a week she lost her eyebrows and lashes; within another all the hair on her head fell to the floor.

Doctor Esperon tried all known methods of treatment without success, and finally, he admitted to himself: "There's nothing else that can be done. Nothing at all." Over a period of days Eufemia's fingernails loosened, and her body emitted a fetid odor that drew flies into the house and caused Fuerte to lose her smile. At that time she sent the doctor to consult the local curanderas who told him to boil the young vines of the strangling fig, and leave a bowl of the green liquid on Eufemia's bedside table.

"Let her drink as much as she wants," he was told. "It will purify the blood."

"Yes," Fuerte agreed, "it will purify the blood, Doctor, but in your wife's case it is only a temporary measure."

After consuming three bowls of the liquid, Eufemia's rancid odor was mitigated. Fuerte regained her smile, and the doctor returned to his practice. But within a week Eufemia, as bald as the day she was born, was once again limping through the slums. She said that she had transcended the malady inflicted upon her and in doing so had been transported to a high, high place where blessed spirits, adorned in Heaven's embroidered cloths, danced on clouds and air. "I have visited deep caverns and high palaces," she told her husband, "and I have bathed in rivers of blood and gold."

"What can I do?" the doctor asked his colleagues at the hospital.

"Keep her at home!" they answered.

Shortly thereafter Eufemia suffered another infection that caused her eyes to bulge and her skin to split in lesions. At that time Fuerte hung wind chimes in every arch surrounding the large courtyard. "She'll contaminate the air we breathe," she told the doctor. "So we must encourage the wind to blow away her infection." This time, Doctor Esperon listened to her.

That evening he locked his wife into her private apartment and hung the key on a post near the stairs. "You're standing in the way of God's work," she screamed through the door. "He needs me to deliver his message of redemption."

"The streets are filled with disease," the doctor said. "For your own good, you cannot leave this house."

"It's another test," Eufemia replied. "And I am ready for it."

After days of confinement she longed for a new obstacle to test her faith. Thus began her series of escapes and nocturnal wanderings. On a rope of twisted curtains and window sashes, she would lower herself over her balcony onto the Street of Merchants and Peddlers, and from there venture into the most desperate neighborhoods to pray with the poor. Night after night the whores and pimps recognized her as she passed and stood to one side out of respect. So did the beggars and thieves for she was bald with holiness and burning with redemption. Children walked in her footprints, and the lame said they were healed by the very sound of her voice. In every part of the city she was recognized, and in every territory of the nation her fame was spreading. Pilgrims came out of the mountains, the jungles, and the marshes for one glimpse of her. They traveled the rivers and byways to camp outside her door or wait under her balcony.

"There's no reason to lock her in her rooms," Fuerte said. "No matter what, she will somehow escape."

With the doctor's consent, the doors to Eufemia's rooms were left unlocked and standing open, but she rarely used them. Instead, she continued lowering herself over the balcony to leave, but always returned through the front door. Finally, bars were placed on all her windows, and from that day forth she considered herself a prisoner. Even when the doors to her apartment were left open and the doors to the street unlocked, Eufemia did not leave the house. She sat in her balcony room and waved through a barred window to the pilgrims who waited for her below. "I am sequestered now," she said to her followers. "Only by withdrawing from the world, can I give you the full power of my thoughts and prayers." Usually she spoke or prayed aloud from her barred window, but on occasions she wrote prayers and messages on colored paper and dropped them onto the heads of her followers. They in turn would sing praises as if she were the Mother of God incarnate. They would speak to her in reverential tones, drop to their knees under her window, and always they left flowers in their wake. When Eufemia tired of their devotion, she would bid them good-bye and retreat to the large courtyard to pray under her orange trees, to study *The Way of Perfection*, and to write her ongoing thoughts.

Always she wrote with both hands, with two pens and on two pads of paper, her arms moving from left to right and back again in an unbroken rhythm until every fleeting thought was recorded in one notebook and every lingering thought was carefully explained in the other.

"Why do you write with both hands?" the doctor asked.

"Because I have been given the burden of two sets of thoughts," Eufemia answered, "and I must capture both. One is like a prayer, and the other is more instructive than inspirational, but both are inspired."

While she sat there peacefully recording her dual thoughts or staring into the lotus pool, Fuerte scrubbed the house, washed the clothes, and cooked the food with Josefina at her side. And during siesta when the child slept, Fuerte sat on the floor and wove with her face inches from the loom. Already Josefina had begun to walk without support, and Fuerte's eyesight had degenerated beyond the doctor's expectations. "You must wear glasses," he said. But he could not find a pair that would stay on her broad face, and besides, glasses did not improve her vision in the least. With or without them she was unable to see her own body from the waist down.

"How will you keep up with my daughter now that she's walking?" the doctor asked.

"I will use a rope, Señor," Fuerte replied.

With one end of a rope tied around her own waist and the other end around Josefina's, Fuerte went about her daily routine of maintaining the doctor's house. While making lunch, washing clothes, or sweeping the forty-three rooms, two courtyards, and four balconies, she tugged on the rope, which she had softened in boiling water, and the child followed along. Connected this way, they shopped along the Street of Merchants and Peddlers, visited the municipal market for vegetables, and for one hour each week they sat in the cathedral and listened to a choir of young boys whose voices, Fuerte said, would soon change and then they would become quite ordinary, like everyone else. But it was not the choir that interested Josefina, it was the statues of the virgin and the angels. They had beautiful faces like Eufemia's face during moments of repose, faces that were calm and peaceful but likely to change into terror at any given moment. Who is that woman who sits in the courtyard, she wondered. Why is she there? And why does she look like the statues of the angels and Madonna?

"We must go now," Fuerte would say after the choir had sung. Reluctantly, Josefina would be pulled along to the next stopping place: the city market, the lace maker's shop, which was always cool, or the little store that sold paper goods where the owner offered her regular customers a glass of guava water or tamarind.

Wherever Fuerte went, the doctor's daughter accompanied her, connected by a rope that gave the child no freedom to explore. They washed the sidewalk together, swept the stairs, and scrubbed the outside of the house with a long handled broom that reached above the balconies and almost to the eaves.

Their days were broken by siesta and a few hours of sleep each night, and never once did Fuerte complain of fatigue or the failing vision that forced her to inspect her work over and over to make sure that it was properly done. Leaving the house in her charge, the doctor made his hospital rounds each morning and returned home before noon to receive patients until the first hour of siesta. Then he retired to his private quarters to entertain one of his five mistresses, all of whom were well known along the Street of Merchants and Peddlers.

"Which one do you suppose is his favorite?" the button maker asked the knife sharpener.

"And what do you think is required of them?" the knife sharpener asked the wheelwright.

"When does the doctor find time to rest?" the tinsmith wanted to know.

"And how is it possible to satisfy so many women?" asked the candle maker. "Sometimes as many as three in a single afternoon."

"But not at the same time," came a voice from needles and

threads.

"No," cried the soap vendor, "but close enough to make you wonder."

From Independence Monument on one end of the street all the way to the great cathedral on the other, the five mistresses provided the merchants and peddlers with much to talk about, and at the same time they diverted the doctor's mind from the suffering he saw by day and the loneliness that slept with him by night. Each mistress was showered with great local fanfare. Merchants and shoppers lined the street to wave them along as though they were queens come to reclaim their rightful throne. They arrived by carriage or by foot moving briskly down the middle of the street and around the corner to the side entrance where spectators gathered to express their approval or place bets as to which mistress might eventually replace the doctor's bald but still beautiful wife.

The peddlers and merchants referred to each of the women by a cherished name starting with the actress Carlota Montejo. To her fans, she was the *Startling Treasure*, but because she arrived at the doctor's door in long skirts and trailing capes the merchants and peddlers renamed her *The Street Sweeper*.

"She," they said, "unlike the others, is a total woman."

"Every year she makes a generous donation to her orphanage."

"And it is not just money she donates either."

"Sometimes it is a baby in swaddling."

"Sometimes it is two."

"And always her own."

"Oh, yes, she can be very dangerous and should be watched carefully. Only *The Infant* is truly innocent."

All the merchants agreed: *The Infant* was the youngest and most childlike, as well as the most beautiful. At the appointed time she arrived with her dolls, with her stuffed animals, and her mother who waited in the courtyard until the doctor dismissed them both with a few coins and a kiss. "Surely," the peddlers said, "*The Infant* is the doctor's favorite." But that was not the case. Although he enjoyed her beautiful complexion and her naïve charm, she was no more beautiful to him than Maria de la Luz, who was called the *Mother of God*, and far less exciting than Maria Aparacida who was called *The Mustache*. Last of all there was Maria Dolores, who in spite of her coarse features and ever expanding waist, was said to have won the doctor's heart. Among the spectators she was called *The Stinking Flower* because the perfume Doctor Esperon had chosen especially for her turned rancid on her skin, an essence that pleased him immensely, for he was a man who thrived on variety, but one that caused the merchants to remark that the doctor preferred his favorite woman unwashed.

"Even the sweetest things turn sour," said the lace maker, the eldest merchant on the street. "Our doctor's festering lily smells far worse than weeds."

"Everyone gives them too much attention," Fuerte replied. "No one should receive so much attention as those five intruders."

Fuerte considered the mistresses an expendable interruption in the daily workings of the street and not necessarily the best distraction for her employer who needed the siesta hours for sleep. "All these visitors are a strain on your father's heart," she told Josefina, "but at least they're not his enemies. He will not die by the hand of a woman; that I can promise you."

Although Josefina could speak simple sentences and recite short nursery rhymes, she could not fully grasp the meaning of what Fuerte was telling her, but she would remember Fuerte's words and the tone in which they were spoken in association with her father's special visitors each of whom filled the house with a different essence. The mistresses intrigued her, but the sight of her mother wandering through the house or writing in the courtyard was frightening, especially when Eufemia's cold blue eyes glowed with the intensity of fire. On occasions when they met face to face Josefina avoided eye contact. She lowered her head, pretended that Eufemia was not present, that she did not live in the house. Sometimes she ran the other way. Sometimes she hid behind a door while Eufemia passed, silently gliding like a contented spirit or ranting like a restless ghost. And while attempting to avoid her mother, whose wraith-like image was unsettling, she gave all her attention to her father's special visitors who were beautiful and always smiling in anticipation of that which awaited them. When any of the mistresses visited the doctor, the house of forty-three rooms seemed to expand from the inside out. To the young Josefina it seemed to breathe as if it had become a living thing, a creature whose breaths were long and satisfying, like a sigh followed by another and another.

While resting during the heat of the day, Josefina would lie awake waiting for the first sound of a creaking door followed by the scent of jasmine, gardenia, or Madre Selva wafting through the courtyards and up the stairs to the weaving room. The anticipation of her father's women, and the scent of their arrival prohibited sleep and quickened her breath. While Fuerte wove Josefina lay on her pallet and listened. Excited beyond her understanding, she dreamed of escape, of following her father into his private quarters to sit beside the lavishly dressed and sweet-smelling women whom she had observed from her window as they arrived at the office door.

"Mother," she said one day when she saw one of the mistresses cross the small courtyard and disappear with flashing colors into her father's chambers.

"No," Fuerte answered. "You mother is in her room. Maybe she's writing today. Maybe she's praying to the people outside, or talking to her little dog. You must never disturb her or she will become very angry."

"She is not my mother," the child said. "My mother is with my father." But why, she wondered, did she have only one father when she had five mothers.

"Which one is really Mother?" she asked her father.

"None of them," he answered. "Your mother is the beautiful lady with a head like the full moon and eyes like the ocean."

"Why doesn't she talk to me?" she asked.

"Because," the doctor answered, "she is always listening to

voices from another world."

"Why does she see things that I cannot see? And why does she hear things that I cannot hear?" Josefina asked.

With a long sigh, her father answered: "It is too difficult to explain right now."

No matter what he said, his words served only to develop a fearful curiosity about her real mother who had the face of a Madonna and the anger of a vengeful god. One minute she might be singing sweetly to the angels, or praying with the pilgrims standing below her window, and the next moment exploding in anger at a demon crossing the courtyard.

"She scares me," Josefina told her father.

"It is best," he replied, "to leave her alone."

"I like the others, Father. They don't frighten me."

The five mistresses, dressed in gowns and jewels and fragrance, continued to capture her young heart. She wanted to know each of them and she wanted them to recognize her, to give her presents and kisses on the cheek. She wanted to hear them speak her name, and she wanted to speak theirs. Before long she found ways to gain their attention.

While Fuerte scrubbed the floors or darned clothing, which she held inches from her face, Josefina removed the rope from her waist and tied it around a pillow, which Fuerte dragged behind her as she made her rounds. "Come along," she would say to the pillow. "You can move faster than that."

Seizing her freedom this way, Josefina often visited her father's side of the house in order to watch his patients come and go and listen to him diagnose their ills. During the hours of siesta when Fuerte was bending over her loom, Josefina would linger in the dark passage between the courtyards, and after the arrival of a mistress she would crouch outside the closed door to her father's bedroom, or press an ear to a windowpane that barely muffled the sighs and laughter. What are they doing in there? she would wonder. Will I be in there one day, also? When the door opened and a scented lady was escorted across the small courtyard, Josefina would then wave or speak or step suddenly into the path of her father's lover, and he, pretending to be greatly annoyed, would chase her around the courtyard before grabbing her about the waist with his strong hands.

"I want to be just like them," she told him. "One day I will be."

Once when she was resting on her narrow bed and Fuerte was weaving a thread of hope into her 153rd panel, Josefina untied her end of the rope that connected them, and in her place she tied the monkey Angel. Then she slipped away to sit outside her father's bedroom door. To return before the end of siesta had been her plan, but that day, Fuerte, whose internal clock had lost its count, put away her weaving after the first hour of siesta. Thinking it was morning instead of late afternoon she dragged the monkey downstairs and prepared breakfast for the second time that day. While water for the doctor's coffee was coming to a boil, she sliced papaya, mamey, and mango into a wood bowl and called Josefina to the table. When the child did not respond to the first call, Fuerte sat down like a fisherman hauling in his catch and pulled the monkey into her lap. Cautiously, she stroked his head, ran her fingers to the tip of his tail, and on coming to the conclusion that the child placed in her charge had been turned into an animal with coarse body hair, sharp teeth, and fetid breath, she threw the monkey against the kitchen wall and screamed for the doctor.

"Something terrible has happened," she said, arousing him from his pleasure. By then Josefina had returned to her end of the rope, and Angel, racing through the house, was knocking over every lamp and table in his path. "Doctor," Fuerte said. "Look at this child and tell me she's not an animal."

"She's not an animal," the doctor sighed, but offered no other words of comfort to the housekeeper who had interrupted his only joy of the day.

At once he disappeared into his office to prepare an injection, and while his daughter watched with the cold blue eyes she had inherited from her mother, Doctor Esperon put the monkey to sleep forever. Then he returned to Maria de la Luz, bathing in water scented with oil of Madre Selva, a fragrance that soon filled the house with such intoxicating sweetness that Fuerte was forced to lie down for the rest of the afternoon.

That evening, while Doctor Esperon dug a shallow grave in the large courtyard, Eufemia dressed her departed Angel in his lace gown, his crinoline wings, and halo. From the gallery above the large courtyard Josefina watched her. "He has gone to Heaven, at last," Eufemia said happily. "He was made to wait such a long time for this reward, but when his hour came his passing was as sweet as a caress. May God bless us, likewise."

"Likewise," Josefina repeated.

"Thank you," Eufemia replied, looking up with a smile at the daughter she would one day recognize as her own.

"This is the first of many graves," Fuerte said.

"And who will be next?" Doctor Esperon asked, but Fuerte answered with silence.

She had already heard more than she cared to know and more than she wished to reveal. She knew who would be next, and the next after the next. Burdened with the knowledge of a tumultuous future that she could do nothing to prevent, she sat down, she wept, she became distracted, not by her household work but by the events she knew would come to pass. And from that time until the far-off day when the tapestry was finished, she withdrew further and further inside herself. Frequently she sat down to weave; fell into deep thought and on awakening could not remember what she had been thinking or what she had woven. She could not remember the day of the week, the house chore she had just completed, or what she was supposed to do next. "When do I sweep the stairs?" she would ask herself. "When do I prune the orange trees? When do I feed the fish in the lotus pool?" She allowed pots to boil over and dinner to burn, and although she never lost her steadfast smile it was clear to Doctor Esperon that his housekeeper was walking though fallen clouds.

"This house," she muttered constantly. "This house has too

many rooms. Too many empty rooms. Too many doors. Too many stairs, and courtyards, and arches. No house should have so many rooms and stairs and arches."

"I like rooms," Josefina said.

"But not so many," Fuerte replied. She was sitting on a gallery bench, her hands resting on her knees and her head thrust forward as if watching Josefina's every move, though she could see nothing except clouds of gray smoke fading and running together. She could not see, but she could hear, and her hearing told her everything she needed to know. The sound of Josefina's footsteps echoing through the house was a loud affirmation of freedom.

"Now that you have your liberty, we'll soon find out what you will do with it," Fuerte said, forgetting that she already knew.

"I will enjoy it," Josefina answered.

"Will you?" Fuerte asked.

"I already am," she replied.

Without the rope tied around her waist, she was free at last, to roam the house she would live in the rest of her life. More by instinct than by chance, she found the warm places inhabited by good spirits and all the cold corners where, Fuerte said, someone had died tragically, if not in the past certainly in the future, though she could no longer determine who the victim was or would be because her mind had become cloudy with questions that were not her own and answers that no one wished to receive.

"You must stay nearby so I can hear you," she would say. "Don't go near your mother; if you do, she might start screaming again. And don't visit your father. He's busy in his little rooms."

Her father's little rooms were the ones that interested her the most. His laboratory shelves were filled with bottles of colored liquids and jars of leaves, bark, and flowers preserved in gelatinous substances. Botanical drawings hung on every wall and bunches of herbs and medicinal plants were tied on poles high over head where they could dry slowly in order to preserve their properties. The sometimes sweet, sometimes pungent aroma of the drying plants filled his laboratory, permeated his clothing, and drew his curious daughter even closer to him. His work fascinated her. She wanted to understand it, all of it. On especially hot days the scent of drying herbs wafted into all parts of the house and led her into his laboratory where she observed him at work. There in his little rooms filled with books and bottles and tubes of fermenting liquids, he sat in a wicker wheelchair and rolled from table to table far more quickly than he could walk. When he vacated the chair, she took it over, but she was still too small to maneuver the chair with alacrity. Often he allowed her to sit in his lap while he wheeled himself around the laboratory, or recorded the daily progress of his patients and the drugs he was using to treat them. At the end of the day she would beg to visit the courtyard, and off they would go in his rolling chair to water and weed his special garden.

Sitting in the wicker chair in the cool of the courtyard, the doctor introduced her to Spanish literature of the Golden Age, beginning with *The Life of Lazarillo de Tormes and of His Fortunes and Adversities*. "We call this the picaresque novel," he explained, "because it is the life of a rogue whose purpose it is to expose injustice while amusing the reader. It is a book for all ages and is beloved by everyone." From there he moved on to the poems of Lope de Vega followed by selections from *Don Quixote*, which he read in a voice that transported her into another world. While he read to her she imagined herself as the characters: she was Sancho Panza; she was Dulcinea del Toboso; she was Quiteria, Lazarillo, his mother, the blind man, the pardoner, and the Moor.

"More," she begged when he closed a book. "Read more."

One day when he was tired and could read no more, he said, "Now it's time for you to learn to read. Tomorrow we will start with the alphabet."

By her sixth year she was reading simple stories and poems and at seven she was writing her own stories and performing them for Carlota Montejo, who praised her delivery. By her eighth year her vocabulary was extensive, due to her father's constant tutelage and Carlota's spontaneous recitations of poetry and drama. Declaiming speeches from The House of Thebes and The House of

Atreus, she transformed herself into Cassandra, Antigone, Electra, and Iphigenia while Josefina sat spellbound, not by the content of the speeches, for she could hardly grasp a word, but by the intoxicating cadence of Carlota's delivery that often interrupted Eufemia's concentration and sent her on a rampage of screaming.

"Literature is important," the doctor said. "It is the heart of a nation. But you must know more."

It was then that he decided to introduce her to his closet of specimens. "You're old enough to see this," he said. "It will interest you." Inside the closet he pointed out jars containing human hearts, kidneys, livers, and spleens. He showed her severed fingers and toes and the diseased lungs of a child who had died in his arms.

"Did you know all these people?" she asked.

"Yes," he replied. "All of them."

She pressed her face close to a jar containing a fetus with delicately formed fingers and toes. "It's like a doll," she said. "Is this what we're supposed to look like?"

"Yes, after five months in the womb," he replied.

None of this repulsed her. Every specimen was preserved in a murky compound that placed the preserved organ at a clinical distance from the actual body of the patient so she was able to see everything with detachment and great interest. She stared into every bottle. She turned them for a better view and then she closed the door and walked into the garden. "I like the garden better than the closet," she said. "The plants are beautiful."

"And they are useful," he replied. "One day I will tell you all about them."

Before long she was visiting her father's clinic and observing him with patients. She would sit quietly in a corner and listen. In the clinic her thoughts did not wander, for there, a certain urgency filled the air and her father's voice, although calm and even in cadence, dropped into a deeper register and remained there until the last wound was closed and the last injection administered.

"Many of my injections are fatal," he once told her. "During intense suffering patients often beg for death, and I, as a medical doctor, have taken it upon myself to assist them. My views, however, are not equally shared and must not be discussed with others."

Josefina kept track of the minute changes in her father's schedule. When he was home she contrived to be with him at all times, and he welcomed her presence in all places except his bedroom. Even though she had never set foot in that room, she knew that his bedspread was indigo, his bed was carved oak, and the walls were the color of lightly toasted bread. She had seen all of this not only in her dreams but from a little room on the second floor where she peered between cracks in the floorboards to watch her father entertain and be pleasured. Lying on her stomach in that upper room, which was filled with spiders and centuries of dust, she learned many things, particularly from Carlota Montejo, the eldest and most experienced of the doctor's mistresses. Carlota mounted him as she would a stallion, locked her legs under his thighs and rode him, galloping through clouds of pillows and bedsheets. And at a precise moment, one that Josefina could never quite predict, the actress would grasp her lover's throat with both hands and gradually tighten her grip to intensify and prolong the doctor's ecstasy. From the room above, Josefina watched her father's pale complexion turn red. She could see the veins in his forehead throbbing and white foam gathering at the corners of his mouth. When she was certain that he was dying in the hands of the *Startling Treasure*, Carlota Montejo released her grip and a deathlike pallor swept over the doctor's face. Her crimson nails left dark crevices in his neck.

He's dead, Josefina would think. She's killed my father.

And although she remembered Fuerte saying that her father would not die by the hands of a woman, she could not allow herself an easy breath until the natural color had returned to his face and his heavy breathing subsided.

From the upstairs room, Josefina noticed, for the first time, that her father was a small man: frail wrists and ankles, sunken cheeks, heavily lidded and deep-set eyes. He had no hair on his chest, which was slightly concave, but surrounding his penis the hair was long and thick, and his erection curved upward extending well beyond his navel.

Do all men, she wondered, look like my father?

She also wondered which mistress he loved the most. Surely it was not *The Infant*, for she could do little beyond lying there to be undressed and petted like a house cat. Receiving the doctor was impossible for her, but the others accepted him with pleasure, particularly *The Mustache* whose known attribute was the extraordinary size of her lips and mouth into which the doctor completely disappeared.

He will be eaten alive, Josefina thought.

The Mustache was not a favorite, and neither was *The Mother of God*, who was ordinary in every possible way. She demanded too many presents, too many caresses, and too many sweet words, which the doctor uttered in the hollow voice of a man who had become bored with his choices. And unlike the others, she preferred making love under the sheets. Even on the hottest days when no breeze could be felt and the air was still with dust and perfume, sun-dried sheets as stiff as parchment, shielded the lovers from Josefina's disappointed eyes. *The Stinking Flower* was far more exciting to watch, for her limber body could bend to the doctor's delight, but the rancid odor of her perfume filled his apartment and wafted into the upstairs room where his daughter, lying with dust mites and spiders, chose her favorite of all the mistresses, the dangerous Carlota.

"Which one do you love the most?" she asked her father. "I hope it's not the one who smells like rotting fruit."

"I like them all," he replied. "But you are the one I love."

"What's the difference between liking and loving?" she asked, and the doctor, sensing that she needed something worthwhile on which to fasten her curiosity, came to the conclusion that it was time for the second phase of her education.

From that day until the hour of his death when her formal education came to an abrupt end and her life turned unexpectedly in another direction, they dined together each evening of the week. During dinner he talked about his latest laboratory experiments with herbs and poisonous plants, and after the meal Fuerte cleared the table for the study of history, geography, politics, mathematics and philosophy, world literature, the history of art, and the myths of the ancient Greeks, much of it on levels well beyond Josefina's comprehension at that time.

After two years of study with her father, she was sent to music teachers who taught her to play Beethoven and Chopin on the piano, and Mozart and Bach on the harpsichord. Later on she learned to sing simple airs in French and Italian, which the doctor enjoyed before retiring. During the season, he escorted her to the opera twice a month and more often than that to the National Theatre where the classics were performed. Once after a performance of *Phèdre*, Carlota Montejo placed her hands on Josefina's head and pressed her sharp fingernails into the young girl's scalp as if secrets were being transplanted directly into her brain. "What you must remember about Phèdre," Carlota said, "is that she is the first to be horrified by her actions over which she has no control. She is ensnared in her destiny by the wrath of Aphrodite, and her crime, if it must be called that, is one of relentless passion, a divine punishment rather than the product of her own free will."

During a late supper in her suite at the Carmina, Carlota directed Josefina's attention toward a portrait of Rachel hanging on one wall and Bernhardt on the other. "Phèdre was their most famous role, and it is mine as well," Carlota said. "Much has been written about our interpretations. Rachel's Phèdre was small, intense and fragile. But Bernhardt's Phèdre was monumental. She possessed the power of a goddess coupled with the fragility of a woman. I, Carlota Montejo, possess the best of both actresses and that is why Bernhardt refused to perform *Phèdre* when she visited our country."

Inspired by Carlota's performance, Josefina wondered if she, like Phèdre would ever be caught in a struggle of power between two jealous goddesses, Aphrodite of the heart and Artemis of the hunt. Searching for answers she studied Racine's couplets, memorized one of Phèdre's longest speeches and delivered it from a balcony overlooking the Street of Merchants and Peddlers.

"Ah, the doctor's daughter," the old lace maker said, "She is quite an actress. But who could be surprised? She has the *Startling Treasure* to guide her."

One afternoon when Carlota was breezing down the street to visit the doctor she overheard his daughter reciting loudly:

> "The Gods have lit within my breast,
> A fatal flame that gives no rest.
> Those evil Gods who torture my day,
> Have carried my fragile heart away."

"Do not speak so rapidly," Carlota shouted from the busy street. "You must enjoy each word. Make us believe that they are priceless jewels dropping from your tongue."

"Teach me to recite it the way you do," Josefina begged.

"No, no," Carlota scolded. "You must learn to deliver the speech your own way. Everything you do must represent you, no one else."

Inspired by the actress's attentions, Josefina dreamed of a life in the theatre, of living vicariously through the great tragic heroines as well as their interpreters. Like Montejo, she was Phèdre. She was Cassandra, Antigone, Electra, and Iphigenia. She would make a name for herself on the stage, and her father, perhaps even her real mother, would applaud her with pride. This was her first glimpse into a future that would be denied her, her first brush with unrelenting ambition. Carlota Montejo was her idol and the mother she wanted. Everything Carlota was, Josefina wished to be. Day and night she dreamed of becoming an actress, a tragedienne not unlike her famous mentor, but this dream, like so many others, would be momentarily eclipsed by another passion, one that did not meet the doctor's approval.

Doctor Esperon was not an aficionado of the corrida, but he

insisted on exposing his daughter to every cultural event, and to his regret she responded to the pageantry of the corrida with un-contained excitement, alarming nearby spectators with a sudden display of ferocity upon such a young and otherwise placid face. For her eleventh birthday she was taken to watch José Maria de Vega face what was to be his last bull, an event that would go down in history, in part because the matador, accounting for his delayed appearance in the capital city, told the press upon arrival that the bull he was to face the following day was nothing more than an underfed cow, no challenge to his bravery or the boldness of his style.

"One must never boast in the face of peril," Doctor Esperon said after he had read the article to his daughter. "Fate does not allow it."

As if the afternoon had been specially planned to add em-phasis to his statement, driving it even further into his daughter's mind, that Fate plays evil tricks on the braggart, the overconfident matador, performing before a crowd of three thousand spectators, was gored to death by the most ferocious bull in the country, a bull the leading newspaper would refer to the next day as "one of our underfed cows, Señor de Vega must now wish he had never met especially on the afternoon when his second son was born."

Without once averting her eyes, Josefina witnessed to the end what would come to be remembered as de Vega's blood bath. In an instant his suit of lights was stained, coils of intestines spilled from his abdomen, and his body was dragged seven yards before the bull hurled it high into the air. Josefina watched the matador fall like a rag doll that had been stuffed with red stockings, blue-green ribbons, and old cotton padding yellow with age. Unlike the spectators surrounding her, she was not sickened by what she saw; death was nothing new to her. Blood dripping from the veins of her father's patients, diseased organs removed to a side table and in some cases preserved in glass jars were familiar sights in her father's clinic and for that reason the matador's mutilated body did not repel her. On the contrary, the blood-spattered sand, the running of the bull, and the ribbons of intestines and blood, filled her with an explosive energy that lasted through many sleepless nights, stimulating her appetite and causing her to consume enormous quantities of food without gaining a single pound.

In the following days, Josefina talked of nothing except her ambition to become a famous matador. "You must not be too interested in these foolish things," Fuerte said. "Only an idiot would chase a bull, and besides that, your father needs you more than ever. Soon you will miss him very much."

Ignoring Fuerte's warning, Josefina ran through the house with a red tablecloth challenging imaginary bulls, stabbing them with a long pole, overturning pots of flowers, tables, chairs, and stools. The commotion broke Eufemia's concentration as never before. Her dual thoughts were shattered, and her notebooks went flying across the courtyard. Suddenly she was awakened to the presence of a daughter she had never acknowledged.

"Who is that girl?" Eufemia cried. "Tell her to be quiet. I am writing."

"She is your daughter," Fuerte said.

"How can you be my child?" Eufemia asked Josefina. "You are too noisy. Sit quietly! Be still! Give the angels a chance to speak to you."

"Why should I?" Josefina said.

"The angels will tell you something you need to know," Eufemia replied. Then she threw a handful of pencils at the daughter she had never accepted and tore through the house on a fit of screaming, "I must have silence! Why is there no silence in this house?" She galloped like a mad animal around the galleries of both courtyards and finally, when she looked down upon her daughter's angelic face, the rampage was suddenly over.

Eufemia calmly returned to her chair near the lotus pool, and Josefina watched her for a few a few moments before she spoke. "Why haven't you ever talked to me?" she asked.

"Because I am always listening to God, to the angels, and to my saint," Eufemia replied calmly.

Then Josefina came forward and stood before her. She stared into her mother's watery eyes and sank to her knees. "I'm sorry I bothered you," she said.

"I am seeing you as if for the first time," Eufemia replied. "You are no longer energetic and noisy. You are calm and beautiful like the angels."

Josefina took her mother's hand and said again, "I'm sorry I bothered you, *Mother*." The word fell from her lips unexpectedly. The sound of it shocked her and she tried to back away but Eufemia grabbed her by both hands.

"Oh, you are my daughter," she exclaimed. "I recognize you now. At first I did not. You are beautiful as I once was beautiful."

"And you still are," Josefina said.

And then for the first time they embraced.

After that, the large courtyard was reserved exclusively for Eufemia's daily meditation and Josefina tiptoed around her in unspeakable silence as she made her way to the laboratory to assist her father. He had forced her to abandon her reckless ambition to be a matador once and for all and return to the clinic where she was needed. "And besides," he added, "your mother does not enjoy noise, loud voices, or lots of commotion. She must have quiet in order to write and meditate. After all, she is a saint."

"A real saint?" Josefina asked.

"Well," her father replied, "the people think so. And it is the people, after all, who decide these things."

"Aren't saints created by God, Father?"

"I am convinced that nothing is created by God anymore, my daughter."

"Well then, is she a real saint or not?" Josefina asked.

"She's as real as any saint ever was," the doctor answered as if the question had exhausted him.

With every question and every enigmatic answer, Josefina's fascination for her mother developed beyond the doctor's expectations. More and more, her interest in Eufemia surpassed that of her father's laboratory and his jars of specimens, his plants, patients and even his mistresses. Several times during the course of an afternoon, she would slip away from the laboratory to watch Eufemia sitting in the garden and writing with both hands. One day she inched her way toward her. "What are you writing with your left hand?" she asked in a quiet voice.

Eufemia answered, "I am praising the creator of this world with my left hand, my daughter."

"And what are you writing with your right hand, Mother?"

"With my right hand I am condemning the evildoers. They must always be punished; banished to the fires of Hell."

"Can you see the angels?" Josefina whispered.

"Yes," Eufemia said. "You are one of them."

"And can you see the evildoers?" the daughter asked.

"No Daughter, they are not allowed to enter the house. Now sit with me and do not talk. Your presence calms me while I write. You are my angel now."

Several times a day Josefina would slip away from her father's clinic to sit with her mother in deep meditation. Presently, her father would call to her, "Come back. I need you to fill the medicine bottles and to shape the corks. I have many things to do that I cannot accomplish myself."

One August afternoon when the heat was unrelenting and every plant in the courtyards had wilted Josefina escaped from the laboratory to find her mother standing on the elevated edge of the lotus pool. One leg was dangling in space, while she held tightly to the branches of an orange tree. "Help me," she cried. "My daughter, help me before I float away to Heaven. The Blessed Spirits are begging me to join them, but I cannot leave you yet. My time is not yet come."

Josefina helped her return to the writing chair. "Hold me tightly Daughter," she cried, "or I will surely float away."

"Not if I put this pot of begonias in your lap Mother," Josefina said. "Hold to it, and you will be anchored."

"Daughter," the doctor called. "Come quickly. You must return."

Back in the laboratory he explained to his daughter that Eufemia had convinced herself that she was lighter than air. "It is possible that this floating sensation arises from extreme weight loss," he said. "The same thing happened to her patron, St. Teresa of Ávila. She was said to have levitated while holding on to the bars of a convent window. Your mother believes she has that ability also. In that regard she is truly a saint, but you must realize that saints are not exempted from evil. They have their dark sides as well. They are human."

"Sometimes she looks at me but she doesn't see me," Josefina said.

"She's looking beyond you," her father replied. "Her thoughts rarely dwell in this world. She has renounced the world and all worldly possessions. On our voyage here she threw almost all of her priceless jewelry into the ocean to calm the waves."

When Josefina celebrated her twelfth year her father gave her what was left of the family jewels, a diamond brooch and a necklace of rubies. "I took them from your mother only moments before she emptied her jewelry box into the sea," he said. "Now they're yours, but you must not wear them until you become a woman."

For her twelfth birthday, she also received a white silk dress, eight lessons for the Viennese waltz, and permission to choose one piece of jewelry to wear to the first performance of *Tosca*. She chose the ruby necklace because it was something that Tosca, herself, might wear; and although she wanted to wear it entwined in her hair, her father refused to allow her that freedom.

With her voice teacher she had thoroughly studied the arias and the libretto. Repeatedly, she had begged her father to hire an artist to paint a picture of the Madonna for which her mother would be the model. "It will be just like the opera," she said. But again he refused to give in.

"How did I manage to create such a child?" he asked Carlota Montejo.

"One day," Carlota said, "she will be remembered."

"But for what?" the doctor asked.

"For things you would not approve of today," she replied. "Take her to the opera and forget the things you cannot control."

On the afternoon of the performance Josefina stood on a balcony overlooking the Street of Merchants and Peddlers and sang *"Vissi d'arte"*. Her sharp voice grated on Eufemia's already shattered nerves. "Silence! she screamed. "Daughter, sing the Ave Maria. Please. You have the voice of an angel. Use it to praise God and the Blessed Virgin.

Immediately Josefina switched to the Ave Maria and Eufemia entered into state of ecstasy. "I will fly away," she said. "I will fly away on this voice of an angel." Euphoric, she ran through her apartment and onto the gallery where she threw herself with outstretched arms into the courtyard. "I fly with God," she said. "Only with God and the Angels."

The doctor looked up in time to see his wife framed by the courtyard and the cloudless blue sky, and in that moment, which seemed to last for eternity, he confessed his regret: he should have been impervious to her strange beauty and unworldly charm, he should have turned his head when he first saw her and never begged for her hand; then she would have remained in Spain where she was content to sit for hours embroidering, playing with the monkey, and talking to God in her family chapel. Surely, he thought, she will not live past this day. Surely, the ground is too hard to cushion her fall. In the next instant the regret he momentarily felt turned to relief, then to disappointment, and finally, to rage: her fall was broken by a hammock.

A shoulder was dislocated and both wrists were badly sprained, but after Doctor Esperon braced them with splints and wrapped them with gauze soaked in camphor, Eufemia returned to her rooms, to her notebooks, and her dual thoughts. "I will continue to write," she said, but she was barely able to hold her pencils. "Even if no one can read my scrawl except me. I will continue to write."

"Allow yourself to rest," the doctor said. "You have fever.

You can write tomorrow."

"Tomorrow," Eufemia answered, "may never arrive."

Shaking from having witnessed his wife falling into the courtyard, and from having entertained many conflicting regrets, the doctor suggested to his daughter that they go to the opera another night, but she refused to stay home. It was her birthday, and she was ready to celebrate. She had studied the libretto, memorized the arias, and had carefully painted Carlota's mole above her right lip.

"What will happen if we are not here and your mother decides to fly again?" he asked.

"She will not fly if we are not there to watch her," Josefina replied.

"How do you know?" her father asked.

"I don't know how I know," she answered. "I just do."

Before they left for the opera, Doctor Esperon cut down all the hammocks in the courtyard, and after walking with his daughter to the next corner he paid one of the peddlers to go back and hang them up again.

"Why did you do that, Father?" Josefina asked.

"Just in case you are wrong," he said. "What's your favorite aria?"

On her father's arm, she entered the opera house and ascended the grand staircase. With her cheeks rouged, her lips lightly painted, and her mother's rubies around her neck, she sat with her father in their private box and waited for the curtain to go up. All day she had felt a burning in her stomach, and by curtain time the bottoms of her feet were tender, her legs ached, and her eardrums pounded with the roar of ocean waves. It seemed as though the orchestra would never stop tuning, the lights would never dim, and the conductor would never make his entrance into the pit.

That night Odette Jupien was singing *Tosca* for the first time in the capital city, and Josefina sat on the edge of her seat waiting for the curtain to rise. She was eager to know exactly how Tosca would stab Scarpio and how she would jump from the parapet.

Would she throw herself into the air head first as her mother had done that afternoon, or would she fall backward with one hand on her brow? "Do you think she will face the audience to jump or will she turn her back on us?" she asked her father. "And what will break her fall? Will it be a hammock? Will it be a giant pillow? What will keep her from hurting herself?" She wondered how many sopranos had accidentally fallen to their deaths while merely acting a role, how many tenors had actually died of broken hearts, how many baritones had been stabbed on stage, and how many had survived the stabbing? Her father could not answer any of these questions, and Josefina failed to understand why. "What did they teach you in school?" she asked. "What is the point of school if you don't study these important things?"

When the curtain came down on the first act, Josefina, weak with excitement and from having entered her time, stood up to applaud the singers and realized that she was bleeding. "No," she whispered to her father. "Not now. Not tonight." Only then did the doctor notice blood stains on his daughter's chair and white dress. "We have to go home at once," he said. "Fuerte should have prepared you for this."

"She did prepare me but not at the opera! Not on my birthday!"

He put his suit coat around her shoulders and led her from their box into the Gran Sala where she collapsed in tears on the powder blue carpet, leaving there another stain.

"Do you need a doctor?" someone asked.

"He is a doctor," someone else replied.

"I need to take her home," Doctor Esperon said. "Please clear a path." With his daughter in his arms he hurried through the crowd and down the grand staircase. Three blocks later they arrived at the Street of Merchants and Peddlers, and two blocks after that they were home. The hammocks were hanging, and Eufemia was sleeping peacefully in one of them.

"Thank God," Doctor Esperon said when he saw her. Then he kissed his daughter on each cheek and turned her over to Fuerte.

"Tonight," he said, "You have become a woman."

"I have always been a woman, Father," she replied defiantly. And the next day she wore her mother's necklace for the second time.

Within that year she grew much taller. Her hair turned from dark brown to ebony black, and her complexion acquired the tone and translucence of alabaster.

Who will be the first man to love me? she wondered.

Lying in bed at night, her hands exploring her ever changing body, she dreamed of all the men she would know, but never once did she entertain thoughts of marriage. The men of her dreams showered riches upon her, took her to the opera, to concerts and the corrida, but none of them expected more than a few hours of pleasure, and always in the afternoon for they knew instinctively that afternoon was the best time of day for love.

By the end of Josefina's twelfth year, the doctor recognized her keen intelligence, her steady eye, and the alacrity with which she used her hands. "You will become my laboratory assistant," he said. "I'll teach you everything. I will even teach you to mix compounds and who knows, perhaps you'll become a doctor yourself."

One afternoon, just before her thirteenth birthday, their visit to the garden took on a more important tone. "Today we will have a serious lesson in botany," he said. There was urgency in his voice that made her uncomfortable. He gave her a notebook and told her to sit in his wicker chair. Then he pushed her through the garden. "You already know the names of most of the plants but now you must know something of their worth," he said. "We will start here. This is called Contribo." She wrote the name in her book. "The flower," the doctor continued, "smells of rotting flesh to attract flies for pollination. In every cantina you will see it soaking in rum. One shot will cure a hangover, two shots will clear away indigestion, and three will kill every amoebae living in the intestines. That's what the curanderas say, and by all accounts they are right."

He held the stinking flower to her nose; she pushed it away with disgust. Then he pushed the chair to the other side of the courtyard naming each plant along the way while she recorded, with meticulous penmanship, everything he said.

"This is called Buttonwood. The leaves added to a hot bath will reduce the aches of rheumatism and the swellings of the skin. This is Dog's Tongue. It alleviates rashes. This is Cocomecca, used to treat ailments of the urinary tract. This is Gumbo limbo for stomach cramps and kidney infections. This is Negrito for dysentery, and this is China root, which is good for the blood. Here we have *Papaver somniferum*, the opium poppy, and over there *Datura stramonium*, which is extremely toxic but in the right dosage can be salubrious as well, particularly when traveling rough seas."

Then they came to a small plant with a three-pointed leaf. "This is commonly called *Tres Puntas*. Boil the leaves for ten minutes to produce a liquid that is quite effective in the treatment fungus, ringworms, and amoebaes. Along with vervain it is also used as a vaginal douche to treat venereal diseases, and the local women sometimes use it to prevent pregnancy. This is called *Chichibe*. It's used to treat gonorrhea, and this plant is used to combat male impotency." At the end of the lesson he said: "Now the garden is yours. You are the new gardener."

Under her careful attention, the garden of medicinal plants thrived beyond the doctor's expectations, and on sensing her acute interest in such matters, he insisted that she accompany him on his visits to the curanderas who set up stalls outside the municipal market. Having already tested many of the local remedies he taught his daughter that the efficacy of some relied purely on faith, whereas others contained medicinal properties that could be scientifically proven. With the curanderas they discussed the curative power of incantations, of certain fragrances, sounds, and places. They recorded the various names of illnesses along with the best of the available cures, and each week they bought powders, plants, and seeds to be planted in the courtyard or analyzed in the laboratory. Her two most useful tools were the garden hoe and the microscope and she was never far from either.

One day when she was transplanting seedlings from small pots to the courtyard soil, Doctor Esperon took the opportunity to warn her once again that many of the plants were deadly if ingested in the wrong proportions. "This one for instance is called *planta mala*. The Indian word for it is *Xcoch*. The seeds and to some extent the foliage contain ricin. In pure form it is one of the most poisonous substances known to man. And this one with a complex leaf is called Flower of Utopia. According to a local formula four unopened buds steeped for ten days in one cup of water will produce a clear, greenish liquid, only three drops of which will produce a euphoria leading to a peaceful death."

"And when do you use it?" she asked.

"When a patient is suffering but cannot die," he answered.

"And are there others like it?" She put down her garden hoe and opened her notebook, which she carried in an apron pocket. The notebook was almost full. She turned to a blank page and began recording everything her father had just told her.

"This one with the dark green leaves and small white flowers is somewhat similar," he replied. "The locals call it the Valley of Death, and they use it to rid the body of impurities that give rise to boils and infections of the joints. A little water added to one gram of the powdered root will make a thick paste from which five small pills can be molded. One will clear the stomach and bowels, but two will stop the heart."

"What is the most poisonous tree in the world, Father?" Quickly she turned a page without looking up or missing a word.

"I would say the curare," Doctor Esperon answered. "The Indians used it to poison their arrows. But then you also have the water hemlock, which is called snakeroot and in some places cowbane."

"And what is the most poisonous mushroom?" Again she turned a page and continued writing.

"They are too many to name," he said, "but as far as I know, we only need to worry about three, the Deadly Amanita, the Destroying Angel and the Fetid Russula. They can be found in the forest just beyond the marsh and must always be avoided, in spite of what the curanderas will tell you."

"And what is the most poisonous insect?"

"Why has your mind turned to poison, Daughter?" he asked.

"Because," she said, "I may need to know these things."

"Not likely," the doctor answered. "Now return your thoughts to the garden and the importance of these plants before your mother calls you."

In a few minutes Eufemia called to her. "Sing me a Heavenly song," she said. "Please Daughter. I shall scream and tear out my hair if you don't."

"You have no hair, Mother," Josefina said but only to herself as she hurried through the narrow passage to the large courtyard. She sang a lullaby. Eufemia drifted away. And then Josefina returned to her father who was calling to her from the laboratory.

There he showed her a shelf of bottles containing murky liquids with residues of leaves and bark and on another shelf he pointed out sealed jars containing dried matter ready to be boiled in water or steeped in cane alcohol. Each bottle was carefully labeled, and those containing toxic compounds, which could be misused easily, were kept on a high shelf, faraway from reach. "You have seen all this many times before," he said, "but today I want to emphasize one important fact. The only difference between a drug and a poison is dosage. The secret to being a good doctor is knowing what to prescribe, how much to prescribe, and for how long. The body is like a storage house and the accumulation of a drug can sometimes be fatal."

Every morning she watered the plants; she moved the seedlings in or out of direct sunlight, and in a leather-bound journal she recorded the slightest changes in color and growth. Later on in the laboratory she recorded her father's experiments, and when the patients arrived she sat unobtrusively in a corner chair to observe his methods of treatment. Before long, she was dressing wounds, assisting with broken limbs, and performing general examinations of the eyes, ears, nose, and mouth. Suffering did not turn her head and neither did the smell of blood on her fingers, nor the eyes of death staring into her own.

"So what do you think?" her father once asked. "This patient cannot live more than a month. It is possible to ease his pain today, but in doing so he will surely die tomorrow. What would you do?"

"One day without pain is better than a month of suffering," she answered.

And the decision was made.

No matter how busy she was in her father's clinic and laboratory, she took a few minutes to sit with her mother and to bring back a report to her father. "She is all right," she would say. Or, "Today she imagined that she was floating again. I tied a rope around her waist and the other end to one of the trees. That seemed to satisfy her. The rope makes her feel secure. I think she is beginning to trust me more. Last night she called to me from her bedroom."

"And what did she want?" the doctor asked.

"She wanted me to tie her to her bed. She said she was floating out the window. And after I tied her to the bed, she said the bed was floating out the window with her own it. And do you know what Father? I believed her. She convinced me. So I tied her and the bed to the doorknob, and then she went back to sleep."

"She is very delicate," he said.

"I want to read the writings of St. Teresa of Ávila," Josefina replied.

"Then it's time," he said. And he put the books in her hands.

After she had read The Way of Perfection, the poems, and selected writings on ecstasy, she told her father, "Now, I can accept so many things, but I cannot understand them. St. Teresa said that ecstasy was like a 'detachable death,' and during these experiences her soul became awake to God as never before."

She opened a biography of the saint and read aloud to her father: "'Mother Maria Baptista, a Carmelite nun, said that she witnessed Teresa raised up from the ground on two occasions. She once resisted a rapture during communion by grabbing the bars of a window as she rose in the air, crying out for deliverance from her ecstasy. The levitations frightened her but there was nothing she could do to control them.' "Really, Father," she protested, "do you really think St. Teresa levitated or was it only in her dreams and in the eyes of the other Carmelites?"

"A mere suggestion can create the greatest of all realities, Daughter. We cannot deny the power of the mind. You yourself have said that you once thought your mother was actually floating away."

"Yes," she said. "I suppose I did. But *only* for a moment. She convinced me it was true only for a moment."

"If you were a believer," he said, "if you truly needed to believe what you thought you saw, that moment would have lasted forever."

"But when I read St. Teresa, I want it to be true. Her language is poetic and with poetry . . ."

". . . all things are possible." Her father finished her thought.

Every morning Josefina studied her lessons beginning with literature, her favorite subject. She gave ample time to the poems of Lope de Vega and St. John of the Cross and the visionary writing of St. Teresa of Ávila, which instilled in her a sense of well-being and purpose even though she could not bring herself to believe in God the Father, God the Son, and God the Holy Ghost.

After literature, she moved on to geography, mathematics, and history, and in the early afternoon she checked on her mother before reporting to her father's laboratory. If her mother felt the sensation of levitation, she would cry out, "Daughter, help me! I feel a great force beneath my feet." For by then Eufemia had accepted the fact that she not only had a daughter, she had a responsible daughter who would come when called. When she felt as if she were floating away, her daughter would tie her to the chair, or to one of the orange trees, kiss her bald head, and return to the laboratory only to be summoned again in a few minutes.

"Daughter, I need you. I am ready to return to my chapel. Untie me please. I need to read St. Teresa's holy words."

"Daughter, I am being lifted up, come quickly."

"Daughter, I thirst like Christ on the Cross."

"Daughter, I need you to hold my hand. I am suddenly afraid."

"Daughter I need a pot of flowers on my lap. I am not ready to fly away."

"You seem to have learned to appreciate her," the doctor said one evening after the last patient had left the consultation room.

"In ways I cannot easily explain," she confessed. "I have grown to love her."

"If for no other reason," the doctor said, "she is unlike anyone else in the world, and she is, after all, your mother. That cannot be denied."

"I think," she said, "I am like her in one important way, we are both dedicated, but to different things."

While Eufemia meditated in the garden Josefina continued assisting her father with great seriousness. She approached her work with a steady gaze, a confident hand, and she kept detailed notes on all the patients and their treatments. Finally, the doctor taught her to close wounds. She handled the needle and thread as if she had been born to sew and at the age of fifteen, she was closing one of the nastiest wounds her father had ever seen and with the neatest sutures he could possibly imagine.

The patient was the president of the nation. The first of many presidents to enter the doctor's house.

Josefina was helping her father set a broken leg when Carlos Serrano, campaigning for a second presidential term, was carried to the front door by four bodyguards dressed as civilians. Only minutes before his arrival he had been delivering a speech on the plaza when an assassin's bullet narrowly missed his heart.

"He will not enter this house," Fuerte said when she answered the door. "This man will never be welcomed here." She stomped her feet and advanced on the guards. "You must leave. The doctor is not home!"

"Silence!" Eufemia pleaded. "I'm sitting with my trees."

"Of course I'm home," Doctor Esperon called from the passage between the courtyards. "Who's there?"

"No one," Fuerte answered.

"Yes," Eufemia replied. "Someone is there, and I must have silence. There are too many voices in this house."

"Allow them to come in," the doctor said when he saw the wounded man.

Only then did Fuerte step aside. "It's your house, Doctor, not mine." Turning her back on the president, his guards, and Doctor Esperon as well, she retreated to her dark bedroom and her loom.

> *The first president has come.*
> *And on allowing him to enter.*
> *The doctor has sealed his fate.*
> *On allowing him to enter,*
> *The house will be forever changed.*

The president was carried into the small courtyard and laid to rest on a long table. "He's lost too much blood to be carried any farther," Doctor Esperon told the bodyguards. "My daughter and I will operate here."

A tent of mosquito netting was hung over the makeshift surgery, and toward the end of the operation Carlota Montejo swept into the courtyard as if floating on a breeze. Doctor Esperon did not once look up to greet her. He had located the bullet and was slowly extracting it, while Carlota, dancing for the benefit of the bodyguards, swirled her way toward the doctor's chambers to make herself ready to receive him. "If he is too busy to pay attention to me this afternoon," she said to the guards, "I'm sure I can count on one or all of you to take his place. And then you, too, will have your names recorded in my little red book." She waved her leather-bound journal in their faces and disappeared into the doctor's apartment leaving the guards standing at attention as if before a commanding officer.

Minutes later, Doctor Esperon extracted the bullet and Josefina prepared to dress the wound. "He's very handsome," she said while closing the incision with perfectly executed sutures. "And his breath smells of mint. Do you think he has many lovers, Father? As many as you?"

The guards laughed. "How many lovers do you have, Doctor?" one of them asked.

"He is a man who needs many women," Carlota answered from the doorway to the doctor's rooms. "But I am his favorite."

"And mine too," Josefina added.

"You see," Carlota said. "I am favored in this house and not only by the doctor, but by his pretty daughter as well. She is so pretty she could easily be my own child."

"How many children do you have?" Josefina asked.

"If you listen to rumor," Carlota said. "I have given birth to everyone in the country. If you believe everything you hear it is because of me that my orphanage is constantly filled with beautiful babies and pretty young girls but none prettier than you."

She stepped forward to admire Josefina's stitches, and only then did she understand why the doctor had ignored her. "My president," she gasped.

"You know him?" Josefina asked.

"Of course," Carlota replied. "I am his favorite actress. I even have a letter to prove this. He has given me many contributions and pleasures."

While the last stitches were being tied and cut, Doctor Esperon, Carlota, and the four guards sat on benches arranged in a circle near the makeshift surgery, and over many glasses of brandy they discussed the political unrest that was far from resolved. "He will never be reelected," Carlota said, "not unless everyone joins his campaign and the counting of the ballots is supervised. I am standing guard at the voting booths where everyone will see me.

I am counting ballots in the plaza where my presence will be noticed, and I am pasting posters on walls and doorways. What are you doing, my dear doctor?"

"He's saving lives," Josefina said.

"But is he saving the right ones?" Carlota asked. "We must encourage your father to take a position, even it is the wrong one, but of course, it will not be the wrong one, not as long as I am allowed to enter this house. You are his daughter; he will listen to you. 'Try every means of persuasion. Words of thine will find him far more agreeable than mine. Beg! Plead! Give him no rest. Weep, wail and beat thy breasts.'"

"She is always the actress," Doctor Esperon said. "And she's never above taking liberties with Racine's couplets. But the truth is: I am not given to political campaigns and public gatherings. My place is in the hospital and here in my clinic."

"Your father is a very stubborn man," Carlota said. "But he has many fine attributes as well. His greatest, of course, cannot be discussed in public, for even I would lower my head at the mention of it. Oh, yes, it is true. When I first saw him, 'I stared, I blushed, I paled. A sudden turmoil set my mind aswim. My eyes no longer saw, my lips were dumb; my body burned, and yet was cold and numb.'"

"She is without shame, to quote Racine out of context," the doctor said.

The gods laughed.
And the brandy was poured.
And the weaver of this cloth waited for her turn to speak.

Soon the moon was floating above the courtyard, and Eufemia was strolling along the gallery like a pilgrim lost in a wilderness of thoughts. In one hand she carried a silver spoon and in the other a burgundy ribbon, which fell from her fingers like a stream of blood. Serrano was watching her. Through veils of mosquito netting and half-sleep she glided like a wraith on thin clouds, her bare head floating like another moon above frail shoulders. "Even if the

whole world should blame you," she said, to the wounded president, "even if the whole world should despise you, defeat you, and
deafen you with its cries, what does it matter so long as you are
embraced by the arms of righteousness?"

"Now this one," Carlota said to the bodyguards. "The doctor's beautiful wife, she is worshipped among the poor and better known throughout the country than I, myself. People walk for
miles just to see her sitting on the balcony. Put her to work, and we
will get plenty of votes."

"And everyone will be shot," Fuerte said. She was standing in
the dark passage between the courtyards. No one heard her.

"Yes," Serrano said, before sleep overtook him. "Put her
to work."

During his convalescence the president and Doctor Esperon
became steadfast friends, and Josefina grew to love the man
who bore the markings of her perfect stitches on his chest. "Let
me see them again today," she would beg, and the president would
unbutton his shirt for the doctor's daughter to gaze with approval
upon the results of her fine needlework. In turn, he gazed with
approval upon her delicate but determined lips, her translucent
skin, her long neck and raven hair, and most especially, the glow
of intelligence in her eyes, but it was her mother, as bald as the
full moon, who won his heart as the most beautiful woman he
had ever seen, even more beautiful than his own wife, who was,
like himself, an Indian from the highlands. Maria Asuncion, a
woman of considerable stature and unconventional beauty, was
greatly admired for her glistening copper skin and hooded eyes,
for her high forehead and prominent nose, her tapering fingers and
long earlobes adorned with loops of pure gold, given to her by her
mother's mother for whom she had been named.

"You belong to the earth," her husband had told her more
times than she needed to hear, "not the sky, not the clouds, not
even the water. The very center of the earth is your home."

"No," she said, "the center of my home is my husband, and

you must never forget it."

She gave him four children, born in his own image, and he gave her his heart, forever. "Forever," he said "Forever and forever more."

And this he had believed without a moment's doubt until the day he was brought bleeding to the doctor's house, and there, after the bullet had been removed, he awakened to see Eufemia for the first time. She held a dark ribbon in one hand and a silver spoon in the other. The ribbon slipped through her fingers and fell into the courtyard, but she held the silver spoon before her as if it were an instrument of navigation. Then she spoke and forever was no more. On hearing her voice for the first time, Serrano's heart ached and his breath shortened. Suddenly, his wife's terrestrial beauty seemed all too familiar, and the corner of his mind that once belonged only to her was invaded by another.

During his recovery he spent entire afternoons in the large courtyard where he listened to the music of wind chimes and watched Eufemia record her dueling thoughts. With a pen in each hand and two notebooks on her lap, she drew her words with graceful flourishes, lifting her arms ceremoniously at the end of each line and moving them quickly to the left. For the president, the measured repetition of Eufemia's arms calmed his labored mind and transported him through portals of many unrealized desires. Hour after hour he listened to the chimes and waited for her to look up, longing for their eyes to meet, not realizing that when she wrote her reasoning was suspended, conscious thoughts surrendered, and the pounding of her troubled heart was silenced.

If only, he thought, I had married such a woman.

But in a week's time, after witnessing Eufemia's sudden and tearful awakenings that sent her screaming across the courtyard, the president began uttering prayers of thanks that Eufemia was not his wife after all. In so few years, he thought, and for little more than awakening from a coma or walking down a dark and muddy street, she has become as famous as the nation's *Startling Treasure*.

On realizing that the president was falling under the dark spell of Eufemia's beauty, the doctor enlisted his mistresses to turn the leader's head. "It will be good for your heart," he said, "to lie back and allow yourself to be pleasured without putting undue strain on the body. You may enjoy all of them except Carlota. I will not allow her to come to you."

"Carlota and I met long ago, Doctor," Serrano said. "You have no worry. What's done is done."

"Well then," the doctor replied. "Things without all remedy, should be without regard."

Under doctor's orders, a mistress visited the president each afternoon, and while lying on his bed he was undressed, bathed and covered with soft kisses. The bodyguards stationed outside his door searched each woman before allowing her to enter and only Maria Aparacida was turned away. Because of her thick mustache they suspected her of being a man, a possible assassin.

"Only the doctor," she said, "knows how to appreciate what I have to give."

"Only the doctor," Serrano said, "knows the true meaning of generosity. The day I leave his house will be one of the saddest of my life."

In the evenings, after his last patient had been treated, the doctor and his daughter sat in the small courtyard and listened to the president talk endlessly of politics. Until then, and in spite of Carlota's insistence, Doctor Esperon had not participated in the politics of the country. "Voting is a complete waste of time," he said, "especially in a nation where all officials are appointed."

In due course, however, the convalescing president, who would be remembered as one of the country's great humanitarians, turned the doctor's head. "This country is founded on murder and slavery," he said. "For almost four centuries the endless pattern of oppression followed by rebellion and mass annihilation has been repeated while the dictators who call themselves presidents speak sweetly of democracy. This is what I want to change."

He said that the country had been founded by five wealthy

families including the Serranos who adopted him without reservation, but he had never considered himself one of them, not even when he had tried to be. At the age of ten, he had entered the family by chance when one of the Serrano daughters, traveling the highlands in search of a cure, saw him sitting on a rock. She was thirty-eight years old, had miscarried six times, and had visited every oracle in the highlands only to learn that it was not her destiny to bear children. "You will have a child," she was told by three seers. "But it will not be your own."

On her way home her party stopped at a stream to rest the horses, and it was there that she saw him: an Indian boy of extraordinary presence who represented the combined souls of her lost children. She dismounted and approached him with outstretched arms. "You are my son and my sons. I have found you. I have found you at last. From now on, you will call me Mother."

In that day it meant nothing to kidnap an Indian, and the president made it clear that nothing had changed, not even he. His origin was Indian and so was his point of view, and even though he had been educated as a Serrano and had been given jobs that would further the family's empire, he continued speaking his first language every day.

"I was encouraged to forget my past," he told the doctor, "so for years I spoke only to myself knowing that one day I would return to my village without having lost a single word of my language, but first I had many obligations to my adopted family."

On one hand he harbored resentment and on the other gratitude to his foster mother and every last Serrano who claimed him as their own, educated him, and saw to it that he had many opportunities to prove his loyalty. Putting his resentment aside he quickly advanced among them, first in education and then in political ambition. His first job was in a local branch of the Public Revenue Office, and from there at the age of twenty-one he joined the military. Within a year he rose to the rank of captain, and under his command there were no rebellions and no uprisings because he used his influence among the Indians and his knowledge of their dialects to assure them that they had not been forgotten in spite of how it might seem. When he was thirty the president of the day chose him to reorganize the National Party, and in a short time he had transformed it from a loose confederation of territorial claques into a cohesive, well-run machine. Then the five families convened as they did every seven years, and after a short debate they chose him to be the youngest president in the nation's history.

"Although my election was assured," he told the doctor and his attentive daughter, "I spent a year between nomination and polling day carrying out an extensive campaign."

"The more I hear of such things," Doctor Esperon said, "the more content I am to spend the rest of my life in my clinic and laboratory."

Serrano sighed. Josefina loosened his bandage. And then he continued, expounding endlessly, or so it seemed to the doctor, on what he called a very expensive charade that sent him campaigning across the country. He visited virtually every village and outpost, met with local leaders, and assured them that they would be remembered if he were elected. And at last he visited his own mountain village only to find that his family had been slain, their land appropriated by the governor, their houses burned, and their bodies thrown to the dogs. "We were not allowed to bury our dead," one of the survivors told him. "Had we done so we would have been shot, and so the bodies rotted by the side of the road, and the vultures filled the skies as well as their stomachs, and even the dogs went mad from the stench."

"We were not even allowed to weave our cloth," an old woman told him. "Because in our designs we talk to each other in a silent language."

After only a few weeks in office he began carrying out a wide range of reforms, all of which angered his family and supporters. He redistributed land; wrangled it away from the nobility, and placed it in the hands of landless farmers. He also extended the services of government banks, so the Indians who had received land could borrow money. And by the time he came to know the doctor, he was well on his way to expropriating the nation's railroads from foreign hands.

"You're extending your hospitality to a very unpopular man," he told his host. "I have too often voiced my disapproval of foreign industries moving into our country and making large profits from which we will eventually suffer side effects that will far outweigh the loss of money. If we are not careful, one day our spirits will be ripped from our bodies. Now I am speaking as an Indian not as a Spaniard, not even as a mestizo."

"What has kept you alive?" Josefina asked.

"Very little," Serrano replied. He pointed to his guards, two at the side entrance and two more on the gallery. "One of them knows who fired the bullet that struck me. I would wager a fortune on it."

"Nonsense," the doctor said. "The thought is astonishing." His wife wandered into the moonlit courtyard and answered him with the words of her saint:

"For human nature is such that we scarcely notice what we see frequently but are astounded at what we see seldom or hardly at all. And the devils themselves encourage this astonishment, for if a single soul attains perfection it robs them of many others."

Two days later, the president stood on one of the balconies that overlooked the Street of Merchants and Peddlers, and while he addressed the crowd standing below, Eufemia scribbled prayers on colored paper and threw them into the air with the uninhibited joy of a child whose birthday was being celebrated. "Remember my prayers," she said. "They'll be important when I am dead, and that's why I'm leaving them to you in writing."

"She belongs to us," said the merchants and peddlers, "far more than to her husband, or the strangers who have invaded our street."

Every afternoon they waited for her, and every afternoon she allowed herself to be seen with the president at her side. She distributed her hand-written prayers while he delivered a campaign speech, and one afternoon Doctor Esperon reluctantly agreed to join them.

"President Serrano is a perfect patient," he said to the crowd of merchants, peddlers, and newspaper reporters. "He's a perfect friend as well. I am in the business of saving lives, and he is in the business of maintaining life on its highest level of democracy."

The following morning, the doctor's words appeared in print. They were repeated in the cafés and plazas, and later that day he stood on the balcony for the second time. "I'm not a public figure," he said. "My place is in the hospital, and here in my private practice, but now that I have been given an opportunity to speak my mind, I wish to say that the coming election will go down as the most important one in the history of this nation. At last we will have the power to choose and elect, and the voice of the people will be heard for the first time."

Within a few days the president was escorting Eufemia into the desperate streets and dark allies where her most ardent followers resided. She had not been seen wandering the streets for a long time so her visit was a great event that drew devoted crowds. Along the way, she distributed written prayers and quoted from *The Way of Perfection*:

"I do not say this without good reason, for, as I have said, it is very important for us to realize that God does not lead us all by the same road, and perhaps he who believes himself to be going along the lowest of roads is the highest in the Lord's eyes. It is when I possess least that I have the fewest worries."

On these excursions into the slums and surrounding countryside, she wore a brimmed hat to shield her baldness from the tropical sun, and a veil to protect her sensitive eyes from insects and dust. She wore gloves to cover her delicate hands and sack dresses of coarse cotton with ragged hems, long sleeves and high necklines. She wore stockings of heavy wool that scratched her legs and sandals that pierced her feet and reminded her of the suffering Christ. "That which we are made to suffer is so little in comparison to His," she told her followers. "To suffer without making excuses is a habit of great perfection, and very edifying and meritorious."

Wherever they went, the people demanded a reminder of their visit: a thread from her garment, a word written on a piece of paper, a leaf she had touched, a rock she had stooped to pick up, or a feather she had found along the way. And of the president, they demanded the same: a button from his shirt, a strand of hair, a handkerchief to be divided among them, or a coin that would never be spent for fear its significance would vanish into thin air.

Finally, the doctor conceded. "I'll help you also," he said. "I can certainly take the time to make a few more speeches."

Plans were made for a campaign that would take the two men across the country, and the night before they departed, the president gave Josefina a small pistol with an ivory handle. "In two weeks we'll return," he promised, "and then I will teach you to use it."

"I'll teach myself," she said. And she did.

While her father and the president were away she ran the clinic, worked the garden, and looked after her mother while Fuerte cooked, cleaned, and wove in the afternoon heat. In her spare time Josefina practiced her first shots on sparrows flying over the courtyards. Lying on hammocks or on the hot sand, she learned to bring down the tiny birds with an accuracy that made Fuerte's fingers tremble across her loom, and Eufemia scream for mercy under a shower of dead sparrows.

"The doctor's beautiful daughter," said the merchants and peddlers. "She's a very dangerous one indeed. Especially if you happen to be a sparrow."

"Not all of the birds are sparrows," said the food vendors. "Some are pigeons, and some are gulls, but the sparrows are the tastiest."

The pilgrims picked up all the birds that fell into the street and roasted them until their bones melted and they could be eaten in a single bite, and Fuerte raked up all the birds that fell into the courtyards and buried them under the bougainvillea. "Before long," she said, "the entire world will smell of gun smoke and singed feathers."

She begged Josefina to aim at something else. "Your father's medicine bottles would make nice targets, and so would his hats." But no target was as challenging as a flock of birds flying over the courtyards.

"I have less than ten seconds to take aim and fire," she said. "Father will be very impressed with what I've taught myself."

Dead birds rained from the afternoon sky. They fell into the lotus pool with a loud splash that sent water flying all over Eufemia's notebooks. "No, Daughter," she begged repeatedly. "Put away your weapons and sing praises."

"In a moment, Mother, I promise."

"Silence your weapon, Daughter. I cannot think."

"Yes Mother, I'm listening, but I cannot stop."

"The courtyards smell of blood!"

"The lotus pool is filled with feathers."

"Everywhere there is death."

Unable to cross the courtyard without stepping on a dead bird, she screamed for help. "Daughter, I am in blood. Stepped in so far that I should wade no more. Daughter, hear me: I am in blood. Help me."

"I will be there in just a moment, Mother."

But Eufemia could wait no longer. Screaming as if she were dying of pain, she tore through the house and threw herself into her bed. There she stayed sheltered from the gunshots, smoke, and the smell of fresh blood until the doctor came home.

On the afternoon of his return dead birds littered the courtyards and street. "Can there be any sparrows left in the sky?" the merchants asked the peddlers, and the pilgrims replied, "No, they are all in our stomachs."

Stepping deftly around the sparrows, Doctor Esperon stood behind his daughter and watched her fire the pistol with astonishing accuracy. "Teach me how to aim so quickly," he said, "one day I may need to defend myself."

"No, Daughter," Eufemia said from the gallery. "Teach him naught. We have too much blood in this house."

"And there will be more," the weaver said.

He loaded his own pistol, and together they brought down their flying targets. Eufemia screamed for silence and retreated to her chapel, and Fuerte, whose ears were plugged with rags, swept up the bloody carcasses and left them in buckets outside the front door to be fought over by food vendors and pilgrims. From that day until the hour she left the doctor's employment, Fuerte lived with rags in her ears and a pillow tied over her head, but even with these precautions, she heard the pistol every time it was fired, and the shots reminded her of many things she was certain would come to pass, things she had seen but could not express, not even with her threads.

Finally, the day arrived when she could no longer tolerate the sound of bullets singing toward living targets, or the lingering smell of gun smoke and blood. "I cannot stay where I am not heard," she said, but only to her loom. Having reached this conclusion, she left the doctor's house without a moment's notice. On a sunny afternoon when sparrows were being shot from the sky and the courtyards were redolent of smoke and singed feathers, she threw her apron on the floor and walked out. She left pots boiling on the stove, the dinner table already set, and the wash hanging from clotheslines stretched across the roof. In a two-wheeled cart, she carried her tapestry of 167 panels rolled up around its loom and secured with a yellow cord. A bag of colored thread was tied to her waist, and panel 168 was folded into a triangle and balanced on her head to shade her face from the blazing sun.

On the corner of Merchants and Peddlers and the Avenue of Saint Michael and All Angels, she paused momentarily to consider her direction. Beyond her extended arm, the world was a blur, but her feet knew the way to the city market, so she started in that direction, and after wandering about for many hours someone pointed her toward her mountain village. "Don't leave this road; it will take you there," she was told, and the next morning she was sitting with her six paddle-footed sisters who had always listened to her. "Next time, maybe you will listen to us," they said. "This is where you belong."

"The doctor," she kept telling them. "He is the one who refuses to listen."

The house of forty-three rooms seemed empty without Fuerte. And on the Street of Merchants and Peddlers, something was missing. All the merchants felt it. Fuerte was not there. "She'll come back," Josefina said. "This is where she belongs."

"I wouldn't be too sure of it," Doctor Esperon replied. "She misses her people."

"We are her people," Josefina argued."

The night after Fuerte walked out, Eufemia dreamed that her husband had left her and Fuerte had returned. "He flew away on a chariot racing across the sky," she said, "and Fuerte returned after the world had stopped smoking and all the armies had marched away." The next afternoon during siesta she dreamed that the armies had returned to loot the city. "Bar the doors," she screamed. "No one must enter or leave this house. Do not allow anyone inside. Where is Fuerte? She will guard the door." The doctor gave his wife a sedative, and after she was soundly sleeping he left for the French park where he was scheduled to deliver a speech written by the president.

At sundown he returned filled with enthusiasm over the response his speech had received, but on entering his house of forty-three rooms, he realized at once that something was different. The air was heavy with unknown expectations, with silent concerns, and with the foreboding perfume of night-blooming jasmine. Both Eufemia and Josefina were standing like statues in front of the lotus pool. As if waiting to be brought to life with a single touch of the doctor's hand, they stood there staring at him as though he had already entered the kingdom of the shades.

"We've been waiting for you," Eufemia said, speaking as if she had a message to deliver, or as if they all knew something that could not be spoken.

"Waiting for what?" the doctor asked.

"Waiting for you to sit with us in the garden," Eufemia said. Her voice did not come from her body. It came from the evening shadows, from the depths of the lotus pool from the narrow dark passage that connected the courtyards.

"Yes," Josefina repeated in her mother's tone. "In the garden. We want to sit with you in the garden."

It seemed to the doctor that his wife was asleep. Did I give her too much sedative? he wondered. But then he quickly realized that his daughter's voice was also receding into the distance, as if she were backing away from an inevitable calling.

The courtyard was filled with fireflies and singing crickets. The frogs in the lotus pool were croaking and scorpions were scurrying across the courtyard toward distant shadows. The doctor, his wife, and daughter sat beneath the orange trees, which had grown to the level of the gallery but had not yet bloomed. For the first time they sat together as a family and for what reason none of them could say. "The world is so peaceful tonight," Eufemia said. With both hands she captured her dueling thoughts, while her husband spoke with pride about the speech he had given a few hours earlier. Soon a night wind, blowing through the narrow passage that connected the courtyards, played warring melodies on the chimes, and after the wind had moved on and the courtyard was silent once again, the doctor began telling his daughter about a compound he had discovered that could put an end to malaria once and for all. "Its base is *Cinchona*," he said, "but I have added to it three herbs the curanderas use; one is the leaves of *Quebracho*, and another is called *Yaxnik*, the exact translation of which I am uncertain." For a few moments he waited to hear a response. Josefina was about to say, "Continue, Father," when three loud knocks on the front door interrupted her thoughts. In the wake of the knocks an unsettling silence reverberated throughout the courtyard. Suddenly the crickets stopped singing and the frogs disappeared under the water. Again someone knocked at the door.

"Let us not answer it," Eufemia said. "The world is too peaceful right now."

"Maybe it's Fuerte," Josefina said. "Maybe we are waiting for Fuerte."

"It isn't Fuerte's knock," the doctor replied. "We are waiting for something else."

"Let us not answer it," Eufemia said. "I want this moment to last forever. We are together, at last, and the night is still."

Again, there was a knock, much louder this time, more demanding and urgent.

Doctor Esperon got up to answer the door. "Your greatest treasure is your purity," he said to his daughter. "It's worth more than silver and gold." She looked at him in astonishment for he was a man who rarely changed the topic of conversation so abruptly.

"What do you mean, Father?"

"There's a great price on your head," he replied. And then he took a deep breath and walked to the door.

"No, Father," she said. "Please don't go."

But the doctor did not turn back.

"You're needed at the hospital," came a voice through the door. "There has been an accident. Many people are injured."

At once the doctor prepared to leave, and Josefina prepared to leave with him, but he held her back. "Stay here with your mother," he said. "We cannot leave her alone."

The doctor left by the front door. Josefina bolted it behind him and ran upstairs to her bedroom. From her balcony she could see her father standing in the middle of the street and talking quietly to a hospital official in a white lab coat. For a moment a feeling of relief swept though her. It had rained earlier in the evening, and the air was still fresh and damp. The moon reflected off the tile roofs, the wet cobblestones, and a knife blade in the official's hand. Seeing her father backing away, she drew Serrano's pistol from her pocket, aimed quickly and fired. The bullet entered the traitor's temple, and he fell face down on the street. Blood flowed from his head like a devil's halo, and the street was washed in silence.

"Well done," said the doctor to his daughter who was leaning over the balcony with her pistol drawn. Somewhere just beyond the corner someone was emerging from the shadows, and at that moment she uttered her first prayer, the only one she would ever speak with sincerity. "Our Heavenly Father," she whispered. "Please let him come a little closer."

Realizing that she was taking aim again, the doctor turned around abruptly, and the man in shadows fired the next shot. Doctor Esperon dropped to his knees and rolled over onto his side. He lay there motionless. The gunman stumbled forward, and Josefina fired her second bullet. In the shadows she saw the gunman swaying on his feet. He raised one arm to surrender, but instead he took a few staggering steps and disappeared around the corner.

Did he drop his gun? she wondered. Did something fall from his hands? Soon she heard the sound of an automobile being driven at high speed. Whose automobile? she asked herself. There are so few in this country.

When the noise of the automobile faded into the distance a crushing silence fell upon the Street of Merchants and Peddlers.

"Father!" Josefina said. "Can you hear me?"

The doctor did not answer.

The rag pickers and the tinsmith carried Doctor Esperon's body to a narrow bench in the large courtyard. "You must not stay with us," Josefina said. "We need to be alone now." After they left, Eufemia bathed the doctor with a sea sponge soaked in vinegar. An oil lamp hanging from a pole cast a circle of saffron light around them, a circle of light Josefina could not bring herself to enter. "Tonight he is dead," Eufemia said. "But tomorrow he will live again."

Fireflies entered the courtyard and swarmed over the doctor's body and in every corner crickets sang as if screaming for relief.

"Did you ever love him?" the daughter asked and was suddenly shamed by the content and the abruptness of her question.

"At times he was my greatest opponent, but he became my

greatest ally," Eufemia answered. "He knew that I had to lose myself in order to regain my soul. To enter the highest level of contemplation is to give up everything, every last shred of worldly gain."

She flung herself over her husband's body and thanked him for bringing her to a new country and a new life filled with many trials. "You cannot die," she sobbed. "I was resurrected and so you will be also. As long as I have eyes to see, I will never cease my dirge and sorrowful laments until you have risen."

Josefina refused to step inside the circle of lamplight for then she would face the truth that she could not allow herself to acknowledge: her father was dead, his body was bathed in saffron light, and her mother was praying for his resurrection. In the shadows, none of these things could touch her; they existed only in light. She drifted silently from shadow to shadow and finally returned to the street. The body of the man she shot had been taken away, and there were two bloody stains on the cobblestones, his and her father's. She walked around them and straight to the corner where the second man had stood. She was sure that her bullet had hit him, and that he had left something behind. She had seen something fall from his hands. She was sure of it. Picking among the shinning cobblestones, she retrieved what seemed to be a piece of leather. The collar of a jacket, she thought, something that could be identified and traced. Under a street lamp, she examined the object in the palm of her hand. She pushed away clotted blood and strands of hair to reveal a round curve that she recognized as an earlobe.

"I have marked you," she said. "And now I will hunt you down."

Only then did she weep. She was sixteen years old and her mother had gone mad, her father was dead, and the future appeared before her as a wall of shadows. She had killed a man, marked another, and she would find him, she promised herself and her dead father that she would.

When the police arrived they found her crying face down in

the middle of the street.

"This is no hour to be outside," they said. "There's trouble in every district of the city."

She stood to face them, and from that moment on, her search began. "Why is your hat pulled down over your ears?" she asked an officer. "You would be far more handsome if you wore it tilted back." The officer pushed back his hat, and when Josefina saw both ears were whole and perfectly shaped, she wept again for at that moment she understood that her search could be a long one, that it could extend through a lifetime, and that she would not die or rest until she had found the man who had killed her father.

But what if I should find him tonight? she asked herself. What would that mean? Surely, he does not represent himself alone. Surely, he was a hired assassin and nothing more, so why search for one man when so many are responsible?

The officers escorted her to the door, and after she had entered the house they waited until the lock turned and a heavy bolt fell into place. Then they walked away, and Josefina, listening to their receding footsteps, waited until they had turned the corner before she returned to the courtyard where her mother, bending into the saffron light, was combing the doctor's hair. "I used to have beautiful hair too," she said. "And when I die again, I will have hair again, and when I live again, the hair will still be there."

"And it will be beautiful," Josefina said.

"And it will be beautiful," her mother replied.

Lying on a hammock that hung in darkness she watched her mother comb and recomb her father's hair. In the distance she heard rifles, sirens, and galloping horses, and in her sleep she heard wagon wheels on cobblestones, a choir of angels, and church bells ringing under water. An hour before dawn she was awakened by loud voices coming from the street. Eufemia was still combing the doctor's hair. "I will comb his hair until there is no hair left to comb," she said. "When he is bald like me, he will resurrect."

Someone knocked loudly at the front door. "The saints are here," Eufemia said. "Let them in. We are bald and ready for blessing."

"It must be Fuerte," Josefina said. "Please let it be."

Shoved under the door was the front page of a newspaper that told her more than she cared to know. The president had been assassinated, decapitated with an axe while he slept. His wife and four sons had been lined up in front of the official residence, stripped of their bed clothing, and shot. Carlota Montejo had been hanged in the plaza, her orphanage burned, her suite of rooms looted, and the Hotel Carmina was in ruins.

While she stood there with the newspaper in hand, hardly able to believe what she had just read, someone knocked loudly on the door once again. When she opened it the president's decapitated body fell into the entry. "See how much you love him, now," said a hooded soldier whose voice was all too familiar. He threw Serrano's head at her feet. "See if your perfect stitches can hold him together this time."

"Bring me Carlota also," Josefina demanded. "If you don't I will kill you."

"A smart talker," the hooded soldier said. "We have already thought of that." Turning to his men, he shouted for them to bring in the *Treasure*, and within seconds Carlota Montejo's body was thrown to Josefina's feet.

"Put them all in the same grave," the soldier said.

"I will bury them with the dignity you lack and they deserve," Josefina said. "Do not try to stop me."

She dragged Carlota into the courtyard and leaned her against a column. "Carlota, Carlota," she cried embracing the body. "You cannot die. Your voice cannot be silenced." She opened Carlota's mouth and closed it and opened it again, but no sound came out. "Please," she said, moving the actress's lips, "please say something. Recite Racine, please. Just one more time. 'The Gods have lit within my breast, a fatal flame that gives no rest.' Say it! Say it! Just one more time." Carlota's head rolled back and Josefina saw, the rope burns on her neck. Then she wailed loudly.

"Silence Daughter," Eufemia cried. "We must have faith."

Josefina wept over Carlota's body until dawn arrived and the fireflies departed and the crickets were also silenced.

"Daughter," Eufemia shouted to her. "It is dawn. Get up! The door. The door is still open."

Josefina stumbled to the entry and bolted the door. She dragged Serrano into the courtyard and lay him outstretched near the lotus pool. Then she returned to the entry to retrieve the head. She held it with both hands and stared into his open eyes. "I will bury you with dignity," she said. Holding the severed head before her she walked, as if in a trance, back to the courtyard. "Bring the head to me," Eufemia said. "I will comb the blood from his hair, and he too will resurrect and live."

"No Mother," Josefina said. "It is over. They are both dead. Nothing can be done."

"Have faith child," Eufemia cried. "Without faith there is nothing."

"Faith left me long ago, Mother," Josefina said.

She placed Serrano's head in its proper place against his bloody neck but the head would not stay in place. It rolled across the courtyard.

"Bring it to me, Daughter," Eufemia pleaded. "I must comb his hair also. I will comb him until he is as bald as the moon."

Josefina took the first steps to retrieve Serrano's head but her legs weakened and would not support her. It seemed as if the entire world was spinning and she was standing still and at the same time falling. She collapsed over the president's body.

"No Daughter," Eufemia cried. "You cannot leave me. Get up. Bring me Serrano's head. I will comb his hair. Daughter get up."

Josefina did not hear her.

"Daughter, wake up!" Eufemia pleaded. "I need you, Daughter. Do you hear me?"

Josefina did not move.

"I will go for help," Eufemia said. "I will find someone to help us."

She wandered into the street in search of sisters of a holy order. "Sisters!" she called. "Come forth and assist your own."

The Street of Merchants and Peddlers was empty. Stores were
locked and vendor carts, some with fruits and vegetables still in
them, were scattered about. "Sisters," she cried, "where are you?
Why have you abandoned me in an hour of need?" She climbed
into a vegetable cart to survey the street from one end to the other.
"This is a holy war," she shouted. "We are ready." Standing on a
pile of rotting vegetables, she called on her Order to stand at attention like soldiers. When a military patrol came whistling around
the corner she stopped them as if she were their commanding officer. "Sisters, halt there," she cried. "Sisters, listen to me. We are
warriors for Christ. Our mission is a holy one."

The five soldiers stopped to listen to her.

"She's the one they call a saint," one of the men said.

"A lunatic," said another. And all five laughed heartily.

"Sisters," she said to the men in uniforms. "You must assist
me. My husband will live again. We must take him to the highest
mountain." She climbed down from the cart and led the laughing
men to her front door. There she cautioned them to follow her into
the courtyard, quickly and silently, for at any moment angry eyes
might fall upon them from the open sky. "We're soldiers," they
said. "We know what to do." With their rifles drawn they walked
around Carlota Montejo's body, and stepped over Josefina who
held Serrano tightly in her arms. One of the soldiers kicked Serrano's head as if it were a ball and it rolled back toward its body.
"Come this way and do not tarry," Eufemia commanded and they
followed her to the bench where the doctor lay. "He too will live
again," she said, kissing him on the brow.

"Oh yes, he will rise like Lazarus," a soldier said mockingly.

"If only we can get him to a high place," Eufemia replied.
"He will resurrect in tomorrow's dawn. Take him to the cart and
then to that high mountain."

"To what high mountain, Sister?"

"To the mountain in whose shadow we live," Eufemia answered. "He will rise again. I too am a soldier. I have fought many battles. Who will help me?"

"We will help you!" The soldier's saluted, clicked their heels together, and carried the doctor's body to the vegetable cart. There they sat him upright against a pyramid of pineapples. They crossed his legs, and folded his arms, and when Eufemia's back was turned they forced a half-smoked cigar into his mouth.

"And now, Sisters, we are ready," she said, climbing back into the cart. "Bring me a wreath of lightening bolts for my head and winged sandals for my feet. Go at once and bring me my horse for he is anxiously awaiting our departure."

"And where will we find your horse, Your Majesty?"

"In yonder stables, of course."

"And what may we call your horse, Your Highness?"

"You may call him Thunder."

"And what may we call your chariot?

"My chariot is Destiny, and my mission is divine."

Two soldiers laughed their way to the stables and returned with a white horse. They hitched the frightened animal to the vendor's cart, and after a long rope was tied around its neck and the two ends placed in Eufemia's hands someone crowned her with a wreath of onion greens. "Be on your way," they shouted. "You're chariot is ready."

"Believe me, Sisters," she said, "the soldiers of Christ, namely, those who experience contemplation and practice prayer, are always ready for the hour of conflict."

The soldiers fired their rifles into the sky, and the horse galloped away.

"So what if someone shoots her," said a soldier. "It will save us the trouble of killing a living saint."

Three blocks away, the horse bolted. The cart was overturned, and pineapples rolled like severed heads down the street and into the gutters. Eufemia was thrown headfirst onto the cobblestones. Blood gushed from her nose and mouth.

"So ends the life of a saint!" a soldier said.

"So much for perfection!" said another.

And they all marched away singing.

The tinsmith and the knife sharpener carried the bodies of the doctor and the saint back to the house of forty-three rooms where they found Josefina sitting on the edge of the lotus pool with Serrano's head in her lap. "They are heroes," she said. "And we will bury them as such." With the help of the button vendor, the husband of the lace maker, and the son of the tailor, four graves were dug in the large courtyard.

"I cannot speak for the president," Josefina said, "but for my father, there will be no prayers. That was not his way. He would be offended if anyone uttered the semblance of a prayer over his grave. As for my mother, prayers may be said. She would be offended if we did not pray for her. But to Carlota we will drink a toast."

In separate corners of the courtyard the doctor, the president, and the *Startling Treasure* were laid to rest with nothing more than a linen cloth covering their bodies, and when it was time to bury Eufemia, the merchants turned to the bench where they had left her body, and it was no longer there.

"Surely," Josefina sighed, "she will not live forever."

"Nothing will ever kill her," said the knife sharpener, "because she is one of the immortals."

While Carlota's grave was being covered, Eufemia had been awakened by a voice calling her to her balcony. "Arise," the voice had said. "You cannot die yet. The people await your prayers." On legs that barely supported her frail body, she had climbed the stairs without anyone noticing, but at the door to her room she had collapsed on the gallery floor.

"Water," she cried when Josefina found her. "I thirst."

That evening Josefina sat at her mother's bedside and fed her rich broth with a spoon. "I must rise," she said. "I must go forth. I have a mission."

"No, Mother," Josefina whispered. "You must rest, now. The mission will wait. Perfect Ones need rest, also."

Hearing this, Eufemia closed her eyes and slept. On a pallet near her mother's bed Josefina lay awake listening to sirens and gunfire, to explosions coming from the harbor, and to a heavy rain falling like bullets onto new graves. Whose graves? she asked herself, as if what she had just lived could not possibly have occurred. How could it be? she wondered. How could it be that she was sixteen years old, that she had shot a man, marked another and had no more tears, neither for her father, who was buried under the bougainvillea, nor for her mother who had died countless times, or so it seemed. Would she go on dying, and dying and dying? And if so how many times would she die before she died? And how many times more would she resurrect? And what was to be done with her open grave? Fill it with sand or leave it open?

She rolled over on her pallet. "At the rate we are going, the grave will soon be filled. But with whom?"

"Are you talking to me?" Eufemia asked in her sleep.

"No Mother."

"Who then? To the rain?"

"No, it has stopped. No one is here except us. We are together. We have a roof. We have two courtyards, forty-three rooms, and four balconies, Mother."

"We are rich in land," she said, "but what of our spirits?"

"Our spirits will be replenished, Mother."

Eufemia smiled and returned to a full sleep, and her daughter, lying on the hard floor, wondered how it could be possible that only yesterday her father had been shooting sparrows from the sky and now was dead, and not only dead but already buried. She had wrapped him in linen and had watched the merchants lower him on ropes into the narrow grave, but she could not believe what she had seen, for at the time, she had felt nothing, not even the sting of mosquitoes or the sickness that swelled her heart and stomach. And now, only hours later, lying on the pallet and listening to her mother breathing peacefully while sirens sounded in the distance and a trail of smoke wafted like one continuous ribbon through the many rooms, she wondered if what she had just lived had actually occurred, and if it had occurred, how would she ever survive it. Sleep, if only she could sleep and never wake up again. She begged for sleep and pleasant dreams. And at last they came.

At dawn Eufemia arose and descended the stairs into the courtyard that now seemed so much like her family home, the courtyard her grandmother had kept, the pool of lilies and goldfish, the elephant ear begonias blooming from clay pots, and the trumpet vines and Madre Selva that grew up the staircase and across the gallery banisters. "I have come home," she said. "But the house is empty."

When Josefina awakened she found her mother standing before the open grave. "It is mine," she said in a clear voice that betrayed no uncertainty. "My hour has arrived."

From the staircase leading into the courtyard, Josefina looked down at her mother enveloped in golden light. For the first time she saw her as she must have appeared to the doctor long ago: ravishingly beautiful, lucid, and pure of heart.

"It is as if I've been away for a long time," she said. "And now I have returned to something I cannot quite remember. Where is the ship that brought us here? Where is the harbor? The crinoline wings, the halo. and the star? What has happened to them? Where is my beautiful hair? My handsome doctor? My beloved saint? My Angel? Surely, they are waiting for me somewhere."

"They are with you, Mother," Josefina answered.

"Where is the day of my arrival?" Eufemia asked.

"Is it not today, Mother?"

"No. It was long ago, my daughter. Where have you been, and where is my Angel?"

She fell to her knees, and then into her own grave. And her daughter, who was sixteen years old, who had shot a man and marked another, and who had watched her father die on a street of moonlit stones, waited one hour for her mother to open her eyes, to raise a hand, to utter so little as a sigh. And after one silent hour that stopped just short of eternity, it seemed to Josefina that the entire world, as she knew it, had stopped breathing. No breeze rattled the branches of her mother's beloved orange trees, and no ripples scared the surface of the lotus pool. There were no sirens, no gunfire, and no church bells. Even the wind chimes were silent. "It is over," she said, "finished." Then and only then did she drop a linen cloth over her mother's body, and in a very short time the grave was covered with sand and flowers.

PART II

The Daughter's Revenge

Fuerte's three sisters celebrated her return with a feast cooked over an open fire: a fat pig, a pot of camotes sweetened with honey, corn cakes stuffed with cheese, peppers and black mushrooms gathered by the sheepherders in the high meadows. Everyone in the village welcomed Fuerte back home. "Your place is here with us," they said. "You must not go away again."

After the feast, a rock ball bigger than a fist was placed in a circle of straw and the players kicked it toward a center hole. "This is how we developed feet like paddles," said Fuerte as she kicked the ball she could not see into the far hole in the ground. "You were always the best ballplayer in the village," said her old aunt, the last of her mother's sisters. "She was always a good dancer, too," said a cousin. After the ball game the sisters danced together for the first time in many years. They slapped their paddle-like feet against the earth to awaken the spring. They clapped their hands and twirled around laughing. They were together again, and all was well.

All of a sudden Fuerte's smile vanished. She stopped laughing. She stumbled over her feet. She bumped into her sisters. "What's wrong?" one of them asked. "What are you thinking?"

"Something terrible has happened," Fuerte said. "The daughter needs me. She's alone now. Everything has changed. Today I cannot dance."

On her last morning in The Place Where Clouds Gather, Fuerte climbed the steep slope on which her village had been built, and when she came to the stream that flowed into a lake far below, her feet recognized a familiar path that led her into a green valley where she visited the wives of herdsmen who sold wool spun into fine threads dyed with annatto, indigo, cochineal, and caracol.

Having made her purchases she accepted a bowl of curds and honey. "Sustenance for the mountains," one of the wives said. "You'll need it."

Loaded with sacks, two on her back and one under each arm, she climbed to the rim of the valley, and from there she began the slow descent toward her village of stone houses and stick roofs.

On her way down she heard rifle shots thundering through the canyons, the stampeding of horses, and the screaming of women and children followed by long blasts on trumpets the men of her village made from rams' horns. The trumpets were used on Holy Days, but this day, Fuerte knew, was not a holy one.

Soon her youngest sister, Rufina Amaya, met her on the narrow path. She was carrying Fuerte's rolled-up tapestry on her head, the loom, and two bags of thread in both arms. "Take this and go," she said. "Do not return."

In the distance a child cried, "Mama Rufina, help me! They are killing us!"

Rufina Amaya kissed her sister good-bye and returned to the burning village, and to her son who stood before a wall of blood.

For the rest of the morning and much of the afternoon, Fuerte sat on a rock high above her village and listened to the firing squad discharging round upon round of ammunition. On command and at regular intervals the squadron fired, and fired again and again; seemingly with each breath that Fuerte drew, another round of ammunition exploded in the thin mountain air and echoed through the canyons and caves where the herdsmen lived. Above the gunfire she heard women, children, and old men pleading for mercy, and high above them, eagles were screaming their way to the other side of the mountain. Soon the air was thick with smoke that carried the scent of blood up the rocky slopes and into the high meadows.

The next day Fuerte returned to the Street of Merchants and Peddlers. Carrying her loom, her tapestry, and many bags of colored threads, she arrived with the dust and sparrows of late afternoon. "I have come back," she said, "because you do not need to be alone in this house. And I have come back for another reason also. My work is not finished. There are things I must do; there is no waiting to do them, and there are things I cannot do alone."

"How are your sisters?" Josefina asked.

"They are living, but only in the threads I carry on my back," Fuerte replied. "I will never see my village again. We had land.

We had a school. A place to vote and talk. We had a better way of thinking about ourselves and were learning to speak our minds. Now everything has been destroyed once again."

From one of her bags she brought forth a small basket. "In this basket there are spiders," she said. "The most poisonous the world has ever known. I will keep them well fed and one day you will need them. They are not aggressive, but can be made aggressive with little effort. They are my contribution to your revenge that is also mine." She returned the basket to her bag of threads. "Spider woman taught us the art of weaving," she said. "And now I must begin again."

She tied her loom to one of the orange trees and called for her threads, the green, the red, purple, and indigo.

"I will arrange the colors for you," Josefina said. She placed the skeins of thread across Fuerte's lap. "Green, red, purple, indigo," she said. "They're in order now. For the rest of your life you will not be required to do anything except weave."

"And you?" Fuerte asked. "What will you do?"

"I," Josefina replied, "will arrange your threads."

Only minutes after returning to the doctor's house, Fuerte began work on the 169th panel. At that hour in the late afternoon on the second Wednesday of the month there were no sirens, no rifle shots, no explosions or clouds of smoke drifting over the capital. In the large courtyard birds were singing once again, and Fuerte was bending over her colored threads. "See the red going in," she said. "This is cochineal. The blue is indigo; the green, avocado. The purple is given to us by a very special snail, and the orange comes from urine of cows that have feasted on mango. But I am not using that color today."

While Fuerte wove, Josefina Esperon learned to maintain the house on a meager inheritance. What little money her father had managed to save, the banks had appropriated, leaving her nothing except a house of forty-three rooms including a clinic, a medical laboratory, and a library where she found a small box of silver coins; barely enough, a banker told her, to last five, possibly six years, certainly no more. "I will make it last a lifetime, if I have to," she replied, and from then on she bargained her way through the municipal market, cooked and served the food herself, cleaned the rooms they lived in, raked the courtyards and swept the street in front of her house each morning.

"You must stay off the streets," the old lace maker called to her from behind curtains tightly drawn. "Hire yourself a young servant."

"I have no money for servants."

"Well at least make yourself look attractive," the lace maker replied. "You never know what wealthy man might be watching you. A pretty dress would help. A bright color."

She could have told the lace maker that colors reminded her of happier days, and the memory of happier days made her cry, and who could shop the municipal market with tears? Who could sweep the sidewalk while weeping? Who could arrange the colored threads much less find them with eyes that were swollen with a sadness she could not otherwise express except to dress in black; black from her shoes, stockings, and daily dress to her one and only hair ribbon; black accompanied her everywhere, and everywhere she went she was closely observed, not only by the few people in the streets but by the many who watched behind closed curtains. "Look at the doctor's daughter," they said, "she's a brave one indeed. To be alone, so young and on the streets. She's constantly on the streets and always in black."

Disconnected from the memory of happier times, she walked to the market each day, and each day she spoke to the military guards patrolling the city, and each day she chose a different path for going and coming and was often led completely off course by someone who caught her eye, for she was constantly searching for a damaged ear. Often she trailed her suspects to the far edges of the city where she had never ventured before but where her mother was remembered and loved. "Yes, I am her daughter," she told the people who recognized her. "Yes, you may visit her grave any time you need to. Yes, you may do something for me as well.

Have you seen a man with a mangled ear? If you do see him will you come to me without delay and tell me his name? But do not let him know that I am looking for him."

"Yes, yes," they promised, "for the daughter of the saint we will do anything."

"We will keep our eyes wide open."

"And we will come to you in the middle of the night if need be."

"We will even commit murder, but only in the name of our saint."

At night she lay in bed listening to the agonizing silence of waiting, knowing that it could be broken at any moment by a knock at the door, a rock hurled against a bedroom window, or a faint voice whispering a name through a keyhole. And if not in the dead of night, perhaps in broad daylight; on a street of broken glass, or in the municipal market, the French Park, the waterworks, someone might press a piece of paper into her hands and on it, a name. Everyday she expected to be approached. Everyday she was ready for someone to step from a doorway and lead her silently along the right path, or surreptitiously drop an envelope with a name, an address, even a stamp. Everyday she was on the streets, and everyday she was searching through a ransacked city where houses had been burned, churches and municipal buildings ripped to the ground, where every street was strewn with glass and every citizen brave enough to show his face walked with head cast down, half afraid to see or be seen. Only the municipal market had stayed open the entire time; only there had life continued as if nothing out of the ordinary had happened, as if the new regime and the old were just the same, the cart had not been over turned or the wheel broken.

We are accustomed to such things, said the weaver on the 171st panel. *Always when a new family takes office it is the same:*

> *There is a display of power.*
> *There is a loss of blood.*

But what does it matter?
The people, they still buy their fruits and vegetables, and
they enjoy their pozole, their chiles, and their fish from
the sea, but they take their coffee at home instead of in the
cafés, for in the cafés, a bullet can easily find them.
This is the way we live.
But this is not the way we have always lived.

"Gradually, life will return," Fuerte assured Josefina. "Soon
more faces will appear in the windows, then the doors, and then
the streets. Before long the Gran Café will reopen and people will
be talking about love and art once again."

On her daily excursions, Josefina found this hard to believe.
The plazas were all but empty, the opera house boarded up, the
National Theatre reduced to ashes, and the Hotel Carmina to a
mountain of broken stones, and yet, no one else seemed to notice these things. "You should not see so much when you go out,"
Fuerte told her. "This is not the time for seeing, and if you do see,
you must not allow anyone to know that you are seeing anything
at all."

"I will never close my eyes," she said. "I will see everything."

Although constantly exhausted, she traveled the entire city
on foot; back and forth to the market where she studied each face,
to the central plaza where she sat beneath laurels and jacarandas
to read with one eye and watch with the other; back and forth to
the harbor where foreign ships were putting out to sea, and to the
French Park where egrets roosted in cypress trees and homeless
families slept under the stars, under a constant shower of white
feathers falling like snowflakes through a tropical night. The search
led her to the Church of the Holy Earth high on a hill, to the gates
of the president's home, to the river where women washed clothes
on gray rocks, and to the salt marsh where Gypsies lived over the
ruins of an ancient city sinking in mud. Wherever she went her
mission was the same, her route was different, and although she

might seem to be selecting the best of the fruits and vegetables, or studying the colonial architecture, or watching the egrets return to the park, she was doing one thing, and one thing only, searching for a suspicious face, an evil eye, a missing ear.

Her daily schedule was firmly set, and she tolerated little in the way of variation particularly during the morning hours. She arose before dawn to grind coffee and bake sweet bread; Fuerte's preferred breakfast. After the dishes had been washed and the goldfish fed, Fuerte returned to her loom and Josefina to the streets. At one o'clock she came home from her wanderings. At two o'clock she served lunch. At two thirty she allowed the pilgrims to visit their saint. And for the remaining siesta hours Fuerte wove in her bedroom, the pilgrims prayed in the courtyard, and Josefina retreated to her mother's chapel where she studied her father's journals.

The journals were of special interest to her. They were filled with medical notes, family names, preferred menus, and the minute details of laboratory experiments as well as long lists of fragrant barks, roots, seeds, and flowers used in the preparation of perfumes and colognes. Many of the entries had been recorded in her own hand, and in the margins of some of the pages her father had written short notes to himself. The margin notes included the various names of local herbs used for stopping the flow of blood, for clearing the respiratory passages, cleansing the body of poisons and preventing seizures, migraines, and eruptions of the skin. In one of his later journals he had listed various methods used by the curanderas for aborting the fetus, for treating venereal diseases, for stimulating the sexual drive in obstinate men, and for speeding, slowing or stopping the heart.

After studying the handwritten texts until her eyes ached she would send the pilgrims on their way and wait for the sea breezes of late afternoon to cool the courtyards. At that time she began preparation for the evening meal to be served under the orange trees after the light of day had vanished behind the mountains and Fuerte was ready to eat. Normally, they ate in silence, but on occasions Fuerte made comments on the preparation of the food.

Sometimes she suggested amaranth in place of rice, especially for stuffing squash, and she frequently found fault with the red sauce because it needed more tomato, less onion, a touch of garlic, or an additional pepper to add complexity to the flavor.

One afternoon after she had fed a feast of crickets to her spiders, she went into the kitchen to assist the daughter with her cooking. "This sauce is not right," she said. "You need more anchos for sweetness, but do not mix them with tomatoes. They must stand alone. From time to time we need mulatos, and habaneros for fire, and always we need serranos for the sweet memory of our finest president as well as our hatred for the family that adopted him."

There were evenings when the chicken soup was perfect, much better than her own, and there were other evenings when the turkey should have been roasted in another manner: with mango stuffed in the cavity, or avocado leaves under the skin, or a paste prepared with chili pequín, lemon, and honey smeared generously over the bird before and three times during the cooking. "A sprig of epazote would help flavor the beans," she would say. "When you are preparing huitlacoche, epazote is necessary. When you simmer nopales do not use so much water. And if you can find escamoles they will bring us good fortune and good health as well. You should use saffron in the paella and always in the fish stew. Annatto is a poor substitute, but it is better than nothing when the real thing cannot be found. When cool weather comes to the high meadows the wild crocus will bloom. I will take you to them, and we will gather the saffron ourselves. I will also show you how to harvest the little black mushrooms that grow in the high meadows, but that will be a two-day trip so we will not be going there any time soon."

The evening meals were short, lasting no more than thirty minutes, and immediately after the dishes were washed, Fuerte would return to her room to check on her basket of spiders, which were thriving under her care. She would tap on their basket and speak to them sweetly so they would know they had not been forgotten, and on occasions she would remove a female fat with eggs and allow her to walk around the room. Frequently, she reminded the daughter: "The spiders are our friends. You must never fear them. But they have good reason to fear each other. When over-crowded they become cannibals, so only the strongest and most venomous survive. Lately, the population has been diminished."

After the evening meals and the feeding of the spiders that were creatures of the night, Fuerte always returned to her loom to weave in the dark while Josefina prepared for whatever the night might bring. Before retiring, she would open all the windows and the French doors leading to the balconies. She would place a blue jar on her bedside table and in doing so, never failed to wonder if she would be awakened by a knock on the front door, or a calling from the dark street where someone, possibly someone she had never met, might be sitting in one of the flame trees and waiting for the first opportunity to whisper a name through her bedroom window. Each night her expectations rose, and the blue jar was retrieved. It contained an amount of preservative from her father's laboratory, and suspended in the liquid was the ear of his mur-derer. During the day the jar lived in a metal box, but at night she placed it on her bedside table so it might influence her dreams and those of her adversaries as well.

Every night she went to sleep with the same thought wander-ing through her dreams: I will find you. And every morning she awoke to another thought, one no less troubling: And if I do find you what will it matter in the scheme of things?

It was a question she could not answer and a search she could not abandon, even during the rainy season when the avenues lead-ing to the harbor became turbulent rivers that washed donkeys, carts, and beggars out to sea; even then, she kept searching; dis-cretely asking questions, and following anyone who caught her eye, while all around her the capital city struggled to recover.

In what was whispered as an act of magnanimous deceit, the new president conducted a grand rebuilding campaign. He said that he was restoring law and order, commerce and respect, that the capital would have a fleet of sixteen street buses to replace the eight dilapidated trolleys, and that boulevards as well as avenues would be widened to accommodate more automobiles, for soon, every citizen would be able to afford the comforts and luxuries of a modern life. "We will not be ruled by intellectual renegades," he said, "not by liberals, but by liberty. We will spring back to life again."

Lies, lies, lies, Josefina thought, as she made her daily rounds. Nothing but lies.

She searched through the city like a mother looking for a lost child or a beggar intent on finding a coin, a crust of bread, anything to sustain life through one more miserable day. The city, she knew, would never be the same. Military guards were posted in every bank, in every railway station, marketplace, and public park. The prisons were overflowing with those who opposed the new regime, and each week angry citizens were deported over the mountains, or stranded on an island twenty-two miles out to sea. Heavy taxes were levied, prices were rising, and merchants were talking of closing their doors while all around them large parcels of salt marsh were being sold at low prices to foreign investors.

"Who would want to buy wetlands?" Josefina asked, and Fuerte answered with the 173rd panel:

We cannot live without our marshes. Life began there. Everything is born of mud and silence. Soon the entire world will celebrate noise. Soon, noise will separate us all, and soon people will learn to live inside this noise that separates, and they will call it music.

Until the day that President Serrano had entered the house it had seemed to Josefina that her colonial city, bordered by mountains, salt marsh and sea, had been created in the image of perfection. Date palms, jacaranda, and flame trees lined the streets and boulevards leading the wanderer through parks and plazas where music was heard each night and birds sang sweetly at dawn. The streets she had walked as a child had resounded with song and laughter, but as a young woman in mourning she walked streets of desolation and silence; silence broken by the sound of construction and demolition. All along the avenues colonial houses were being torn down and ancient cobblestones ripped up to be replaced with asphalt and cement. And toward the end of the year, just as the president had promised, one thousand new automobiles invaded the capitol; black hooded vehicles driven through the narrowest of streets for no other reason than to call attention to a new age of affluence, an age of loud horns and screeching brakes, noises that could be heard in the courtyard where Fuerte sat with rags stuffed in her ears.

In the courtyard, and in the climate of the changing city, Eufemia's orange trees bloomed for the first time. Suddenly, the courtyard was redolent of orange blossoms; the air was thick with bees, hummingbirds, and butterflies. If only Mother could have seen her trees, Josefina thought. Following her father's written instructions, she picked the largest flowers and steeped them in ambergris to preserve their fragrance, and after she had picked a sufficient amount for perfume she watched the remaining blossoms wither and fall upon the graves; she watched the first fruit appear like stones of jade bending the branches, and she watched the stones grow in size and color.

"One day," Fuerte said, "you will have many orange trees in this courtyard, and all the rooms will be filled with music and laughter."

While weaving through long, unbroken hours she occasionally found reason to remind Josefina that she was responsible for many domestic obligations and had no time to wander the city, to court grief, or dream of revenge, no reason to bathe in sorrow. "Remember why we are here," she said. "Remember what our ancient poets taught us. 'We only come to sleep. We only come to dream. It is not true, it is not true, that we come to live on the earth."

"I will remember, Fuerte."

"Good. Now where are my threads? Where is the blue of the sky, and the green of the sea? Bring them to me."

"Yes, Fuerte."

"And arrange them across my lap like you always do."

"Yes, Fuerte."

"Thank you again my child. You are my eyes, and I am your eyes. I'm here to remind you that lately you have become careless in your chores. You have not swept the street today. You have not washed the clothes. You have not raked the courtyard or fed the fish. If you do not face your responsibilities your mind will dwell in dark places."

My mind, Josefina thought, has always dwelled in dark places.

"I understand," Fuerte replied, having heard every word spoken in silence. "But right now, you must rake the sand in the courtyard, and I must feed our friends. Where are the fat flies I trapped on the bananas yesterday?"

"They are here in this jar.'

"Good, give them to me."

What will we do with so many spiders? Josefina wondered.

"I will tell you when the time comes," Fuerte said. "Now go and rake the courtyards."

Taking up the rake, Josefina wondered if Fuerte could hear all of her thoughts or only some of them, and how far away she needed to stand in order to think without being overheard. While raking patterns into the sand she tried to clear her mind of all anger and resentment, to annihilate hate from her thoughts as her mother had attempted to do, but for Josefina this was impossible. Her mind dwelled helplessly in dark corridors, where desire for vengeance fed her daily thoughts.

The murderer deserves more than a slow, painful demise. With each line she raked into the courtyard sand she plotted his downfall. He must endure everlasting humiliation. Humiliations that lives beyond the grave.

"What are you doing?" Fuerte asked.

"I'm raking the courtyard."

"I can hear your thoughts."

"Do you disapprove?"

"It's not for me to approve or disapprove," Fuerte said. "But if you listen to me, you will not waste so much time thinking of evil returns. Now it is time to water the plants. That's all you need to think about. Test the soil with your fingers first, and if it is dry you may water, but you may not allow the water to spill over the rim of the pots or soak the ground were there are no plants. You must not be wasteful. And after you finish watering you may need to prune the trees and the vines. If you don't we will be living in a jungle before long."

"Perhaps I should hire someone to help me," Josefina said.

"Then you would have too much time for thinking," Fuerte replied. "Allow me to create the dark returns for you; I know the proper way of weaving them into existence; you do not, as yet."

With a bucket of water drawn from the lotus pool, Josefina hurried through the damp passage and into the small courtyard where she might think without being overheard. Fuerte put down her loom and followed her. "Listen to me," she said. "First you must complete your domestic obligations and when you have learned to do them properly everything else, even all the darkness that dwells inside your mind, will find its proper solution."

"Sometimes there's only one solution," Josefina said. "And it's not always the proper one."

"If it's the only one," Fuerte said, "it is, no matter what, the proper one."

According to Fuerte there was only one way to accomplish anything; even the ordinary duties of maintaining a house were governed by rules that were inflexible and had remained so since the beginning of time. There was one way to go to market, one way to wash clothes, one way to cook food and sweep floors, one way and only one way, and that was the right way, and in that house the right way was still and always would be Fuerte's way. She said that her way should never be forgotten or else no one would ever remember the right from the wrong, so if the casaba were too green, or the avocado too ripe, Fuerte spoke up.

"You're forgetting your lessons," she said one evening after they had dined in total silence. "What were you thinking when you went to the market today? I will tell you. Thoughts of revenge have invaded your mind again. Do not think them. I will think them for you. I will weave them into existence. When you sweep you must think only of sweeping, when you cook it is cooking, when you feed the fish, it is only the fish that concern you, and when you go to market you must pay attention. Tomorrow you will take me with you so I can remind you how to choose the freshest herbs and meats, how to recognize a ripe melon and to distinguish one cheese from another. Tomorrow we will go to the market together. Do not argue."

"Yes," Josefina said. "All right. We will go to the market tomorrow, but you must stay very close to me so I will not lose you in the crowds."

Into the market they went, connected by a rope tied around their waists. Josefina led the way, and Fuerte followed her through the aisles to inspect fruits and vegetables and shake eggs to test their freshness.

"Here we'll buy bread," Josefina said.

"No," Fuerte argued. "We must bake our own. If we do not we will forget how. We must never forget how to bake bread."

"Here we will buy mamey," Josefina said.

"But only if it's ripe. Hold it to my nose, and I will tell you for sure."

"No it is too green. Let us move on."

"Here we will buy meat."

"But only if it is moist and there is an abundance of blood," Fuerte said. "If your finger slides across a hard surface, we will not buy. Tell me what color it is."

"Red."

"Dark red or light red?"

"Dark."

"Very dark?"

"Yes,"

"Then we will not eat meat today. Take me to the fish. Tell me about their eyes."

"They are dull and flat."

"Then we will not eat fish today. Take me to the little man who sells the baby goats, he is always reliable."

One afternoon a week Fuerte abandoned her loom and accompanied Josefina to the market to make sure she had not forgotten how to buy melon, papaya, and zapote, or how to distinguish one chili from the other. "It is very important that you know the difference," she said. "With chili pasilla, chili mulato and ancho we make mole, but you must also use almonds, cloves, cinnamon, peppercorns, chocolate, prunes, peanuts, and raisins for sweetness. How many chiles can you name?"

"Chili de arbol, chili de guajillo, cascabel, pasilla, poblano, mulato, pulla, jalapeño and habanero. Then we have chili chipotle, which is very hot and ancho which is sweet."

"And how many can you recognize today?"

"All of them."

"And tomorrow?"

"The same."

"Good. Now tell me this, what herb do we use when we prepare quesadillas de huitlacoche?"

"We use epazote."

"And what do we do with the leaves of avocado?"

"We flavor soups and meat."

"And why do we give albahaca?"

"We give for good luck."

"And when do we pick squash blossoms?"

"In the morning before the dew dries on the petals."

"And what must we find for your mother's grave?"

"We must find a crown of thorns."

"Yes. That will please her so much."

From the curanderas who continued to set up their stalls outside the market, they bought a crown of twisted rose branches and a blue bowl. The crown was placed on Eufemia's grave, and inside the circle of thorns, the blue bowl, filled with water and orange blossoms, was pressed into the earth. "Good," Fuerte said. "She is satisfied now. The others can drink from the lotus pool, but your mother's spirit is too delicate for that. She will always have a bowl of her very own, and every day fresh petals must be sprinkled in the water because she might not find it otherwise."

"Very well," Josefina said. "I will remember."

"I will remember also," Fuerte said and from time to time she put her to task by asking if she had remembered to pick flowers for her mother. If Josefina answered by saying there were no flowers blooming that day, or they were too high up to be picked, Fuerte abandoned her weaving for the flower market. "Your mother cannot rest without flowers in her water," she would say in a scolding voice. "We must go to the market now. The dead do not know how to wait patiently for the living. Your mother is thirsty. Today we must buy flowers, but very soon we will no longer need to buy them. Very soon they will fall upon you like rain."

Very soon, Fuerte's prediction came true. The men of the capital began noticing the doctor's daughter, and from time to time a total stranger handed her a flower, usually a red rose. "A touch of color," they said. "A pretty girl in a black dress needs a touch of color in her life."

"She has always been pretty," said the merchants and peddlers, "but suddenly she has become beautiful, and the men already talk of possessing her. But how blind they are, she is not one to be possessed."

"Soon you will receive letters," Fuerte told her on their way to market. "If this is Wednesday the first one will arrive, maybe today maybe tomorrow."

One week later on a Thursday afternoon, the first letter was left at her door, and soon many more arrived, all of them invitations to dinner, to dances, to masquerade balls; invitations to stroll along the river, to visit the foreign ships in the harbor, to sit in the French Park or in the Gran Café and wile away the hours. The invitations arrived from men whose names she did not recognize and she answered them all with the same two sentences:

I beg you to understand that it is too soon for me to take
part in public entertainment. Festivities make me weep;
therefore, I must decline your kind invitation.

No matter how many invitations she declined, they still kept
arriving three, four, as many as eight in one week, and each was
declined and each was saved. Who are these men? She wondered.
And when did they become aware of me?

Suddenly she became self-conscious on the streets. Every eye
was watching her. Even eyes she could not see were watching her.
She felt them on her skin. Some were hot. Some were cold. Others
were sharper than pins, and they followed her everywhere.

Instead of wandering about the city in search of a mangled ear
or a suspicious face, she began staying home to sit on her mother's
balcony while the sun rose over the green sea and the egrets flew
from the French park back to the marsh. In the distance she could
hear the new street buses screeching along the four major avenues
en route to the harbor, and she could see the structural bones of the
new factory that was being built on the west side of the city. It was
a factory that promised to manufacture over fifty different kinds of
building bricks to be marketed outside the country.

"Ridiculous," Josefina said. "Who needs that many different
kinds of bricks?"

"The church," Fuerte answered. "It's always the church."

Every morning the cathedral bells awakened them, and after their breakfast of sweet bread and black coffee flavored with
cinnamon and dark sugar, Josefina sat on her balcony until the
bells sounded for the second time. Then she stood to watch the
people leaving Mass. Most of them walked along the Street of
Merchants and Peddlers toward the business district, the market,
and the main avenue leading to the harbor, and as they passed
beneath her balcony she studied them, one face at a time, the old
as well as the young.

She came to realize that the entire city passed underneath her balcony. It was her point of view and she would wait there, even if she had to wait a lifetime.

"Are you waiting for someone?" a man once asked her.

"Yes, I am," she replied.

"Who are you waiting for then?"

"I will recognize him when he walks beneath my balcony," she answered, "and certainly not before."

"Then you're waiting for the man you will marry."

"No," she said. "I will never marry."

"Then what is the point of waiting?" The man laughed. His friends laughed with him, and in the Gran Café the story was told and retold and everyone laughed. "Yes," they all agreed, "she's waiting for the man she will not marry, but when the she finds him she will marry him anyway."

A spark of life returned to the capital city. Morning and night, young men and old talked of nothing except the daughter of the doctor and the saint. Attendance at Mass increased, just for an excuse to walk beneath her balcony on the chance that eyes might meet, that words might be exchanged or hearts lost. Every morning she was there, staring with the cold blue eyes she had inherited from her mother, and every morning the men returned; some of them walked slowly, their heads turned upward as if something in the sky had caught their attention, and others, not so circumspect, stared blatantly at her from the time they left the cathedral steps until they reached her balcony. They stared, and she stared, and occasionally words were exchanged or flowers thrown onto the balcony.

"I accept your roses on behalf of my mother," she said to one of her regular admirers. "The saint refuses to drink water, unless it is scented with petals."

"But isn't your mother dead?" the man asked.

"Don't you know," she answered, "the dead thirst just as much, if not more, than the living?"

"She's a spook," the men began saying among themselves.

"A beautiful one at that."

"And she's up there every morning waiting for one of us."

"But who will win her?"

"That's the question."

In cafés, on street corners, all along the harbor and in the many parks and plazas the saint's beautiful daughter was the topic of the day.

"I would desert my wife and children for her."

"I would give half my fortune or more."

"I would sacrifice my mother."

"I would send my father to the asylum."

"And I would sell everything I own just to be alone with her for one hour."

"As long as they can see you every morning," Fuerte said, "they'll keep talking, and the parade will never stop."

"Then I must not disappoint them," Josefina replied.

At dawn she arose with the cathedral bells and took her place on the balcony in order to watch and be seen watching. On occasions, particularly when strangers caught her eye, she dropped colored squares of paper on which she had scribbled lines from her mother's book of prayers. Thrilled to have captured her attention, even if it was only for a moment, the men looked up eagerly to catch the falling prayers and when doing so she could clearly see their important features: the nose, the mouth, the eyes, and most importantly the ears.

The parade continued each morning, and each morning prayers written on colored paper were dropped from the balcony, and each morning faces were studied, and restudied, and newcomers were carefully observed. And after one year of parading faces and falling prayers, it seemed to Josefina that the entire world had walked beneath her balcony, and would continue walking beneath it for the rest of her life. After one year, and hundreds of invitations, none of which she had accepted, and after sending thousands of prayers falling onto the heads of admirers, none of whom she knew by name, she arose on a cloudy Easter Sunday when bells were ringing all over the city and every pew in the cathedral was filled; she arose and stood on her balcony with her pockets filled with squares of colored paper, and when Mass was over and the worshipers passed along her street, she studied each face once again. That day someone she had never seen before caught her eye, a portly man with short legs and a wide forehead. He wore a black suit and a black hat, from which his lamb chops descended like brambles, and he walked with a slight limp that struck her as unusual for a man not yet old. He walked alone. No one spoke to him, and no one passed him. Out of respect? she wondered, or something else? At the balcony he looked up and smiled. His teeth were small and spaced far apart; his eyes were closely set, and his face was covered with dark moles he had attempted to hide with powder. Smiling in return, she dropped a few squares of colored paper, and when he reached up to take one of them from the air his hat fell from his head, and her heart pounded.

I have found you, she thought. And now I must know who you are.

The man paused giving the impression that he had no intention of walking a step farther, and it was then that she noticed his receding hairline; it had been extended with cosmetic paint and his lamb chops, which were long and bushy, had been brushed straight back in an attempt to divert attention from his scar. She blew him a kiss and waved him good-bye, but after he had walked on and was well beyond hearing, she leaned far over the balcony to gain the attention of a young man who was walking through a dream.

"Who is the gentleman just ahead of you?" she asked.

"You have interrupted me," he said curtly.

"Then answer my question and return to yourself," she replied.

"He's, José Maria Serrano, our new mayor," the young man answered.

"What happened to the old mayor?" Josefina asked.

"It's unwise to ask such questions."

"And who are you, may I ask?"

"I am a poet."

"I thought you were all murdered in the revolution."

"Do not speak of such things on the street," he whispered.

"If you are a poet you must visit me," she said. "But only if you are truly a poet. Come to the side door after eight in the evening. Ring the bell only once. I will hear you."

The young man, whose black hair hung in ringlets about his shoulders, and whose damp clothing was covered with the dust of the streets, stood in the shadow of the daughter's balcony and wondered what it would be like to live in such a house. He wondered what the daughter would think of his dark room at the waterworks where he spent his nights opening and closing valves in order to distribute water to various districts in the city. Would she gladly lie with him on his damp mattress? And would she like his poems? He had composed them in his head while walking the dusty streets, and had copied them onto paper late at night while mountain water rushed through the aqueducts and into a city of cisterns.

What if I do not like his poems? she wondered, as she watched him depart. And what if I do?

He walked three blocks before turning to look back, and even from that distance Josefina could recognize the fire of romance burning his eyes. "You will return," she said. "But when?"

That afternoon in the courtyard she was arranging colored threads on Fuerte's lap, when a plan sprung into her mind fully developed. She rushed from the courtyard before the threads were completely arranged but not before Fuerte heard her thinking:

I will open my doors to gentlemen of title and prominence, and no one will leave this house the same as he entered it.

That night she studied all the invitations she had received, and the next day she carried them to the old lady who sold lace on the next corner. "Tell me," she said, "you have lived in the capital all your life, do you recognize these names?"

"Why yes, of course," the lace maker exclaimed, "my foolish heart would stop beating if I said no, for I have made lace for their wives and daughters, their mothers and grandmothers. You have everyone here from the president to the mayor."

"The president, I can do without," Josefina said. "But the mayor must be included."

"Oh, he's a very strange one indeed," the lace maker replied. "The president's half brother José Maria Serrano. He has been accepted into the family, but *illegitimate* is the word. And they say he will do anything to sit on the throne."

Perhaps, Josefina thought, I should invite the president as well.

The lace maker arranged the invitations in order of prominence, beginning with the president, and Josefina removed the mayor's card from the tenth position and placed it on top. "His foster mother was my best customer," the lace maker said. "His real mother was a family servant, my husband's only sister, who disappeared without a trace. Now the mayor has imitated his father, by giving his wife two sons and a daughter, but the daughter is of a different mother. Adopted they say, but *illegitimate* is the word."

"How can you keep account of all these marriages, infidelities, and adoptions?" Josefina asked.

"If you are in my business," the lace maker said. "You must keep track, so you do it."

On returning to her house of two courtyards, Josefina addressed invitations to the twenty-five most prominent men in the nation, and only after she had mailed them did she remember one other thing the lace maker had told her: "None is to be trusted. They will do anything, pay anything, say anything in order to hold your hand."

The Señorita Josefina Pilar Esperon requests the honor
of your presence
in celebration of her nineteenth birthday.
The fifteenth day of March at eight thirty in the evening.
Gentlemen only may attend.

With the last of her father's money, she bought champagne and caviar. She hired a local chef, a ten-piece orchestra, and three waiters in tuxedos. From the dressmaker on the street she borrowed a long gown of black silk and a hair ornament of black feathers. From the shoemaker she borrowed satin slippers, and from her jewel box she chose her mother's rubies.

On the day of the celebration, she covered the graves with tables draped in linen, and around each table she placed hand-carved chairs the furniture maker had loaned her for the occasion. From the gallery level she strung garlands and oil lamps, and at the top of the stairs she placed ten chairs for the orchestra and one extra for Fuerte who said that she did not wish to attend the celebration, preferring instead to weave in her dark room.

"I do not need light to see what I'm doing," she said. "Nor do I need to be told what is about to occur. Twenty-five have been invited, and twenty-five will attend, but twenty-five times twenty-five times twenty-five more are willing to murder for the right to sit at your table."

"I know what I am doing, Fuerte," Josefina said.

"I know what you are doing also," Fuerte replied. "I am here not to judge but to record, and it will be recorded; everything will be woven and woven accurately, down to the very last thread, the very last guest and the very last grape."

"There are no grapes on my tables," Josefina laughed.

"I'm not thinking about your tables right now," Fuerte said. "I've gone beyond your celebration, beyond the grapes, beyond the auction, and above the yellow sky."

"The sky isn't yellow," Josefina said.

"But one day it will be," Fuerte replied.

"You have a chair," she said, "if you care to use it."

"I do not care to use it," Fuerte replied. "Let the gentlemen who are celebrating you use the chair. They will be here soon. All of them will arrive on time. No one will be late except the president. He must be the last to arrive. But he will not be too late."

The guests arrived at eight thirty. Bankers and lawyers and

members of the president's cabinet. Dressed in tuxedos, they entered the courtyard to Handel's Suite for Trumpet and Orchestra. Standing before the lotus pool Josefina greeted each guest with a firm handshake and a kiss on each cheek. "I have admired many of you from my balcony," she said, "and tonight I have the honor of admiring you in my home. Before the evening is over I intend to dance with each of you."

"To dance with you will be a pleasure like none other," said the mayor when he took her hand, "but as you can see I have a lame leg. I cannot move with agility."

"A lame leg must never stop a dancer from dancing," she replied. "As long as you can stand you can dance and you will. It is not the same as a bad ear, for if you are a musician without an ear, you are not a musician, or a tuner of pianos."

"It's safe to say I am neither," the mayor said. He rested a hand over his mangled ear.

"You are the kind of man who understands his limitations," Josefina continued. "A very rare and admirable trait." She touched the hand that covered the remains of his left ear, around which his sideburns had been combed and his irregular hairline had been extended with a cosmetic pencil. A chill passed through her and into the courtyard, and even Fuerte, weaving in her dark room, felt the cold. "He has arrived," she said. "But this will not be his last visit."

"You must promise me that the first dance will be given to my brother the president," the mayor said, removing her hand rapidly. "He'll make it very uncomfortable for all of us unless you honor him first."

"Then I'll dance with him the moment he arrives," Josefina whispered into the mayor's broken ear.

Soon the president of the nation arrived in full military uniform with a bouquet of roses in hand and three guards in attendance. He was a man, much taller than his half brother, with a full head of hair, and a mustache meticulously waxed and curled. Seeing him in the entry, Josefina called for a trumpet fanfare, and after receiving her flowers, she led him to the center of the court-yard for the first dance of the evening. "Forgive my impudence," she said. "I do realize that my eagerness will be frowned upon, but I cannot delay for another moment the thrill of dancing with the president of our nation. I trust you will not find me too aggressive in my approach."

"I trust you will not find me too awkward in my steps," he responded.

Under garlands and lamplight they waltzed around the lotus pool, around the covered graves, and under the orange trees that perfumed the night air with an essence that would forever be asso-ciated with the doctor's beautiful daughter. "You could be one of your trees in bloom," the president said at the end of their waltz.

"Perhaps I am," Josefina replied.

Then he escorted her to his twin brother, the appointed gov-ernor of the state, and the most handsome member of the family, a man whose gray eyes, wavy hair, and sweet breath gave Josefina a moment of reconsideration. With a man so beautiful, she thought, could I live forever and contentedly in his arms? No matter what he has done, or will do, could I go with him for better or worse?"

The governor waltzed in the Viennese style, with great agility and lightness of foot, and when the waltz was over Josefina led him to the center of the courtyard. "I would be pleased to waltz with you for the rest of my life," she said.

"That," he replied, "would be a pleasure, even though it would cause a major war in our little kingdom."

"Your brother, our president, could greatly improve his dance were he to take lessons from you."

"From you and me," the governor added.

Immediately following the governor's dance, champagne was poured, toasts were made, and presents were presented one by one: a box of Swiss chocolates, three gold bracelets, a bolt of blue silk, six bottles of French perfume, a jewel box inlaid with ivory, seven pair of silver earrings, three hand-painted scarves, two pearl necklaces, and a case of wine from the president's vineyards. "I am honored," Josefina replied. "Each gift is truly impressive, but no more so than the giver."

Ringing a bell to summon the waiters, she invited her guests to dine with her under the stars. There were five tables with six chairs at each, and during the first course, which consisted of lobster aspic bathed in saffron sauce and a drop of Pernod, Josefina traveled from table to table, pouring Anjou Blanc and retrieving napkins to blot the lips of her prominent guests who reveled in her attentions. Following the aspic the guests feasted on braised guinea fowl with figs and oranges accompanied by a mélange of nightshade vegetables. While every morsel was being relished, Josefina showered affection from table to table but showed no partiality until the dessert trays arrived. "We have an assortment of thin cakes, tarts, and puffs," she said, "and our president is the first to be served. I will arrange his plate with one of each delicacy, for nothing is too good for our leader, and nothing too rich for his liking."

"How did you grow up so fast?" the president asked. "Only yesterday, you were a precocious little girl who loved the corrida."

"Sometimes," Josefina replied, "one is forced to grow up much faster than one would like."

At every table she was toasted, and in every heart one question continued to beat repeatedly: "Which one of us will she choose?"

"You're the most beautiful woman in the nation," she was told.

"Easily the most beautiful in the entire world."

"You deserve to live in splendor all the days of your life."

"You deserve to be treated as a queen."

"A goddess."

"You are the rare and startling treasure of our day."

She accepted these compliments with modesty by calling for more music and dancing, and after she had danced with every man in her company except the mayor of the city, she invited him to join her for the last waltz of the evening. They held each other closely and swayed in place while every eye was upon them, and every heart beat with jealousy.

"Look how closely she holds him," someone said.

"And how she allows him to rest his head on her shoulder."

"Doesn't she realize that his face powder will stain her gown?"

"What can she possibly see in someone so short, and malformed?"

"Everyone feels pity for our half brother," the president said to the governor. "It is because he has inherited more than his share of ugliness."

"But not from our side of the family," the governor added.

"Of course not," the president replied. "Our side has been blessed with good looks and sound minds."

"Let them say what they will," whispered one banker to another. "The ugly brother is very useful to our president because he will obey without question."

After the last waltz Josefina stooped to kiss the mayor on his forehead and while doing so noticed powder stains on her shoulders. Quickly covering them with strands of hair, she escorted the mayor back to the crowd of applauding guests whom she thanked for attending her celebration. "And now," she said, "I must send you home because your wives are surely anxious for your return, and I do not wish to enrage them with jealousy." She then distributed slips of colored paper folded in half on which her guests assumed they would find a handwritten prayer, but when unfolding the paper they were astonished to discover that nothing was written there. They looked to their hostess for an explanation, and she smiled in the presence of their silent confusion. "Yes," she said, crossing to the marble staircase, "I must, in all good faith, send you home at once, but before you leave, allow me to reveal my selfish purpose for inviting you here."

"Speak," said the governor. "Don't keep us waiting any longer."

"Gentlemen," she continued, "in honor of my beloved father,

who valued my purity beyond silver and gold, I intend to offer my body and soul to the highest bidder."

A thundering silence fell upon the heads of the men standing before her.

"Breathe, gentlemen," Josefina said. "Please do not forget to breathe, for I do not wish another person to expire in my household. You may leave your bids at the door this evening or deliver them tomorrow before eleven. Of course, I will give half of the highest bid to the church; my mother's soul will not rest otherwise."

With all eyes upon her, she slowly ascended the stairs and disappeared into her living quarters. The birthday party was over.

The capital city talked of nothing but the daughter's birthday celebration. For the second time since the revolution she had given even the poorest of citizens something to occupy their thoughts other than death, destitution, and the loss of property.

"The doctor's daughter," they said, "she has entertained in her house, the president of the nation, the man whose administration is responsible for the death of her father."

"And now she expects one of her guests to make her a whore."

"Has she no honor left inside her?"

"Has she no respect for anything her father stood for?"

"And does she even remember her mother's name?"

"Oh yes," the old lace maker said. "She remembers everything. And she holds nothing but respect. Some say her fault is youth, some say wantonness, but if honor can be made a fault, the daughter's fault is honorable."

While the city talked, Josefina sat on her balcony to read her bids. For the privilege of taking her virginity some of the men had offered enough money to live like royalty for an entire year, but it was not the money that interested her, it was the names of the bidders. She studied each square of paper carefully before arranging them in groups of importance.

Why am I studying them so closely? she finally asked herself.

My choice has already been made.

Quickly, she penned the mayor of the city a brief letter:

> Señor José Maria Serrano,
> I am heartbroken to learn that your bid is not
> among the highest, but in my grief I am comforted
> by the hope of one lingering thought: a man whose
> family name is so well known and respected,
> should not risk the embarrassment of having
> the entire country learn that he cannot afford the
> doctor's daughter. Should you care to match the
> highest bid, I would be honored to receive you in
> my home.

Under her name she wrote the amount of money the mayor needed to match: 25,550 lyricos. She perfumed the letter with the scent of orange blossoms, sealed it in a plain envelope, and paid a pilgrim to deliver it to the municipal offices. One hour later the same pilgrim returned with another envelope, one heavily taped and marked with a confidential stamp. In it was a roll of bills and wrapped around them was a handwritten message of three words. "Tonight at eight."

That afternoon Fuerte threaded her loom to begin the 184th panel, and that night, while weaving in the dark, she recorded the arrival of the mayor.

> *A man in his late forties, with a wife and three children,*
> *the half brother of the president of the nation, and one*
> *much given to drink. He has little money, but devious*
> *means of acquiring it, and because of him the daughter*
> *will never be impoverished. Because of him it will be said*
> *that she prefers men who are ugly because then she can*
> *give them so much. But it is not ugliness that she courts,*
> *it is revenge, and the revenge is not solely her own. There*
> *are other hands guiding her. The path has already been*

woven.

The mayor arrived, powdered, perfumed, and dressed for a formal occasion. Earlier that evening a case of wine from the family vineyards had been delivered and was still sitting in the entry. "When you taste this," he said, "you'll know the goodness of wine. What my brother gave you will taste like vinegar in comparison. The best he keeps for himself, but I believe in sharing the goodness of our vines."

She thanked him for his generosity. "You will gain much through my association," she assured him. "And you may trust me to be discreet."

In her bedroom she poured two glasses of the mayor's wine, and he drank in audible swallows that offended her, but she smiled in the face of his boorish manners and replenished his glass. Then for reasons unknown to her at the time, she made inquiries as to the location of the vineyards, the type of grape, and the exact time of harvest. "I know nothing of these things," she said. "Do you enjoy eating the grapes as well?"

"Oh yes," he replied. "During harvest the entire family gathers for a feast and everyday many kinds of grapes are brought to the table."

"A time of enjoyment and celebration," she said.

"Not unlike this one," he replied, and she replenished his glass for the third time, all the while dreading the thought of touching him or giving him the pleasure of touching her—and in her mother's bed.

In her mother's bed, but not without purpose,
She enticed the man who murdered her father.
She undressed him with a smile that was not a smile.
And with a heart that was not given to love.
In her own mother's bed she undressed him.
She passed false admiration upon him,
And she breathed the contaminated air from his fetid lungs.

"Every muscle is visible," she said. "I can see that you take active part in manly activities. No one who sits behind a desk can be expected to possess such a body."

"I am a man of a certain age. And . . ."

"And I am a woman of a certain age," she interrupted, "who admires a certain man of a certain age."

She placed sweet scented pillows under his head, a bottle of wine in his hands, and begged him to turn his head while she undressed. "You are the first," she said when her dress fell to the floor.

"And I will not turn my head," he told her.

"And I will be embarrassed," she replied.

With feigned modesty, her fingers slowly untied the straps on her slip, and after it had fallen to the floor and she stood naked and silent, but with anger that boiled in her stomach, she whispered to him again, saying that she was honored by his presence but much afraid of the sight and smell of a man. Hearing this he stroked his penis and breathed heavily, and the odor of his fetid breath and rancid skin permeated the closed-up room, seeped into her lungs as she stood there naked, silent, and angry; fighting against the sickness that swelled in her stomach. She felt his eyes moving across her breasts and down to her thighs, but not once did she turn her head, not once did she fail to see the dark moles on his face, or the powder stains on her sheets. She watched him lying there, chewing his wet, swollen lips and breathing as if every breath could be his last. Should be his last, she thought. And then she thought again: No, not his last. Not just yet.

Determined not to quit her plan, she breathed deeply the noxious fumes from his lungs and with each breath the room tilted and turned and her temples throbbed and beads of cold sweat appeared above her lips, on her forehead, and on the palms of her hands. She wanted to speak, but could no longer produce a sound for her will to continue was vanishing in the rotting air of her mother's room. She heard the sound of his breathing, like the hissing of many serpents, the sound of the ocean wind pounding against windows, the sound of the creaking bed and of the wind chimes calling her into the courtyard where the air was cool and fresh. She bent down to take her clothes, to put them on again, to leave the room, and quit her plan, but when she reached for her slip he rose up and took her first by the arms and then the legs. In an instant she was on the bed, and he was over her, and in an instant more he entered her with one painful thrust.

She stifled her scream.

He withdrew fully.

And with one thrust more he was finished.

Her mother's bed was wet with his sweat and with her blood, and with the wine that had overturned staining the mattress and scented pillows. For a long time they lay there, his weight pressing against her and his hands clamped around her wrists. Soon his head dropped onto her shoulder, his hands relaxed their grip, and the air reeked with the fumes of his snoring.

"It's over," she said. "And we have only just begun."

While he slept she took his head in both her hands and turned it carefully to examine the remains of his ear. Then she rolled him onto his back, and adjusted the floor lamp so his head rested in a circle of light that held no secrets. Slowly, she unscrewed the lid from the blue bottle, and with long tweezers she removed the fragment of ear to compare it first to the mayor's good ear; then to the mutilated one.

Not a perfect fit, she thought, but close enough to be unmistakable.

Time had distorted the edges of perfection, but had not interfered with her memory of that night and that dark figure stepping from the shadows of the flame trees and limping away, leaving behind something that could be traced. "Yes." She kissed his damaged ear. "I have found you."

The mayor stirred in his sleep. She quickly returned the ear to the bottle and the bottle to its box under the bed. "Please," she begged, "you must wake up. You must wake up at once because you have not yet given me complete satisfaction. Once more.

Please. I must have you once more."

To ensure his return, she mounted him in his half sleep, her legs locked beneath his thighs. Instantly he became erect inside her, but she bore the pain with a smile of pleasure, and at the point of his orgasm she grasped his throat with both hands. Gradually she tightened her grip prolonging his ecstasy and bringing him to the edge of his own death. She watched his temples throb, his face glow red, and his lips turn white with foam. When his eyes rolled back into their sockets, he tried to overpower her, but she held fast to his throat and refused to let go. "I'm dying," he gasped. And she answered him sweetly:

"Not yet, my love. Not yet."

Seconds later she released him, and he took flight, rising above the bed and into a cloudy space where he looked down upon himself and his lover. "I am flying," he said. "Bring me back." She massaged the muscles of his neck, and he returned to his body. He was cold and still but within seconds, beads of sweat appeared on his forehead and his eyes opened wide. He begged for water, for a wet cloth, a cigarette, a shot of brandy anything to let him know that he was still alive. "Surely," she said, "your wife has performed this ancient method of intensification that produces an out-of-the-body experience not unlike that practiced by the yogis."

"Would I be alive to tell it?" he asked.

"By her hands, no," Josefina replied.

"I have never known such . . ."

"Pleasure." She spoke the word for him.

"Pleasure," he repeated.

"A man, such as yourself, needs intense pleasure," she added. "And I am the woman to provide it."

Soon he was sleeping once again, and the fumes from his rotting lungs, and the flatulence of his distended stomach sent her fleeing into the courtyard to walk among the orange trees where the air was sweet, where her mother's bowl overflowed with flowers, and her father's grave was bathed in moonlight. At the lotus pool she performed her ablutions with distilled water in which leaves of *Vervain* and *Tres Puntas* had been boiled and cooled. Over and over she washed herself, and after every trace of the mayor's odor had been removed from her body she bathed herself again using soft spring water scented with orange and cloves.

She hung her hammock from her mother's trees and slept with gentle rocking and cool breezes until the ocean's salty clouds descended and dawn awakened her all too soon. To lie in that garden hammock for the rest of her life, was her morning's wish, but her plan was far from finished. "Now," she said as her feet touched the courtyard earth, "I must prepare breakfast for the president's half brother."

On a silver tray she served coffee and sweet bread toasted with butter and cinnamon. "You must stay in bed," she told him. "For it is the only place to truly enjoy breakfast." She spooned slices of mango onto his toast, and poured his coffee into a silver cup. "I want this breakfast to be as delicious for you as the evening was for me." She spoke with feigned temerity as though embarrassed to be speaking so personally, and for the first time to someone she hardly knew. Then she joined him on the bed. Sitting among crumpled sheets stained by his powdered face and painted hair, she stared at him with love sick eyes while he consumed every grain of sugar, every crust and crumb and drop of coffee with rapacious appetite for the night had left him contented of mind, but ravenous beyond expectation. "You will eat everything in the house," she protested, and he, reveling in her attention, attempted to lick yet another drop of coffee from the bottom of his cup. "Your manners will take some getting used to," she said in a tone of good humor.

"A good man knows how to show his appreciation for good food," he replied, releasing a torrent of gas as further proof of his enjoyment.

"I am flattered," she smiled, "but your behavior will awaken my father and mother, our beloved Angel, and others who must never be named. They are all sleeping in the courtyard."

"What is it out there, a cemetery?" he laughed.

"A hotel," she said. For the departed, she thought.

"And when may I return?" he asked.

"My pleasure is yours," she told him. "But the rules are mine. If you wish to return, you may do so at any time, but you will pay me double what you have already paid me, and after that you will continue to pay double the amount of your last visit. If you cannot afford me do not return, but remember, you will bring disgrace to yourself as a man of wealth and political importance if your opponents learn that you cannot match my worth."

At the front door, she kissed him good-bye, and he promised to return.

"I will expect you soon," she replied. "Do not disappoint me."

And all of this the weaver recorded, down to the very last thread; all of this and more.

> *One week later the mayor returned,*
> *And he paid double.*
> *And one week later he paid double again.*
> *And one week after that he paid double.*
> *And that amount doubled in one week's time.*
> *And in another week it doubled again.*
> *And the money came from here.*
> *And the money came from there.*
> *And when there was little money to be seized,*
> *Neither from the rich nor from the poor,*
> *The daughter refused to accept another coin.*

"You see," she confessed, "I've fallen in love with you. From now on, I can no longer accept your money so tonight I will pay you the same amount you first paid me, and every week hereafter, I will pay you double the amount until I have repaid you completely. That is the only way I can convince you of my love."

Pacing the floor, he reminded her that he was a married man, that his wife had given him two sons and a daughter whom he valued more than life itself, and therefore, he could never return her deepest love. "My eldest son is three and his brother is almost two," he said. "Both are very smart. I will send them away to school, and they will become even smarter. That's the only way they will advance over their half cousins who have the family's total support. Someday one of my sons will become the longest reigning president in the history of this nation, and the other? Who knows what he will do with himself, but one thing is certain, he will succeed. They will all succeed because they will be educated outside this country, unlike their cousins who will know nothing of the world."

"And your daughter?"

"Adopted," he said.

"From the orphanage?"

"Yes," he replied, "from the famous orphanage of the actress. Her mother left her there. She will marry into a family of high rank and her husband will be a man of the modern world even though her real mother may be a rebel."

"And what if she does not agree with your choice of husbands for her?"

"She will marry him anyway."

"A marriage agreement is easy enough to arrange," Josefina said. "But if one of your sons is to lead this nation you will need to precede him. That can be accomplished by eliminating everyone who stands in your way."

"My half brothers," he said jokingly. "Shall I shoot them?"

"Now you are thinking like a man," she said. "You should think like a woman instead. Only men think of guns."

"And what would a woman think?"

"She would think *poison*. Poison is very difficult to trace. One drop is worth a hundred bullets when properly used."

She took him into her father's laboratory and showed him row upon row of bottles containing roots, flowers and bark steeping in murky fluids. "My father," she said, "was a humanitarian who did not believe in suffering, and he often took it upon himself to release a patient from an agonizing death. He was well acquainted with nature's aggressive poisons, such as the root of sanguinaria, the young leaves of cowbane, and the bark of curare, which paralyzes the respiration system and is always fatal. But he was also well acquainted with what he called the gentle poisons and often relied upon them in order to transport his terminal patients into a blissful and everlasting sleep. So many times I watched him exchange suffering with eternal dreams."

She placed a bottle in the mayor's hands. "Annihilate those who stand in your way," she said.

"Poison the wine." he replied.

"Do the children drink wine also?"

"Certainly not," he answered.

"Then why ruin good wine? Poison the fruit instead."

She placed a syringe on her father's desk, and invited the mayor to sit down. Taking the doctor's chair she spoke as if counseling a nervous patient. "It will be very easy. Very simple. You're not to worry about anything. Allow me to create the dark returns for you. I know the proper way of bringing them into existence." Drawing the fluid into the syringe, she showed him how to measure the dosage. "Two cc's into each grape," she explained. "What that means is this: one grape will make you very sick, two a little sicker, three could kill a child, four a small adult, and six an elephant. You are to eat two grapes but no more. You will feel the effects, but you will not die. You will be taken to the hospital, and in a few days you will recover, but the others will not."

"And my wife and three children?"

"Let them eat grapes," Josefina replied. "I will give you new children and better ones."

Later that evening she kept her word by returning the money he had sent to her prior to his first visit. She returned it in the envelope in which it had been delivered, and she sealed it with kisses. "When you are president," she said, "I will be your First Lady, and we will have music in the streets once again."

"Yes," he replied. "We will have music everywhere."

And the weaver recorded the daughter's dark return just as it happened and as she had known it would:

> *The next week she paid him double what she had paid him the week before, and the week thereafter she paid him double once again. And in this way she convinced him of her devotion. In this way she gained his complete trust. And trusting her completely, he followed her advice by taking the syringe, and the bane she had given him in an unmarked bottle. By taking the syringe, the unmarked bane and her advice, he was, without knowledge, designing his own destiny, for one week later he did not come to her and would never come to her again for he had listened well and had trusted her wisdom and had eaten two grapes. And the second was one too many.*

"The daughter's lover," the peddlers cried, "he has been poisoned."

"But they were never lovers," said the lace maker.

But they were never actually lovers, said the weaver of the tapestry.

"You could have relied on the spiders," Fuerte said.

"I am saving them for a special occasion," the daughter replied.

While the Street of Merchants and Peddlers argued over what had or had not occurred, Josefina Esperon sat on her mother's balcony to read a special edition of the daily paper. It had been left on her door at one o'clock in the afternoon, and within the hour every citizen in the capital had heard or read the story: the president, his wife and four sons were dead; his second brother, the governor of the state, was hospitalized, his wife had died instantly, but their three sons had been spared. As for the mayor of the city, he had died before reaching the hospital, but his wife Teresa Elena, two sons José Maria and Jesús Maria and his adopted daughter Maria Concepción were traveling abroad. Appearing on the first page was a photograph of the ex-governor who had become the new president. From his hospital bed he charged the family servants with the crime and called for their execution. By then the faithful cook and her two daughters, the gardener, the chauffeur, and six chambermaids had already fled the country. "Over the mountains," the street sweepers said, "they left at dawn and will surely never return."

"They would be better off in Hell than fettered to such a household," Josefina said. Leaving the newspaper to blow across the balcony she returned to her bedroom, and for the first time since her father's death she observed the siesta hours. "I am very tired," she said when she closed her eyes, and when she opened them again it was morning, and she was still tired; exhausted from having slept so long with one troubling thought: A handsome father with three sons, two mole-faced brothers and their adopted sister—too many seeds have been left, and one day they will return and sprout again.

The governor recovered to assume the presidency, and for one year the house of forty-three rooms, four balconies, and two courtyards, did not see a visitor other than the pilgrims. For one year, the doctor's daughter read from her father's library. She cooked the food and kept the house, and the weaver recorded the events of the day and the days to come.

Every morning the goldfish were fed, the stairs swept, the orange trees watered, and the sand in the large courtyard was raked into swirling patterns around the graves. At noon soup was placed on the stove, the laundry was seen to, and the pilgrims were let in to rest. By five o'clock, when the wind changed its course, the pilgrims departed and smoke from the brick factory invaded the city. At that hour every window was closed and every curtain drawn, and before the falling smoke settled into the courtyards, Eufemia was visited with fresh water and petals.

The factory smoke did not disturb the saint's eternal peace, but when her crown of thorns lost its sting, she refused to rest until it was replaced with a new one. And on restless nights, when a new crown did not please her, the daughter and the weaver were awakened to recitations and heavy footsteps heard throughout the many rooms.

How many nights did the daughter leave her bed to speak to her restless mother in words that could calm a baby? I am with you. I will help you rest."

How many times did she replace one crown of thorns with another? "You will like this one Mother," she said countless times and would continue to say. "These thorns are sharper than needles. They will please you, and you will rest again." Only then would Eufemia return to her grave, only then would she drink from her bowl, and only then would the restless nights turn to sleep.

Since that week of many deaths and accusations, the days passed and passed quickly one attached to the other. That year the rainy season was neither too wet nor too dry, and the dry season did not parch the earth, and when the daughter's twentieth birthday arrived, no one took notice, not even the daughter herself for she was occupied with her mother's journals, her father's medical dictionaries, and the musical instruments she studied as a child. Only one day out of each week did she leave this house, for there was never a reason to leave it more frequently than that, and on that day she visited the market to buy food, which she had learned to do without assistance, never once bringing home a spoil, never once paying more or less than what was reasonable at the time.

And this according to the weaver whose ear was tuned to the street:

She is like her mother, the merchants say.
She has the smile of our saint,
And her heart, saintly also, is without blemish.
No, the peddlers argue, there is something fearful about her.
She is like her father who controlled life.
And she will do anything, say anything,
Stoop to any humiliation,
In order to fulfill her destiny.
Among all this talk, some idle, some not, another year

*has come and gone, and now her twenty-first birthday
approaches and another celebration is planned—because
the daughter has not yet finished her vengeful purpose.*

"I am twenty-one today," she announced to the twenty-five
men who applauded when she entered the courtyard decorated
with garlands of dark roses, gas lamps, and star-shaped mirrors
hanging from the orange trees, the many arches and the open sky.
Wearing a red gown from the lace maker's shop, she stood before
her guests silencing their applause with an up-lifted hand. Everyone of importance had been invited, and everyone of importance
had arrived thinking they would find an orchestra on the gallery
and the courtyard swept for dancing. All week the men had practiced their steps, some had taken private lessons in the Viennese
waltz, and all of them had placed bets on who the daughter would
favor on the dance floor.

"There will be no dancing tonight," she announced to the disappointment of her guests. "Tonight there will be music. Chopin
has agreed to join our celebration, but unfortunately he has not
agreed to concertize. Through a long and arduous exchange of
conflicting opinions, however, he has coerced me into taking his
place at the keyboard."

A baby grand piano, purchased especially for the occasion,
had been moved into the courtyard, and twenty-five high-backed
chairs of carved oak surrounded it. When her audience was seated,
the daughter asked two questions: "How long has it been since
our capital city has heard music? And how much longer can we
survive without it?"

For three quarters of an hour she played Chopin, and for three
quarters of an hour more, her guests would have listened rapturously even if wrong notes had been played and oranges had fallen
onto the keyboard. Even if the earth had trembled and the house of
forty-three rooms had fallen to the ground they would have gone
on listening as if every note were the last to be heard on earth.

On concluding the concert, she begged her guests to cease

applauding her amateurish talent. "Take up your chairs at once and followed me to the tables," she said. "I implore you to reserve harsh judgment on our simple repast, which I have prepared myself."

Having given this cue, five waiters in tuxedos appeared with silver platters arrayed with golden pheasant roasted to perfection, with purple potatoes from the highlands, black mushrooms from the pine groves, and white moon squash stuffed with sweetmeats and mango chutney. During the meal she visited each table to retrieve napkins and shower attentions, and after the men had dined sufficiently, black, bitter coffee as thick as molasses was served along with slices of blood orange powdered with cinnamon, dark sugar, and red chili.

The men shouted with approval, and after receiving their praise, she returned to the keyboard. "The night is filled with moonlight," she said, "so appropriate for Beethoven's most famous sonata."

Watching the daughter's hands glide effortlessly over the keyboard, the president wondered how she could maintain an even tempo against so many hearts pounding like metronomes, each beating a different time. He leaned forward in his chair, and she singled him out with a smile that traveled through the courtyard enticing each gentleman, who received her fleeting attention, to lean forward in anticipation of more.

On finishing the sonata, she stood to receive the applause of her admirers, and when the courtyard was silent once again, she delivered a speech designed to burn out-of-control in the streets and cafés the following day. "Gentlemen," she said, "I intend no harm to any of you, nor do I wish to pay disrespect to our late mayor and dear friend, but tonight, in his honor, and for the sake of our own amusement, I am offering once again, my virginity to the highest bidder."

"How is that possible?" asked the director of the National Bank.

"What do you take us for?" shouted the governor.

"But my brother . . . " said the president.

"The rumors heard along the streets and corridors have little credence!" Josefina replied. "We were never lovers. He was a cavalier, a total gentleman, but incapable of satisfying a woman. In his honor, let it be known that the doctor's daughter is attempting, once again, to relinquish her purity for a charitable price."

Again she distributed squares of colored paper, and while the waiters ushered the guests to the front door Josefina Esperon ascended the stairs to wait for her announcement to flood the city like a rainstorm that was meant to wash everything, even the vegetable carts out to sea, leaving behind that which made life in the capital city almost bearable: another scandal.

"Disgraceful," said the church officials.

"Good news," said the bankers. "Now our economy will soar because everyone is happy once again, and when everyone is happy everyone spends money, even money that does not exist will be spent."

For two days the cafés levitated with laugher and high stakes. "The president will surely place the highest bid," the businessmen said. "For how else can he pay tribute to a brother who could not perform his manly duties, not even on such a lovely woman as Josefina Esperon."

Just as the daughter suspected, the president did not place the highest bid, but she honored him as if he had, and every night crowds of people lined either side of the Street of Merchants and Peddlers for the sole purpose of cheering the president's arrival. Old men salivated at the thought of the president's good fortune, and old women wished that in their youth they had been blessed with the daughter's willful desire.

"Once I was very beautiful also," said the old lace maker. "Even I could have turned a president's head, but I did not know this at the time."

The president's body guards forbade him to leave the official residence. "It's not safe," they said. "There's too much anticipation all over the city." The crowd lining the streets from his front

gates all the way to Josefina's door had become impatient. Bets
had been placed on the exact time of the leader's arrival. Stakes
were high and tempers short. Fights broke out among the bettors.
Knives and clubs appeared. Ambulances were summoned, and the
Hospital of the Sacred Heart was filled with broken heads and
bleeding throats.

"And all because the daughter of our late colleague is so
beautiful," said the doctors.

And all because the daughter controls her destiny, said the
weaver.

Finally, the president sent for Josefina, but she refused to leave
her house, and after a week of delays, after a week of false starts
and refusals, she made a plan, and he carried it forth. Disguised
as a beggar he escaped from the official residence at two a.m. and
passed silently through the dark streets while those who awaited
his arrival were sleeping against walls and on hard cobblestones.
At the appointed time Josefina waited at her side door. She listened
for the sound of approaching footsteps, and on the first knock she
quickly opened the door.

Appearing in a dress of black silk with a burgundy rose in her
dark hair, and Carlota Montejo's mole painted above her upper
lip, she greeted the president with a kiss. "Tonight," she said, "you
will turn me into a woman."

"I've dreamed of this night," he said.

"But you must be gentle," she whispered.

"The first time is never good for the woman," he replied.

"Then let the second time be tonight as well," she begged,
"for I do not wish you to leave me with a memory of pain."

In her sitting room, she fed the president a light meal of mushroom crepes and champagne followed by purple figs and black
coffee. After dinner they lingered at the table amusing themselves
with kisses, cognac, and talk of the seasons. "What must it be
like," she asked, "to experience winter, to know the beauty of au-
tumn foliage?"

"One day you will know first hand," the handsome president

replied. "I will take you on a trip, and we will visit the four seasons."

"Now," she said, "you are speaking as a poet."

"You bring the best out of me," he confessed. "I dare say you have the power to create poets from common military men such as myself."

"A man with such gray eyes must have a poet in him somewhere," she quickly responded.

At that moment his head drooped and fell onto the table; his arms became limp and his eyes closed with sleep. She rolled him onto the floor, unbuttoned his shirt and opened it to his bare chest, which was full and tight with muscles. She tore away the buttons, ripped the shirt from his body and unloosened his pants with a sigh, for they clung to his form like extra layer of skin, leaving little to imagine and everything to behold. A fan of dark hair that began on his chest diminished to a thin line that extended down his stomach to his thick penis, which stood erect.

"This president," she said, "is like none other."

Remembering the night she had first stared into his gray eyes, she once again reconsidered her plan by asking herself if she could take this man, who was built like a god, and love him unconditionally for the rest of her life? "I could love his body," she freely admitted, "but soon his vacuous mind would leave me wanting."

Quickly she ripped the black dress from her body, and left it in a pile on the floor. She scattered her undergarments about the room, pulled ribbons and combs from her hair, and at the feet of the sleeping president she stood, naked and determined. "How you have dreamed of this night," she said. "And so have I."

With a syringe she drew blood from her own veins and dripped it onto the floor, onto the naked president and onto her legs and thighs. When he awakened from the potion she had given him, she cried out in pain and disappointment that he had not waited to finish the supper she had thoughtfully prepared. She accused him of taking her by force, ripping her, dress and entering her as one animal enters another. She pointed to the blood on the floor and demanded to know why he had not withdrawn when she had pleaded and begged for him to have mercy on one as yet unaccustomed to the ways of love.

"As I have already said," he replied, "the first time is never good."

"The next time," Josefina said, "if there is a next time, will cost you double."

"Only if you agree to marry me," he said. "I am a president with three sons. They have no mother, and I have no wife."

"The poor soul," Josefina said with tears in her voice. "She suffered agony at the hands of a murderer who was never found. That should never have been her fate. Such a beautiful woman."

"A good woman, but not a particularly beautiful one," he replied. "Every president in the history of our country has had a wife, but no one has ever had a beautiful wife. You will be the first."

"You must visit me again to help me decide," Josefina said. "And you must give me time."

"It is one hour before dawn," he replied. "How much time will you need?"

"I will inform you when I know," she replied and walked him to the side door.

In the guise of a pauper, the president left the house of forty-three rooms, four balconies, and two courtyards. Presently, he arrived at the official residence, and when the dogs barked his arrival, he fed them with bones from his pocket. He patted them on their heads and passed unnoticed through the house. And later that morning when the sleeping guards awakened they found many white bones at their feet, and many satisfied dogs sleeping contentedly in the hall.

The next week was the same. The president, disguised as a beggar, came and went unnoticed. To spend a few hours with the daughter he paid double the amount he had paid the week before. The week thereafter he paid double again, and in one week's time that amount also doubled. So it continued, week after week until the daughter responded to the president's proposal.

"Yes," she said, "I will marry you."

The next morning she appeared on her balcony to tell the crowd to go home and return again on her wedding day. And to the worshipers leaving early Mass, she said that she would soon become their First Lady.

Hearing this, some of them cheered. And some spat on the daughter's door. Some hurled rocks. And others, roses. And many more shook their fists in everlasting damnation.

"The doctor's daughter has the mind of a whore," it was said in the cafés, the parks and plazas. "And she will become our First Lady."

And this, as it was written on the 193rd panel:

The dead mayor's brother, who was the president of the nation and the fiancé of the doctor's daughter, returned to the house of forty-three rooms, four balconies, and two courtyards. He returned three days after the daughter had accepted his proposal, and he paid his future wife twice what he had paid her the time before, but the following week he did not bring money, he brought, instead, three diamond necklaces that had belonged to his murdered wife, necklaces that he had given to her on the birth of each of their children.

> *The jewels were well received,*
> *And the wedding day was set.*
> *The streets were cleaned.*
> *The people were ready.*
> *And so was the daughter.*
> *The day before her wedding,*
> *She had not yet chosen her dress.*

"No, I will not be seen in your wife's diamonds," she told the president the night before they were to marry. "But I will keep them for a day in the distant future, when we are old and wise and have forgotten our many tragedies; only then will I bring them out, and by the light of a flickering fire, I will dress myself in your diamonds and our world will sparkle again."

When it was time to say good-night she kissed him passionately, and at the door she made him promise to walk in shadows so he would not be detected by the crowd of spectators sleeping in the streets. "You must not walk the avenues," she said. "Follow this map, and you will not be recognized or harmed." She gave him a hand-drawn map. He studied it carefully and gave it back to her.

"You think of everything," he said. "Tomorrow will be a beautiful day for you. I promise."

"Tomorrow will be a beautiful day for us both," she whispered. "The entire capital will be watching us, but tonight you must not travel forth without your cloak. Pull it tightly around your face so no eyes may see and recognize my love."

He arranged the hood of his cloak so it fell over his face. Then he opened the side door and stepped silently into the dark street, and she bolted the door behind him.

"Tomorrow," he whispered through the heavy oak.

"Tomorrow," she whispered in reply.

With his receding footsteps she returned to her bedroom where there was no wedding dress and no bridal veil, no bouquet of flowers and no trousseau. There was nothing in any of her rooms that spoke of marriage, but on her balcony marriage was celebrated in advance with many white ribbons, with wedding bells, lace, and lilies.

"The wedding balcony is ready," she said, "but I am not. In this house there shall be no giving or taking in marriage."

From the decorated balcony she watched the president passing through shadows without once alerting the sleeping crowd.

At the far corner, she watched him turn.
And at the next corner he turned again.
And in her mind she followed him to the next corner,

Where three men waited in three doorways.
Each man carried a knife.
And each knife, a promise.
And each promise had been made
*   to the daughter as well as the saint.*
Who are you? the president asked. Let me pass.

We are disciples of Eufemia, came the answer.
And what do you want with me, a poor beggar?
We want your blood, your flesh, and your bones.
And what will you do with me?

With your blood we will water the red rose.

With your flesh we will summon the vultures from the skies.

With your bones we will feed the dogs in the streets.

It was then that the first blow was struck.
Not once but three times the president was attacked.
The knife blades sang between his ribs,
And the blood flowed from his veins.
Who are my slayers? he asked.
Eagerly, the three men answered:
The daughter of the doctor and our saint.
And the president replied:
Why didn't I know this?
And one of the slayers answered him:

Because you saw only her beauty.

Hearing this the president died with his face in the cobblestones and three knife wounds in his back, and when his slayers
were certain that all life had passed from his body they removed
his bloody cloak, as they had been instructed to do, and from that
dark corner they followed the shadows of their own destinies back
to the house of forty-three rooms where the daughter waited at
the side door. The slayers knocked five times rapidly. The door

opened, and they quickly entered the house.

They told her what they had done. They showed her the blood stained cloak. She touched the wet stains and smiled.

"Well done," she said. "For this you shall be rewarded."

She gave them each a diamond necklace. "For your devoted allegiance," she said, "you shall surely receive many stars in your Heavenly crowns, but until that glorious day arrives, take these stars of my own, which I give you in deepest appreciation and respect for my mother, our saint."

The following morning, after the president's murder was announced, it was the daughter's turn to tear through her house on a fit of screaming. From the windows of every upstairs room she wailed loudly, and the people on the street below followed her cries from one side of the house to the other until she finally emerged onto her wedding balcony, her eyes red and swollen, her fingers tearing her hair. With all eyes upon her, she stripped the balcony of the wedding decorations and hurled them into the crowd below. "Take them," she screamed. "Burn them in the street. There is no happiness in this house."

Before the morning had passed into afternoon she had covered her balcony with black ribbons, her windows with black curtains, and her outside doors with lilies. She then returned to the balcony to sit beneath a dark veil and cry softly to the people on the street. "I will never be seen in a wedding gown. My color is black, and my flower is a rose darker than blood."

Observing this public display of mourning, her admirers praised her for dignity, and her adversaries damned her for bringing dishonor upon herself, her noble family, and the nation.

"Everything she touches," they said, "withers and dies."

"Who could desire such a woman?"

"Her eyes carry a deadly sting."

"And her tongue is forked like a serpent's."

"She's caused men to go mad with love."

"And women to die of jealousy."

While the daughter mourned on her balcony, the weaver wove in darkness, recording everything she saw and heard. For one week the daughter grieved in public, and for one week more the weaver wove without stopping to rest, to lift her head, or feed the spiders. Now the panels were long, twice, three times longer than the first one. "Because," Fuerte said, "there is so much to be woven. And the threads never lie."

Finally Josefina said, "Fuerte, you must rest. You must take food. You must eat something now."

"No my child," replied the weaver. "I cannot stop because I am almost finished with this panel. Please feed the spiders for me, they will not harm you. One day soon we must separate the males from the females. "

At the end of that week when the panel was finished, Fuerte put down her loom and called to the daughter, "You are no longer mourning on your balcony."

"My mourning has been in celebration," Josefina said. "Now I am finished."

"Nothing is ever finished," Fuerte replied. She unrolled the new panel and stretched it across the floor. It was different from the others in that it marked the end of one time and the beginning of another. And it was also the longest. "The future will soon become the present," she said, "and the present and the past will become the future once again, and once again someone will read the signs and will make predictions and some of the predictions will come true."

On hands and knees, Josefina studied the panel. Unlike the others it was dense with long lines that wrapped around the four selvage ends.

"I will read it to you," Fuerte said. She read by touch, beginning with the first word in the left-hand corner and following the lines as they wrapped twelve times around.

The presidential torch has been passed to another family;
a generation of humanitarians, and a new era has begun,

an era that will come to be known as the Forty Years of Peace. During this time all the presidents will be poets and all the poets will be kings, and the Forty Years of Peace will be remembered as a time of great happiness not only by the daughter but by many of her countrymen as well. Once again the opera house will reopen and the National Theatre will be rebuilt, music will return to the streets and to the plazas, and verse will be composed for all occasions. The factory that spits smoke into the air will be closed, and flowering trees will be planted along all the barren streets. During this time the people will turn back to the sea for their wealth and inspiration. The produce from these waters and marshes will be sold around the world, and prosperity will return to the land.

The Forty Years, which will pass like the turning of a page, will be remembered as a time of plenty and gratitude. The disciples of Eufemia will multiply; her grave will forever be visited by pilgrims, and they will leave flowers in her bowl and prayers pinned to her door. And the daughter will leave the prayers on the door, which will come to be known as The Door of Prayers, and she will never fail to invite her mother's disciples to sit in the cool courtyard where the serene fountain, the fragrance of orange blossoms, and the music of wind chimes will transport the voice of the saint from her grave into the open air.

At all hours the pilgrims will come, and none will be turned away. Eufemia's grave will forever be covered with flowers, her blue bowl filled with fresh water, and her crown of thorns often replaced because each pilgrim will know that the thorns must be kept sharp for even in death Eufemia desires to be reminded of the suffering that once consumed the world. And likewise, the pilgrims, particularly during this Forty Years of Peace, must be reminded of the cruelty they once endured, so they too will wear crowns of rose thorns when entering the house of forty-three rooms, four balconies, and two courtyards. Until the walls crumble and fall, the pilgrims will arrive with their foreheads bleeding and the bones of their knees gleaming from having crawled great distances to honor their holy one.

And in this house, these courtyards and rooms of many soft colors, the daughter will welcome her visitors both by day and by night. For four decades she will entertain many loved ones each of whom will shower her with promises, sweet words, and riches, but at the end of the Forty Years of Peace, the world will turn once more, and once more there will be revolution and bloodshed, and once more the face of the city will be scared, and once more the poets will be condemned, and the land will no longer sing.

"What does that red streak represent?" Josefina asked. "It's like an open wound."

"It represents the dying sea. The twelve green moons are the twelve parrots that will pray for you. The eight green moons are the eight parrots that will remain with you and give you wisdom. The blue circle is the wheel that will be built outside your window. The saffron birds represent the return of the yellow clouds, and the thirty stars are the thirty daughters who will love you unconditionally because you saved them."

"Thirty daughters!" Josefina laughed. "Impossible."

"Go to bed and sleep," Fuerte said. "Tomorrow you will not laugh at the impossible."

Having delivered her say, Fuerte rolled up the panel and went to sleep on the hard floor. The next morning she and the daughter separated the males from the females. "Now," Fuerte said, "we have two baskets to feed." That afternoon she strung her loom with threads of brilliant colors. The Forty Years of Peace had begun, and there were many panels waiting to be woven. "For a while," Fuerte said, "we will be happy again."

Part III

The Forty Years of Peace
and
The Coming of the Parrots

For the daughter of the doctor and the saint, the Forty Years of Peace was a deceiving grace; a time of celebration and prosperity that began with a great love and ended with the return of the mole-faced heirs of her father's assassin. And it was recorded, all of it, for the survivor to read: the tragedy of a great love in threads of black, gray, and burgundy, the thirty daughters in the colors of the rainbow, and the mole-faced heirs in threads dyed with blood. Fuerte wove into her tapestry everything she had witnessed as well as the things she would never witness but knew simply by the act of knowing. She recorded the events of the day as they came to her in her room without windows, and she recorded the events of the future as if they were happening simultaneously with the events of the day—and always with the understanding that yesterday, today, and tomorrow live in the same house, under the same sky. "The events of today point to the events of tomorrow and reflect the events of the past," Fuerte told the daughter. "If you understand your day, you understand your past, and if you understand all that has gone before you, the future is a small step forward."

"When your mind is more receptive, I will draw the alphabet and teach you to read the threads. It is not difficult but there is one hill you must climb. In your language you have a different form of the verb to express a different time, but in the language of the threads the verb remains the same; the time changes only with the reader's understanding. You must also pay attention to the short lines as well as the long ones. Both must be read."

She stressed the difference between the two lines and the purpose for both: the short line was used to capture her thoughts before they left her, and the long line was used to expound upon them. In both lines, long and short, Fuerte recorded the coming of the thirty daughters who would bring great riches into the house, and the arrival of the parrots that would draw the mole-faced heirs of the doctor's assassin to the daughter's door. In the long line she recorded the coming of the multitudes, the desires of a servant called Contenta, and the return of the poet, the daughter's first and greatest love.

From the streets came a poet, one the daughter had already met from her balcony. Finally, he returned, and she, thinking it was a pilgrim knocking at eight in the evening, threw opened her door without asking who was there. And it was with surprise and great pleasure that she recognized her visitor, a man not much younger than she, a man of great stature: a lean face; black hair that fell in ringlets; eyes that danced with fire and romance.

She stood to one side.
And the poet entered her house.
And with him she lived five years of pleasure,
And one of sorrow.
And with him she sang five poems of love,
And one of sorrow.
And with him, she wept.

He returned on the Day of All Souls, at one minute past eight in the evening, two years after their eyes first met. He arrived out of the dust of the street and with the dampness of the waterworks clinging to his flesh. Threadbare, soiled, and proud, he was dressed in a black suit with a red ribbon wrapped twice around the collar of his white shirt, wrapped twice with distinction and tied in a loose knot, the ends hanging. He had no hat, no boutonniere, no handkerchief for his pocket, no gift for the daughter except himself.

"You are dusty," she said.

"I am thirsty," he replied.

"How can one who spends so much time at the waterworks be thirsty?"

"It is not water that I desire," he confessed.

"Then why has it taken you so long to return?"

"I have stood before your door six times without knocking," the poet said. "I was not ready to face the inevitable."

It was then that she noticed his damp shoes. Thin but recently polished, the leather was splitting across the instep, and the laces, although they were identical, were much too long for the well-worn shoes, and like his tie, which was merely a discarded ribbon, the laces were threaded twice through the eyelets; threaded twice and tied with ends hanging.

"My father," she said, escorting him into the large courtyard, "had six pair of shoes. Perhaps, they will fit you."

"I did not come here for charity," he replied.

"For what reason then?" she asked.

"To sit before my mother's grave," he answered.

"Your mother?"

"Carlota Montejo." He spoke the name with pride.

For a long time they sat on opposite sides of Carlota's grave, and finally, the poet confessed that he had known neither his mother nor his father, the matador José Maria de Vega. He had been conceived the night before the matador's death and had been taken to the orphanage at birth. That was the story he told.

"Then you can be no more than nine years old," Josefina said. "I was present that afternoon when de Vega faced his last bull."

"And what did you see?" he asked.

"You do not wish to know," she replied.

"I am twenty-two," he said. "I wish to know."

"If you are twenty-two, then I surely must be thirty-four. But I am not thirty-four, and you are not twenty-two, and if you are twenty-two, and de Vega was your father, you were not conceived on the eve of his death."

"I must have a heritage," he said. "I am a poet."

"I will gladly give you a heritage," she replied. "And I will give you many poems as well."

For six years they lived the poem, and the poem was their own, and at the end of their first year the first poem was printed in gold letters on a folio of indigo paper. Bound in red leather and edged in black, the poem, an epic to everlasting love, was read by everyone in the capital. By the rich and the poor it was read and quoted in the cafés and plazas, along the harbor and the streets where people gathered to talk of the day.

For six years they lived the poem, and the poem was their own, and the poem was in six parts, and each part covered one year of life together, a year in the courtyards and on the balconies, a year in their bedroom, and on the tree-lined boulevards as well, for they were often seen together: strolling, listening to music, sitting in their private box at the opera, clothed in shadows that separated them from the world, but not from each other.

For six years they lived the poem, and the poem was their own. And every year for five years another poem was printed on indigo and bound in red. Bound in red leather and edged in black, five poems were published and four were loved. The fifth was read but it was not quoted. It was read, but it was not loved, and the sixth poem would never be published in the daughter's lifetime, for unlike the others, it was a poem of heart-rending sorrow.

And not once during the first five years did the daughter weep. Not once did she fall into despair. Not once did she give herself to remorse or thoughts of evil returns.

Day after day the lovers lived only for each other. Their passion filled every room of the house, and Fuerte, deeply infected by their amorous desires, wove continuously through the days and nights hardly stopping to rest, to eat, or feed the spiders. No one existed except the two lovers, the weaver, and the pilgrims who begged to be let in and were let in, but for the first time they were treated with disregard by the daughter who had eyes only for her poet. He may have been eighteen. He may have been twenty-two, but together they were insatiable; the courtyard was Eden, and they were love. What did they care that the pilgrims were watching them? What did they care if their love infected the entire street, the city, the nation?

"I wish to become a great lover as well as a great poet," he told her.

"With me," she said, "you will realize your dreams."

From the moment he arrived, thirsty and tired, they were locked in each other's arms; only the daily arrival of threadbare pilgrims separated them, but not even the pilgrims in their sack-cloth and thorns could separate them for long. "Yes, you may enter," she would say with ringing irritation. "But if you have come expecting to be fed, you will be disappointed. In this house we do not live by food and food alone, but by love and love alone."

Leaving the pilgrims to wander on their own, she would return to her bedroom where love was created during the heat of the afternoon on a bed that was never made, on carpets forever rumpled, among overturned chairs, and behind drawn curtains. And when they tired of the bedroom and chapel they joined in hammocks, and doorways, on tables and stairs, on the roof under the soft light of the moon or the glaring sun. Often they chased each other through the courtyards; running like naked children, they startled the pilgrims, the priests, and the ordinary citizens who had come out of curiosity to see how many graves were actually there and what the daughter was doing to occupy her time.

On an afternoon when the ocean was restless and three lost pelicans flew into the courtyard to take shelter from an approaching storm, Tomaso Pardo, the president of the nation and a poet himself, followed the pilgrims through the front door. Concealing himself behind a column, he watched the prancing pelicans and listened to the lovers. Their footsteps pounded the gallery floor, and the seabirds fled into the small courtyard and back again as if looking for a place to hide.

"I will catch you," the poet, shouted. "And when I do I will kiss every part of your body. I will cover you with kisses that will burn your flesh. Kisses that will blister your skin. Kisses that will make you go mad with love, and then I will go on kissing you."

Down the stairs they ran, naked and delirious. The pelicans took flight, and the pilgrims screamed at the sight of the naked man chasing the naked woman around the graves, back up the stairway and across the gallery.

"Surely this cannot be the daughter of our saint," they said.

"Surely we have come to the wrong house."

"Surely there's a mistake."

"There's no mistake," Tomaso Pardo told them. "Surely, you will never find a happier pair."

The daughter did not hear what was said and neither did her poet. Nothing that day distracted them, not even the archbishop's flashing robes and trail of incense. Having heard that the daughter's concupiscence, due to its infectious nature, was cause for great concern to the Christian world, the ancient archbishop paid an unexpected visit to the house of forty-three rooms, two courtyards, and four balconies. After the president had slipped away unrecognized, the archbishop arrived in the scorching afternoon heat, and for no other purpose than to investigate the rumors of indecency that surrounded the daughter of the saint and the poet who shared her life. The archbishop had just read the poet's second book which inflamed his mind, and caused him to lose three nights of sleep. "It is not fit for the Christian mind," he told his parish. "It is made for burning."

Adorned in rich robes with a cattleya orchid pinned to his chasuble, the archbishop, whose face was flush with communion wine and glistening with sweat, stood in the courtyard among pilgrims whose heads were circled with thorns and whose feet were bare and bleeding. Prepared to cast out demons, and to intervene with the Heavenly Father on behalf of the daughter, whose iniquities had been enumerated by church officials, the archbishop listened in righteous indignation to the lovers' voices wafting down the stairs.

"Do not stop," the daughter cried. "If you stop making love to me, I shall slay you without forethought."

"Slay me," the poet said. "And then this house shall be a tomb where buried love doth live."

From the bottom of the stairs, the archbishop called for the lovers to cease. "The Lord and all the angels in Heaven are listening to you," he said. "Every word spoken or thought reaches them on high."

Throwing open the bedroom door the daughter ran—flying, it seemed to the archbishop's tired eyes—around the gallery and down the stairs. Without clothes or shame she brushed the archbishop to one side. "Too hot the eye of heaven shines," she said, plucking the orchid from his cape and soaring across the courtyard. Behind her came a swarm of sulfur butterflies and behind the butterflies came the naked poet who also ran as if flying through the air. Without concern for modesty, he chased her through the passageway and into the small courtyard where he threw her into a hammock of many colors.

"Flee youthful lusts!" the archbishop shouted into the dark passage. "Evil men and seducers shall wax worse and worse, deceiving and being always deceived."

Demanding that the visitors leave before evil infiltrated the air they breathed, the archbishop held the front door open, and as the pilgrims departed he touched each of them on the forehead.

After they had all left, Hortencia Flores, who was also in the house that day, came forward to kiss the episcopal ring. "Blessings upon you, Hortencia, and upon your devout mother as well," the archbishop said to the young girl who carried herself with the weight of the cross. She was fifteen years old, but the lines on her face showed her to be a woman twice that age, and her mouse-colored hair, cropped unevenly from ear to ear, gave her the appearance of a boy locked inside the withering body of an older woman.

"Stay in this house, Hortencia," the archbishop commanded. "I will send someone to care for your mother. The Lord God beseeches you to open the door when the pilgrims knock, but only if the inhabitants of this place are fully clothed. It is your mission to prevent lascivious thoughts from escaping into the air, for lascivious thoughts are contagious, and must be obliterated from the earth. Capture them in your heart to make them your own, and then ask God to rid you of them."

"Yes, Your Excellency," Hortencia said.

"And one thing more my child, the poet's books are contaminated with unhealthy desires. They are filled with lustful longings and words that poison the air. Do not read them. Do not touch them. Destroy them at once."

For one week the pious Hortencia remained inside the house unbeknownst to the poet and his lover, who had eyes only for each other. For one week Fuerte wove passionately rarely abandoning her loom, while the young girl, whose face was already washed with wrinkles, hid behind chairs and columns to observe that which she had never allowed herself to imagine. Never before had she seen an unclothed man. Even as a child she had refrained from staring too long at pictures of half-clothed saints for even they carried a wild call, and a clear call, and a call that could not be denied. "Protect me Jesus," she prayed. "The daughter and her poet behave like animals, the lowest of the kingdom."

During the afternoons when the pilgrims begged to be let in, Hortencia sent them home. "There's illness in this house," she told them, closing the door quickly and returning to her watch.

Hiding under tables, behind curtains, and doors, she watched the lovers without ceasing, and without allowing herself to see all there was to see; seeing too much might give rise to a blindness of the soul or a quickening of the heart, so she watched through half-closed eyes, with her head slightly bowed and her ears tuned to harmless sounds: the dripping of water, the flouncing of goldfish, or the fluttering of sparrows, candle moths, butterflies, anything to protect her from hearing what must never be heard. From her various hiding places, she watched without seeing and listened without hearing, and on her fourth afternoon in the house the pilgrims gained her attention by demanding to be recognized. They attacked the door, beating upon it with fists and rocks, and from the middle of the street they cried:

"Let us in!"

"We have walked three days to visit our saint."

"Let us in! We are the living."

"We must let them in," Fuerte called from her dark room. "They will destroy the door if you do not."

Finally, Hortencia allowed the pilgrims to enter the house, but when they saw the naked lovers, flying like angels across the courtyard, they departed rapidly.

"We have knocked on the wrong door," they said.

"We have lost our way."

"Something has confused us."

The next day it was the same. While Fuerte dreamed feverishly over her loom, the pilgrims arrived. When they entered the courtyard and saw the naked lovers playing in a hammock, they were convinced that they had been led astray by Satan.

"Tell me," said the poet, whose right hand rested between the daughter's thighs. "What is the name of this article I hold in my hand?"

"Surely you know by now," said she. "It is my coynte."

"You are destitute of modesty," he laughed. "And what other names is it known by?"

"By the names of exotic flowers and luscious fruits that mellow with age," she answered.

"You are without shame," he cried in jest. "Now tell me what is the name of this concern of mine I hold in my hand?"

"In *The Book of the Thousand Nights and a Night*, it's called a pizzle."

"No, no, that's not its proper name," he teased. "Tell me again."

"In the same book, and on the same night it's called a prickle and a pintle."

"Prickle, pintle, or pizzle," said he, "which do you prefer."

"I prefer them all," she cried, smothering him with kisses and laughter.

"And what would happen," he asked, "should I take you in my arms and never let you go."

"Oh my love," the daughter sighed, "should you do such a

thing, tomorrow will not exist, for this moment will dissolve into eternity."

On hearing this, a pilgrim cried out:

"Let's go outside and turn around to see where we are. Then if we still do not know, someone on the street will direct us."

Thorns falling in their wake, they departed as eagerly as they had arrived, and Hortencia followed them to the door. "Righteousness will be restored to this blessed house," she assured them. "Things are not entirely as they seem," she added, as if trying to convince herself of something she once knew but could no longer believe. But the pilgrims refused to listen to anything she had to say. They fled into the street as if they were a herd of stampeding cattle, and after they had left the house of forty-three rooms, Hortencia closed the door tightly behind them and prayed: "Lord what can I do?"

On the afternoon of her seventh day, which fell on a humid Thursday when the temperature rose beyond expectation and the blue-green sea stood still, Hortencia found a book of poems bound in red leather. The poet had dropped it on the stairs, and she, without questioning her motives, picked up the forbidden book and carried it to the gallery overlooking the lotus pool. There she hid among the flowering vines and read the poet's verse of love, desire and uncontrollable passion. What must it be like to be so in love? she wondered. What must it be like to give yourself to the call of the flesh? She read the book again, and again and after the third time her temperature rose, her breath shortened and she buried herself deeper into the vines as if they might conceal her from the eye of God.

While hiding there she watched the lovers bathing in the lotus pool. "Not even water can cool their flesh," she said. "Lord what must it be like to live with such heat and torment?" When the poet stood up, her heart accelerated and for the first time she allowed herself to see him without once averting her eyes or considering the wrath of God. She saw a collar of lily pads, a flower behind each ear, skin the color of dark honey, and between his legs a patch of dark hair from which his erect penis extended. "Without shame." Hortencia muttered to herself. "Without prudence!" she cried when the daughter took the poet in her mouth and refused to release him.

"No!" he cried, trying to push her away, "go slowly, or you'll devour me."

"Perhaps that's her wish," Hortencia said. From her hiding place on the gallery she watched the daughter wrap her arms around the poet's legs while holding him tightly in her mouth; she watched the color fading by degrees from his face as if all his strength were being siphoned away by a ravenous beast. At the very last, when he was pale and trembling and his legs could no longer support his weight, he threw back his head and howled.

"Holy Mary, Mother of God, they're like savages!" Hortencia cried. "What will it take to tame them?"

The lovers collapsed into the cool water, and the book of verse fell from Hortencia's hands. She had been infected by the lascivious thoughts that filled every page and every room of the house; of this she was certain. Her head ached, her heart pounded, and her body burned with fever. She ran down the stairs and stood before the lovers. "Look at me," she cried to the poet. "I, too, am a woman. Why don't you look at me as well?" The lovers looked up for one moment and quickly returned to their pleasure. "Look at me!" Hortencia cried again. But the lovers refused to turn their heads, not even when she tore off her clothes. "I cannot breathe in these rags!" she shouted. "I cannot breathe in this house. I'm being smothered by lascivious thoughts, and they are not entirely my own."

"Leave then," Fuerte called from the weaving room. "The house is what it is."

Hortencia ran to the front door and threw it open. "God forgive me!" she screamed to a crowd of shoppers. "I have sinned in my thoughts."

"A living skeleton!" someone exclaimed, and the crowd dispersed in all directions leaving behind only the merchants, the peddlers, and the naked girl with breasts no bigger than plums and skin the color of gray, wet clay. Like her father, who had swept the longest street in the city everyday of his adult life, the white bones of her rib cage protruded like harp strings against a thin layer of translucent flesh, and like her mother, who crawled each week to the cathedral, her knees were swollen, bruised, and scarred.

"Take this sheet and cover yourself," the old lace maker said, but Hortencia would not have it.

"I am infected," she cried. "The sins of the daughter have entered me."

"Nonsense," replied the lace maker. "Take this sheet before you're arrested."

"Let them arrest me," Hortencia said. "What does it matter?"

Like a plucked sparrow, she ran down the Street of Merchants and Peddlers. "I am that I am," she shouted. "Let everyone see me." Prudent wives and bashful husbands begged her to step quickly inside their houses, to accept a dress or a blanket for cover, but Hortencia refused. She wanted the entire world to see her, to know that she, too, was a woman.

As if in a state of rapture, she entered the cathedral with her head thrown back, her arms extended, and her fingers splayed. The archbishop was standing at the altar with the communion chalice in hand when he saw her running rapidly toward him. He dropped the chalice. Wine stained his hands, his chasuble, and his silk slippers. "Bring me a cassock," he cried, "a curtain, a bed sheet, a cloth of any kind. Anything, to hide this woman's shame!"

Covered with a white robe, she was led into the archbishop's private courtyard where the poet's books, stacked in every corner, were waiting to be burned. There the archbishop cooled Hortencia's body with holy water and set her mind at ease with prayers.

"I cannot stay in that house," she confessed. "Your Excellency, the poet is like a saint who has not yet received his calling. Always he thinks of one thing: love and nothing but love. Always he is drawn to his full size, and always the daughter receives him, no matter where she might be; standing, sitting, or lying down, she is there for him and him alone; no matter who might be present to witness their spectacle they behave like animals blinded to the presence of others."

"You must return, because your very presence will eventually restore sanctity to the house," the archbishop said. He approached her with trembling fingers, to pick an insect from her shoulder, she assumed, but instead, he removed a speck of dirt from the lip of his *Cattleya gutata*, which was blooming in a cloisonné pot hanging over Hortencia's head.

"Your Excellency, please do not force me to return," Hortencia cried. Her heart accelerated at the mere thought of entering the house again, but the archbishop insisted, and presently, the merchants and peddlers who had gathered outside the cathedral followed them back to the house of forty-three rooms. There on the street he prayed for the purification of the house and the souls therein, and after bathing the door with holy water, he commanded Hortencia to enter the house once again, to retrieve her clothes and stay.

"Allow the Heavenly Father to be your guide," he said. "He will exert his influence over you, and you over these walls and the inhabitants therein."

"No," Hortencia protested, "not even for God will I enter this house again. Last night I dreamed that I was the daughter and the poet was mine. If I return, I will surely kill her."

"Enter the house, my child," the archbishop said. "The angels will protect you."

Disregarding his commands, Hortencia fled down the street in her white robe, her arms outstretched, and her feet hardly touching the cobblestones. "She's returning to the sanctity of the cathedral," the old archbishop said. But at the cathedral Hortencia did not stop or slow her speed; she kept running until the street turned into a footpath that climbed the hills. From the street in front of the daughter's house the archbishop, the merchants, and the peddlers could still see her: one small white spot moving fiercely along the winding path that led to her mother's door.

That night the poet finished his third poem and the archbishop burned copies of the second one on the steps of the cathedral. He was disappointed that so few citizens attended his burning ceremony, and while the ashes cooled he expressed his concern for the souls of his parishioners. Then he sprinkled holy water on the heads of the few who had remained and retired to his chambers. That night he slept peacefully knowing he had done the right thing and that God would take pleasure on his acts. But up on the hill Hortencia tossed and turned in her bed of straw. Finally, she went to sleep with her eyes wide open, and that night she was visited by the poet. "The third poem is finished," he told her. "I hope you will like it." The next morning she wondered if she would be given the opportunity to read the new poem. In a secrete chamber of her heart, she knew she would read it, and in another chamber she promised herself that her eyes would never fall upon those pages.

For many days to come Hortencia talked of nothing but that which she had witnessed in the house on Merchants and Peddlers. "That house is no longer a holy place," she told her mother. "Soon no one will go there again." And to her neighbors she said, "It's a place infected with carnal love. Every room is contaminated with the daughter's spirit."

To a sloe-eyed priest, sent by the archbishop to counsel her, she said that the daughter thought of nothing but herself and her own pleasure. "And the poet," she sighed, "surely he was not created in the image of God."

To herself she said: "I must return. I want to return. But I cannot."

Within a very short time, word of the daughter's prurient existence had spread to every corner of the nation, and for a long time the pilgrims did not enter the house. Instead, they pinned prayers on the front door and departed, for they had heard tales of the naked woman and the naked man, both of whom were too beautiful for mortal eyes to behold; far more beautiful than the angels painted on the ceiling of the great cathedral, which stood like a monument to righteousness only two blocks from the daughter's door.

"The daughter and her poet," said the old lace maker, "they are like one person. She has found her true love."

The daughter and her poet, said the weaver on the 210th panel, *they are like grains of sand washing from shore to shore; falling in lots and familiar patterns.*

This, the weaver witnessed and recorded:

The years came and the years quickly passed, and the daughter and her poet were together always. With eyes only for each other, they sat in cafés and plazas, oblivious to the people around them.

> *And when he laughed,*
> *She laughed.*
> *And when she laughed,*
> *He also laughed.*
> *And laughter was the envy of their admirers.*

> > *If only we could know such happiness, they said.*
> > *If only we could laugh as they laugh.*

> *But toward the end of their fifth year,*
> *The laughter ceased.*
> *And the fifth poem was finished.*
> *The daughter became restless,*
> *And the poet could not please her.*
> *The poem was finished.*
> *And the poet refused to say good-night.*
> *It was finished.*
> *There was no laughter,*
> *And the daughter was weary.*
> *After reading the new poem she said:*
> *No more rhymed couplets.*

I cannot listen to another.
Something new.
Please.
Another kind of verse.
Another kind of love, not in place of,
But in addition to,
That which we already have.
And the sixth year began.

At the beginning of their sixth year, which would be their last together, the second poet arrived, and the poet was the president of the nation, a man who had long admired the daughter's austere beauty. Without invitation, he entered her house for the second time, not for love but for inspiration, but love accompanied him into her secret room, and love was on his breath, and love was in every verse he composed to her honor. And on The Door of Prayers he surreptitiously left poems of love, and on The Door of Prayers, he left poems of promise, and poems to celebrate her beauty: her eyes that glistened like the blue-green seas, her hair as black as a raven's feather, and her skin as translucent as clouds.

And the old merchants and the old peddlers read the poems he had left on the door. And they said:

These poems have been written for our saint.
And the first poet read the poems and said:
These poems have been written by my nemesis.
And he wept on his sleeve,
And on his shadow.
And finally, he discovered her secret door,
The one he would never open again.
And when he found them, unclothed and sleeping,
His heart ached with anger and jealousy.
And when he found them, woven into one body,

His heart bled,
His blood spilled in words of torment,
And his sixth poem,
>   *which he wrote in one night, was a cry.*

How many times did the daughter tell him, that she belonged not to one but many? And to the new poet, who had become her new love, not in place of but in addition to, she said the same, not once but many times—I belong not to one but to many—and he too, as the nation's leader, belonged to many not one, and because of this he could share his love. But the poet of the streets was of a different heart and a different mind. And his heart and mind worked together without argument, for his mind agreed with his heart and his heart with his mind.

There was no confusion.
Nothing but anger,
Torment,
And hurt.

When the new president arrived with reams of love,
The poet of the streets withdrew to a dark corner.
And after a long search the daughter found him
>   *weeping inside a shadow.*

His eyes were swollen,
His face, the color of ashes,
And his flesh, already cold.

There she lay with him, in shadows and in dust. And while he wept onto his sleeve, she promised him that their love was not lost, but shared. She promised him that he could reside in her home of forty-three rooms for the rest of his life for he was her first and great love, but never her only love, for like her father, her heart was insatiable, and like her father, she would always favor one over many.

But the poet of the streets, being of a different heart and a different mind, could not accept her promise, and when they slept together the lingering smell of his rival brought tears to his eyes and angry words to his lips.

He wept in the daughter's arms,
And she gave him comfort by catching his tears on her face,
    And in her hands.
I will save them for you, she said.
One day when you can no longer cry,
I will return your tears.

And the poet replied:

    I will always have more tears than I need.

And it came to pass throughout the remaining days of his life, his eyes were red and swollen, his cheeks the color of dust, his lips yellow with hurt. Throughout the remaining days of his life, his fingers trembled, and his head ached; and each time the new poet, who was the nation's leader, arrived with verse in his hands and love in his heart, the poet of the Streets retreated to his dark corner where he wept without ceasing—unto his death and the world beyond.

Six years after he had entered the house of forty-three rooms and two courtyards, he was ready to leave it, but he could not bring himself to pack his belongings or turn his back and walk away. The poet's heart was broken, his eyes were swollen with jealousy, and his chalk lips quivered when he spoke. For weeks on end he could take little in the way of food. His body wasted. His silver bones pressed against a thin layer of silky flesh and his head drooped forward, his chin resting against his chest. Like a skeleton suspended on a wire he rattled his way through the many rooms dropping tears on his sleeve and on his shadow.

"You must eat," she said. "You cannot live without food."

"No," he told her. "The thought of living is too painful."

"Do you want me to help you?" she asked.

"Please," he begged. "Tonight."

That night, which they both knew would be their last together, they lay in each others arms; peacefully and for hours without speaking they lay there, and after making love for the final time on earth, the poet wept and kept on weeping, and when her hair was wet with his tears, and her heart no longer sad but angry, not with herself but with her love, she stroked his hair and kissed his swollen eyes and told him that he must not be afraid of the dark night, or the half-light of morning or the bright skies of afternoon when truth was exposed by the blazing sun. "I cannot bear your tears," she said, "Nor can I turn my head another way. No matter how it might seem to others, I will remember you always. You will forever be mine."

"But never on this earth," he said. "Should I go on living, my verse of love will be consumed with rage and suspicion. And in time to come, who will love my poems if they are filled with your most high deserts? I must be totally yours. I cannot share you with another."

"If I could give you all my love," she said, "what more would you have? What more would you ask?"

Having said this, she held him tightly in her arms. She comforted him with kisses. And when his body relaxed and sleep descended upon him, she left her mark. From the back of his neck to the end of his spine, her long fingernail pierced his flesh, and a deadly substance flowed through his body. By midnight he was singing with the angels. By morning he was dreaming of Paradise. And by evening he was buried in the small courtyard.

She covered his body with a linen cloth, with sand and gravel. A white stone, carved into a broken heart, was erected to his honor, and before too many days had passed, the Flower of Utopia, which was the sweet herb she had concealed beneath her fingernail, grew blithely over the grave.

Again she put on her black veil, and from her balcony overlooking the Street of Merchants and Peddlers, she announced the poet's death.

"My love has hanged himself for love. He has honored me with his death, and I have honored him with a grave. He has left behind two long poems. The fifth poem will soon be published and with it we will celebrate his life. But the sixth poem I shall never publish, for it is a work of undying love filled with heart-wrenching sorrow. It is a poem drenched in tears."

The fifth poem was eagerly awaited. And the day it appeared in the stores and stalls, it was bought and read. It was read in the cafés, the parks and along the harbor. It was read in doctors' offices, streetcars and in churches behind closed doors. By the young and the old it was read, but as the weaver had predicted, the fifth poem was not loved and not quoted. The readers said that the poet's style had become artificial. A tone of suspicion had entered the verse. There were too many dark clouds on the horizon of love. The verse did not flow smoothly and the poem did not *sing*. "And, this," they agreed, "was the fault of the daughter. While the poem was being written, she became restless and hard to please. She was ready to give her heart to another. And in doing so she destroyed the poet as well as the poem."

The poem was not quoted.
It was not loved,
And the poet returned to the daughter's bedroom to weep.

Josefina was awakened by the sound of his tears falling one by one like diamonds into still water. She arose from her mother's bed to follow the trail of tears into the courtyards, around the galleries, and back into her bedroom where the poet retreated to a dark corner, there to weep alone. "Go to sleep," she said to his shadow, "and forgive me if I have failed you, but I cannot take sole responsibility for what I have done. My sins, if they are sins, are not entirely my own."

"Tonight I weep not for my life that you have taken," the poet replied, "but for my fifth poem that is not loved. While composing it, I saw that your eyes were losing their sparkle and your voice was drifting to another place. And so it is in the poem. The gradual approach of love's suspicion can be felt in every line, and for that reason, the poem is not loved. But it must never be condemned. Do not allow my critics to hate me or my papers to yellow with age. I have not composed antique songs. We are still living in my rhyme."

"I promise you," she said. "All your poems will be read by hundreds and by thousands and tens of thousands. Even the fifth one will one day enter its time of appreciation."

"But what about my sixth poem?" the poet asked.

"I cannot bear to read it again," Josefina cried. "It is filled with oceans of tears. But this, I promise you as well, the day will come when the sixth poem will be read, and, if not loved, admired greatly."

On these promises the weeping poet returned to his grave. And when the night was still once again, and the daughter could no longer hear the sound of falling tears, she lay awake until dawn thinking of her first and only love and the books of verse he had left behind. "Who is this poet who refuses to die?" she asked herself. "Was he in truth the son of Carlota Montejo and José Maria de Vega? Or was he another. Who created him? Was it Fuerte who created him, who created me, who created us all? How many creators are allowed to create at the same time?"

One morning when she was arranging Fuerte's threads, she asked, "What are you weaving now?"

"The return of the dogs," Fuerte said. "See, here is the first one to enter the loom."

"And what is his name?"

"Names are not important," she said.

"And when will he knock on my door?"

"Do not bother me. I am listening to another voice."

Josefina wondered if Fuerte's tapestry had, in some inexplicable way, possibly by its very presence in her house alone, influenced her choices, destroyed them, or predicted them? Why during this Forty Years of Peace did everything seem so familiar, as if she were following a path that had been created especially for her, as if the reins of her destiny were in someone else's hands?

Did Fuerte predict this future? she wondered. Or was she creating it on her loom? Is this life nothing but a dream? And if so, whose dream? Who is the poet? And who is the daughter? Was the saint truly a saint, the doctor, a doctor, the weaver, a weaver of cloth or destiny?

She felt as though her life had been dreamed by someone else and transplanted into her body or whispered into her ears in such a way that there was no choice but to follow the prescribed path; even when she was uncertain what path she was following, or where exactly it might lead, she knew instinctively that she was following a path she had not chosen but was, none the less, her own, and would lead to her final act of revenge.

Who made the choices? she wondered. Was it Fuerte? Was it the saint, the doctor, or the poet who cries in the dark? And who was this poet if not the son of Carlota Montejo? Surely the weaver knew all the answers?

"No," Fuerte, said, "I do not know the answers. The loom hears everything, the poet's verse as well as his tears."

Many times throughout her long life, Josefina Esperon was awakened by the poet's tears falling like frozen stars into a tropical night. Many times, even after the return of the dogs, she was awakened by the poet's shadow passing rapidly over her bed. And many times more, his voice called to her at dusk when the light of day was crawling on its knees from the small courtyard into the shadows of night. "No matter what you have done, I will continue to love you," he assured her. "There will never be another."

"You were not my only love," she constantly reminded him. "But you were, and continue to be, my greatest love. Your heart could never be mended. I had little choice but to help you do that which you could never have done alone."

"What is this article I hold in my hand?" he once asked her in the dark of night. She heard him clearly as if his voice had been trapped for eternity inside the thick walls of her house. "Does it have a name, and if so, what is it?"

Laughing as if she had never stopped, the daughter answered, "In *The Book of the Thousand Nights and a Night*, it is called a pintle."

The poet laughed, and the walls of the house shook with his laughter, and the ground on which the house had been built trembled as if the gods were laughing far below. So often he came to her in darkness and the half light of evening, and on occasions she called him forth, unknowingly at first, by allowing her thoughts to drift through the six years they had spent together, through the love and desolation that had guided them to the last night of their union and to the last poem that made her weep, almost without ceasing. Composed of fifteen hundred lines, it was too beautiful for the eye to behold, too sad for the human heart to endure, and for those reasons, she refused to read it a second time, preferring instead to arrange the weaver's colored threads so that she might have the final say:

Did the daughter grieve?
Did she mourn the passing of her great love?
Yes, the daughter mourned, and yes, the daughter grieved.
The shadow of grief followed her into every room,
And every hour.

"No more be grieved," she had once written in the margin of one of her mother's journals. "Roses have thorns. Clouds and eclipses stain both moon and sun." And on another page she stated her only recourse: "To embrace life as it is, filled with shades and shadows, to live within what fleeting happiness might be left, for happiness, unlike sorrow, is slow to arrive and quick to depart. It is ephemeral; hard to capture, impossible to hold."

And on the next page she had written this:

"No one will take his place. He will always be the first and the greatest love among many."

"If you love me you must also share me," she said to those

who followed the path of the first, "for there are many who knock at my door, and my heart burns with a fire that cannot be extinguished by water alone. But remember this: Few are allowed to speak my given name, and most are turned away before their shadows darken my door, for now I, too, must fall in love before I can give myself, and I can only fall in love with poets."

Because of her, each president who followed within the Pardo family was a practicing poet, a lover, and a king. So were their fathers, their father's fathers, their uncles and their sons. All of them. They entered her house to read their romantic verse and woo her with precious jewels, raiment of scarlet and purple, coins of silver and gold, which she stored in secret places.

"Each gift is very impressive," she said, "and each reflects the heart of the giver."

Pertaining to that time, to that place, and to those with whom the daughter found favor, the weaver, on the 215th panel, recorded the coming of the multitudes and the daughter's first cry for help.

The years passed, and the lovers came and went.
They multiplied by the week,
By the month
And by the year.

They multiplied.
Their gifts multiplied.
And the pilgrims multiplied with them.

We cannot desert her, they said.
No matter what she has done,
She is still the daughter of our saint.
Returning in great numbers,
*   they swept the courtyards and the streets.*
They brought flowers for Eufemia's bowl,
Prayers for her door,
Rose branches for her crown.
And before leaving they ate from a pot of stew the daughter

had prepared herself. From now on, she said, every pilgrim
who visits my house shall not leave hungry.

Seeking food for their stomachs and food for their souls,
They came out of rejoicing and hunger.
They came.
They kept coming.
They returned in great numbers.
And soon the day arrived
  when they were too many and too demanding.
The pot of stew was always empty.
The courtyard was always full.
The daughter was always tired.
And yet, the pilgrims came and kept coming.
They demanded both day and night to be let in,
To sit before the grave of Eufemia,
To sleep with their heads resting above hers,
To replenish her bowl of water,
To sing,
To pray,
To plant flowers.

I must have help, the daughter prayed,
And her prayer was heard.

Here the weaver ended the 215th panel. And here Hortencia
returned to the house of forty-three rooms. With a bundle of clothes
tied to her back she entered the house with a group of pilgrims,
and when they departed she remained; sleeping that first night of
her return in a hammock that she hung over the poet's grave.

"He was so beautiful," she said, when Josefina found her
bathed by the amber light of the moon. "And I loved him, too."

"Why do I know you?" Josefina asked.

"Because I have lived here before," Hortencia said. "And this
time I shall not leave."

"And why are you here?"

"To be near his grave," she answered.

"You must leave," the daughter insisted, but Hortencia wept at the thought of leaving, and Josefina allowed her to stay. "At least," she said, "for one night."

She was given a bedroom overlooking the small courtyard, but she preferred sleeping in the hammock, which brushed the poet's grave. "He'll keep you awake," Josefina warned her. "His shadow is restless. It's impossible to stop his tears."

"I'll comfort him," Hortencia replied. And that night when the poet wept in his grave she silenced him. "Let me cry for you," she whispered. "Give me your tears."

The weeping poet obeyed her.
His tears poured from her eyes.
And because of this she was content.

One night turned into two; two into three, and three into a promise. "Yes, you may stay," Josefina said. "I'll hire you to help me keep this house, but you must not interfere with my life. My way has already been determined, and there are no turns. The decisions have already been made, and surely not by me alone."

"We're God's creation," Hortencia said. "He has given us a path to follow, and we must obey."

"God is not the only creator of destinies," Josefina replied. "There are others, far less suspecting."

"Do not release such thoughts into the air," Hortencia pleaded. "God is the sole creator of man and Earth; if you think otherwise, keep your thoughts to yourself; if they escape they will surely infect us all."

"So be it," Josefina said. "My thoughts, though they may not be entirely my own, are now beyond my control and so is my life. Now I must occupy myself while I wait for their return. And then I will destroy them."

"Destroy who?"

"Anyone with a face covered with moles and the eyes of a mad dog. You must come to me if you see visitors who meet this description."

And what will you do?"

"I will not use guns, knives, or clubs. I will use words and whatever may be given to me on the day of arrival. I will lay a trap. And in my trap there will be no escape."

"Are you speaking of murder?"

"No, merely retribution."

From that day forward Hortencia took it upon herself to purify the air in all the rooms and courtyards. To capture evil thoughts that should never have been released she placed empty bottles on windowsills, above doorways, and in all dark corners where the dust of temptation lay waiting. She tied rosaries around the legs of tables and chairs, hung teacups on the branches of the orange trees, and pinned pillowcases filled with Madre Selva on the clotheslines. Throughout the day she inspected her traps, and if need be, she burned the Madre Selva, poured scalding water into the cups and bottles and replaced the ones her employer had removed.

"They are unsightly," Josefina said.

"They are necessary," Hortencia argued. "I cannot live in this house without protection. And the pilgrims! Think of the pilgrims! How can you ask them to breathe this air? It is infected with your evil turns."

"Then you must find a way to protect yourself," Josefina replied.

For protection, Hortencia draped rosary upon rosary around her neck. She wrapped them around her wrists and ankles. She filled her pockets with statues of the Blessed Virgin, and she washed her clothes in holy water, which the archbishop provided. It did not take Josefina Esperon long to realize that her housekeeper's fear of a vengeful God was beyond reconciliation. Although she was given to complaining and prone to sudden bouts of fitful discontent, on rare occasions a smile would cross her face. Observing this, the daughter decided to give her servant a new name, one that she hoped would influence her disposition for the rest of her life. She was called Contenta.

Before long it became apparent that Contenta would never be happy working in such a house, and yet she refused to leave, protesting loudly at the mere suggestion of more suitable employment. She said that someone had to pour scalding water into the bottles and cups, and someone had to pick Madre Selva for the pillowcases, and someone had to welcome the pilgrims. And beside those things, which occupied much of her time, there was another concern: the poet. She was certain he would never rest unless she slept near his grave.

"And what about your mother?" Josefina asked. "Surely she needs you."

"The Sisters of the Church look after her now," Contenta said. "My place is here. You need me to rid the air of ungodly thoughts. The pilgrims need me to feed them. And the poet needs me to cry his tears."

For these reasons Contenta remained in the house of forty-three rooms where she wept for the poet by night and tended her traps by day. And each week, or so it seemed to Josefina, Contenta draped herself with more rosaries circling her wrists, ankles, and neck. Each week she carried new religious statues in her apron pockets along with an ever changing variety of fragrant herbs to purify the air. Wherever she went in the house she announced herself by the clanking of her rosaries and a cloud of fragrance, sometimes sweet, sometimes pungent. "At least," Josefina Esperon said, "I always know where you are." Continually pushing against the demands of sleep, Contenta neglected her domestic work in favor of prayer and the visiting poets in favor of the pilgrims. And she interrogated everyone who aroused her suspicion.

"I must have your purpose for being here," she said to any pilgrim who seemed oddly out of step with the others. "If you have come for food and food alone you will be found out."

"We're not expecting you," she said to all the poets. "We have one poet in this house, and even though he's no longer living, we need no others."

But the poets could not be discouraged anymore or any less

than the few suspicious pilgrims, and as time quickly passed Contenta became increasingly more discontent because the poets multiplied by the week, by the month, and by the year. They multiplied, their gifts multiplied, and the daughter's wealth increased with each visitor. With every knock at the door, Contenta prayed for the daughter's soul, and the daughter prayed for solitude counting the seconds until she could be alone again.

Her life had become series of dreaded events, a festival of scheduling and rescheduling, of refusing to answer the front door until someone had left through the side door, or refusing to answer the side door until she had kissed the visitor at the front door good-bye. Back and forth she ran from one entrance to the other, traveling rapidly through the narrow passage connecting her courtyards, and on occasions when two or more lovers arrived at once, each expecting to find her alone, she had no choice but to entertain them. "What am I to do in such a situation?" she asked them. "I cannot say no to either of you because it is my fate to love many not one, and I cannot, not for all the gold in the world refuse a poet."

"You should entertain us together," the men of fortune agreed. "We have wives to give us children, but you inspire our poems, and by our poems we shall be remembered."

Poems were written,
And poems were recited.
They were dedicated and published,
And left in stacks and piles on tables and chairs,
On benches and sofas.
Poems were found on the staircase,
And in kitchen cabinets.
The wind scattered them through every room of the house,
And into the courtyards as well.

One day Contenta opened a pantry and found a folio of fifty-six poems along with a proposal of marriage and a blank check signed and dated. "There are too many poets in this house!" she screamed. "Too many poets and too many poems!" She threw the folio out the window and the poems were blown away. One was found in the French Park, another along the harbor, and a third was shredded by an electric fan at the police headquarters. Out on the street the granddaughter of the lace maker found the proposal and the check stuck in her windowsill. Within the hour she returned both. "I will burn them under the orange trees," Contenta said. And she did.

Starting that day, she kept a record of all the poets who visited the house. On a kitchen wall she made a mark for each visitor who knocked at the door, and at the end of one year, she counted 553 men of fortune and letters who had visited the daughter seeking her as a muse, as a wife, a lover or a friend.

"Your mathematical ability is sadly lacking," Josefina said. "You have obviously counted some of the callers twice, maybe as many as ten times."

"That is not the point," Contenta argued. "You have too much company. No one can live with so many intruders."

Reluctantly, Josefina agreed. "Yes," she sighed. "You're right."

With scrupulous judgment she sorted through a list of one hundred names and chose to favor thirty men of fortune, seven from the ruling family, five from the world of banking, and eighteen from the sea. And of them all, it was the sea captains she came to prefer because their visits were infrequent and their gifts priceless: pearls from the Orient, diamonds from Africa, rubies and sapphires from India, bars of silver and gold wrapped in fine silks or Persian carpets and transported in teakwood chests or smuggled inside pillows embroidered with tiny mirrors to reflect the light of the soul.

In addition to the thirty men of fortune, each of whom composed verse to her honor, but none was in her estimation a true poet, there were sixteen others, eight of whom claimed to be the son of Carlota Montejo. Of the sixteen, none was wealthy but each composed verse that made her laugh or weep. "I will dress you in silks and crowns of flowers," she told them. "And I will provide for each of you a room facing the sea, for only the sea can inspire a poet."

"Oh, no," they said. "We are inspired by you and you alone."

"You are the subject of all our poems."

"Well, then," she replied, "when you sit before your windows and gaze out to sea, you will think of me, and each time I receive a poem that is truly exceptional I will honor that poet in a special way. None of you shall ever want for anything as long as I am here and the thirty men of fortune find favor in me."

She lived for her sixteen poets who were poets, and she entertained lavishly the thirty lovers who were not poets but desired to be, and she accepted from one and gave to the other, and in return she received poems that pleased her and riches that purchased her freedom as well as the freedom of the sixteen who met at her house each Friday evening to drink champagne, to read from their work, and to listen rapturously to any one of the thirty men of wealth who might choose to read also.

"No matter what you think of their verse," Josefina told the chosen sixteen, "you must praise it lavishly, for they are the men of fame and fortune who make our lives pleasurable during forty years of peace."

"Yes," the poets who were poets agreed.

"We will say the right things."

"You can depend on us."

Supporting her wishes, they gave comments generously, singing their words of praise, even when they did not mean them, and at the daughter's thirty-fifth birthday celebration, they turned their attention away from her and onto her men of fortune.

On the daughter's thirty-fifth birthday the sixteen poets who were poets vowed their ever lasting allegiance to the daughter, their muse, and then they sang praises not to her but to the men of fortune who made the Forty Years possible. They sang not to their wealth, but to their verse.

"The phrase, *walking silently as if stepping on clouds*," one of the chosen said to Clemente Pardo who had succeeded his father as the nation's leader. "It is too beautiful to be used only once."

"Yes," Josefina agreed. "Don't deprive us of the joy of hearing it again. You shall surely go down in history, not only as a great president but as a great poet as well."

"And your birthday sonnet," said a poet to the mayor of the city. "Should you read it one more time I am certain to die of envy."

"And I of pleasure," Josefina added.

"I will stab myself if I have to hear it again," said one of the sixteen.

"Only because he cannot live with the competition," said another.

"We are all jealous beyond redemption," said a third.

"Your poem is too wonderful for words," said Josefina.

"You must have many more birthdays," declared one of the shaggy-haired poets who was a poet as well as a lover. "We cannot exist without you. If our muse should die, none of us will ever write again."

"What a tragedy," Josefina replied. "I suppose I have no choice but to live even when I'm dying of pleasure."

"Your life has been touched by the gods," the governor told her. "And then you touch us as well."

But my life has become so predictable, she thought. Without the excitement of variety and the unexpected, this cannot be called life. The visitors are fewer, but their demands seem greater; their jealousies unrivaled. And what has it all amounted to anyway? Thirty lovers who fancy themselves poets, sixteen poets who fancy themselves lovers, a house of forty-three rooms, reams of poetry, more than a human being could possibly read, chests of priceless jewels, a courtyard filled with pilgrims, and thirty-five years lived under the same sky. And the long wait continues. When will they come? When will it end?

"Nothing ever ends," Fuerte had once told her. "Everything

begins again."

"Life must be enjoyed," she told her birthday guests. "If it is not enjoyed of what good is it? Now we are living through forty years of peace. The streets are filled with music and everyone is in love once again."

But too much love, she thought, can be a burden on the heart and so can riches. Now the poor have a little more and the rich have a little less, and for awhile we will continue living within the shadow of Paradise, but as some of us already know, this forty years will not last forever. One day the mad dogs will return. And I will be here to greet them.

On this thought, the daughter ended the celebration of her thirty-fifth year, and the weaver began a new panel.

> *The days became long.*
> *The nights longer.*
> *And the hour arrived*
> *When the daughter refused to open her door.*

"I am very tired," she said. "Come back another time."

From that hour forth, she said this freely to everyone except the president of the nation, but his two sons, three brothers, and father were turned away as often as not. And yet, they continued knocking at her door along with the bankers, the sea captains, and the many strangers who were determined to stand in her circle. Some gained entry by climbing ladders to balconies and windows. Some entered over the roof, lowering themselves into the court-yards like spiders dangling from thin ropes, and others disguised themselves as pilgrims with flowers in their hands and crowns of thorns wrapped around their shrouded heads.

Almost every peaceful afternoon was shattered by the invasion of a jealous admirer dressed in sackcloth and thorns. Some-times Contenta would catch one of them climbing through a side window. "You are not a pilgrim," she would rant. "You are an im-postor. You must leave at once." Her angry voice and the rattling of many rosaries could be heard throughout the house.

"Please escort the intruder to the door," Josefina would call out in a loud and commanding voice. "Only my mother's devoted may enter this house today."

The presence of impostors made Contenta more fitful than ever. "Nothing in this house is as it seems," she said. "It is impossible to trust anyone anymore. Sometimes the pilgrims are not pilgrims. Sometimes they are lovers. Sometimes I cannot tell one from the other. What's wrong with this world? What's the meaning of this house? Why am I here?"

"You are here because I need you to welcome the guests," Josefina said, "but only those we wish to receive. Keep the windows locked. Try to be more discerning when the pilgrims arrive. Do not allow them to deceive you."

But the servant was always deceived.
And the house was always filled,
Filled with pilgrims who were not poets,
And poets who were not pilgrims.
They came and kept coming in great numbers.
And their presence in the house
angered the devout servant,
And exhausted the daughter.
Her eyes lost their sparkle.
Her lips lost their smile.
And once again she prayed for help.

"Lord, send me some nice girls who can relieve me," she prayed from her morning balcony. "If I'm not the oldest living member of my sacred profession, I'm certainly the busiest, and I've been operating single-handedly far too long."

Two blocks away Mass was being said in the cathedral, and on the street in front of the Esperon House, Contenta, who had just entered her thirty-first year, was scrubbing the sidewalk. Hearing the prayer spoken, and in such a loud voice, she dropped her brush and pail. "Cease praying at once!" she exclaimed. "How many times have you made this unreasonable demand?"

"Once, Contenta," Josefina answered. "Only once."

"Then let it be no more," Contenta begged. "What you do with your own life is one thing, but what you choose to do with another is a very serious matter. Something terrible will come to us if you make such demands of God."

She was convinced that the house, even though it was made of stone, would surely burn to the ground or that lightening would strike without warning if her employer introduced innocent girls to the ways of the flesh. Abandoning her chores, she hurried to the cathedral, and minutes later she returned with a bucket of holy water into which she added a strong measure of disinfectant, and for the better part of an hour, she cleansed the balcony where the terrible prayer had been uttered.

"This prayer is a contagious one," she said. "It must not live beyond this house."

"The prayer was released long before you went to all your trouble," Josefina reminded her. "Right now, somewhere in this capital city, my prayer is being heard, possibly answered."

On the following Monday, at precisely two o'clock in the afternoon, exactly one week from the day the prayer had been released, Contenta was bathing her swollen eyes, when she heard someone knocking at the front door. "No one is home," she shouted. But the knocking continued persistently, and in a steady cadence. "Who's there?" Contenta asked, but there came no answer other than the constant knocking. Expecting to find one of the sixteen poets or even the president of the nation, she opened the door on three young girls in sackcloth. To her surprise she saw spindly legs, unwashed hair, and dirty faces brightened by beatific smiles and circles of golden light. Taking two steps backward, she made the sign of the cross and blocked the door with her broom.

"You have not been sent by God," Contenta said. "You have been sent by the Archangel Lucifer, and you shall not enter this house."

"We are not Devils," said the tallest of the three girls. "But we are poor. And we are willing to work."

Contenta stood firm. The girls persisted, and because they seemed so earnest, almost evangelical, in their need to see the daughter of the house, Contenta decided that they must be Protestant missionaries. Until that day, she had never uttered kind words for the Protestant movement sweeping the country, but on staring into the faces of those three girls, she came to the conclusion that for her mistress a Protestant doctrine was better than none at all. "I'll let you come in," she said, "but only if you promise to provide the Señorita with a list of all the things that should never be requested in prayer."

The promise was made, and Contenta, still somewhat reluctant, stood to one side while those girls, the very first three, entered the house of forty-three rooms, four balconies, and two courtyards.

"I've been expecting you," Josefina said. "Contenta should be happy to know that even my prayers are answered."

She took the girls into her house, treated them as her own daughters, and to Contenta's astonishment, within four days three more girls arrived, and after the second three came six, and after the six came nine, and nine again made thirty.

"And now," Josefina said, "all my bedrooms are filled, and we may begin our formal training. If you choose to remain with me you will speak formally and without grammatical error. You will enjoy concerts, opera, and the classical theatre. You will each play a musical instrument, the piano, the harp, or the harpsichord, and if one or more of you is blessed with a beautiful voice you will be expected to sing, not for your supper but for your own enjoyment as well as the enjoyment of the class of gentlemen we intend to attract. And two things more: Firstly, you will learn to arrange the colored thread so our weaver may continue her work, but you may not open the two baskets in her room. They are filled with venom. Secondly, you must be vigilant. A family of mad dogs may return at any moment. If you entertain one of them, you must question his purpose for choosing to enter our house and I must be informed at once."

Seven days a week she lectured her daughters on the necessity of proper and elegant speech, on poise and carriage, laying emphasis on dropping the shoulders, lengthening the neck, and lifting the chin so the face may be seen in all its glory. She insisted that they read classical literature, know the stories of the great operas, commit quantities of poetry to memory, and glide up and down the stairs as if supported by a wire. She hired music teachers, dancing teachers, acting coaches, and culinary experts to lecture on the world's great wines and cuisines. She preached the benefits of daily exercise to firm the body and slow the process of aging, of deep breathing to improve the complexion, and the juice of sea grass to purify the blood. She encouraged a modest diet during the day, a breakfast of fruit and a lunch of consommé, so the pleasures of a rich evening meal might be thoroughly savored without expanding the waist.

The moment this period of training was established and well underway, she turned her attention to the house. She hired electricians to wire every room for light and decorators to cover the walls with silk damask. She hired marble cleaners to polish the stairs, carpenters to build kitchen cupboards, and roofers to stop the many leaks the daughters had discovered on rainy nights. Long before the renovation was completed she ordered six crystal chandeliers, forty-two floor lamps, seventy-nine sconces, and thirty double beds all of which arrived on the same day along with a grand piano, two harpsichords, four harps, six lutes, thirty gilded music stands, and two Victorian sofas covered with burgundy silk.

"You must slow down," Fuerte said. "You're living faster than I can weave. You're living beyond my vision, and I cannot keep up."

"We are slowing down," the Daughter said. "Very soon we'll be back to our normal pace."

"And what is that?" Fuerte asked. "Not even I know for sure."

"The house is being improved and so are we," Josefina told

her daughters, "but there's still much work to be done. For one year you will not be permitted an idle moment. You will devote yourself to learning, and every subject will be yours, otherwise how can you expect to interest men of importance if you have nothing to say, and no means of saying it? If you listen to me, you will learn how to enjoy the riches that will be lavished upon you."

While the girls gave themselves willingly to be re-created, Josefina Esperon refused to entertain the men of fortune who loved her and sought her as a muse. When they came calling she informed them, without apology, that her present situation made social intercourse totally impossible. "I'm a forty-year-old mother of thirty young virgins," she explained. "I must give myself to my girls. It's with your interests in mind that I take this year to be with them and to train them properly for your pleasure." With that she closed her doors and barred her windows to the men of fortune and letters. She covered her roof with broken glass, tangles of wire, and signs threatening to trespassers.

"Do not forget that Serrano's pistol is always with me and that my aim is perfect," she told the men who waited under her balcony. "Even the sparrows remember that."

For one year only the sixteen poets were permitted to enter the Esperon house, and the thirty daughters were not permitted to leave it. The poets came every Wednesday and Friday evening. They entered through the side door being careful not to be noticed by the men of fortune. The poets taught the daughters to recite poems of love as if singing an aria, and to insert poetic phrases into ordinary conversations. They taught them to speak quietly as if whispering secrets into a loved one's ear. And they also taught them the art of calligraphy, a skill that should never be overlooked in the opinion of the sixteen as well as their muse.

During that year the daughters continued their education, according to Josefina's rigid standards. Music, art, and literature were taught during the morning hours and in the afternoon, history, science and politics, the only subject they would never be allowed to discuss with a guest, but none the less a topic to which they were instructed to keep their ears attuned. They studied from dawn until dusk, and by lamplight for three hours more until they dropped into their beds with fatigue. And at the close of that one year of long days and endless nights, Josefina stood back to admire her creations, individually at first, and then as a whole.

"Finished," she said. "My work is finished."

And the poets agreed: the thirty daughters had been recreated in the image of the creator, and yet, each of them displayed an individual personality with a talent for conversation.

By then the daughters understood completely what was expected of them; how they were required to behave when gentlemen entered the house, what to say and more importantly what not to say. They had been taught to laugh melodiously, to change a topic of conversation with grace, and to drink quantities of champagne without intoxication. "Gentlemen," Josefina Esperon insisted, "do not enjoy drinking alone, in spite of what they may say. And remember: you are my eyes when I have no eyes. In due time, I will teach you what to look for—the faces you must learn to recognize."

Pronouncing her daughters ready to be introduced, she ushered them off to the dressmaker. "This is a woman who knows her business," she said, taking every opportunity to dispense knowledge. "See how she cuts a fitted bodice. On the bias so the body can breathe. All the seams are French, all the underskirts are silk, and the simplicity of line accentuates the natural beauty of the body rather than obscuring it."

In one afternoon measurements were taken for dresses to be worn during the evening, and dresses to be worn during the day, dresses to be presented in, dresses to work in, and dresses for attending Mass and high civic ceremonies. In one afternoon fabrics and colors were chosen, and two weeks later the first fittings were scheduled at which time Josefina Esperon turned her attention to other pressing matters. "Hair," she said. "Hair is as important as the dress." The following morning she escorted her daughters to the Parlor of the Three Sisters where the recently trained beauticians were eager to demonstrate everything they had learned.

"Our goal is to make everyone beautiful," said one of the young sisters whose black curls hung like fat sausages over her shoulders.

"Even people who have never been beautiful before will be beautiful when we show them how to achieve it," replied the second sister. "This week I've been experimenting with beauty patches. They can add a certain allure to the right occasions."

"We're here to bring you the latest styles and cuts," said sister number three.

"You're also here to take subtle suggestions as if they are orders," Josefina added.

For a few minutes she observed the sisters at work and then she made her wishes known. "My suggestion to you is this: Too long on top." Snatching scissors from the hands of the sister, she made the next cuts herself. "The face must be exposed. These eyes alone are worth a million lyricos. Do you know how much a man will pay merely to stare into such lovely eyes? A fortune, I tell you, fortune for sure."

"No, no," she said to another sister, "you're one step from ruining a perfect face. The hair must be kept long and swept up off the neck with ribbons and ornaments of the most priceless variety. The forehead must be seen. The nose, the lips and the cheeks must be framed with curls, but not overpowered by them."

"Who are the beauticians here?" a sister demanded to know.

"Supposedly you," Josefina said, pointing to the three round sisters whose young faces captured the rainbow. "But remember: I am the customer, and the customer must be pleased at all cost. Nothing can be left to chance. Every last curl must be accounted for. My daughters will be perfect in every way."

"Your daughters?" the beauticians exclaimed in unison. "Surely not all of them."

"Yes, all of them," Josefina replied with implacable sobriety. "They are mine."

"You have adopted them, of course."

"Oh, no," Josefina said. "I gave birth to each of them, as many as five at a time."

"What a story this will make," the three sisters whispered among themselves. "Every woman in the capital will make an appointment just to hear us tell it."

After three days in the Parlor of the Three Sisters and six more fittings with the dressmaker, Josefina Esperon dispatched handwritten invitations to the thirty richest and most influential men living in the capital.

On the twenty-third day of April at eight in the evening,
The Señorita Josefina Esperon y Blanco
Requests the honor of your presence
for dinner and dancing
Formal attire

When the president of the nation, his brothers, sons, uncles, and father, arrived at the daughter's house, they were greeted with trumpet fanfares that shook the walls and activated every wind chime in every arch. On their arrival the weaver put down her loom and pulled a chair close to the marble staircase where she could hear the symphony of voices in the courtyard. "They're arriving," she said to the daughters, "and they will continue to arrive, for they have endured a year without their muse."

During the last year, only a few of the men had glimpsed the daughter hurrying along the streets in her black dresses, shopping at the market, buying yarn from the wool merchants, or sitting on her balcony in the early morning before the city had awakened. None of them had exchanged with her more than a few passing remarks and suddenly, or so it seemed, she was ready to receive them once again. Eagerly they entered her house, which sparkled with riches and lights of many colors. They followed a Persian runner, woven for an endless hallway, and where it ended, only a few feet from the lotus pool, the daughter received her guests. From the gallery Fuerte watched through vacant amber eyes that saw little and everything. She listened to the cacophony of merry voices, to the pleasant exchanges and to the rhythm of the daughter's heart-beat. "This night will be remembered," she said to the nervous daughters awaiting their cue to enter. "And it will be written about for many years to come. Mine will not be the only account, but it will be the most difficult for the survivor to decipher."

To each man the daughter seemed much older and more for-mal in her greeting, but far more beautiful than ever. She wore a black silk gown trimmed in black feathers and in her hands she carried a burgundy rose. Her hair was fashioned into a tight bun at the nape of her neck, the style in which she would wear it for the rest of her life, and her throat was circled with diamonds.

"You may have already noticed a few improvements to my house," she announced after the guests had arrived and the front door bolted. "Every choice was made with your comfort in mind. It has been a long and arduous year, and now we are most anxious to please you."

"Surely," whispered the governor, who was the president's first cousin, "she will not attempt to pawn her virginity again."

"Surely," whispered the mayor, who was the governor's brother, "she intends to introduce us to her virgin daughters. Ru-mor has it she brought them into this world five at a time."

"Impossible," said the director of the National Bank. "Who would believe such a thing?"

"You would be surprised," replied the president who carried in his breast pocket a copy of his latest poem. "An uninspired son-net," he said, "created during a year of deprivation."

Presently, the orchestra began the overture from Purcell's "The Indian Queen," and on musical cue the daughters appeared one at a time at the top of the stairs. Fuerte stood as they descended in long dresses and on clouds of perfume. "Straighten your backs!" she reminded them. "Drop your shoulders and stretch your necks. Carry your heads as if they are jewels to be admired. The occasion is a high one—but not the highest this house will ever know."

As each daughter descended the marble stairs, her name was announced by a baritone, standing in the courtyard.

"Areli, of the House of Esperon, Adela of the House of Esperon. Clara, Dolores, and Elena, of the House of Esperon, Anahí of the House of Esperon."

After the daughters had been introduced and were posed in twos and threes under the many arches that surrounded the courtyard, the invited guests demanded personal introductions at once.

"You're far too anxious," Josefina laughed. "Personal introductions will certainly be made, and assignations as well, but later, my friends, a little later please."

"The one whose hair is like flames," said the mayor of the city. "Surely that's not her natural color."

"All my daughters are natural," replied Josefina.

"And the one called, Anahí," said the president's father. "Surely you have created her in your own image."

"They are the better part of me," she answered.

Each daughter chose a gentleman at random, and led him to a long table draped in white linen and covered with lace. The table was appointed with hand-painted china, family silver, and crystal stemware, four to each setting. The chairs were carved oak, the napkins were embroidered with the Esperon family crest, and the meal was prepared by a French chef who scrubbed the kitchen from ceiling to floor and rearranged the pantry before boiling the first pan of water or chopping the first shallot. The chef, who had traveled over the mountains and through the marsh especially for the occasion, had arrived with wagons loaded with spices, wines, and herbs as well as five waiters costumed in eighteenth century livery with powdered faces and periwigs, with lips like rosebuds, and cheeks the color of crushed cherries. Like specters floating under the flickering lamplight, they came and went; invisible to the guests who had eyes only for Josefina Esperon and her lovely daughters.

Moving silently from kitchen to table, the five waiters served a first course of lobster soufflé. Minutes later it was followed by a sorbet of passion fruit to cleanse the palate in preparation for Duckling Rabelais, the chef's specialty. The young birds, expertly deboned and meticulously reformed with a stuffing of pâté de foie gras and truffle, were thinly sliced and served in the French style by the five powdered waiters, their hands clothed in white silk gloves and their eyes glistening with belladonna.

"The dinner is as intoxicating as the company," said the president's youngest brother. "Poems will be composed about this night."

Glasses were raised in honor of the beautiful daughters, in honor of their creator, and in honor of the night brightened by stars and fireflies swarming through the orange trees. After the last toast had been pronounced and the glasses emptied, the gentlemen, thinking the dinner was over, stood ready to mingle among the beautiful daughters, but Josefina Esperon begged them to take their seats again. "Why do you presume that I should invite you to dinner and fail to serve the main course?" she asked. The men sat down quickly, and the five waiters appeared with medallions of beef crowned with thin slices of bone marrow, served with a thatch work of asparagus and a hearty burgundy.

After every morsel had been enjoyed, gloved hands appeared again to ready the table for a dessert created especially for the evening. The smallest glasses were coated with twelve drops of absinthe, filled half way with sparkling water, and swirled before the eyes of each guest. Then Josefina Pilar lifted her glass to make a toast, and when all eyes were on her, an orange cake soaked in rum was ignited and carried into the courtyard. "This cake," she said, "has been created in memory of my mother, who was called a living saint. She brought three orange trees from Andalucia, and now look: all of them are blooming at once."

"Blooming with teacups," observed the director of the National Bank.

"For the purpose of capturing your thoughts," Josefina replied. "When you leave I'll consult the cups and they will not lie."

After the cake was consumed and every drop of absinthe

enjoyed, Josefina lifted her glass to the orchestra, a signal to begin the first waltz of the evening. "Tonight I shall not dance with any of you," she announced. "The celebration belongs to my daughters."

For one hour she stood on the marble stairs and watched the dancers. For one hour nothing moved except her eyes that saw everything. She observed the ease with which the daughters changed partners, and continued dancing without the struggle of adapting to a new leader, and at the same time, she observed the difficulty some of the men experienced when suddenly confronted with the energy and movement of another partner. In this way, Josefina Esperon selected thirty compatible couples to further the celebration, and when the last waltz of the evening had been danced and only the wind chimes could be heard singing in the arches, she passed among her guests for the purpose of pairing them off.

"You, my dear Governor," she said. "You must spend more time with Alicia. She has such a beautiful voice. One evening soon, you shall hear her sing. And you, my dear Banker, you must get to know Clara because she is very talented on the keyboard, and Julia on the harp. Where is the father of our president? He will surely appreciate Julia's talent, and where is his youngest son? I want him to know Adela who possesses a striking wit. I want our president to deliver a sonnet to Isabela who is a poet of remarkable invention. And I want the director of our National Theatre to know Ursula because she is capable of reciting Racine like none other since Carlota Montejo. All of my daughters have special talents. But surely you have come to this conclusion already. If they had no talents at all they would not be my daughters, nor would they interest you, for gentlemen of the world, though they may be worshipers of beauty, are not given to the worship of beauty alone, but beauty combined with quick minds, talent, and gracious manners."

After making her selections, she sent the couples to their rooms with a warning to the gentlemen. "In my house you shall never enter a bedroom with the same daughter until you have enjoyed each of her sisters. I insist that you treasure them all without partiality. I'm standing by to keep record of your enchantments."

The couples ascended the staircase to their rooms and when every door was closed and Josefina was standing alone in the large courtyard, Fuerte descended the staircase to be with her. Sitting on the ledge of the lotus pool they listened to many sighs of pleasure accompanied by one sacrificial cry from each of the daughters. "Let this night end rapidly," Josefina said. "Let it be the shortest and the quickest passing."

"It will soon pass," Fuerte said. "You must be patient and let the evening dictate its own rhythm. Still your heart. Have you learned nothing in all the years I've been with you?"

When each daughter cried out, Josefina felt the pain like a sharp memory stabbing her heart. She counted the cries one by one, and Fuerte identified them by name: "Adela, Digna, Micaella, Andrea, Veronica, and Remedios."

"It is almost over," Josefina said, wishing the daughters could hear her. "Very soon we will all sleep again."

For a few minutes there was silence and then another cacophony of sighs and stifled cries. "Magaly, Ursula, Clara, Anahí, Julia, and Dolores." Fuerte whispered the names into her folded hands and waited for more. Again there was a spell of tense silence broken, at last, by the sound of seven short screams. "Elena, Areli, and Esperanza, Lilianna, Marta, Maria, and Luisa. The night is passing rapidly, and we are very tired."

For a few minutes the house was silent, as if all the inhabitants therein were slumbering peacefully, but the silence was soon broken by the cries of Aïda, Modesta, Ofelia, and Teresa. "Soon," Josefina said. "Very soon the sun will shine. Tomorrow is already here." Then she listened for Lourdes, Malena, Rosita, and Helena, for Isabela, Rubendella, and Felicia. Only when she heard them did she allow herself to draw one deep breath. "At last," she said, "it is over."

For a long time the rooms were silent, and the courtyard air did not tremble in the presence of the moon, which floated overhead like a winged ship, plowing the seven seas in search of the Heavens. "At last," Josefina said again. "At last it's over."

"At last," Fuerte said. She kissed the daughter good-night and returned to her loom.

Josefina watched the moon floating on the lotus pool, until the desire to sleep blurred her vision, and the granite walls of her ancient house suddenly appeared unbearably fragile. It was as though the house had sprung to life around her, as though she were sitting inside a creature from the sea, a creature with a giant rib cage of columns and arches, with doors and windows for breathing and a gaping mouth, which opened onto the night skies for the very purpose of swallowing the Heavens.

"This house," she said, "has taken a painful breath of pleasure."

At three hours past midnight the gentlemen prepared to take their leave. One by one they were escorted by a livery man into the courtyard to say good-night to their hostess. She stood to receive them, and to each she delivered the same speech.

"Tonight, you are our invited guests, but tomorrow evening, and the evening thereafter, and all the evenings to come, you need no invitation to enter this house, but you must remember: The rules and standards I have set for myself, apply equally to my daughters."

After the last guest left the house of forty-three rooms and the daughters were performing their ablutions, Josefina visited the small courtyard where Contenta, who had been given tincture of *Papaver somniferum*, was dreaming in her hammock. Her cheeks were wet with tears, and her gray lips trembled with each breath. Her tiny arms were folded over her body, and her thin legs were crossed at the ankles. Around her wrists, neck, and ankles there were rosaries, dozens and dozens of rosaries, glistening in the moonlight. And in her apron pockets there were statues of the Blessed Virgin, the Christ Child, and the Archangels Gabriel, San Miguel, and San Rafael.

Speaking through the voice of the dead poet, Josefina Esperon whispered Contenta's name over and over, first into the left ear then into the right one. "Weep no more Contenta," she said. "You must return to your mother, now. She needs you more than she needs the Sisters of the Church. You have cried my last tear, and yours as well. You have given me comfort. You have walked with me through many dark shadows, but now, you are needed far more by another. Weep no more."

Leaving Contenta to dream on what she just heard, Josefina returned to her daughters, to kiss them good-night and beg them to sleep until the sun was high. Soon the house was slumbering in silence, but all too quickly the golden fingers of dawn descended into the courtyards, and with the first light that fell upon Contenta's face, she arose and went straightway into the bedroom of Josefina Esperon. "I've dreamed a dream that cannot be questioned," she said. "I must leave you now. But, even still, no matter what I have dreamed, I do not wish to leave the poet's grave."

"The poet," Josefina said, "is no longer in his grave, but in his books. He lives there, and so should you." She gave Contenta the five books of love the poet had written in her house; the five published books plus a dusty manuscript tied with a purple ribbon. Into her arms she deposited these volumes and then, considering what she had done, she took back the manuscript. "You must not read this now," she said. "It will surely make you weep all the more. The five books are more than enough. Come to me with words you don't understand."

"May I also come back to greet the pilgrims each afternoon?" Contenta begged.

"Yes," Josefina Esperon agreed. "That would be very helpful."

After Contenta returned to her mother, the daughter of the doctor and the saint removed the empty bottles from the windowsills and the Madre Selva from the clothesline, but she left the teacups hanging on the orange trees. "The cups," she said, "are useful."

From that day until the end of the Forty Years of Peace, Contenta lived with her mother whose name was Lourdes. In their three room house of rock and clay, she read aloud from the poet's books, and Lourdes, believing she was hearing the Song of Solomon, slept with the poet's stanzas of love roiling like the ocean in her ears. Morning and night Contenta read aloud, believing that she had inspired the poems herself, and in her sleep she embraced the poet in the lotus pool, giving herself to a love she would never know outside her dream.

"My dreams put me to sleep and wake me up," she told Josefina one afternoon while preparing the pilgrims' stew. "My dreams are the best part of my night but the worst part of my day."

"But without them we are nothing," Josefina replied.

"I do not wish to remember my dreams," Contenta said. "I wish only to dream them."

"What happens when you remember them?" Josefina asked.

"I'm reminded of my sins," Contenta confessed.

"You have no sins," Josefina insisted. "No sins at all."

"If only the archbishop would say the same thing," Contenta sighed. "Then I would not be so confused."

"Confusion is Satan's tool," the archbishop warned her. He had summoned her into his private courtyard to discuss the daughter, the daughter's daughters, and the sanctity of the daughter's house. Surrounded by the orchids he loved, the archbishop sat on an ebony chair inlaid with ivory. In his lap he held a porcelain pot from which his prized *Cattleya labiata* was blooming for the first time. "You must remember your purpose for being in the daughter's house," he said. His fingers caressed the crimson petals of the *Cattleya* as he spoke in solemn and confidential tones. "Do not allow the daughter to dwell on things dark and nefarious. Take her sins into your body and each evening when you return to your mother's house, spit them into the fire. Those that are not expelled by the flames will be expelled in your dreams.

"How many dreams must I dream before there are no more left," she asked, "and how many times must I spit before I put out the flames?"

"You will dream hundreds, and you will dream thousands," he replied speaking more to the *Cattleya* than Contenta. "You will spit fountains, rivers, and oceans into the fire. And you must remember that you are expelling not only the daughter's sins but the sins of the daughter's daughters as well."

After sending her on her way, the archbishop kissed his beloved *Cattleya labiata*, and Contenta returned to her mother's house with shoulders heavy with sins that carried no name, only the burden of their weight. She built a fire in the garden and she spat into it, but no matter how hard she tried, she could not spit out the flames, and even after the fire had died down, it continued burning in her dreams.

> *By day the dreams confused her,*
> *But by night she embraced them with sleep.*
> *And the dreams were the poet.*
> *And the poet was love.*
> *And the daughter who dreamed the dreams,*
> *Was no longer the daughter who created them.*

On a steamy afternoon during the rainy season when the courtyard was reduced to mud and sixty-five pilgrims had trampled across the graves, the daughter Elena, known to be the most congenial of them all, asked Contenta what she had dreamed the night before. Contenta, who was by then exhausted from herding too many pilgrims through the mud, dreaming too many conflicting dreams, and trying without success to extinguish too many blazing fires, answered Elena in an angry voice that drew every daughter from every room:

"I do not wish to remember my dreams. They are too many. And I don't know anymore which ones are mine and which ones are not mine."

"Come quickly," Elena shouted. "Contenta needs a song to lift her spirits."

Just as she had done so many times before, and would do so many times again, Josefina Esperon summoned her thirty daughters

to the staircase where they arranged themselves in choir formation
and sent Contenta home on the wings of her favorite song:

> Make us true servants to all those in need,
> Filled with compassion in thought, word, and deed;
> Loving our neighbor, whatever the cost,
> Feeding the hungry and finding the lost.

Supported by this choir of angels, Contenta left the House
of Esperon with a smile on her face and the glory of God in her
heart. All the way down the street and into the far hills she floated
on alleluias, on the solemnity of the Holy Trinity and the glory of
the life to come.

"Now that Contenta is happy once again," Josefina said, "we
must make ready for our evening. Tonight we shall have a melody
on the harp. We shall have a poem, a song, and many toasts. Tonight this house shall levitate with laughter, priceless gifts, and
songs of love."

At ten o'clock that evening the guests began arriving in formal attire and one of them was a young boy of twenty-two years
who, it seemed to the daughters, still had the round fleshy body
of a well-fed child. His hair was thin and his sideburns were extended with feathery strokes of a grease pencil and his face was
dotted with moles. He wore a tuxedo of ill-fit and carried a pocket
of cash that he flashed by the fistful. "I will find out who he is,"
said Elena. She took the boy to her room and relaxed him with caresses and sweet words. "My grandfather," he told her, "was once
the mayor of this city. He knew Josefina Esperon quite well. Do
you think I might be able to meet her?"

"Of course," replied Elena.

When Josefina entered the room she was dressed in black lace
with a burgundy rose pinned to her bosom. Her fingernails had
been lacquered to match the rose, and in her hair she wore a jade
comb inlaid with diamonds. Her austere presence startled the boy
and for a moment he was speechless. He chewed both sides of his

tongue and nervously twisted his tie.

"You are unmistakably your grandfather," she said. "I see him in you."

"I also favor my father," the boy replied with difficulty.

"And where is he?"

Again he was speechless. His lips moved as if trying to form the words. "Here let me help you," Josefina said. She gave him a kiss on both cheeks and his tongue suddenly loosened. Words spilled out of his mouth as if they had been trapped inside his head for centuries.

"My father is still living abroad and so are my uncles; but they will return soon. That is their plan. I'm here with my brother and cousins. We're getting the hacienda ready. I'm afraid it is in ruins."

"Oh, and what a beautiful hacienda it was. I remember it well."

"We are still fond of it. The younger generation, especially."

"The younger generation, meaning you, and your cousins?"

"My cousins, my brother and I. The grandchildren."

"Oh, how many grandchildren are in your family now?" she asked, as if bewildered by the count when in actuality she had learned to follow every thread through the maze of marriages, infidelities, births, adoptions, and deaths.

"Only nine of us are left," he replied. "I am one of two brothers. Two of my uncles had three sons each. One had four. Three of my cousins died of small pox. And the third uncle is an archbishop who, of course, has no children."

"That we know of," said Josefina.

After a pause she added, "Don't tell me there are no sisters of the church in your family."

"Well, yes and no." He paused to scratch his palms.

"Please continue," she begged. "In my house we discuss everything. No topic is overlooked."

Again the boy spoke in a torrent of words as if he could not control himself.

"At some point my grandfather adopted a young girl who went on to have a daughter out of wedlock. But no one in the family talks about it. My adopted aunt is no longer living, but the daughter is a Carmelite who is rising rapidly in her order."

"Then she is your half cousin?"

"Cousin by adoption."

"How complicated it must be to come from such a large family. I am an only child, and therefore, I can only imagine the difficulty of keeping up with everyone."

"It is not easy," he replied.

"And what of your immediate family," she inquired. "You must tell me everything because I knew and adored your grandfather and his brothers. And therefore, I wish to know more about you and your children."

"My older brother will marry next year. One of our cousins will marry next month. The rest of us are single and unattached."

"Well, what are you waiting for? You must get busy before the family extinguishes itself."

"Our fathers married late in life," the boy explained. "It seems we're following the example. But we do have plans."

"As do I," Josefina sternly replied. "Now I must leave you to your pleasure. You are invited to return again and often. Bring your brother and cousins next time. We are discreet here."

Having found out all she needed to know, she kissed the boy on both cheeks and left the room to visit Fuerte. "I am waiting for you," the weaver said when the daughter entered the dark room. "We will send only the males. They are the smallest, and their venom is the most powerful this time of year because they are getting ready to breed."

"How many do we have?" Josefina asked.

"More than enough," Fuerte answered. "And they are restless, but first we must remove one leg from each spider in order to promote aggressiveness."

With long tweezers they set about selecting the spiders and removing their legs. "They will grow back within a few days,"

Fuerte said. "But until then they will be very angry."

When the young man was ready to leave, Josefina walked him to the door. "Your grandfather and I were friends," she said. "Your great-uncle and I were engaged to be married. But Fate had other plans in store for us. It is too painful to remember." Then she presented him with a basket of fruit wrapped in red paper tied with purple ribbons. "A gift," she said, "for you, your brother, and cousins. While you worry with the hacienda in ruins you will need something nourishing."

> *And the young man accepted the basket of fruit.*
> *And it was eaten at dawn.*
> *By his brother and cousins, it was consumed,*
> *Enjoyed,*
> *Fought over without suspicion.*
> *At the bottom of the basket came the angry attackers,*
> *With fangs exposed and on hind legs they struck,*
> *Leaving their marks on hands and fingers.*
> *And within minutes the nine became two.*

"Another tragedy has stuck the Serrano hacienda," reported the afternoon paper. "Yesterday seven sons died from the bite of the Brazilian Wanderer, a usually docile spider that has entered this country on bananas and other tropical fruits. According to Dr. Joseph White, the British entomologist, the Brazilian Wanderer is the most poisonous spider in the world. Without immediate treatment it has been known to kill a human being in less than thirty minutes. The Serrano hacienda, which has not been occupied in many decades is said to be infested with them. The deaths of these young men mark another tragic chapter of an ongoing curse this family has endured."

"And it has not ended," Josefina Esperon said when she put down the paper and proceeded with her day.

"It is time to give the spiders their freedom," Fuerte said. "In the future we will not need them. The future is filled with other poisons."

A picnic was planned at the edge of the jungle. And while the thirty daughters enjoyed crusty bread, fruit, cheese, and wine, Josefina and Fuerte walked into the jungle and released the spiders. "Thank you," they said in unison. "Now you have freedom." The spiders entered the jungle on vines and tree trunks and when the last one had disappeared from sight Fuerte reminded them to choose their victims wisely.

On returning to the picnic, they found the daughters singing, strumming lutes, and dancing barefoot on the grass. "We must not linger here much longer," Josefina said. "Evening is quickly approaching and we have our guests to think about. Because of them we have riches. We must prepare for the night."

Every night except Sunday, the guests gathered in the drawing rooms and courtyards to be entertained with music and poetry, with vast quantities of champagne, caviar, and love perfumed with a touch of avarice. It was a house of earthly pleasures and heavenly delights where the richest businessmen, the most powerful politicians, and a long list of celebrated poets, painters, and musicians came to celebrate the remaining years of peace, to while away their leisure hours with Josefina Esperon and her beautiful daughters. The nights were given to celebration: dancing in the courtyards, assignations on the stairs, a classical monologue delivered by one of the daughters, an aria, a poem, a promise fulfilled.

It was during this time of increased affluence and celebrity, that Josefina first introduced herself as *Señora*. "I've been married only once; more by spirit than by law," she told a group of prominent businessmen who visited her house. "But I shall marry no more. From now until the end of my life, I am Señora Josefina Pilar Esperon y Blanco."

The Señora's notoriety had already reached well beyond her nation, into the neighboring countries, and many corners of the world. Her dark reputation was the topic of discussion not only in newspapers, cafes, and plazas but also in the weaver's threads.

Her father was called a doctor of mercy,

Her mother, a living saint.
But the daughter was called a whore.

And her house was a called a house of whores.
And her whores were called the Jewels of the Nation.

For whores, it was said in the cafés and plazas are
necessary, particularly during times of great happiness.
And the Señora's whores, it was also said, are the most
versatile in the kingdom of whores, and if you can afford
their services you will not be disappointed, for everyone
who leaves the house of Señora Esperon leaves with a
smile on his face even though his pockets may be empty.

"Harlots and strumpets!" the archbishop cried. "Women arrayed in purple and scarlet color and decked with gold and precious stones. They with whom the kings of the earth have committed fornication and the inhabitants of the earth have been made drunk. Harlots and strumpets and women of wanton leanings have defiled this earth and cast a blight upon our land!"

With tears in his eyes, because his beloved *Cattleya guttata* had died the day before, the archbishop welcomed Contenta into his courtyard to tell her that she must build larger fires in order to extinguish the daughter's sins, which he believed to be multiplying rapidly. "You must spit and spit until every coal has lost its shine," he said. "And when you dream of Epicurean habitudes you must cast those dreams into the fire also."

"Your Excellency, I cannot put out the flames," Contenta said. "They are too many. And they are not mine. I have no tears left in my eyes, no moisture in my mouth. I cannot cry. I cannot swallow without water to wet my tongue. I cannot take food that is dry. My eyes are deserts, and my tongue is parched from spitting."

Vowing that she would never consult the archbishop on another matter, she left him to his grief. "I will not be attending Mass until that archbishop is replaced," she told Señora Esperon. "He's more concerned with his *guttata* than he is with his people. He can weep rivers and oceans over a wilted plant, but I can no longer shed a single tear."

"Your tears will return when you need them the most," Señora Esperon said. "In the meantime, my daughters and I will attend Mass in your place, and we will remember you in our prayers."

While operating her establishment within the shadow of the cathedral Señora Esperon solicited the protection of the church by contributing to the restoration fund, by occasionally presenting the archbishop with a new orchid, by attending Mass regularly and accompanying her girls to confession with a list of minor transgressions.

During the sixteenth week in Ordinary Time, when Saint Mary Magdalene, disciple of the Lord, was being remembered, Señora Esperon, who had recently been accused by high church officials of flaunting her ill-gained riches within the shadow of the cathedral, arrived at confession with her thirty daughters. "Our right to exist has been threatened by those invested with ecumenical powers," she had told her daughters earlier that day. "Because they are incapable of receiving our gifts they wish to destroy us, and in order to appease them a little longer we must confess our sins in voices to be heard; and we will be long about it."

Into the confessional booths they marched, and in voices wracked with atonement they loudly enumerated their transgressions, angering the parishioners who were waiting to be heard and arousing the pigeons nesting in the apse.

"This week envy entered my heart, Father. I coveted the blue eyes of my best friend, and failed to thank the Creator for my own God-given attributes."

"Today I spoke in an angry voice to the Señora who has given me a Christian home."

"Twice I have denied my God-given talent by refusing to sing to someone who was ill."

"Yesterday, I sinned in my thoughts. I entertained carnal desires, but they were quickly extinguished by the Señora who is always present to protect us."

Although the number of parishioners waiting to be heard became greater by the minute, the daughters did not hurry through their confessions and neither did Señora Esperon.

"Father forgive me for the sin of anger," she confessed to her favorite priest, a young man whose dark eyes were deeply set and whose perfect mouth was shaped like an archer's bow. "This week I slapped a beloved daughter. She spoke to me in harsh words, and I returned her anger with my own. Twice I spoke ill of my saintly mother, who dedicated her life to achieving perfection. And once again I did not wish to pay my tithe because my heart, given to unmitigated greed, remained closed to generosity. But my beloved daughters encouraged me to pay double the amount, and when I did so the Lord softened my heart and made me glad. Father forgive me, I am guilty of the sins of pride, avarice, anger, gluttony, envy, and sloth."

"Father forgive me," each of the daughters said. Their voices echoed through the cavernous space. "I am guilty of the sins of pride, avarice, anger, gluttony, envy, and sloth."

"You'll notice," said one of the brightly painted beauticians waiting to enter a booth, "they left out the sin of lust."

"You'll also notice," said her sister whose sausage curls were holding in spite of the humidity, "that they're wearing dark colored dresses with a touch of red or pink around the neckline."

"Just enough," added the third sister, "to remind us all who they really are."

The Señora did not insist that her daughters attend confession each week, but she did insist on regular public appearances made in the spirit of holiness. No matter how late they had entertained the night before, on Sunday morning they arose early and were ready to sing to the people passing along the Street of Merchants and Peddlers. Squeezed onto the four balconies, the thirty delicately painted daughters, wearing dresses of reverent colors, lifted their voices in many songs of praise that could be heard all the way to Independence Monument, and from there to the cathedral, to the harbor and to the French Park as well.

O Jesus, we adore you, Who in your love divine,
Conceal your mighty Godhead in forms of bread and wine.
O sacrament most holy, O sacrament divine,
All praise and all thanksgiving, Be every moment thine!

After singing to the passers-by and to the spectators, who gathered beneath the balconies, the Señora hurried her daughters off to Mass. Down the Street of Merchants and Peddlers they strolled like birds of respectful plumage making their first stop at the police headquarters where wrecked automobiles from the previous week were kept on public display. Through dark veils and beneath brimmed hats, they examined the wreckage speculating loudly on the exact cause of each accident.

"Drunkenness," they would say in pitiable tones for the benefit of the spectators who strained to catch every word.

"Sleeping behind the wheel."

"Driving too fast."

"And on streets that were not made for automobiles."

"When will it all end? This appalling recklessness."

"This shameless waste of life."

They lifted their long veils and lowered them quickly as if the sight of a demolished automobile were too gruesome for their tender eyes. Then Señora Esperon, supported by the arm of the chief of police, would step closer to the wreckage for the purpose of searching dashboards and car seats for bloodstains, shattered windshields for strands of hair, and dented fenders for clues to the cause of collision. On finding evidence of human suffering, and possibly death, she would swoon into the arms of the police chief, who went to great lengths to convince her that automobiles were not as dangerous as they seemed.

"There are more accidents at home, than on the roads." He was fond of saying this. As if, Señora Esperon thought, it represented the only idea of substance he had ever entertained.

"Walking through a kitchen is far more dangerous than driving one of our latest automobiles over cobblestones," was another of his favorite sayings.

"Crossing under an arch may not seem hazardous," he frequently reminded her, "but I assure you, it is far more dangerous than taking a leisurely drive through the mountains."

"When will you believe me," he said countless times, "automobiles have been invented for pleasure and pleasure alone. Descending a staircase is far more perilous than steering a moving vehicle."

At last the Sunday arrived when Señora Esperon had heard enough. "I refuse to listen to another word of this," she cried. "Your philosophy, as comforting as it may be, will never restore the loss of human life."

Pointing with her parasol to the charred remains of an automobile that had exploded on impact, she called on her daughters to play close attention to this reminder of a life driven at high speed.

There were four wrecked automobiles on display that day, and Señora Esperon quickly inspected each of them.

"Look at this one!" she exclaimed, leaning heavily on the chief of police, a man whose shadow had not yet been permitted to darken her courtyards. "How could anyone survive so hideous a crash? See how the steering wheel was ripped away, leaving only the rod to pierce the driver's chest. Oh, how torturous a death it must have been. And look at this. You cannot convince me that every bone was not broken by the collapsed roof. And over there, that unfortunate person must have been thrown against the windshield. Notice the shape of his head on the shattered glass."

"There was no way of escaping," said a daughter.

"Death was inevitable," cried another.

"How could this have been the will of God?" wept a third.

The chief of police, who had developed a fondness for Areli, took the young girl's arm and walked her around the wreckage. "The victim," he told her, "was the only remaining grandson of the late José Maria Serrano who was once the mayor of the city."

"Oh!" Areli replied. "The poor boy. Did I know him? Did he

have a face full of moles and the disposition of an angel."

"I cannot speak for his disposition," said the chief of police, "but like his father he had a face of moles."

"And was his face lean?"

"Anything but," said the police chief. "His face was round and full like a ripe melon."

"And his father?"

"The same."

"I supposed I am confusing him with another," said Areli. "Where is the family now?"

"They have returned," said the chief of police, "and are looking for a house."

"What kind of house?"

"A large house in the city. There has been too much tragedy in their family hacienda. It is up for sale but no one who knows the history of that house will buy it."

"I will inform the Señora ," said Areli.

"Oh, no," said the chief of police. "She is troubled enough. Long ago she was in love with the victim's grandfather who was the mayor of the city. She has mourned his death all these years. If she knew his family had returned she would be greatly troubled by thoughts of the past."

"I shall not speak a word, then," said Areli.

Suddenly the Señora interrupted them:

"Let us go quickly to Mass and pray for these departed souls," she cried. And off they went weeping loudly over the tragic loss of life.

"I have something to report," said Areli as they walked rapidly to the cathedral. "Another son is dead. The victim of this crash is the grandson of the once mayor."

"Then there is only one grandson left."

"Yes, Señora, and the family has returned."

"And what do they want?" asked Josefina.

"A grand house free of their family curse."

"My house, of course," said Josefina.

"Yours, I'm sure." said Areli.

"Only one grandson is left," the Señora mused. "One day he will enter my house and he will leave it but he will never return."

And with that, they continued on their way to Mass. With somber faces they entered the cathedral to kneel in prayer. And they were watched, and followed, and discussed by everyone who saw them, as well as by those who did not.

Before long, the small following of spectators had grown into a large crowd of admirers and a scattering of detractors who occasionally threw rocks as well as malicious remarks and were immediately apprehended by police who eagerly awaited the arrival of Señora Esperon and her thirty daughters. Their presence at the police station was a Sunday event not to be missed by a few and meticulously chronicled in all the daily newspapers. "We will always make the most of our outings," she told her girls. "For who knows when we may need additional acquaintances to assist us. I've lived long enough to know that peace is not forever lasting, and that forty years is a billion times less than a grain of sand on the ocean floor. Allow them to take your pictures, and to hear you pray for the victims, and if they speak unkindly to you do not return unkindness with unkindness, for unkindness returned will serve no purpose but to solicit more unkindness in return."

"It would be my greatest pleasure," said the chief of police, "if I and a few of my officers might be permitted to visit you and your daughters at home." He delivered this request on a Sunday morning after he had planned and rehearsed it all week.

"But my daughters are priceless jewels," the Señora said as though stunned by what she had just heard.

"We are not men of great means," the chief reminded her.

"But you are men who are capable of offering ladies a certain protection," she replied. "And therefore, we will reserve an afternoon especially for you."

The afternoon was arranged, and the officers arrived with flowers and perfumes. First they were plied with rich morsels and strong drink. Then they were bathed and patted dry with towels as soft as clouds. Next they were oiled and massaged and bathed again. At last they were given cardamom to sweeten the breath, and after tender kisses had been exchanged they each were escorted to a bedroom for more earthly delights. Two hours after their arrival, they felt as though the bones in their bodies had melted away, leaving nothing but a spirit devoid of aches and pains, inured to the problems of the day.

"Thank you," said the chief of police when he said good-bye to Señora Esperon. "How can we ever repay you?

"We are a house of women who appreciate a strong arm to lean on," she answered. "You and your men have always treated us with respect, and it is our honor to repay it."

That evening when the Señora opened her doors to the public, her regular clients arrived to be entertained and pampered and after midnight when the door was locked for the day and the guests were preparing to leave someone else arrived, a handsome man in his twenties. "There is no need to tell me who he is," Señora Esperon said. "I see the resemblance in his face and stature. His grandfather was a man of heart-stopping beauty."

The young man was paired with Clara who learned that the he was living in a hotel by the sea on the outskirts of the city. "Our family house is a disaster," he said. "I do not even wish to park my car there."

"And what kind of car do you own?

"A black Cadillac."

"It is too large a car for these narrow streets."

"Yes," he replied, "but I was able to park without too much trouble near the side door."

On receiving this information Señora Esperon summoned the repairman who lived on the Street of Merchants and Peddlers. "The car," she said, "is parked outside my side door. You know what to do."

That night the young man was sent home, not with a basket of fruit, but with a kiss. "And now," the Señora said, "we wait."

On arriving at the station the following Sunday, Señora Esperon and her daughters were greeted effusively by the policemen they continued to entertain. "We have something to show you," said the chief of police. "It's a black Cadillac reputedly to have once belonged to an American president but who knows which one. "A wheel came off when the driver was crossing the new bridge," said an officer.

"The poor victim," wailed Señora Esperon when she saw the flattened car. "Surely he did not survive."

"No indeed," said the chief of police. "The car plunged thirty feet off the bridge. Death came instantly. His grandfather was said to be the most handsome president in the history of this country. He was murdered on a dark street."

"Do not remind me of this!" Josefina cried. "The memory is too painful. We were engaged to be married."

"Forgive me," said the chief of police. "But it is fortunate that you did not marry him. This entire family has endured too much tragedy and now it is said that their house is cursed."

"Yes, I know," Señora replied. "I read the papers. Seven grandsons suffered agonizing deaths due to the bite of poisonous spiders, and now two have died behind the wheel of their cars. But where are their fathers?"

"They are living somewhere in the city," the chief of police said.

"My daughters and I will go at once and pray for the souls of these victims, and for the safety of their fathers."

And off they went under the protection of seven policemen.

The policemen were with them constantly no matter where they went. Like guardian angels, they accompanied the Señora and her daughters on their daily rounds and their movements were closely watched. On Mondays they visited the Hospital of the Sacred Heart where they entertained the patients with song and verse. On Tuesdays they visited the poor districts and distributed baskets of food. On Wednesdays they visited the convents and monasteries to sing with the brothers and sisters, and on Thursdays they showed up at the orphanage with stuffed animals they had made themselves. On Fridays they lingered at a home for the elderly where they read newspapers and letters to those who had lost their sight, and on Saturdays they visited the municipal market to buy food for the entire week.

"The Señora and her daughters," the merchants said. "They have hearts as big as the world. Ask the policemen if you doubt it."

The policemen carried the daughter's purchases, their baskets of food for the poor, their books and newspapers to be read to the elderly, and often after a long day of many good deeds, the men were invited back to the house of forty-three rooms where they were lavishly entertained and sent on their way before the evening guests arrived.

"When all else fails, you're our greatest allies and protectors," Señora Esperon told them. "Even when the final trumpet sounds and these walls crumble, we will still have you."

Sitting in her dark room Fuerte called for the daughter. "Visit me. I have heard what you said today." Josefina was sitting in her mother's chapel. She got up at once and went to Fuerte's room. It was empty except for a bedroll, and a hook on the wall for anchoring the loom. Empty except for row after row of colored threads the daughters had meticulously arranged. There she sat, her amber eyes glowing in the dark, her hands moving across the loom like two spiders plucking the strings of an ancient musical instrument that had been silenced by time.

"You've been talking about the final trumpet," Fuerte said. "I heard you. No matter how far away you are, I can still hear. Yes, the trumpet will sound. That day is not far off. And this forty years of peace will end the same way it so violently began. But you know that already. This pattern is woven into all things and not difficult to recognize."

"Have you already woven the final day?" Josefina asked.

Fuerte answered: "Oh yes. It was woven long ago, but it has not been finished."

"And what do you think will come to pass?"

"I do not think," Fuerte replied, "I weave."
So said the weaver on the 217th panel:

Through many peaceful days, nights of pleasure, and years
of good fortune, the Señora presided over her house, the
welfare of her daughters, and the comfort of her guests
who came to sing songs, to read verse, and be entertained
with music, caresses, and soft words. The nights were
given to romance, and the days to anticipation, and all
departed souls who watched over the house, watched also
for the coming of the end.

Two mole-faced brothers returned to bury their sons,
To remember their dog-eared father,
And to rule the land.
And behind them came their three cousins.
Two returned to bury their sons,
To honor their dead father,
And to govern the country of their birth.
The third came to represent the church.
Behind the mole-faced sons,
And behind the three cousins,
Came the daughter of an adopted sister.
With their coming, the Forty Years of Peace ended.
And once again the days were long,
The streets were empty,
And the nights were filled with terror.
Lost threads had returned to rule with vengeance and dread.
They took the nation without election and with force,
With swords and clubs,
And bombs that exploded at all hours of day and night.
In one week the sons of the humanitarians were murdered,
Their bodies hung from poles that circled the plaza.
And the ancient archbishop was among them.
Even the poets who sat before windows facing the sea,
Even they were tortured

For having nothing to give other than their verse.
Their tongues were cut out.
Their ears removed.
And their mutilated bodies
    were thrown against The Door of Prayers.
How many were thrown there dead or to die?
Not one and not six,
Not twelve but sixteen.
For three days the door was stained with blood.
The doorstep was covered with bodies.
And they were buried in the small courtyard.

"From now on," Señora Esperon said, "this courtyard shall be called the Tomb of the Poets."

Then she wept loudly and her daughters wept with her. Their weeping was heard in every room of the house, in the streets and avenues as well. And it came to pass that on the third night of wailing a military guard, patrolling the Street of Merchants and Peddlers, knocked on the Señora's door.

"Let us visit your house of pleasure," they said. "We each have something that will make you smile again."

Señora Esperon refused to open her doors. "Not one of you shall touch my daughters," she said. "You may murder me or torture me in a public square, but my daughters shall never be touched."

The military patrol stormed the door and broke it down, and to their surprise, the Señora and her daughters greeted them as if they were poets, as if they were gods to be entertained.

"Look," they exclaimed. "They're so handsome."

"They're not animals, after all."

"They're men of letters and swords."

"And we need their protection."

"Welcome, welcome to our house."

"Our doors are always open to men seeking pleasure."

"Upstairs there's a room for each of you."

"We'll take you there and gladly go."

"But first a kiss. Many kisses. And then more."

While locked in deadly embrace, each daughter, according to a well-laid plan, made a deep scratch on the neck of her chosen. And not one of them mounted the stairs. Not one of them lived till morning. And once again the Street of Merchants and Peddlers was covered with bodies, twenty-eight in all, and none of them poets.

"The poets are gone," Fuerte said, "and now your daughters must go also. They deserve far better things than you or this country can now offer them."

In the dead of night Josefina sent her daughters away. With purses filled with riches, she sent them into various corners of the world. By twos and by threes, they left weeping, and after they were gone Señora Esperon wept also. She wept and kept weeping, and not even Contenta could stop her tears. "I could fill an ocean with weeping," the Señora said. "Nothing is left but sadness."

There was no laughter.
No dancing in the streets.
There was nothing but noise,
Noise and new faces,
And more automobiles,
And sirens and smokestacks,
And a circle of factories surrounding the capital.

How can this be possible? Señora Esperon wondered. Who built all those factories? And so quickly. And the new streets? Did they appear overnight? Why do we need so many and why are they numbered instead of named? Oh where are the poets? We need them to give our streets beautiful names. When will they return? How can we live without them? And where are my mother's pilgrims. They have stopped visiting her grave. When will they return? Will they ever return?"

Soon the sky was filled with yellow smoke.

The merchants and peddlers were driven from their street.
Old stores were given to new businesses,
And the new businesses were given to new merchandise,
And the new merchandise was not made to last forever.
And the people cried:
Where is the knife sharpener?
The tinsmith and the cobbler?
Where is the wheelwright
The candle maker
And the daughter of the lace maker's daughter?
Where are our ancient cobblestones?
Our flowering trees?
Our narrow streets?
Our marsh?
Our old ways of living?
And the daughter of the doctor answered:
Who can be surprised or angry?
Who can be bitter?
For is it not the way of all things?
So it is,
So it has always been,
And so it will always be.
A new day will arrive at the end of the old,
And the world will continue,
At least for a while longer.
But nothing will be the same,
Because the new merchants have arrived,
And with them we have noise, which is called music,
And with the music, which is noise, we have loud voices.
Everyone shouts.
And no one whispers.
Not even a poem.
Everything has changed and nothing has changed.
Seeds were left.
Seeds have returned.

But they will not grow forever.

"Nothing grows anymore," Contenta said. "Not even the flowers on my mother's grave. Not one violet not one anemone. Nothing. Even if I watered them with the tears I no longer have, they still would not grow."

On the second day of the revolution Contenta's mother had crawled down the hills to pray in the cathedral and was shot four times while crossing the plaza on her knees. Without the comfort of a tear, Contenta buried her in a small cemetery in the hills. Her father had been buried there also, and Contenta wished to be buried between them, but until that day arrived, she had returned to the house of four balconies to live in a room overlooking the small courtyard that contained not one but seventeen graves; all of them marked with white stones carved into hearts.

"Why have you come back?" Señora Esperon asked on the day of Contenta's return.

"To find my lost tears," Contenta said. "Maybe the poet will help me cry again."

"But the poet no longer weeps. Now he is resting with his companions."

When Contenta looked down upon that graveyard of seventeen marble hearts rising like white sails on a sea of red poppies, she wanted to weep without stopping, to wail in a loud voice that could be heard to the ends of the earth, but she had no tears to give. "Too many people are buried here," she said. "How will I ever recognize the grave of my beloved. Nothing will ever be the way it once was."

"Everything will return," Señora Esperon said, but Contenta was never convinced of this.

"We are in mourning," she said, "for the days that will never return and for the end that will never come, and for the pilgrims who have stopped coming. And while we wait, for who knows what, the factory smoke fills our lungs, and our trees die, and our ocean turns red, and not even the goldfish in the lotus pool are happy anymore."

"Perhaps you should wear more rosaries," the Señora said.

"Not even that," Contenta said, "would do any good now."

"I am very worried," said Señora Esperon

"You are spending too much time thinking about the wrong things," said Fuerte. "Now you will learn to read the threads."

On a long table in Eufemia's chapel, Fuerte unrolled a panel, and the first of many lessons began. On a tablet she drew the alphabet and a list of words, pictures, and patterns. With a magnifying glass Josefina studied every thread while Fuerte read the panel aloud, stopping now and then to offer explanations. She read by passing her fingers over the threads, occasionally pressing her face close to a difficult passage in order to read with what little eyesight she had left.

> *And so it was, day after day.*
> *The Señora in her mother's chapel,*
> *The weaver at her side,*
> *A panel was unrolled,*
> *A panel was read,*
> *The alphabet was studied,*
> *The patterns were learned,*
> *The pictures interpreted,*
> *And then the panel was read again.*
> *Again*
> *Again*
> *And yet again,*
> *And then another panel was unrolled,*
> *The alphabet was studied,*
> *The patterns were learned,*
> *The pictures interpreted,*
> *And the panel was read, studied,*
> *And read again.*
> *Again*
> *Again*

And again.

Day after day, the Señora studied the threads while just outside her door the city she once loved continued to dissolve into a fog of yellow smoke. One by one the leaders of the country came calling. Several times a week they knocked on The Door of Prayers, but Señora Esperon did not allow them to enter. "We are not ready to receive the dogs," she told Contenta. "They must wait."

Still they knocked; the president of the nation, José Maria Serrano, who was named for his dog-eared father, and who resembled him in every way—he continued to knock and knock loudly.

"Who is there and what do you want?" Contenta would call through the door.

"I am the president," José Maria Serrano would say, and Contenta would answer: "And I am the Archangel Gabriel. Go away."

Several times a week the president called upon the Señora to no avail; the door was never opened onto him. His brother came calling along with his first cousins and the daughter of his adopted sister who was a Carmelite, but they, too, were turned away.

"The Señora is studying the old weaver's carpet," Contenta would say. "Her mind is troubled. She is mourning the loss of her two great loves."

And who might they have been," asked one of the cousins.

"The once mayor of our city, and the once president of this country," Contenta answered as she had been instructed. "Her heart was broken long ago and it has never mended."

"I have something long and hard that will heal a broken heart," said the president's brother. "And I will show it to her. She will smile when she sees my saber of love."

"The Señora has no interest in knives and weapons," Contenta replied. "You must go away. She is old and deeply troubled by her past."

One day Contenta had had enough. She opened the door and faced the president without fear. "Leave us alone! The parrots have not come. I cannot allow you to enter this house until the parrots arrive. The old weaver who knows how to read the future said so."

"What do parrots have to do with this?" asked the president. "There are no more parrots in the jungles."

"Do not ask me to explain," said Contenta. "I do not have the words for this subject. Now go away. The Señora is busy learning something new." Then she slammed the door so hard flowerpots fell from the balconies and into the street.

Nothing stopped them: they came again, and again they were turned away, and they kept on coming. "We are here to see the Señora," the secretary of tourism said one morning moments after the Señora opened her bedroom window. "We can help her maintain her large house. It is a national monument in need of repair."

"The whole world is anxious to see the Señora," Contenta replied, speaking through the thick door. "And why? Because she has trunks of jewels and a house of many rooms?"

"Because she is a national treasure," said the secretary of natural resources. "She has no heirs and we can assist her in the preservation of her property."

"Her heirs will arrive," Contenta said. "And they will have feathers and wings. Parrots will inherit the Señora's riches. The crazy old weaver said so. The Señora read all about it. It is written on a rug."

"How can parrots maintain a house of this size or any size?" asked the secretary of commerce.

"You must ask the weaver these questions," Contenta replied in a sharp tone. "The Señora says she weaves magic carpets."

In this manner Contenta continued to hold the ruling family at bay. "But how much longer can this go on, Señora?" she asked.

And Señora Esperon replied. "It will go on until the parrots arrive and even after they arrive. This house is to be their home. I have read this in the carpet."

Months passed. Another year arrived. And on a stifling afternoon when Señora Esperon and Fuerte were busy stitching two panels together, three pilgrims knocked at the door. With great joy, Contenta welcomed their return. She let them in to sit at the grave of the saint where they prayed for clean water, more rain, and less scorching sun. They wailed loudly in voices that could be heard on the street and after they left, Contenta returned to the courtyard to find that the goldfish had jumped out of the lotus pool and were flouncing on the hot sand. She picked them up with her bare hands and returned them to the water but they jumped out again, and finally, after she had returned them to the water for the third time, she covered the pool with a sheer cloth.

Señora Esperon, who had recently observed her seventy-fourth birthday, looked down from the gallery to see the pool draped with the cloth of Heaven.

"You see, Señora," Contenta said. "Even the goldfish are anxious for the end. Every living thing is dissatisfied."

"The air is poison and so the water is also," Señora Esperon signed. "We will need to protect ourselves with a roof."

She called for contractors, for glass and metal workers, and within a few days a grid of steel ribs had been constructed over her courtyards. Glass panes were fitted into the steel panels, and after the structures were finished, Señora Esperon sat in her large court-yard and breathed the fresh air from her garden. "Now we're hermetically sealed," she said. "And we are waiting for the parrots. How will they ever find us if we are closed off from the world?"

"That's not your problem," Fuerte said. "It's the parrots' problem. Soon they will come and the world will start all over again. First there will be twelve parrots and then eight. They will attract the wrong people to this house at the right time. And the survivor will be among them. When the twelve become eight the president will be invited to lunch. He will come and many others will accompany him here, for they do not want a flock of parrots to inherit this house and all it contains. And they will do anything to prevent it."

"Have you seen parrots today, Contenta?" Josefina Esperon continually asked. "We must watch for them. They're the inheritors of my life and fortune."

"No Señora, why do you keep asking me this? I have not seen parrots anywhere," Contenta said. "You know I'll tell you the minute I see one."

Every morning Señora Esperon asked the same question. "Where are the parrots? Only they are my true heirs."

And Contenta answered, "They're flying through the jungle but not our jungle."

And Fuerte replied: "They're in cages. We're all in cages."

And Señora Esperon replied, "Cages or not, bring them to me. First twelve and then eight. I want to end this waiting."

"I don't know how to catch them," Contenta said repeatedly. "If I knew how to catch birds, I'd have caught them long ago because I'm also tired of waiting."

To the new archbishop, who was one of the seeds returned, Contenta expressed many opinions regarding her employer's state of mind. Sitting in his private courtyard, stripped of every blooming plant, the archbishop, once famous for his needlepoint, was teaching himself to knit. "We need socks for the boys at my orphanage," he told Contenta. "Do you understand knitting?"

"Yes, Your Excellency," Contenta said. "Let me help you."

She took the needles into her hands to demonstrate the purl stitch, and while the archbishop looked over her shoulder, they discussed the Señora's health. "She makes no sense anymore," Contenta said. "She talks about parrots and nothing but parrots. Twelve are supposed to be given to her. But who would give anyone twelve parrots? Even one is too many."

"She is old," said the archbishop. Taking the needles into his hands he attempted to repeat what he had just seen. "She is old. She is confused. And she has no heirs. You must convince her to leave everything she owns to the church. Her house would make a fine residence for my orphans."

"Her will has already been made," Contenta said, "and her heirs are eight parrots. Eight parrots she has not yet seen will inherit everything she owns. The weaver has put this idea in her head. It is crazy, but that is the way it is in that house."

"This has been the talk for a long time," the archbishop said, "but it cannot be true."

"But it is true, Your Excellency," replied Contenta. "You must believe me when I say this. Her heirs are a flock of parrots. I will swear on my dead mother's soul that this is true."

"Then the time has come to take these matters into our own hands," said the archbishop. He summoned a meeting with his brothers and cousins.

"She has bequeathed her house and entire fortune to a flock of unseen parrots," he told his kinsmen. "This has been the rumor for years, and the rumor has been substantiated. It is true. And now we must do something about it."

"She's gone mad," said the president, "but who'll be surprised to hear it? I will try once more time to talk sense to her. This time I will approach her on her own terms."

In a formal letter he requested an audience with the Señora for the purpose of discussing the arrival of her parrots. To his surprise and great joy the audience was granted. The day and time of their meeting was decided upon, but when the president arrived at the Señora's house, she refused to receive him. Through a barred window in the center of her door she stared at the leader whose military jacket was decorated with medals and whose face, like his dead father's, was spotted with dark moles he had attempted to conceal with powder.

"I knew your despicable father, the murderer of my father," she wanted to say. "I knew him well, and he knew me not so well, and at this time I do not wish to know you."

But she did not say this.

"Your father was a great man," she said instead. "We were the closest of friends, and in your face I see his face. Do me the honor of leaving me to my own suffering and loneliness. Your presence reminds me of many happy hours, and such memories make me weep."

Having said this, she closed the window and returned to her

rooms, but the president was unwilling to be so easily defeated. The next day he sent his brother the secretary of commerce, to the house of forty-three rooms, but he was also told to leave. "Your presence is imbued with memories of too many glorious days and enchanted nights that will never return," she said. "All these memories do nothing but fill me with despair."

Still unwilling to be defeated, the president sent his cousins, the secretaries of natural resources and tourism to the Señora's door, and when she opened her barred window and saw their medals and braids, she sent them away also.

"I entertain poets not capitalists," she wanted to say, but she did not say this. Instead she reminded the men that she had been engaged to their handsome father, who was the president of the nation. "Our wedding day was set. Crowds had already gathered along the street, and on the eve of our marriage . . . do not force me to remember these things . . . I was one of the last to see him alive." After a long pause, during which the men could hear her sobbing through the door, she spoke again. "I have nothing more to say to anyone, not until the parrots arrive and perhaps not even then. They will be my only heirs. It is written in Fuerte's tapestry that parrots will inherit my houses. And that I will not die until twelve become eight."

Sending them on their way, she returned to her rooms, her mid-morning coffee and her daydreams filled with parrots of many colors flying through her courtyards. "How I wish they would arrive today," she said when Contenta cleared the dishes from the serving table. "I'm tired of waiting. I'm tired of living."

"Who're you talking to now, Señora?" Contenta asked. "I hope it's God."

"Myself," Josefina answered. "My daughters are gone. My poets are dead. There is no one else to talk to except myself. I am a prisoner in my own home for the world beyond these walls is not to my liking. Day and night this street is noisy with automobiles, delivery trucks, and buses of tourists coming to visit the smallest country in the world, a country of one city with a baroque opera house but no opera, a country with a national museum but no living painters, a country with magazines and newspapers but no libraries and no poets and no singers strolling the boulevards and plazas."

"And so, why do the tourists come here?" Contenta asked.

"Just to say that they have survived the world's most inhospitable city," the Señora replied.

"You think about things too much," Contenta said.

"I have nothing else to think about other than the destruction of my country and the ruination of the world."

"You have many things to think about," Fuerte reminded her. "We are still reading the threads."

Again the Señora turned her thoughts to the tapestry and while studying the threads, she rarely considered the fact that it was her life she was reading, and only once during the next year of intense study did she suddenly remember the parrots, the survivor, and the coming of the end. One day she read this aloud to Fuerte:

First there will be twelve,
And then there will be eight.
When there are eight parrots,
The daughter will choose her day,
And only then will she know what to serve the president
When he comes to lunch.
Only then will she recognize the survivor.

"Here we are again?" Josefina said in exasperation. She threw the panel to the floor. "Who is the survivor? The survivor of what?"

"I don't know all the answers," Fuerte said. "I wove this tapestry but I did not create everything that is in it. The survivor will come. And will be recognized. But first the parrots."

"Why parrots?" asked Señora Esperon.

"In our calendar we use parrots and other animals to mark the passage of ages," Fuerte said. "The Age of the Parrot is not far away."

"How many ages make a year, or how many years make an age?" asked the Señora.

"One age can be as long as twelve years," Fuerte said. "But you must not think in years, you must think in moons. Eight moons make one year in our time. One of your months can have two full moons sometimes none. Sometimes the moon is there but cannot be seen. This all goes into the count. When the age of the parrot arrives twelve birds will come to you. Then four will go away, and then you will be in the fourth of twelve parrots, and in this time of many full moons you will be able to make important decisions. The parrots will inherit your house, yes. But who will inherit the parrots? The tapestry does not know everything.

"Twelve years and how many moons? Twelve parrots, then only eight. When we have only eight parrots we will be in the eighth year of the parrot. Yes?"

"No," Fuerte answered, "we will be in the fourth parrot in an age of twelve.

Who can possibly figure it all out," the Señora said.

"It is merely a method of marking the passage of time," said Fuerte.

"No," Señora Esperon said, "there must be more to it than that? Why parrots?"

"They are at the top of the tree," Fuerte answered. "Among the wisest of all inhabitants of the animal kingdom. They can recognize the truth. They can recognize the lie. And they can speak their mind. We who are trapped on this earth are always deceived but the parrot is never deceived. And for that reason we eagerly await the Age of the Parrot."

"And why do I have to wait for twelve to become eight?"

"Eight is the number for new beginnings."

"Now the parrots are too much on my mind again. How will I be able to forget them and go on with our lessons?"

Another year passed rapidly during which Señora Esperon studied the threads and waited. From her balcony she watched for the slightest flutter of any bird that might be a parrot. She saw nothing. "It is because the Age of the Parrot has not yet arrived," Fuerte said, "but it is upon us."

And then one afternoon in the following year a tourist bus scraped the side of her house. Tiles fell from the roof and flower-pots from the balconies. The front door was demolished and two windows shattered. With repair work heavy on her mind the par-rots flew from her thoughts, and one week later they suddenly ar-rived, not at her door, and not on her balcony but on the Street of Merchants and Peddlers, a street whose face continued to change from year to year.

"There are too many changes now," she said on the morn-ing the parrots arrived. Earlier that week a group of men came to break up the sidewalks that had been poured only the year before. They worked with hydraulic drills that shook the foundation of the Señora's house and caused oranges to fall prematurely from her trees. And when the sidewalks were demolished and twelve flame trees torn out by their roots, a metal pipe was cemented into the places where the trees had grown. On top of each pipe was an iron cage, and inside each cage the secretary of urban development, who was not a member of the ruling family, placed nine green par-rots and three macaws. "For the enjoyment of Señora Esperon," the secretary said in a public ceremony which she watched from her balcony. "The Señora has been expecting these parrots for a long time. They belong to the city, but the city is happy to share them with her."

"I have a correction to make," said the secretary of com-merce when he was called on to say a few words about the par-rots. "These birds belong to the nation. They were purchased from a private collection and are very rare."

"I have another correction to make," said the president when he was called on to end the ceremony. "The parrots are from my own aviary, and I have not yet sold them to anyone."

Everyone claims to own the heirs to my fortune, Señora Espe-ron thought. But who will assume their care?

From her balcony she waited to see who had been appointed

to feed the birds and change their water, and how many times a day they would be tended. For three days she waited and no one came, and on the third afternoon when she discovered that there were no seeds or water in any of the cages she took it upon herself to care for the birds in her own way. "They have arrived," she said. "And now they are mine."

At dawn she fed them and changed their water, and when the sun was hot and they could not fan themselves with their wings, for their cages were too small for wingspread, the Señora fanned them herself. She scratched their heads, spoke to them affectionately, and finally after one week of staring into their sad eyes, she took matters into her own hands. After midnight she broke the locks on their cages and the next morning when she opened the doors to her balcony, the parrots, all twelve of them, entered her house as if it were their own.

They perched on open doors, chairs, and balcony rails. They drank water from the lotus pool and ate every piece of fruit in the kitchen. They even found their way into the weaver's room and scattered her colored threads. "It doesn't matter, if the threads are scattered," Fuerte said. "The parrots have arrived. That is all that matters."

Contenta did not like the parrots because they imitated the jangling sounds of her many rosaries. "They're laughing at me," she said. "But worst of all they're laughing at God." From time to time a parrot would fly to her shoulders and rip a rosary from her neck, sending the beads rolling across the floor and the crucifix falling into her hands. But when the birds learned to speak proper words, her opinion of them quickly changed. "The Lord has sent these talking parrots to the Señora for a reason," she told the archbishop. "I'll teach them to pray, and the Señora will listen to them. She will never listen to anyone else, but she will listen to her parrots. They are her new daughters."

Within a short time, Contenta had taught each parrot to recite a phrase from the Hail Mary, but teaching them to recite in correct order was far more difficult than she had imagined. The macaws, she found out, were the most stubborn and refused to cooperate. She lined up the birds on a banister and pointed to the keeper of the first phrase. "Speak," she said, "the Lord commands it." The first parrot refused to talk, but the third, a scarlet macaw, did not hesitate. "Blessed art thou among women," it said repeatedly, and Contenta screamed, "You're too early! Wait until I point to you!" The sound of her shrill voice encouraged all twelve parrots to commence speaking at once, and Contenta chastised them for not cooperating with the will of God.

After many failed attempts to teach the parrots to recite the phrases in order, she took the problem to the archbishop, and while she helped him finish a pair of socks, he convinced her that words divinely inspired had never been known to lose their sanction even when spoken out of sequence.

Believing him to be the voice of right and reason, Contenta allowed the parrots to chatter on in whatever order they pleased, never once scolding them for anything other than lapsing into an hour of silence. Silence she could not tolerate. "The Señora doesn't have many years left," she reminded them when they refused to talk. "You must take every opportunity to expose her to the word of God."

"What are those birds saying, now?" Señora Esperon asked. Her frail voice carried through the thick walls of her house and into the courtyard where Contenta was feeding the goldfish. "Are they asking questions? Do they require a response, if so I cannot give one." It was one week before her eightieth birthday, and she was sitting in her mother's chapel with Fuerte at her side. Panels of the tapestry were at their feet and they were busy stitching them together in the proper order. "I must have silence," she said. "I cannot work with all these parrot voices. What are they saying? Contenta, what have you taught them now?"

"Almost all of the Lord's Prayer," she said. "If they're constantly praying it could be because they think your soul is in need of redemption."

"I am not concerned with redemption," Señora Esperon

replied. "I am concerned with numbers. How many parrots are there today?"

"There are twelve."

"Are you sure?"

"Yes, Señora. I am sure."

"Count them again please. Let me hear you."

"At this hour there are twelve parrots, and all of them would like to recite the Lord's Prayer just for you?"

"Parrots I need," the Señora said. "Prayers no. How many did you count this morning?"

"Twelve."

"And just now?"

"Twelve."

"And tomorrow, will there still be twelve also?"

"I cannot speak for tomorrow, Señora."

"Nor can this tapestry," Fuerte sighed. "Not with regard to the parrots and when they will die or fly away. We know they will, but when? And so we wait."

"Yes," Contenta said. "We wait and we wait."

And while they waited, the leaders of the nation continued to knock at the Señora's door, and each time they were turned away because Josefina Esperon was studying the threads and Fuerte was weaving the final panels and Contenta was teaching the parrots whatever she thought the Señora needed to hear. The entire house was busy, and could not be disturbed, not even by the president of the nation.

And then the morning came when Contenta, going about her daily routine of feeding the parrots and scratching their heads, noticed that one of the macaws could not grasp its perch. Within the hour the bird was dead and Contenta, who had grown old and stiff in her joints, came running into the chapel as if she were sixteen once again. Finding Señora Esperon bent over the tapestry, she spoke out with great excitement, "Señora, Señora, a parrot has died! Now we have eleven. Does that make you happy?"

"Yes," she replied. "For I am very tired."

The next day the secretary of commerce sent the Señora a sympathy card. "We are in mourning for your beloved parrot," the card read.

"And how did they learn of the death of my parrot?" the Señora asked Contenta.

"I do not know, Señora," Contenta replied. "I did not mention it to the archbishop when I saw him yesterday."

"Just as I suspected," Josefina Esperon replied.

One year later Contenta could hardly make it up the stairs without stopping to rest, but when she discovered that another parrot had died, her strength was momentarily restored. She came running into the chapel, where the Señora was studying the threads, and called out excitedly: "Señora, Señora. Today there are only ten parrots! One of them died during the night."

"Good," the Señora said. "We are getting closer."

Nine months later, seemingly for no reason at all, another parrot fell off its perch and was dead. On discovering it, Contenta screamed, "Señora, now we have nine."

"Good," the Señora replied, "very soon there will be only eight."

For another year she waited for the next parrot to die. During that year she received letters and visits from the nation's leaders but they were turned away without apology. And yet they returned and kept on returning. All the while Fuerte worked at her loom, Contenta greeted the few pilgrims who visited the house, the birds recited the Scriptures and Señora Esperon screamed for silence.

"They have recited the Hail Mary more times than it has ever been heard in all the cathedrals of the world. When will they cease? How many are there now? When did you last count them? Contenta, I'm speaking to you. I said, How many parrots are still living? Why don't you answer me anymore?"

If Contenta ignored her long enough Señora Esperon would inevitably count the parrots herself, but never trusting her diminishing eyesight, she would beat her cane furiously against a banister, a door facing, or a piece of furniture until Contenta arrived to make her own count. "Yes, you're right," she would say, "there are nine parrots. Nine and only nine."

"No more and no less?"

"No more and no less."

"Then we're forced to wait a while longer."

Long after the tenth parrot had died, Señora Esperon became disgusted with the interminable pace of her final days. Shortly after beginning her eighty-second year she came to the conclusion that it was time to stop counting the parrots. From her balcony she announced to the city that she would wait no longer.

While Contenta was stirring a pot of stew, and pilgrims were praying in the courtyard, the Señora chose a bird at random, and on the kitchen table she removed its head with one blow of a hatchet. Flapping its bloody wings, the headless parrot danced over the kitchen floor. A spray of blood splattered the walls, the tables, and chairs. The parrots in the courtyard screamed as if they too had been attacked, and Contenta, dropped her spoon into the pilgrims' stew and screamed with them.

"Señora, you have killed the most sacred parrot of them all. This bird prayed to you so sweetly, Señora, why didn't you listen? Why didn't you kill one of the contrary macaws instead?"

After all signs of life had passed from the bird's body the Señora replied:

"Now I will invite the president to lunch."

Part IV

The Day the President Came to Lunch

The second Friday after observing her eighty-second year, Señora Esperon arose before dawn. The president was coming
to lunch. The nation was celebrating its independence, and the
she was determined to make her luncheon a memorable one. That
morning all the clocks in the house seemed to be ticking louder
than usual as if they were nervously counting the seconds until the
president arrived. Even before she had fully awakened she was
aware of the steady ticking. If only, she thought, they would go silent; if only they would wind down. Wearing a threadbare kimono
that smelled faintly of camphor, she entered her mother's chapel
and sat in front of Fuerte's tapestry. It had taken the two of them
an entire afternoon to roll it up, and this day it would be hung for
the first time.

A few minutes before dawn she called for breakfast, and
when Contenta served it she spilled coffee on the long table and
on the tapestry as well. "Forgive me, Señora," she said. "I cannot
see what I am doing this morning. My eyes are dry and burning. I
need my drops."

"That's no excuse for clumsiness!" Señora Esperon responded quickly. "Your life is recorded in these threads. You do not wish
to stain your life with coffee do you?"

"I wish to prepare a delicious lunch," Contenta answered. "I
wish to please the president."

"Though he may be the longest reigning president in the history of this country," the Señora said, "he is not worth pleasing. I
will prepare lunch myself, and with the greatest of pleasure, but
only when I am ready."

"But Señora we have not shopped. There's no food in the
house worth serving to a president.

"Are there pilgrims waiting outside?" Señora Esperon asked
"Yes, Señora."

"Invite two of them in. Strong ones. This tapestry must be
hung now while the day is cool."

While she calmed her excitement with an early brandy, two
pilgrims wearing sackcloth and thorns, entered the chapel to carry

the tapestry into the courtyard. "Let it hang three times around from arch to arch," Señora Esperon said. "I want the president and his kinsmen to see it. I want them surrounded by their destiny."

After she was alone again, she retreated to her balcony to bleach her face with rice powder, to color her lips, her cheeks, her eyelids, and finally, to acknowledge the remains of her city and the day she had long awaited.

Looking east over the tile rooftops she saw the gray sea and red algae floating like ribbons of blood toward the harbor. To the north she saw oil derricks and storage tanks, the control tower at the new international airport and the white windowless walls of a missile plant. To the south she saw smokestacks, skyscrapers, and steel supports for an elevated highway that was being built around the city and through the western mountains. Through the mountains, to where? She wondered.

That day the mountaintops could barely be seen. They were crowned with yellow clouds ready to descend, and when Señora Esperon saw them hovering overhead she decided to smoke her morning cigarette before the air became too heavy to breathe.

Presently, Contenta returned with a tray of sweet bread and another pot of coffee. "Señora," she said. "I have searched the cupboards again, and I found nothing except a few slices of stale bread. The cupboards are empty, Señora. How many times have I reminded you that the president is coming this afternoon, and there's no food in this house? Yesterday the pilgrims were very hungry, and they ate everything."

"Not quite everything," Señora Esperon replied. "Somewhere we'll find a jar of caviar, and one loaf of bread. Surely, they won't require more than that."

"They?" Contenta gasped. "Señora, who else will be coming?"

"Everyone I invited, I'm sure. The secretaries of commerce, natural resources, and tourism. Counting the president and me, that comes to five, but set the table for seven because the archbishop and the young mother superior will show up when they learn that everyone else has accepted." She handed Contenta a slip of paper on which she had indicated the exact placement of the table as well as the linens, the crystal, and the china she wished to use. But at that hour, Contenta was far more concerned with food than appearances.

"What shall I buy at the market?" she asked. "And how may I assist you with all the cooking?"

Calmly, Señora Esperon assured her that marketing and cooking were the least of their problems, but Contenta was not convinced.

While she was setting the table for seven and worrying about the menu, her employer stood up with the help of a sturdy cane and went back inside the house. She opened the double doors onto the gallery, and a green parrot flew through the apartment and perched on the back of a chair. "Give us this day," the bird said in Contenta's voice.

"We already have it," Señora Esperon replied.

Behind the parrot came seven more, all of them reciting, "Thy will be done," "Blessed is the fruit," and "Forgive us our trespasses."

"We have no trespasses," Señora Esperon said, "and we also have no fruit."

When she returned to her balcony chair, the birds perched on her arms, lap, and shoulders, ate crusts of sweet bread from her hands, and drank warm coffee from her cup. After satisfying their hunger, they preened themselves for the day to come while Señora Esperon smoked a second cigarette, something she rarely needed to do. "Smoking," she confessed to the parrots, "is a very bad habit, especially since the air is already filled with smoke, but today it is necessary."

"Thy Kingdom come, thy will be done," a macaw sang out, and the Señora rewarded the bird by scratching its head.

While the other parrots fought for equal attention, she watched the yellow haze descending upon the city. "Even on a national holiday," she said, "the factories don't close."

The Independence Day celebration was scheduled to begin

at five o'clock and last through the night, but already there was a sense of celebration in the air. Carnival rides were being assembled for three blocks on either side of the Señora's house, and directly in front of her balcony a group of men on scaffolds were erecting a blue Ferris wheel. Next to it a carousel of twelve horses and two swan boats was being unloaded piece by piece, and next to the carousel, a house of mirrors was ready for visitors. From Independence Monument all the way to Our Lady of the Sea, food vendors were claiming leftover space, and merchants were nailing boards over display windows.

Under normal circumstances Señora Esperon would have sent Contenta into the street to complain about the noise, but that day, the private celebration she had planned was occupying her thoughts. She intended for her luncheon to be written up in all the newspapers and talked about for many years to come.

Scratching the heads of her parrots, she attempted to walk through the entire day in her mind, but there were still too many uncertainties, too many blank places, gaps that would be filled at the last minute. For someone who planned everything down to the last detail, the blanks did not fall easily on the nerves. She felt secure with only one thing: the menu, which she had planned in accordance with Fuerte's instructions.

> *The president will expect pheasant under glass,*
> *But he will not be served it.*
> *He will expect roasted pig,*
> *Or poached fish,*
> *But his expectations will not be fulfilled.*
> *Knowing this house, he will be apprehensive.*
> *At the last moment he will not wish to come.*
> *But he will come.*
> *And he will wish to leave, long before his time.*

The dining table had been placed under the orange trees and in full view of the graves. Señora Esperon had chosen the china and the silver her mother had brought from Spain, and the crystal stems that had belonged to her father's family. They were the finest in the house and the most fragile. "But what does it matter?" she asked one of the parrots. "Of what good are they now?"

The seating arrangement concerned her more than the place settings, and far more than the main course. She intended to place the president on one end of the table and herself on the other. But the remaining guests? How should they be seated? In what order?

"What would you do if the president were coming to your house for lunch?" she asked one of her parrots. "Who would sit on your left, and who would sit on your right?"

"God the Father, God the Son," the parrot replied.

"I'm speaking seriously," Señora Esperon protested.

"Look she's talking to herself again," one of the carnival workers said.

"No," replied another. "She's talking to God."

Señora Esperon heard them. "The God to whom you refer and I have never been on speaking terms," she said. "It is true, I have been known to pray but that is quite different. Prayer is nothing more than releasing the power of words into the air."

"And who answers your prayers, Señora."

"I am not stupid enough to attempt an explanation of the inexplicable," she said. "No one knows all the answers, not even Fuerte. The tapestry, however, is a work of some kind of divine inspiration."

"Our president believes in prayer. He prays with his cabinet everyday."

"He also believes in destroying our world in order to fill his purse," the Señora said emphatically. "When necessity prevails, he, his entire cabinet, and the leaders of the church, are completely comfortable with any contradiction that seems convenient at the time."

"If you weren't talking to God who were you talking to Señora?"

"To my parrots, of course!" she said with irritation. "Who

else is there? My daughters no longer live here and my poets have been murdered. There's no one else with whom to have an intelligent conversation, no one except the parrots and Fuerte."

Every morning while Fuerte wove, the Señora sat on her balcony and ranted to her parrots as if they understood every word she said. Her daily complaints turned into vehement diatribes against foreign industrialists who had poisoned the air, and the government officials who had allowed them to enter the country with money, power, and false promises. She ranted against the church for instilling fear into those already afraid, against an amusement park filled with artificial shade trees, and against all the new merchants who sold shoes, belts, and sunglasses for the price of a month's rent. "How could you allow this indecency to occur?" she shouted to a carnival worker as if he were responsible for all the ills of the world. "Why would anyone want to live here? The egrets have been poisoned. The trees are dying. The water is no longer fit to drink."

"Señora, I can hear you all over the house." Contenta called from the large courtyard. "You must cease this foolish chatter and give me the menu."

"How many times do I have to tell you I am not concerned with the menu? I am concerned with the seating arrangement, the serving of the food, and the difficult task of bringing a disgraceful luncheon to a graceful end."

"Señora, I must remind you that this luncheon is very important. The guests wish to talk to you about your house and the ownership of the parrots. Señora, your house is very important."

"And very famous," she said. "I am aware of that."

"You need to make a provision," Señora. "The parrots are a poor excuse."

"The parrots are no excuse," she replied. "They will attract the wrong people to this house at the right time. Fuerte said so."

"You need someone to help you make decisions, Señora. You are all alone. You have no one."

"Why have I put up with you all these years," she muttered to herself. "I am not all alone, but I am lonely!"

The loneliness of her last years was mitigated by the reminder that long after she had closed her doors to the public and kissed the last of her daughters good-bye, her colonial house of forty-three rooms, two courtyards, and four balconies was still regarded as the most famous house in the nation, even more famous than the president's mansion. It was said that more presidents had slept under her roof than in the official residence, but when questioned on this hearsay, the Señora issued the same comment.

"I am afraid there is a misunderstanding. I have only entertained four presidents and in ways they are not likely to forget unless, of course, they are no longer living. And they are not!"

Even on the day of the presidential luncheon, a day when her mind dwelled on issues far removed from the men with whom she had slept, the question regarding the exact number of presidents she had known intimately was put to her by a young man in an orange jumpsuit. Tightening nuts and bolts as he went along, he was climbing through the inner workings of the Ferris wheel when he saw the Señora sitting on the balcony with her parrots. At eye level and with no more than a few feet separating them, he asked what she considered the most tiresome question, a question that defined for her the mentality of the day, and to make matters worse, it was not a single question but a double one.

"How many presidents have slept in your house, Señora, and how many still come back to visit you?"

Coming unexpectedly, and from such close range, it was not so much the question that startled her, but the tone of the man's voice. Sharp and impersonal, it made her gasp, and sent the parrots fluttering to the floor. She stared at the young man with cold eyes while the birds slowly climbed up the chair and settled on her arms and lap once again.

"Well, then," the worker said, after a long pause, "is it true that you carry weapons concealed in your clothing?"

In answer to that, the Señora drew a black silk fan from the pocket of her kimono. With quick movements of her wrist, the fan opened and closed like the flapping of a wing, and when she tapped it on the balcony rail a long silver knife came shooting forth. "As thin as a blade of grass," she said in a tired voice; and the worker was silenced.

By then the yellow cloud of factory smoke had settled over the tall buildings of glass and steel. The observation deck of the New Hotel Carmina, a tower of thirty-five stories, had all but disappeared into the golden haze.

"Today," the Señora said, "children believe that the sky is yellow."

"The sky is yellow," came a voice from the street.

"But it is not supposed to be," Señora Esperon replied.

Within the hour, tourists were covering their faces with scarves, hats, and handkerchiefs. The carnival workers on the high scaffolding were wearing masks to filter the air, and the walk-in oxygen tents located on every corner were filled to capacity.

"It is the same everyday," she said to her birds. "And now it's time to go inside."

Under the weight of eight fat parrots she stood with the help of her cane and returned to her apartment. She closed the French doors leading to the balcony and all the windows giving onto the street. With parrots clinging to her shoulders or walking pigeon-toed behind her, she inched her way through the apartment and across the gallery to Fuerte's room. She was strapped to her loom but her eyes were closed and her hands were still. Silently, Señora Esperon arranged the colored threads according to Fuerte's final instructions. This, she knew, was to be the last panel, and it called for six shades of red, four shades of purple, and just as many blues, greens, and blue greens. Only one shade of yellow. A terrible yellow, Señora thought, as she bent over to place the threads in the correct order. The yellow of the clouds. The yellow of a dead man's eyes. Leaving Fuerte to rest, she returned to the gallery and the stairs leading into the courtyard. There she stopped to take a deep breath before continuing. At one time she had been able to take those stairs on the run. How well she remembered it.

But at the age of eighty-two she was thankful to take four steps down or up without stopping to rest.

Halfway down she paused to admire the hanging tapestry. Who will be the next to read it? She wondered. Who will survive me?

From arch to arch, 293 connected panels hung three times around the courtyard where hummingbirds and yellow butterflies swarmed through rays of golden light filtered through the glass ceiling. Every plant and tree was flowering, and the panels of many colors hung within the profusion of blooms as if both the courtyard and the tapestry were the same creation.

"It is all very beautiful," Señora Esperon said to her parrots. "If this president has forgotten beauty, today he will be reminded of it once again. And if he has never known beauty, today he will see it for the first time." She sighed heavily. "But does he have the eyes to recognize anything?"

A cool breeze blew up the stairs and around the gallery playing contrapuntal melodies on the wind chimes. The Señora looked up to the glass ceiling of her courtyard, and to the flowering trumpet vines that grew across the steel beams. The maestro who had constructed the glass roof had been against the project. "Open courtyards," he had said, "bring cool breezes into a house. If we close them off your wind chimes will be silenced forever."

"There will always be a breeze in my courtyards," Señora Esperon had replied. "Please begin work at once."

Within a few weeks the glass ceilings had been completed. They sealed the house from the outside world and captured a breeze that traveled back and forth through the narrow passages.

Under the glass ceilings, the wind chimes were as active as they had ever been, and the Señora's plants thrived beyond expectation. The orange trees were blooming for the second time that year, and the hummingbirds trapped inside her walls had already raised a third family to feast upon lotus blossoms, trumpet flowers, hibiscus, and poppies. The large courtyard was her favorite of the two, the place where she retreated each morning to contemplate her long life and short future.

Beneath the orange trees was her father's wicker wheelchair. "No I do not need a wheelchair," she heard him explaining to a patient. "It provides me rapid accessibility to my files and tables of laboratory equipment." The speed with which he had rolled around his study and into the courtyards had amazed his young daughter, and now long after his death, she had appropriated the chair as her own. Two of her parrots had already perched on the armrests and were screaming for her to join them with more food and caresses. For a moment she ignored their demands in order to listen to her father, the resident doctor, and to her mother, the living saint. Their voices lived with her each day, and not only through memory, through many dialogues she had not heard but had been recorded for her; woven out of time, and with colored threads that transcended all time.

And the doctor said:

I will give you a child for each bedroom.
And to this the saint inquired:

How many bedrooms are there, my husband?
And when the doctor answered:

Enough to make you very happy,
She threw the Angel across the courtyard
And mounted the stairs like an animal.
Galloping with madness and rage
She slammed doors open
And slammed doors shut
And after she had counted forty-three rooms
She threw herself at her husband's feet and cried:

How could you?
Have you no respect?
Please take me home!

"By then it was too late to go home." The Señora sighed and continued on her way to the bottom of the stairs.

Six anxious parrots flew to the wicker chair and screamed for her attention, but she did not give it. She paused before her mother's grave, which was marked with a cypress cross. The blue bowl was filled with fresh water and flowers, and the thorns on the crown were sharper than needles. "As they should be," she said. A few steps away was an obelisk with *Angel* carved vertically on all four sides, but the Señora did not pause there, she moved on in her slow pace toward two marble columns she had recently commissioned. One was in honor of Serrano, and the other marked the grave of Carlota Montejo. "Gone is the National Theatre," she said. "Now which mirror will the people hold up to reflect their lives?"

A little farther on, she paused before her father. His grave was marked with a rough stone of pink granite, and his name was chiseled within a small polished surface. On the other side of the stone was an open grave. "It is mine," she said as though she were answering someone else's question. The grave had been recently dug and roped off, so Contenta, in her perpetual distraction, would be reminded to walk around it. It was marked with a smooth river stone with her name carved into it.

Turning away from her own grave, she stood for a moment before Fuerte's. It was close to the lotus pool because she had asked to be buried near fish, frogs, turtles, and snails, and all other creatures that lived in water and mud. Fuerte's grave, also roped off for Contenta's protection, was marked with a smooth river stone but nothing was carved into it. No name, no date. Nothing. Names were not relevant to Fuerte, and time did not mean to her what it meant to most people.

Four of the parrots were also buried in the courtyard, their graves hidden beneath bougainvillea that had forced its way into the house to cover walls and furniture in almost every room. But Señora Esperon was not much concerned with the condition of her house, particularly the rooms she no longer used.

"One day," she said, "this house will be restored with my money, but not by me."

The hour of her death, she realized, was rapidly approaching, and a final provision for her house, in spite of what everyone believed, had not yet been made. Yes, the parrots were her heirs, but who would inherit the parrots? Who would survive her? Who would care for the parrots, the house, the tapestry, and the pilgrims? She knew all too well that her property, should it fall into the hands of the city developers, would be turned into a hotel for tourists, an emporium for foreign goods, or something even more distasteful: a presidential residence. On further consideration, however, she had decided that a presidential residence was no more or less distasteful than a restaurant no one could afford, a bank without tellers, or a hospital for the rich.

"Please accept this invitation to lunch on the afternoon of our independence," she had written to the president. "At that time we may discuss the future of my property." She had sent the same invitation to the president's secretaries as well as the clergy and all but the clergy had responded.

"They will arrive at two thirty," she said, as if reminding herself of something that could easily be forgotten. "There is so much to be done between now and then. The beauty parlor is on the schedule, but first I must rest."

Under latticed light, she sat in her father's chair and stared into the lotus pool taken over by frogs. How did they get there? she wondered. And how have the goldfish survived this invasion?

The pool was circled with pots of begonias, and partially shaded by a fern tree that grazed the glass ceiling. Bromeliads sprouted from cracks in the upper walls, and along the banisters that circled the courtyard, orchids of every color bloomed the year round. Somewhere in the high corners, under the eaves and away from the light of day, bats could be heard fluttering about.

"Only they," the Señora said, "know how to find the exit."

The large courtyard was a sanctuary for sulfur butterflies, hummingbirds, and honey bees weaving their way through threads of golden light. And for Señora Esperon the courtyard was a place of solace, especially when sitting in her father's chair wheeled close to the pool and the flowering trees. Every morning she sat there until sleep visited her tired eyes, but that day she had no time for sleep; her mind was restless with preparations that needed to be made without the interruption of the carnival worker who continued to invade her thoughts. "If you can believe what you hear, knives, guns, and vials of poison are hidden all over this house," she said as if the man in the orange jump suit were standing before her. "Thanks to the beauty parlor it should come as no surprise to anyone that this Señora is well acquainted with self-protection. Go ask those three sisters if you do not believe me."

"How many guns do you own?" she imagined the carnival worker asking. "How many of your daughters were really your daughters? And were the sixteen poets your lovers or your sons?"

"I am not in the business of entertaining questions," Señora Esperon replied. She closed her eyes for a few moments and when she opened them again the man in the jump suit was no longer there: the parrots were preening in the latticed light, and the courtyard was silent.

"I must look my best," she told the parrots. "That's the only reason to subject myself to the sisters and their endless interrogations." With one hand on her cane and the other on the arm of her chair she slowly pushed herself to a standing position.

"You're late," Contenta called from the kitchen. "The sisters will be angry."

"The sisters have been accused of many things," Señora Esperon said, "but anger has never been on of them. Now come with me to the door. I cannot open it myself."

Still located on Independence Avenue, only two blocks from the Señora's front door, the Parlor of the Three Sisters was one of the few businesses that had survived the advent of the industrialists. "We will last forever because we will not resist the changing world," the sisters had always told their customers. During her years in business, Señora Esperon had visited their parlor four times a week, but after closing her doors to the public she informed the sisters that weekly forays into their changing world were not worth the effort, and therefore, one appointment a month would be more than sufficient because her hair was still as black as the day she was born and her style had not changed: a tight bun at the nape of her neck, an ornamental comb or a jeweled hair clip, but only if the occasion merited it.

"Today the president is coming and I will wear hair ornaments of all varieties," she said. Contenta held the front door wide open. "That will make the sisters very happy because they will have an excuse to charge a higher price."

Señora Esperon stepped from the cool air of her courtyard into the heat of mid-morning and the noisy confusion of the carnival. Across the street a family of midgets was rehearsing a balancing act against a wall of graffiti. A sword swallower was roping off his allotted space, and a tightrope artist was testing his cables. Paying them no mind, the Señora picked her way through a corps of electricians, carpenters, and firework technicians. She dodged a school of six plaster mermaids swimming on the shoulders of six strongmen, and she stepped deftly around a sign pointing the way to an exhibit of anomalies and curiosities.

When she reached the corner, the young man in the jumpsuit shouted an apology. "Forgive me for bothering you with too many questions, Señora. Let me make it up to you this evening. I invite you to take the first ride on our Ferris wheel." He was standing on the high ribs of the blue wheel, and all around him the yellow sky was falling, but this surprised the Señora no more than the invitation.

"Thank you," she said with all the voice she had to spare.

Holding a black scarf to her nose, she walked hurriedly down Independence Avenue toward the beauty salon's neon sign. Exhaust fumes and smoke from three landfills slowed her pace. "The air is abrasive," she said. "No one should be out of doors today. It is like breathing sand and fire." When she entered the salon, the three plump sisters abandoned their customers without apology to escort their most famous client into the changing room. The sisters, Señora Esperon noticed, were waging a losing battle against time. They had chosen their weapons carefully, but not carefully enough: hair dyes and facial paints, necklines cut low, hem lines cut high, and shoes that pinched their swollen feet.

Recently the sisters had equipped their salon with five television sets and ten telephones with cords long enough to stretch from the waiting room to the changing room, all the way to the shampoo sinks and back again. Stepping through this maze of electrical cords and multiple conversations, the Señora reminded the three beauticians that her hearing was permanently impaired. "As you surely must know," she added in a loud voice, "but I feel compelled to say it again, I have removed my hearing device for the sake of shampooing, and cannot understand a word you say. I have brought four ornaments, and I wish to wear them all, but I forbid you to change my style. I am too old for changes, but not too old to know what's going on around me."

"And what's the occasion for so many hair ornaments, Señora," one of the sisters shouted into her ear. "Where are you going this evening?"

"I'm going nowhere. Only back home to my house of two courtyards, many rooms, and lovely dreams."

"That's what you say every time," the sisters said in loud voices.

"Then there's no reason to ask the question again," Señora Esperon replied.

After she was dressed in a cotton smock and escorted to her chair, the beauticians told their new customers from the north that the Señora was the richest woman in the nation, that she had had more wealthy lovers than anyone in the history of mankind, and that she was old, yes very old, but not too old for love. "She's the most famous woman in the city," they said. "Indeed the entire country!"

"But when she dies what will happen to her bars of silver and gold stored in every room?" one sister asked another.

"And what will happen to her dresses?"

"And her jewelry?"

"And all the expensive pictures they say are hanging in her house?"

"And what will happen to her house?" a long-time customer asked. "That's the important thing."

"They say she will leave everything to her parrots."

"But surely this cannot be true!"

"Only time will tell."

"Oh, yes, everyone wants to know what will happen to her house."

What will happen, indeed? Josefina Esperon thought. The entire city wants to know if I will bequeath my fortune to eight parrots, and if so, who will own the parrots after my death.

She was well aware of what was said about her, who was saying it, and how often, because the sisters she visited once a week kept her informed on everything she needed to know. While her hair was being washed and rinsed, she held tightly to the bag of priceless ornaments, and the sisters chattered on, telling their customers, old and new, that the Señora lived in a house of spiders, scorpions, and serpents, that three of her most accomplished lovers had been bitten and died, eight pilgrims had been paralyzed by stings, and one had been stabbed, possibly by the Señora herself. They said that she had murdered, robbed, and loved more men than Cleopatra and ever dreamed of meeting, and had annihilated more than one betrayer with a box of tarantulas captured with her bare hands. To her face they called her the Beautiful Old Whore, the Dangerous One, and the Deformed. And to all their new customers, who were unaware of the Señora's legend, they said that she was stone deaf, that her hearing had been permanently destroyed by the disease of her profession, and that she was a woman of extraordinary anatomy, unlike any other on the face of the earth, for she had been born not with one but with two and had, without any difficulty at all, given birth from each.

"Oh yes," one of the sisters eagerly added, "it is true. Not a word can be denied. Go to the opera house if you don't believe us. Walk through the dress shop on the first floor and up the grand staircase, past the boutiques and into the restaurant. Ask the maitre 'd if you can see dining box number three. Pay him two lyricos if he says no, and he will be sure to show you the bloodstained seat where one of her children was born, and then, if he likes you, he will show you another stain, this time on the carpet where five minutes after the first, another child, which surely belonged to a different father, entered the world through a second gateway. Oh, yes, this is the way it happened. This is the way God made her, and no one realized it, not even her very own father, not until the moment he delivered her second child on the opera house floor, not until then did he know the truth: she was twice the woman she should have been."

"How else could she have sold her virginity the second time?" asked one of the regular customers.

"It would have been impossible otherwise," the sisters exclaimed.

"And her mother, they say, was a saint."

"A living saint."

"And nothing but a saint."

Señora Esperon did not respond, not even to lift an eyebrow or raise a finger. For years she had feigned deafness while the beauticians talked incessantly, repeating not so much what they had heard but what they imagined she was hiding inside herself and her house of forty-three rooms.

That day, however, one of the sisters became suspicious and put the Señora to test by asking questions that demanded responses. "Don't you think we should cut all this ugly dead hair today, Señora? Don't you think we should try something new? Do you think you might enjoy having red hair for a little while?" The Señora did not react to these questions, but when a bottle of dye was passed before her face, she shook a finger of disapproval.

"You will not make a circus clown of me," she protested loudly. "Perhaps I belong in a house of freaks, but for better reasons than any of you can imagine."

"Did you hear? Did you hear?" a beautician exclaimed. "The Señora has confessed. She belongs in the freak house, and she thinks we do not know why, but of course, we do. It was her deformity that made her so tireless in her profession, and now she has all but said so herself; she belongs in the circus."

"A freak house."

"A sideshow."

"But she would not have made as much money as a circus freak," one of the customers argued.

And to this the beauticians replied:

"Oh, yes you are so right."

"She knew her place in life."

"She knew where her talents would be most appreciated."

"She used her God-given attributes to good advantage."

"And they were not *one* but *two*."

While the Señora's hair was drying, the sisters called attention to her long lacquered fingernails. They let it be known, and known without doubt, that the Beautiful Old Whore had, on sundry occasions, scratched snake venom into the veins of customers who refused to pay her fee, and that she carried a deadly poison concealed within the petals of a burgundy rose wilting on her bosom. They said, with certainty, that she knew how to produce knives, hat pins and ice picks from thin air. They bore witness to the fact that they had combed razor blades from her hair, and that her earrings, even the ones she always wore to the beauty parlor and refused to remove for shampooing, were nothing more than containers for deadly substances.

"Oh yes," they said with swoons and sighs.

"It is true."

"Our Señora is no fool."

"She's not to be misjudged, not even in her old age."

"And to this day she carries a loaded pistol."

"And it's so tiny she is able to conceal it in one of two places not even our Heavenly Father would think to look."

Señora Esperon, who had trained herself to delay all reactions, listened attentively as the three sisters reminded each other that their most famous customer was a whore and nothing but a whore and a whore would always be a whore and nothing better.

"And her daughters," a sister said, "the whores who lived with her. They were beautiful beyond imagination, but only after she trained them and made them over."

"She turned them into goddesses."

"She invested them with supernatural powers."

"And they too could defend themselves with a glance."

"But underneath it all they were still whores."

"Whores, whores, and nothing but whores."

"The most beautiful."

"Most talented."

"And most wicked whores this nation will ever know."

While Señora Esperon sat with eyes closed and a face that registered no emotion except the fatigue that comes from having lived a long time, she listened to the sisters tell their new customers from the North that she had kidnapped thirty innocent girls who had faces like starved dogs and bodies like snakes, but within one short year she had transformed them into creatures whose beauty could never be denied.

"How did she find them?" a newcomer asked.

"In the most devious ways," the sisters said.

"She searched the orphanages."

"The foreign ships."

"The Gypsy camps."

"She prowled the city's most desperate streets."

"And in the dead of night she knocked on doors in search of pretty daughters to buy for a wink and a promise half made."

"She took them home and scrubbed them clean."

"And groomed their hair."

"And bought their clothes."

"And forced them to swallow a foul-tasting liquid that turned their skin yellow, but in one week's time, the parasites living in their stomachs were gone forever."

Had she been one to confess such things, the Señora could have said that many of the stories the beauticians told did, in fact, contain a seed of truth. Because of her father she had learned a thing or two about poisons, and her earrings were indeed containers for deadly substances, but she had never robbed a snake of its venom or captured spiders with her bare hands. She had, however, made a practice of concealing tiny vials of a deadly potion in flowers and lamp shades or glued beneath her long fingernails. Then there were the rumors about her knives and where she kept them, sometimes in a fan, sometimes in the binding of a book, the lining of a coat, the brim of a hat, or brought forth when necessary from the depths of her long delicate throat.

"She always keeps a dagger concealed here," said one of the sisters as she stuck a finger into her opened mouth, "and she will spit it up and kill you with it if you cross her."

So many lies, Señora Esperon thought, while the ornaments were being placed in her hair. So many beautiful, beautiful lies, but at the same time so close to the truth.

She could have set the sisters straight on many points where reality stopped and legend began, but her legend interested her far more than the reality of her life, so she allowed the beauticians to ramble on and on, inventing what they wanted around the particle of truth they already knew, and they seemed to know everything. Everything more or less, Señora Esperon thought. They do not know how I acquired my girls.

Contrary to what the sisters said, she had never traveled on a broomstick for the purpose of purchasing young virgins for the price of a kiss and a promise half made. Nor had she cast a hypnotic spell with her eyes that lured them back to her house where she reshaped their young faces by forcing them to wear plaster masks for an entire year. "My daughters," she could have said, "were sent to me by the ancient gods who do not require a name, a cross, a holy trinity, or a church filled with gold."

But she did not say this. She sat quietly until her hair was perfectly arranged, until the sisters became exhausted with talk, and the last jeweled clip and ornamental comb were placed to her liking.

"These diamonds," a sister informed a customer, "they are real. Don't fool yourself by thinking there are not. And the rubies, they are real also. The occasion must be very special for Señora Esperon to bring her good jewels into the streets."

"Cover her head with a scarf, or else she'll be robbed at the front door," the customer said. "She's entertaining the president today, and I have been told by reliable sources that she will present him with a very impressive gift."

Yes, the president is coming to lunch, Señora Esperon thought. And I will give him a gift, but he will never know how truly impressive it is.

"The president will adore you," one of the sisters shouted into the Señora's ear. "You look sixteen years old today,"

"But I do not feel sixteen," she answered. "Given the life I've lived, it is impossible to feel sixteen because I was never allowed to be sixteen."

Having said that, she paid the sisters their normal fee plus extra for the placing of the ornaments, and with a black scarf tied around her head, she departed rapidly; the morning was already passing into afternoon and there was still so much to do.

Along the avenue a crowd had gathered to watch a marching band, but Señora Esperon did not recognize one familiar face. Most of the spectators, even the Indians, were dressed in T-shirts with words she did not understand printed across the front. "What is this word on your shirt?" she asked a young girl. "Is it the name of your village?"

"No," she answered.

"The name of your family then?"

"No," came the reply in a haughty tone of voice, "it's the name of the person who designed this shirt."

"And what does this say about you?" Señora Esperon inquired, and the girl answered by turning her head.

"Everything," the Señora sighed. "It says everything." With an anxious heart and one hand covering her mouth and nose, she continued on her way, dropping coins into the hands of beggars, while trying not to notice the garbage accumulating along the avenue.

At her front door, the carnival employee called to her once again. "Remember, Señora, I'm saving the first ride for you."

"If we live that long," she answered. "The air has been poisoned and so have we." Quickly she entered her house and the cool green of her courtyard where the air did not sting her lungs and the tapestry of many colors hung like a banner to celebrate in advance the passing of a great day.

Fuerte was standing on the gallery. "Can you see it?" Señora Esperon asked.

"I can see enough to know," Fuerte said. "One more panel and we can rest."

"Give me one of your dresses to wear. The day calls for more colors than I have in my closet."

Fuerte gave her a dress heavily embroidered with the history of her village. Señora Esperon read it aloud.

> *Three times we were invaded.*
> *Three times we were burned.*
> *And three times our temples were destroyed.*
> *And after the third time,*
> *New temples were built on top of old temples.*
> *And the conquerors said:*
> *This is very good.*
> *The old gods will be forgotten,*
> *And the new will be remembered.*
> *And only the saved will go to Heaven.*
> *But the people said:*
> *Heaven is for all.*
> *And the old gods did not vanish with the new,*
> *And the new gods did not vanish with the old.*

Wearing Fuerte's dress, which fell to her ankles, she returned to the wicker chair, the calling parrots, and sweet memories of beautiful daughters arranged on the staircase like birds of paradise ready to greet the visitors of the evening. "Every night," she said, "there was champagne to wash away the day and salute the darkness. Every night this house was filled with poetry. Every night these rooms came alive with singing."

"Such things must be forgotten," Contenta replied in a scolding voice when she came to feed the fish. "The president will soon arrive, and then what will we do?" In desperation, she flung a handful of crumbs into the pool, and the surface of the water boiled with hungry goldfish and tiny frogs. "There is too much agitation today," she said, "even the fish and the frogs feel it. Watching them fight for the tiniest crumb makes me very nervous."

"Then I advise you not to watch them," Señora Esperon told her. "Today will be over tomorrow. That should be a relief to you."

Contenta reminded her that the only recognizable relief was the promise of Eternity, and without faith in that promise, life would be meaningless. While expounding upon the necessity of faith she noticed for the first time that her employer had changed dresses. "Señora!" she cried, "Why are you wearing so many colors? At your age it is not becoming; it is not done!"

"What has become of senility?" Señora Esperon asked. "By now, I expected to be living in a mindless bliss."

"You have not answered my question," Contenta protested. "Try not to think so much about yourself. And when you've learned to do that, try not to think at all. Thinking too much is a bad thing, especially for you."

"Not thinking is impossible." Señora Esperon raised her voice. "Why do you thrust the impossible upon me at my age? She closed her eyes to dream of glorious tropical nights and beautiful daughters singing to her from distant chambers. "The years I spent with my girls were the most satisfying years of my life. Their presence in this grand house kept me from sinking into despair and uncontrollable rage while I waited for this day."

"Ask God to relieve you of your anger," Contenta said.

"There is no relief for this anger," Señora Esperon sighed. "Even at my age, anger is my unwanted but constant companion, but today I will put it to rest."

"What will happen today, Señora?" Contenta asked. "And what will we serve? You have not yet given me the menu, and it's almost too late to make a plan."

"Every question has already been answered," the Señora assured her, "and there is no escaping the past or the future. My father was murdered. My mother's character distorted. Our great president Carlos Serrano was tortured and killed along with Carlota Montejo and countless poets who gave us hope and something sublime to live for. And now my city is overrun with smoking factories and tall buildings that interrupt the view to the open sea, to the mountains, and our once golden marshes. I am a prisoner in my own home because the air outside is poison, and the noise of the modern day has caused my head to ache without ceasing. So what must I do? Dream pleasantly of days gone by? Or become too angry to die in peace?"

"Pray," Contenta said.

"Dream," the Señora replied. "Long ago, I chose the dream. Without it the present day would be unbearable."

"Dreams are foolish," Contenta argued.

"Dreams are necessary, Contenta, and tears also."

"If only my tears would return," she sighed. "The only tears my eyes know are artificial ones." She squeezed drops into each eye and blinked aggressively. "When will I be able to cry again?"

"I don't know, Contenta," Señora Esperon said. She leaned back in her father's chair and tried to relax her restless mind. She closed her eyes, and once again she was with her daughters, and once again her dream was interrupted by the memory of cannons and guns that rocked the foundation of her house.

"The Forty Years of Peace is over," she said as Contenta was returning to the kitchen.

"Who are you talking to this time?" she asked.

"My Daughters," the Señora continued, "this country will never be what it once was, and even if it should be again, it would not be the place for any of you because even when it was it was no better than it has become. I will send you away with purses filled with riches. Some of you will marry, and some of you will continue in my tradition, but one thing is certain, each week you shall write to me, and each day I shall write to one of you, and long after you are no longer here, I shall be sustained by the sweetest memories."

"The mail has not been delivered today," Contenta said, thinking this might bring her employer back to the present.

"Of course not," she answered. "It is a national holiday, and the industrialists have arrived. The factories are open, but the post office is closed. Everything has changed, but I shall not change with it."

Contenta returned to the kitchen, and Señora Esperon chased away shadows by rereading letters of the previous week. All thirty daughters had written to her from various corners of the world. She could remember their names, addresses, and faces almost better than she could remember her own, and over the years her desire to see them had increased considerably, but not to the extent that she would allow one of them to visit her. In her letters she reminded them that she was too old to endure the strain of a visitor, but she appreciated kind thoughts as well as boxes of chocolate that the postman had been instructed to deliver before the heat of the day touched them.

"No, you must not visit me now," she had recently written to the eldest daughter who had been the first to leave.

The Street of Merchants and Peddlers is not the same. The opera house is a shopping mall, the National Theatre is long destroyed, and the museums are closed forever, their collections sold to foreign investors. Now the streets, even the narrow ones, are congested with buses, and the trees in the French Park are covered with plastic bags that have blown in from the landfills. There are no more egrets. There is no singing in the streets. Few flowering trees shade our avenues and boulevards. And the beaches are rotting with dead fish. More than twenty years have passed since I last saw you, and suddenly, or so it seems, everything has been reinvented. No, you may not call me because I still do not have a telephone. The need for one escapes me. No, I do not understand what you have written about popular entertainment. The world has gone mad for television, and the three sisters, who speak of you affectionately, own a total of five sets, and they are always turned on because they have obviously lost the instructions or the good sense for turning them off.

Yes, Fuerte is still with me. Yes, I arrange her threads every day. Yes, she is almost finished. We are all almost finished and soon we will rest. Yes everything is different now, and you must not return. Do not visit me, I beg you. You would recognize Fuerte and Contenta but you would not recognize me. You would not even recognize the city. Of this, I am quite certain.

When the exiled daughter received the letter she responded at once:

But the house, surely I would recognize the house, and the rooms, those beautiful rooms. Surely they have not been destroyed also.

To this Señora Esperon replied:

The house is still standing but only barely. Yes, we manage to dust some of the rooms each week, but Contenta has grown too old to take care of them properly, as have I. Yes, there are leaks in the roof, and the bougainvillea has invaded a room or two, but nothing has been damaged that cannot be easily repaired, and therefore, nothing has changed. Yes, I am lonely without you. Yes, the solitude has crept into my bones. The marrow has been loosened and rattles like seeds in a gourd when I walk. My joints are stiff, but I can still take the stairs. No, you would not recognize me now.

On the marble staircase she could still see her daughters arranged like exotic birds. Her sweet memories drifted along the gallery to the many bedrooms that she entered without leaving her father's chair. In each room the lace curtains, the silk walls, the bedspreads, and lamp shades had been touched by the mellow fingers of age and all the mirrors were dark. Somewhere not far away she heard champagne being poured into long-stemmed glasses. She heard her favorite poems recited by the poet himself, and she heard her daughters laughing or singing as they led gentlemen into the splendidly furnished rooms where girls of ordinary birth became goddesses in the eyes of presidents and poets who had slept there.

From time to time throughout her retirement she had considered opening her doors to the public once again, but each time the consideration surfaced, she quickly realized her limitations. She had neither the strength to train another round of girls, nor the desire to adjust to a new clientele. "Today people would come here only to satisfy their curiosity," she said to her preening parrots. "They would complain of high prices, and speak in a slang I do not care to hear in my home."

"The Lord be with you," one of the parrots screamed.

"There shall be no discussion of religion in this house." The Señora, spoke not to the bird but to her daughters who had returned to visit her afternoon dream. "We have four rules governing proper behavior, and the other three are as follows: There shall be no discussion of politics with a guest. There shall be no show of partiality by allowing love to interfere with our work. And there shall be no coarse words spoken in this house. We shall not indulge in common language."

"Hail Mary full of grace," a parrot replied, but Señora Espe-ron did not hear what the bird had said. Her eyes were closed and her daughters were listening attentively.

"Of these four rules, my Daughters, one is considered far more serious than the others. I can understand falling in love. I can forgive the expressing of political opinions and religious mores, but speaking in the vernacular is most egregious and will never be tolerated inside this house."

"Señora, wake up!" Contenta came running from the kitch-en. "You're talking in your sleep again. I hope you're dreaming about your luncheon." She gave the Señora a hard shake to wake her up.

The parrots fluttered to the ground, and Señora Esperon sat upright in her chair. "I was dreaming about my daughters," she answered. "And you rudely interrupted me."

"You should have been dreaming about the menu," Contenta said in a scolding voice.

"I dream of my daughters every day," the Señora replied. "I dream of the days when this house was filled with the rich and the talented. You remember those days, don't you?"

"Oh, I try not to, Señora," Contenta confessed without shame. "That is not such a good thing to dream about. At your age you should dream only of Paradise."

"I was dreaming of Paradise," Señora Esperon answered sharply. "You seem to be confused again. Wake up Contenta."

"I woke up early this morning," she replied. "The sun did not confuse me today. I knew it was morning."

"Then I am wrong," Señora Esperon responded in exaspera-tion. "Pay me no mind."

"You remember too many things that you should forget," Contenta said. "You must put all your memories behind you."

"Memories are my only solace against the greed that walks these streets, Contenta. Memories are my shield, and your God is my sounding board. Everyday I remind him of the disgrace he has allowed to visit this city."

"The disgrace," Contenta said, "is part of God's plan. We should not question Him for doing what He does because His purpose will be revealed at the right time. Even in my own mother's tragic death there is a divine purpose."

After speaking her mind, Contenta took a bottle of eye drops from her pocket and squeezed three tears into each eye.

"I shall discuss this tiresome subject no more," Señora Esperon said.

She returned to her dream, and Contenta returned to her kitchen, there to worry over the state of the Señora's soul and to wait anxiously for the president. While waiting she rewashed the morning dishes, swept the floor, and dusted the vigas with a rag tied to a pole. At two o'clock, she doctored her eyes once again. At two fifteen she boiled a pot of water. And at two thirty, she was nervously rearranging the contents of a kitchen cupboard when a loud knock at the front door shattered the peaceful courtyard and reverberated through the kitchen causing Contenta's hands to tremble and cups to rattle in their saucers.

"Señora," Contenta shouted from the kitchen. "Señora, they are here and we're not ready. What shall I do?"

"We are ready, Contenta." Señora Esperon rose to her feet. "Invite them into the sala. I will do the rest."

Contenta raced to the door and froze before it. "I cannot move! I cannot open the door! We are not ready!"

"Move!" Señora Esperon demanded. "Open it at once!"

"No," Contenta argued. "I can't. I do not wish to disappoint them."

"When all is said and done disappointment will be the last thing on their minds," the Señora said. "Now let them in!"

Against her better judgment, Contenta threw open the door and in marched the secretary of commerce, the secretary of natural resources, and the secretary of tourism, all corpulent men in military uniform with ribbons and medals decorating their chests. Behind them came mother superior of the Carmelite order, and behind her came the archbishop, sweating under the weight of his vestments. On entering the foyer that led to the courtyard, they stood to one side and waited for the president to make his entrance. Half first cousin to natural resources, the archbishop, and tourism; brother of the secretary of commerce and uncle of the Carmelite, the president, who had spent the better part of the morning covering his moles and lowering his hairline, waited outside the door until his advisers were standing in place. After the secretary of commerce blew three sharp blasts on a whistle, two presidential guards in plumed helmets marched through the entrance. Directly behind them, the president, also decorated with medals, ribbons, and gold braids, entered the house with military dispatch, his ceremonial saber scraping the wall. In one hand he carried a folio of legal documents requiring signatures, and in the other a fountain pen filled with indelible ink. Behind him came two more guards in plumed helmets, and when all four were standing in place, two on either side of the president, Contenta closed the door and bolted it.

The guards remained at the entrance, and the dignitaries were led into the gran sala filled with Persian carpets overlapping Persian carpets and cathedral chairs pushed against the four walls covered with burgundy silk and many layers of dust. In the center of the room was a Divan Circulaire upholstered in royal blue, and on either side of it matching Victorian sofas with lion-paw feet were covered with fringed scarves, embroidered saris, and mantillas, all gifts from sea captains, bankers, and diplomats. Next to one of the sofas was a teakwood table, on which Señora Esperon had displayed Eufemia's well-worn copy of *The Way of Perfection*.

"The Señora will be slightly delayed," Contenta announced. She hurried from the room closing the double doors behind her and leaving the guests to themselves.

The air in the sala was stale with mildew and heat. Two windows giving onto the street were closed, and when the president ordered them opened, his first cousin, the secretary of natural resources, discovered that they were nailed shut and further secured with chains and padlocks. "If we ever become as wealthy as our friend," the president said, "and as crazy, I might add, we'll probably nail our windows shut also."

Striving to make a good impression, Contenta reentered the room with a tray of glasses, two bottles of wine, and news that the Señora would be along shortly. "At this moment a beautiful soup is being prepared," she said. "I think it will please you very much." She assured them once more that the wait would not be a long one, and after she had left the room, the secretary of tourism filled the glasses. "Wine from our family vineyards," he said. "This bottle is almost sixty years old. She thinks of everything, or so they say."

In the airless room they drank to the prosperity of the nation and to the nation's church, to their ruling family and their own good fortune in being invited to the Señora's house to hear her important announcement.

"Why do you suppose she has suddenly decided to receive us?" asked the secretary of commerce. "She's very cunning. Do you think we're in danger?"

"Certainly not," the president replied in a distracted tone. He was reviewing the legal documents that controlled the ownership of her house and all its contents, her bank accounts, if any existed, and the use of her name for purposes of advertising. "She's too old and sentimental to be dangerous. We're here because she knew my father. In her advanced age she misses him and wishes to bestow upon us a few tokens of gratitude."

"Oh, yes," mother superior added, "I have been told that she knew your father, my grandfather, quite well."

"She knew *our* father even better," replied the archbishop.

"Indeed she did," added natural resources.

"Yes, indeed," echoed tourism.

"You are speaking of your father, who was murdered the night before he was to wed the Señora," the president said. "Yes, she knew him quite well. But she knew my father, the mayor of the city, before she knew yours."

"The Señora knows everyone quite well," mother superior spoke up quickly. "Even the people she does not know, she knows quite well; at least that's what I've been told." The Carmelite, who was entering her fortieth year, and her first as mother superior, was overcome by the heat and alcohol. Beads of sweat appeared on her upper lip and dropped into her wine that she drank rapaciously. On emptying her glass, she asked for a bit more, and the archbishop, who at the age of sixty-five still had the face of a choir boy and the soft delicate hands of a dilettante, poured another glass for her, and himself as well, while the secretary of natural resources inspected the liquor cabinet in search of something stronger. The president preferred Jamaican rum and ordered natural resources to pour a round for everyone.

"No more for me," mother superior said, and the president replied, "Yes, more. Give it to her."

After emptying their glasses the men stood to loosen their ties and remove their coats. Their starched, white shirts had already gone limp in the humidity, and sweat stains were beginning to appear under their arms, but neither the heat nor the lack of fresh air stopped them from filling their glasses again.

In the kitchen just across the courtyard, Señora Esperon, who was far more prepared for this day than Contenta had ever imagined, was issuing instructions as to the final preparation of the soup. "It's a cold soup," she explained, "but I do not mean to imply that it is uncooked. Its flavors are heightened by the fervor of our prayers."

"A soup of prayers?" Contenta asked.

"No," the Señora replied. "A soup to be prayed over. The more it is prayed over, the more delicious it becomes. But the lid must not be lifted until the tureen reaches the table otherwise the flavors will escape."

That being said, she turned her attention to the hors d'oeuvres. Half a loaf of stale bread was sliced into thin rounds, and on each she spread a generous portion of black caviar. Then she arranged the appetizers on two plates, a gold one for the president, the secretary of commerce, and mother superior, and a silver one for the archbishop, the secretaries of natural resources and tourism.

"In this house immediate family members are expected to share the same plate," she explained.

"The bread is very old," Contenta said.

"But the soup is very fresh," the Señora replied.

Her most devoted parrot alighted on her head and accompanied her across the courtyard and into the sala. The guests rose to their feet when she entered the room, and the parrot flapped its wings as if it were about to fly away with her jeweled head in its claws.

"Your fathers were great friends of mine," Señora Esperon reminded the men. "And for that reason I find it astonishing that we have never broken bread or shared a bottle of wine. During the FortyYears of Peace, none of you visited my salon, but of course, music and poetry did not speak to you then as they do now so we must quickly make up for lost time." In the dim light the jewels in her hair sparkled like a crown of stars, and the parrot, inching its way down her arm toward one of the plates, cried loudly, "The Lord be with you."

"What a divine creature," mother superior said excitedly.

"No! No!" The Señora scolded her pet for stealing a crust of bread. "This is not for you. This is for our president to enjoy." The parrot flew to mother superior with the bread in its beak and landed on her lap. She received the bread in both hands and the parrot exclaimed. "Pray for us sinners!"

"This is a holy bird," the Carmelite exclaimed. She put the bread on her tongue as if it were a sacrament and the bird burrowed into the folds of her habit.

"I believe you have a new friend," Señora Esperon said. Then she presented the president with the gold plate, and begged him to share freely with his closest kin. Reluctantly, the president received the plate in both hands and offered the morsels of food to his brother who was not so hesitant.

"What is it?" the president asked.

"Caviar," the archbishop replied cheerfully.

"Thank God it's something edible," the president whispered as the first hors d'oeuvre disappeared into his mouth.

"Delicious," added the secretary of commerce. "But what unusual bread. Who baked it, Señora?"

"Our Father who art in Heaven," the parrot replied emerging from the nun's habit.

Mother superior forced an hors d'oeuvre into her mouth and made the sign of the cross. "This bird is a saint," she exclaimed.

"Yes," Señora Esperon replied. "It's surprising where the next saint will turn up, isn't it?" Without pausing for response she proceeded to the business at hand. "I have called you here for personal reasons. As you must know, I have no desire to live forever, and today, the day of our independence, I am prepared to distribute a portion of my wealth, but first we must get to know one another a little better."

She sat on one of the scarf-covered sofas and faced her guests. The parrot flapped its wings and took to the air. The archbishop let out a piercing shriek when the bird flew past him, and he fanned his face in relief when it alighted on the chandelier of Venetian glass. Gasping for his breath, he requested a bit of fresh air, and Señora Esperon, after apologizing for the stuffiness of the room, advised him to make an appeal to his brother the secretary of natural resources.

"I have already tried to open the window," he said.

"It is not the inside air, to which I refer," the Señora replied.

Speaking around his hors d'oeuvre, natural resources answered her rapidly. "The air quality has greatly improved within the last few months. In fact we are looking into the possibility of covering the entire historical district, including the harbor, with a dome made of the latest hard plastic manufactured here in our plant."

"And where is our beautiful plant located?" the Señora inquired.

"It was built over the marsh," the president replied chewing rigorously.

"From mud and silence," Señora Esperon said. "Life began in the marsh so why not plastic as well."

"The Lord bless you and keep you," the parrot chanted in Contenta's voice.

Mother superior looked up reverently at the parrot on the chandelier and the parrot looked down upon her and said, "I thirst. I thirst."

"We all thirst," said the nun. "The entire world is in need of spiritual sustenance."

"Enough of that," said the president.

"Silence! Give me silence!" the parrot said in the voice of Señora Esperon.

"I must remind you, that sacred animals have long been part of my family's tradition," Señora Esperon said. "My mother, a Carmelite at heart, arrived in our capital with three orange trees, a husband who was a doctor, and a monkey who was an angel." She opened Eufemia's copy of *The Way of Perfection* and read aloud a handwritten note on the endpapers:

"The voyage to our new home was long and tumultuous. Everyday this book was read to my beloved Angel because only the words of our dear saint would calm his anxiety on the high seas."

"The words of our blessed Eufemia give comfort to us all," the Carmelite said. Her eyes drifted around the room, which she had already transformed into a library for her order. "Your mother," she added, "would surely be pleased to know that her house was being used to promote Saint Teresa's teachings. With its many rooms, it would make a fine convent."

"Perhaps not," Señora Esperon replied thoughtfully. She opened the book to a marked page and read:

". . . let our houses be small and poor in every way. Let us to some extent resemble our King who had no house save the porch in Bethlehem where He was born and the Cross on which He died. These were houses where little comfort could be found. Those who erect large houses will no doubt have good reasons for doing so. I do not utterly condemn them: they are moved by various holy intentions. But as for a large ornate convent—God preserve us from that. Always remember that these things will all fall down on the Day of Judgment, and who knows how soon that will be?"

"Saint Teresa's words are most profound," mother superior stated emphatically, "but we must also take into consideration that it was a different day that inspired them."

"Yes, it was," Josefina Esperon replied. "But we must remember that the very same scroll is wound and rewound throughout time. Nothing is new. Nothing is old."

For a moment she drifted away. Where do I go from here? she wondered. And then she remembered the sandals. "The hour has come to present the first gift of the day." The guests leaned forward in nervous anticipation. "Mother superior, allow me to honor you before I honor the gentlemen?" From beneath the sofa she brought forth a pair of Eufemia's sandals and invited the Carmelite to try them on.

With pleasure the nun removed her own sandals and slipped her feet into Eufemia's. "If you wear them for any length of time," the Señora said, "you may notice that there are many sharp tacks that penetrate the soles and pierce the feet. In this way my mother was constantly reminded of the suffering Jesus."

Suddenly she stood up, "Enough of this melancholia. Come, I wish to give you a tour of my house, there are no fewer than forty-three rooms, so fortify yourselves now or bring your glasses along, which ever you prefer." Armed with *The Way of Perfection*, she crossed to the double doors and threw them open. "God give us relief from the darkness of this world and this room," she said. "What we need is some light to lift our spirits."

"Light, light, let there be light," the parrot exclaimed and the Carmelite applauded its performance.

The president swallowed an hors d'oeuvre and refilled his glass. His brothers and cousins did likewise, and presently, they followed their hostess into the courtyard where she called their attention to the glass ceiling, and the fresh air. "It is the air," she said to natural resources, "mine not yours, that has kept me alive so long."

"When we build our dome," he said, "our entire city will be

protected like your courtyard."

"I *live* for that day," the Señora replied.

"If I may say so," added the secretary of tourism, "your house would make a splendid hotel. Named in your honor of course."

"I *live* for that day, also," she added and turned abruptly to the archbishop. "Under the protection of your church, this became the most famous house in the nation, and possibly because of you it will go on enjoying a certain fame."

"Oh, yes," he responded eagerly, "an orphanage for my young boys."

"The younger the better, I'm sure." Señora Esperon smiled, leading her guests rapidly toward the orange trees. "Three of them are almost a hundred years old," she said. "Their life span, of course, has to do with their enclosure. The poison rain has never touched them."

"The problem is being rectified," the secretary of natural resources assured her.

"If I could only believe that," the Señora replied, "my problems would be over. I would leave my house and fortune to science."

"May I suggest an academy for the preservation of the environment?" Natural resources spoke up quickly. "I would be honored to administrate."

"The upstairs rooms are quite interesting," the Señora responded. "Come let me show them."

The men followed her to the staircase leaving mother superior standing between the graves of Carlota Montejo and Eufemia Esperon. "Each woman made an indelible impression on this country," she said. "Every historian has said so; they are unavoidable. Unfortunately, I was born too late to have known them."

"Too late to have known them, yes, but not too late," Señora Esperon said. "I will show you photographs of them. Come along."

"I have something to show you as well," the Carmelite said in a conspiratorial whisper.

"I'm sure you do," Señora Esperon replied.

On the gallery level she led the visitors into various chambers with high ceilings and narrow windows giving onto the courtyard. In each room the bed was carefully made, and the silk damask that covered ceilings and walls was rotting with mold. Shade-loving ferns grew from cracks above the doors, from window facings, and bookcases, the contents of which were decaying rapidly. While the afternoon visitors searched for something to say, the room they were inspecting filled with an oppressive silence, broken at last by a wasp buzzing through shreds of blue silk hanging from the ceiling.

"At one time each room in this half of the house was a different shade of red, yellow, or blue," the Señora said, "but in the second half, the rooms were shades of orange, green, and purple. The colors were not garish but pastel; in some of the rooms there was only a hint of color."

"All of them could be beautifully restored," said the secretary of tourism. "I could send someone over to record each color and take samples. Then we could send you around the world to buy the perfect silk and accessories."

"For the official residency, of course," interrupted the president.

"I was thinking in terms of a hotel-spa that would attract a world-class traveler," replied the secretary of tourism.

"A bank and a stock exchange would be more practical," added the secretary of commerce.

Ignoring the differences of opinion, Señora Esperon gestured to a wall of photographs: men in military uniform standing on the steps of the National Palace, men in tuxedos on the grand staircase of the opera house, and policemen sitting in the courtyard on an afternoon of celebration. "Here is a picture of your father who at the time of his tragic death was the mayor of this city," she said to the president and the secretary of commerce. "Your grandfather," she added for the benefit of the Carmelite. "And the man standing next to him is the father of Our Excellency, the archbishop, as well as the father of our secretaries of tourism and natural resources. He was governor at the time of this photograph, but after the unspeakable tragedy that took most of your family he became the president of the country and my fiancé who was brutally assassinated on a dark street. See what handsome brothers they were. The city mourned their deaths for weeks on end. Every flag flew at half-mast, and every window was darkened. What a tragedy it was; depriving you of the opportunity to know them well."

Watching her guests crowd around the picture convinced her that she was correct if not accurate in her identification of the two men. The photograph had faded beyond recognition, but she insisted again that the two men standing before a spiral staircase were easily recognized as her dearest friends. Mother superior stepped closer for a better view of her grandfather and great-uncle. Her kinsmen, edging her to one side, pressed their faces close to the frame and adjusted their glasses while Señora Esperon bowed her head and pronounced the two brothers the greatest of men. "Great in all ways of greatness."

"May I have this photograph?" the president asked.

She wiped her eyes with a lace handkerchief but did not raise her head. "Take it," she wept. "It is yours."

"We were children when they were murdered," the president said. "If we had only known them, they could have taught us so much."

Quickly rearranging her history to serve her immediate purpose, Señora Esperon spoke as if every word carried a sad memory. "All the men on this wall of photographs did not come to my house to learn. They came for pleasure. But I took it upon myself to instill in them a sense of equality and the true meaning of democracy as I understood it from my father and his friend, the great president Carlos Serrano, who was adopted into your family. But everything I said to these seekers of pleasure was immediately forgotten once they were elected to public office, for it is the nature of men in high places to misuse wisdom."

"Not always," the secretaries spoke up in unison.

"Oh yes, always," Señora Esperon replied in a forceful voice, giving her attention to another wall of pictures. "The men in this photograph, for example. Do you recognize them?"

"It's hard to say," said the president. "The photo is very faded."

"When they were young," Josefina Esperon replied, "they belonged to your opposition, and they were mine. When they were young they sang and recited poetry, but when they were older and famous, they changed their affiliation and lost their sweet voices; they lost their love for verse, and they declared war on the poets who once frequented these rooms along with them."

"Those poets," the president said, "were rebels."

"Subversives," argued the secretary of natural resources.

"Traitors," shouted the secretary of commerce.

"And truthful," added mother superior.

Silence descended under the weight of her disclosure, which she realized had been too candid for the occasion. "Yes," she said in defiance. "I have read them all." Turning abruptly to leave the room, rather than face the wrath of her family, she walked rapidly toward the door but was stopped by a photograph of Carlota Montejo. Inscribed to Josefina Esperon on her twelfth birthday, the photograph hung in a gilded frame and had been given a wall of its own. Captured in her most famous role, the actress was wearing a Grecian tunic. Her arms were outstretched, begging the gods for mercy, and her eyes were focused deliriously upon the Heavens. Across the costume she had written one line from Racine. "The Gods have lit within my breast, a fatal flame that gives no rest."

As if she had stepped into the shoes of the actress rather than the saint, mother superior read the inscription aloud and added to it. "'Those evil Gods who torture my day, have carried my fragile heart away.'"

"How do you come to know that line?" Señora Esperon asked.

"It is a story too long for the telling," the Carmelite answered and left the room quickly.

"Don't get her started," said the secretary of commerce.

"Another time, perhaps," the Señora replied.

"You must remember," the president said, "that my late sister was not exactly one of us. She was adopted at birth, and her daughter, though she may have risen rapidly and to a very high place within the church, has much of her mother inside her."

"Her grandmother as well," said the secretary of commerce.

"Let us not discuss this subject again," pleaded the archbishop.

"What a family you do have," Señora Esperon replied. "It makes my head swim to think of it; all of these half brothers, half cousins, and adopted sisters not to mention stepmothers, foster mothers, no mothers, superior mothers. How do manage to keep up with yourselves?"

Without soliciting a response she led her guests around the gallery and through the upper passage where they could look down on the small courtyard overgrown with weedy plants and flowering vines that she identified as if she were a doctor herself. "*Passiflora incarnata* for your aching nerves. Contribo for your terrible hangovers. *Lobelia cardinalis* to indurate ulcers, to treat stomach ache, syphilis, and parasites. *Picaria* for sweet blood, and *Datura stramonium* for sickness at sea. Here we have *Atropa belladonna* to brighten your eyes as well as your mind, and over there the Flower of Utopia will see you gracefully on your way."

Rising above the plants were seventeen marble hearts, and balanced on top of each was a blue bowl filled with water and petals. "Like my mother," Señora Esperon explained, "the poets must have their own water, and it must be scented with petals because their spirits are far too delicate to drink at the fountain. My father's spirit drinks at the fountain. The great president Serrano drinks there with him, and so does Carlota Montejo. On still nights you can hear them discussing equality among all men, and from time to time Montejo, not unlike our mother superior, will recite a few lines from Racine's *Phèdre*. On those occasions the poets will gladly join in. They were not citizens of this world, and for that reason they were poets, and for that reason your administration threw their dead bodies against my door. One by one I buried them myself, and their spirits will protect this place forevermore. Should this house crumble to dust, the poets will continue to sing."

"A fantastic ghost story, Señora," exclaimed the secretary of tourism. "If we convert your house into a luxury hotel, tourists from all over the world will come to drink at the fountain along with your ghosts, and you will be remembered forever."

"Perhaps you are right after all," said the president.

"There is no danger in my ever being forgotten," Señora Esperon reminded them. Then she motioned for her guests to follow her around the gallery, but mother superior, complaining that the tacks were beginning to pierce the soles of her feet, sat down on a bench for relief. "I'm afraid I will leave a trail of blood all over your floors and carpets," she said.

"What of it?" Señora Esperon replied. "My mother would approve of that."

"God is permitting me to remove your mother's shoes, now," mother superior insisted.

"You're still young, you can bear it," Señora Esperon responded. "My carpets and floors have seen much bloodshed already. If you remember your history, you will recall that this house was once a convent. During the long struggle to gain independence, your Carmelite sisters were executed along with the insurgents in this very courtyard. A few drops of blood from your sanctified veins will be a blessing to the future of this edifice."

"I am not mentally prepared to receive the Lord's pain today," the Carmelite said, and Señora Esperon, already armed with her answer, opened *The Way of Perfection* and read from a marked page:

"Now what I have just been doing—namely, excusing myself—is very bad for me, and I beg you not to copy it, for to suffer without making excuses is a habit of great perfection, and very edifying and meritorious."

On finishing the passage she placed the book into the Carmelite's hands. "Perhaps, you should keep this copy of St. Teresa's inspired words. Perhaps you need to be reminded of all that is required of your order." Refusing to delay the tour any longer, she quickly led the nun around the gallery that circled the small courtyard. "Look!" she said, pointing upward.

"Yes, yes," the secretary of natural resources responded. "Another glass ceiling."

"This seems to be the appropriate time to bestow my next gift." Señora Esperon turned to face her guests. "Secretary of natural resources, to you I bequeath the air rights above my house."

"Air rights?" he gasped. "Señora, what exactly do you have in mind?"

"Another skyscraper, of course," she replied, "one that will graze the ceiling of your plastic dome and bear your name in lights."

"The air rights should be included in the acquisition of the property," argued the secretary of tourism. "A first-class hotel with two courtyards cannot exist with an office building on top of it."

"But a bank and stock exchange could make good use of air rights," added the secretary of commerce. "Señora, it is my hope that you will reconsider."

"And mine also," the president said emphatically.

"No," argued Natural Resources. "She has stated her wishes very clearly."

"Come, come," the Señora insisted. "This silly discussion can wait."

Beyond a narrow door, she led them through a maze of rooms overgrown with bougainvillea, which had all but obscured a long damp corridor inhabited by bats. At the end of the corridor was a small window no bigger than a head, through which a shaft of light fell upon a door of reinforced steel. With five keys, the Señora opened the door to a dark closet and asked the five men to retrieve the five strong boxes she had stored there. "The contents of these chests will thrill you," she said, "but we must take them into my apartment where there's enough light for you to enjoy the treasures I have accumulated."

The archbishop's opulent vestments and delicate hands did not exclude him from the task at hand, nor was mother superior exempt from carrying a small inlaid box placed directly into her arms. But the locked chests were far too heavy for the men to lift so they resorted to pushing them down the narrow passage and onto the gallery.

"Let us stop here," the president said. "Here we have light to see your treasures."

"In my apartment there are comfortable chairs," Señora Esperon replied. "You haven't much farther to go."

Once in the sitting room, she opened the door to Eufemia's chapel and the Carmelite, whose soles were indeed bleeding on the carpet, fell prostrate before the altar, while the men, reeking of sweat and cigars, collapsed on sofas and soft chairs covered in rich brocades and fringed scarves. "Rest, rest," the Señora, said. "Even you deserve to rest on occasion." Passing through the room, she stirred pots of sweet incense to give the air a pleasant aroma, which she promised would awaken lost powers in the most obstinate of men.

Hearing this, the secretary of commerce asked where she might have acquired such a potion, and whether or not it had been medically proven, but the Señora, ignoring his sudden interest in her essence, smiled knowingly and proceeded to open the five chests. In two of them paper notes were carefully bundled according to denomination. "Still as crisp as the day they were earned," she said. In the other three there were coins of silver and gold.

The contents of the boxes brought the men to their feet. "There's enough wealth here to cover our entire country in a plastic dome," Señora Esperon said. "Please do not tax yourselves with excitement."

The president dropped to his knees to touch the coins. "Can they be real?" he asked his brother.

The secretary of commerce held up a gold coin for inspection. "Good God!" he said. "The year fifteen thirty-five! Here we have a small fortune, in one coin alone."

While the men of government inspected the riches, Señora Esperon deposited the small box into the archbishop's hands and opened it with a key. The box was filled with loose jewels, opals, rubies, diamonds, and sapphires as large as quail eggs. On seeing them the archbishop squealed with happiness and dropped the box onto the floor. Diamonds, rubies, and emeralds rolled across the Persian carpets, and the archbishop, confessing his weakness for precious stones, fell to his knees to scoop them up. Holding a large emerald against his third finger he trembled. "I am overcome," he said, suddenly making the sign of the cross.

"I see we share the same weakness for precious jewels," Señora Esperon sighed. Circling the room, she removed a scarf covering a bowl of fire opals, another of pearls, and yet another of rubies. "It would seem to me that your love for jewels might far exceed your love for our ever suffering Christ."

"Oh no," the archbishop argued. "Precious jewels reflect the glory and salvation that shines forth through the eyes of our Lord's Son who suffered that we might live."

"It would seem to me," said the president, who no longer realized he was tired, "that you need a financial adviser. Someone to assist you with banking and investment procedures."

"Modern banking and investment procedures, particularly as they exist in our country," replied the Señora, "have never inspired my confidence. Were I to deposit my money in your bank, I would then be forced to pay heavy taxes to a nation that prefers to squander great fortunes on missiles rather than music, on plastic domes rather than poetry."

Having heard little of what she said, the president turned to the secretary of commerce and asked for an estimation of the Señora's worth. After making a few calculations on paper, the secretary said that one box of coins alone would easily pay the national debt.

To this, the Señora replied, "What good would that do? Tomorrow there would be another debt three times as big as the current one."

Before anyone could make a reply, the clocks struck the hour of five o'clock, and Señora Esperon apologized for delaying the lunch. "If we do not proceed to the table at once," she said, "we will not make it there before dinner."

Down the staircase they went, the Señora springing forward with forced energy toward a meal for which she would always be remembered. The president and his secretaries followed her closely, and some distance behind them came the archbishop who had interrupted his niece's meditation by forcing her to rejoin the group. "It is humbling," she confessed, "to wear the sandals of one I have long admired."

The table, covered with linen and lace, was set with Chinese porcelain bowls on which hand-painted peonies attracted swarms of Sulfur butterflies and sea-green hummingbirds that seemed to spawn from the 293 panels.

"None of you has yet admired the tapestry." Señora Esperon said admonishingly. "It's not merely a design but the history of our world from beginning to end. Everything is contained in it, for as you know, we are continually repeating ourselves, and therefore, it is possible to capture the essence of our small planet and all the choices of mankind within two hundred and ninety-three panels written in a language the world has all but forgotten."

"The Indians do not have a written language," said the president.

"Perhaps the few who remain do not," Señora Esperon contended. "But once they did. And I understand every thread of it. The patterns on my dress recount the history of Fuerte's village. Fuerte was my nurse and is my friend. This tapestry is hers, and she is watching us now." She pointed upward. Fuerte was standing on the gallery.

"She has no pupils," said mother superior. "Can she see?"

"She can see everything," the Señora replied. "She's working on the very last panel that will chronicle this day, and days to come."

Deciding to put her to test, the secretary of commerce pointed to a row of dots and designs on the last panel. "What does this say?" he asked.

Only this much did Señora Esperon read aloud and in the current time:

> *The table is set,*
> *The guests have arrived,*
> *And their appetite for riches is strong.*
> *The table is set,*
> *And the feast will begin,*
> *And all the bowls will be filled with precious foods.*

This she did not read:

> *The guests will pray for the food,*
> *But they will not consume it.*
> *They will pray as believers,*
> *And they will pray as nonbelievers.*
> *And when they see that the food*
> *   has not responded to their prayers,*
> *All but one will drink wine,*
> *All but one will make toasts,*
> *And all but one will sing false praises*
> *Until the parrots speak,*
> *And the messenger arrives.*

"It's very interesting," said the president, "but hardly what I call a language."

Disregarding his remarks, Señora Esperon took her place at the head of the table. She invited mother superior to join her on her left, the archbishop on her right, and the president to take the seat directly across from her. "Now I will be able to keep an eye on you," she said to him, as if flirting. "The rest of you must choose for yourself any one of the three remaining chairs, but please, I beg of you, make your choices without a show of conflict."

"What a difficult task that will be," mother superior whispered.

"It is part of their test," Señora Esperon whispered in reply.

"And what is mine?" the Carmelite asked.

"Yours," she was told, "will be ongoing."

Once they were comfortably seated, the eight parrots flew to the orange tree behind the Carmelite. They perched in the branches directly over her head and stared in unison first at one visitor and then another.

"I feel as though we're being watched," said mother superior.

"Not only watched but judged," replied Señora Esperon.

Your parrots are so silent," the president said.

"They know when to speak and when not to speak," the Señora replied.

"Now they're staring at our mother superior," said the archbishop jealously.

"They are fascinated by my habit," she replied. She lifted a hand to one of the birds and they all scrambled along the branches to touch it with their leathery tongues.

"They will bite you," said the secretary of natural resources.

"My parrots do not bite, they kiss," replied Señora Esperon. Then she rang a crystal bell for Contenta to serve the soup, but Contenta did not respond to her employer's call. The bell was rung again. And again the soup did not arrive. The bell was rung yet again. And yet again the soup was not served.

"It must not be ready," the Señora said. Excusing herself from the table she hastened to the kitchen where she found Contenta kneeling before the tureen. "I have prayed and prayed," she said. "But my prayers have not been answered. Yes, I have opened the lid. Yes, I have seen what you did when my back was turned, and yes, I continued praying anyway, but this soup is still not ready and never will be because God is displeased with what you have done."

"How dare you be so presumptuous as to speak for a god," Señora Esperon responded. "Give me the soup at once, and bring candles for the table. The afternoon sun cannot be found."

Returning to her guests with the tureen of soup in hand, Señora Esperon placed it in the center of the table with an apology, not for the added delay but for the soup itself. "It's called Soup of the Transfiguration," she explained. "It has been prepared with loving hands and has been prayed over by glad hearts, but my Contenta tells me that the soup has not yet reached perfection and must be prayed for by a higher authority, someone whose heart is brimming with gladness." Her eyes fell upon the archbishop who folded his hands and delivered a prayer for the perfection of their souls and for the soup as well.

After his prayer, Señora Esperon called for Contenta, whose shattered nerves sent her running to a far corner of the kitchen, to come forward and serve the salubrious concoction. Moments later, Contenta arrived at the table with a candelabra and six burning candles that she placed on a side table and backed away. "The soup," Señora Esperon said. "Surely it's ready by now."

Contenta leaned over the table and slowly removed the lid on a dark and viscous mixture. For a moment, it seemed possible to her that a miracle of transfiguration had indeed taken place for the brown soup appeared to be a hearty brew containing many roots and green vegetables. Serving the president first, she dipped a silver ladle into the tureen and brought it up filled with water plants and movement. A tiny frog jumped from the ladle onto the table."

"Catch it quickly!" the Señora commanded. "The small ones are the most flavorful."

Contenta dropped the ladle into the soup, and ran back to the kitchen where she collapsed on the floor. The men sprung to their feet and backed away from the table while Señora Esperon and the Carmelite focused their attention on the frog. Scooping it up in both hands the nun deposited it back into the soup while the Señora scolded the archbishop for praying with artificial gladness in his heart. "For shame, Your Excellency, your mind is too much on gemstones. Somewhere on your path to Heaven's gates you have veered off course, and now you expect me, of all people, to right you."

"I told you she was mad," the president whispered to his Secretaries. "Now will you believe me."

Three goldfish jumped from the tureen onto the table, and the Señora chased them with her spidery arms. "I did not know there were so many fish in my pool." she said, "I thought for certain that the frogs had taken care of the overpopulation of fish. Will someone explain to me why they did not? Secretary of natural resources, surely you will be able to answer my scientific inquiry."

The secretary attempted an explanation, and the president, whispering to the others, reminded them that the Señora was certifiably insane, possibly due to the disease of her profession, and that they must pacify her in order to reap the benefits of their visit. On issuing this advice, they all returned joyfully to their seats, and Señora Esperon, assuming the responsibility of the server, balanced the president's bowl in the palm of her hand and brought forth from the tureen one ladle of water grass, one of slime, and yet another containing a spotted goldfish. "Where are the frogs?" she asked mother superior. "Are you hiding them in your habit?"

"I have hidden many things in this habit," mother superior replied with a hearty laugh. "But never a frog."

"She must be drunk," the secretary of commerce whispered to the president.

"She is not drunk," the president said. "She is merely being herself. I knew we should have left her behind."

"Can't you shut her up," natural resources whispered to the archbishop.

"Not even the pope could close her mouth," the archbishop replied.

"What a shame there are so few frogs," Señora Esperon continued. "I wanted frogs in abundance just for our president." Fishing in the tureen with a small net, she added tiny lily pads into the bowl along with a few petals. "Water lilies," she said. "Pretty, pretty. Especially for our guest of honor."

The bowl was passed to the president who quickly covered it

with his napkin. "I am honored to be here," he said. "My brother and cousins join me in thanking you, as does my niece, the daughter of my adopted sister who is with us in spirit."

"God rest my mother's soul," said the Carmelite. "And my grandmother's as well."

"Let us not discuss our extended family tree at table," the archbishop pleaded. "We have other things far more important to discuss."

"Yes, we do," Señora Esperon agreed. "And one of them is food. I am sure you are starving by now."

"Oh, no," the men replied.

"Oh, yes." mother superior spoke as if taking a solemn vow. "We are starving. All of us."

The second to be served, she accepted her soup with steady hands, held the bowl to her lips, and declared her faith. "I believe in the miracle of the Transfiguration." On uttering this declaration she took a sip from the bowl before placing it on the plate. "It is perfectly tasty," she said. "A soup to purify the souls of my kinsmen." A baby goldfish no bigger than a shirt button swam to the surface of her soup. "Oh, no!" she exclaimed, "This child has not yet been transfigured. She captured the fish in a spoon and added it to the archbishop's bowl. "Your prayers are far more favorable than mine," she said. "Perhaps you should give this creature of God some of your purest thoughts."

Suddenly the archbishop was burning hot, but the perspiration running down his face was cold. The churning movement in his bowl of soup bowl caused his stomach to turn sour and his head to swim.

"Poor, poor archbishop," said Señora Esperon. "This day has been a difficult one for Our Excellency, but with the help of his Savior I'm sure he will endure to the last and will be rewarded with a storehouse of good things. Yes, this house could make a splendid orphanage for his young boys."

In response, the archbishop apologized for his inability to digest fish. "It's a reminder of our Lord's only begotten Son," he said. "Only on Friday will my body accept this most holy of feasts."

"What a good thing to know." Señora Esperon stirred the soup vigorously. "Surely I put something in here you can eat, a few snails perhaps?" Into his bowl she deposited snails, algae, and a tiny, red worm whose moral character was questionable but would provide a delicate flavor when mashed with a spoon.

"Thank you graciously," the archbishop managed to say.

Speaking rapidly, the secretary of commerce apologized for his allergy to goldfish, snails, and worms, and the secretary of natural resources as well as the secretary of tourism confessed to the same allergy. "Isn't that unusual," the Señora exclaimed, "three of you at the same table. But, of course, you do come from the same family."

"As far as we know," mother superior added slyly.

Another heavy silence descended upon the Carmelite, but the silence was rapidly broken by the Señora's promise that delicate palates and fragile stomachs would not be exacerbated by her table offerings. She dipped her net far into the soup and brought forth three servings of frog eggs encased in long streamers of gelatinous protein. "The only food guaranteed to combat impotency," she whispered to the secretary of commerce.

"Then you had better give him my portion as well." The secretary of tourism spoke up quickly. "He needs it more than I."

"I will donate mine to the cause also," replied the secretary of natural resources. "In no way do my brother and I wish to deprive our dear cousin of this life-sustaining delicacy. In addition to his cabinet position he is also our Vice president. Should our leader meet an untimely death, the Vice president would be called on take over immediately without physical restraint or debilitation of any kind."

The Señora applauded the donations. "You are generous beyond avarice," she exclaimed. "Both of you."

Then she redistributed the eggs, giving all of them to the secretary of commerce, while resources and tourism were left with green water, mosquito larva, and the Señora's sympathy. "Unfortunately, this is your lot in life." She spoke as though a tragedy had just occurred. "When we over exercise our generosity we often deprive ourselves, but fear not, your rewards are forthcoming. Look! What did I tell you, I have found two tiny frogs, one for each of you. What a pity, neither seems to be breathing very well, so I encourage you to enjoy them while they last."

"I recommend that we put our meal on hold," said the president. "Let us adjourn into your sala, Señora. There we will discuss important matters."

"No! No!" The Señora protested. "We must enjoy our lunch, which is quickly becoming our dinner."

"No! No!" The president stood. His brother and cousins did likewise, and the two women remained seated. "Food can always wait. Let us go into the sala. I have brought along papers requiring signatures."

"We will dine first," Señora Esperon argued. "With our stomachs filled with riches, we will enjoy signing our names to even greater riches."

"We will dine later!" said the president.

"'Try every means of persuasion,'" mother superior advised her hostess. "'Words of thine will find him far more agreeable than mine. Beg! Plead! Give him no rest. Weep, wail and beat thy breasts. Convince him with a piteous show. In thy hands you hold my fate. Go! Decide it, while I wait.'"

"Perfectly spoken!" Señora Esperon exclaimed in astonishment. "But there are no stories in this house too long for the telling. How do you come to know these lines that ripple off your tongue?"

"You are asking me to confess," mother superior replied in a grave voice. "And even I am not given to confessions. But since I have begun to speak at last, I must continue . . ."

"Oh shut up," the president insisted. "Whose side are you on?"

"The truth is," the Carmelite continued, "like so many others who learned to accept this cloistered existence, I did not pass through the convent doors by choice, and neither did some of our most beloved saints. In my case it was the safest choice among many. I am a poet."

"My niece has always expressed ideas entirely her own," said the president.

"We can only guess where they came from," commerce quickly added.

"Tell me this," Señora Esperon asked, "do you find Phèdre sympathetic?"

"The most sympathetic of all tragic heroines," came the answer. "Because she's trapped by the gods in a tapestry that has not been woven by her own hands, she's neither completely innocent nor completely guilty."

"Who are you?" she whispered to the Carmelite. "And what exactly is your name?"

She replied, also in whispers, "I am Josefina Maria de la Paz Serrano y Montejo. It was the name my mother gave me. She chose it for reasons we cannot discuss at this table."

"Then we shall discuss Phèdre," the Señora replied.

The two women continued to discuss the tangled threads of Phèdre's tragedy, and the men, whispering among themselves, agreed to toast the Señora until she collapsed with fatigue and inebriation. "Once she is too drunk to know what she's doing," the president said, "it will be much easier to acquire her signature."

Agreeing to this plan, the gentlemen sat down and the president remained standing to deliver the first tribute.

"Before we begin this wonderful and most generous repast," he said, "I would like to pay my personal respect to a great lady." He spoke on and on, punctuating his speech with an upheld glass and frequent sips of wine. "Enjoy the fruit of our vines," he encouraged the Señora. "Ours is the finest vineyard in the world."

"Oh yes, the very finest," mother superior added. "But that does not mean we must drink as much as the rest of you."

"The alcohol content in our wines is very low," the secretary of commerce interjected. "Therefore, one may drink as much as one likes."

"Please do," Señora Esperon encouraged. "In my house I have always served the best of everything."

While glasses were emptied, the president rambled on in celebration of the Señora's generosity and beauty, but Señora Esperon neither lifted her glass nor closed her eyes; she fixed her gaze attentively not on the president but on the last panel hanging behind him. She read it to herself using near future time rather than the past or the present.

> *Soon the messenger will come.*
> *The guests will depart.*
> *And the food uneaten,*
> *Will be returned to its bowl.*

After the men had raised and emptied many glasses, the president sat down and the secretary of commerce stood up. Extolling upon the pleasures of the Señora's company and her well-appointed table, he held forth with toast after toast. Gesturing and bowing, he painted flowers in the air with his words alone, and when he saw that the Señora was neither inebriated nor fatigued, he bowed to the secretary of natural resources who picked up the threads of praise that had been dropped and spun them into a eulogy of such magnificence, the Señora felt obligated to remind him that she was still counted among the living.

"This is not my funeral," she said, "though it may soon be yours. Please continue."

With a sense of defeat, natural resources sat down and tourism stood up. Light headed with drink, he broke into a cold sweat after his second toast and could not continue. Coming to his rescue, the president, who had also imbibed beyond his capacity, stood quickly only to sit down again.

"I suggest that you remain seated in order to say whatever it is you assume I need to hear," Señora Esperon advised him.

Thanking her for considering his comfort, the president proposed another toast to a great lady. Again glasses were raised and glasses were emptied, at which time the archbishop who had not yet spoken, stood to deliver his personal appreciation.

By then night had descended and fireflies were swarming from the vacant rooms. It was time for the parrots to sleep but their eyes were open and focused on the table. From the bottom of the soup a baby turtle came up for air.

"I'm honored to recapitulate," said the archbishop. Swaying on his feet, he began on a high note of praise and was fast interrupted by a knock at the door.

"The messenger!" Señora Esperon exclaimed with relief. "He has come at last."

The excitement in her voice sent the turtle back to the bottom of the soup and Contenta to the front door. Presently she announced the arrival of another guest, a man from the carnival.

"Show him in," the Señora replied. "He is expected."

The young man, still wearing his orange jumpsuit, was escorted into the courtyard, by one of the presidential guards. "Señora," he said, "the fireworks display will begin shortly, and I have reserved the first ride on the Ferris wheel for you."

The Señora responded:

> *The wheel is blue.*
> *The sky is yellow.*
> *And the night is filled with man made stars.*

"What did you say?" the young man asked.

"I said, that I might be successful in persuading my honored guests to ride the wheel with me. What better place can we find to sign our important papers?"

"None whatever," said the president. "Let us leave this table at once."

"Splendid," cried the archbishop.

And all the secretaries replied:

"Yes."

"Yes."

"Yes. Let us take a ride."

"I never have," mother superior confessed.

"Then you will enjoy yourself all the more," said the president.

"She will stay here," Señora Esperon said firmly. "Surely we have no papers requiring *her* signature. In my bedroom there is a couch facing the window. She will be comfortable there. And she can watch us sign these celebratory documents."

"Very well," agreed the president. "But the rest of us must make an appearance at the carnival. The people expect it. We will sign our documents in the air, and after we return we will enjoy our meal all the more."

"What a splendid plan," the Señora exclaimed. "The soup will surely keep for a later hour."

Resigned to walking in Eufemia's sandals, mother superior chose the shortest path to the marble staircase. The eight parrots flew ahead of her to the gallery. And the honored guests followed the carnival worker and the presidential guards onto the street where barricades had been positioned to clear a direct path from the Señora's house to the Ferris wheel. At the end of the corridor of barricades, they climbed six steps onto a platform and waited for the wheel to turn. Soon the first chair rocked into place, and Señora Esperon offered it to the president who hesitated. Seeing his reluctance she motioned for the crowd to applaud the leader, and the people responded with a thunderous ovation. Flattered by the attention, the president graciously waved to the people, and as further proof that he was a man of good nature, he took the first seat and invited the Señora to join him. "I will take a seat below you," she said. "We will be able to pass the documents back and forth. What a sight it will be for our countrymen."

The crowd continued to applaud, and the president commanded the Señora to ride in his chair. "Give me your papers," she said, "I shall sign one of them now." The president handed her a folio of papers, and she quickly signed over the deed to her property.

Smiling broadly, the president applauded the Señora's generosity, and reminded her that more signatures were required. "I have marked the pages," he said.

"I will sign them all," she replied. Then she lifted an arm to signal the attendant.

"Take him up!" she said.

The lever was pulled. The wheel turned. The president fell back into his seat. And the next chair was moved into position.

"The secretary of commerce," she announced. The people applauded on cue. The secretary sat down, and the Señora signed another document before crying out, "Take him up!"

Again the wheel turned, and the next seat appeared, and the secretary of natural resources stepped forward. The crowd applauded when he sat down, and again the Señora signed her name, and yet again she signaled the attendant to take him up

"Next! The secretary of tourism."

The crowd applauded. The daughter signed her name. And the wheel took him up.

"Next! The archbishop in magnificent robes."

Again the crowd applauded. Again she signed her name.

And the wheel turned.
And the yellow sky descended on the celebration.

"Give them a long ride," Señora Esperon said to the young man. He pulled the lever. The first round of fireworks exploded in the evening sky, and the next seat swung into position, but the Señora refused to accept it.

"You do not wish to ride also?" he asked. "I promised the first to you."

"I thank you in ways you may never understand," she replied. "But I do not accept rides on nights when the stars are made by man."

The attendant pulled the lever again, and the wheel entered the first of many revolutions.

"What will happen," the Señora asked, "if that lever is removed?"

"The wheel will go on spinning forever," the attendant told her.

"Then give it to me," she said.

"My boss will not like that," he replied. But he gave her the lever anyway and she concealed it in the folds of Fuerte's tunic.

"Your boss need never know," she whispered. Holding tightly to the lever and the signed documents, she offered her free arm to the attendant who escorted her off the platform and back to the door. "My table was not to their liking," she said, "but your invitation was both timely and well received. You have played an important role in a drama that we did not create but were obligated to finish."

"May I visit you one day, Señora, I promise not to stay very long."

"It is too late for visits," she answered. "Why is your Ferris wheel blue?"

"Because it always has been," he replied.

"Just as I suspected," she said. "Everything is, and always will be. Nothing was, that will not be again."

Behind them the presidential party completed its second revolution on the wheel and far above them fireworks lit up the sky. "Look, Señora!" The young man pointed to a column of sparks falling into the crowd, but Señora Esperon had already stepped inside her house and was closing the door. "Forgive me for leaving you so abruptly," she said. "The day has been a very long one. And it is not yet over."

"Wait," he said. "Don't leave me. I want to be a great lover, a great poet, and a great president."

"Then you will need this." From the pocket of her dress she removed Serrano's pistol and placed it in the young man's hands. "Promise me that it will never be used as anything other than a reminder of our greatest president."

"I was born in his village," the young man replied.

"This comes as no surprise," Señora Esperon said and quickly closed the door behind her.

Relieved to be alone again, she paused in the courtyard to admire the tapestry hanging three times around in candlelight and in shadows. For a moment she questioned her fate: How can I just leave it hanging here? Surely, there's a better way.

There is no other way, Fuerte reminded her. Her voice emanated from the threads of the tapestry, from her dark room, and open grave.

Let it hang three times around your courtyard. After my death it will be read, and read again. And the first reader will be the survivor. And the survivor will carry it forth into the world.

Señora Esperon looked up to the opened door of the weaver's room. "Fuerte, are you there?"

"Yes, my daughter," came the answer. "I am in my room. I am coming to the last line, the very last thread."

"And so am I," sighed the Señora.

While Roman candles exploded in the night and sparks fell like a rain of fire on the glass ceiling, Señora Esperon poured the soup and every living creature back into the lotus pool. Supported by the soft breeze eternally trapped inside her courtyards, and accompanied by constellations of fireflies, which she knew to be the souls of her dead loves, she climbed the stairs to her apartment redolent of dust, of many pots of smoldering incense, of sandalwood, copal, and time. There she opened the French doors onto her balcony and stepped outside to view the city she had once loved, now a noisy crush of citizens forced to work too hard and for little reason other than diverting their minds from the inevitable. A dark night had settled over the capital, and the aromas from many food stalls had obliterated the acrid smell of factory smoke. "But it will return," she reminded herself, "and all too soon."

Leaning over the balcony she waved to her guests, barely touching their hands as they passed before her. "This night will be remembered always," she called to them. "Never has there been such a celebration."

In the parlor mother superior was laughing like a young girl and the parrots perched on tables and chairs were chattering madly among themselves. "I should have gone with them," she said. "What fun this would have been."

"Your place is here with me," Señora Esperon said. "I am reminding you of something you should already know."

From the wheel, the presidential party could see her sweeping the floor.

"Why has she chosen this moment to clean her house?" the archbishop shouted to his brothers. Before his startled eyes, she swept gemstones over the balcony and into the street. Rubies, diamonds, sapphires, and opals fell into the crowd. Behind the jewels came silver coins, and behind the silver coins came gold ones, and behind the gold came paper notes of all denominations.

And in the final panel, the weaver wove that which she had already predicted and had now come to pass:

And the blue wheel turned and kept turning.
The yellow sky slowly descended.
And the crowd was made happy by extraordinary gifts.

The presidential guards abandoned their posts to stuff their pockets and hats. The people scrambled on hands and knees to fill their purses, their shoes, anything that would contain one more coin, one more jewel, one more paper note.

"No!" the members of the president's party shouted from the wheel.

"Do not give everything away!"

"Think of your friends!"

"There are better ways to distribute your wealth!"

In response, Señora Esperon hurled fists of paper notes into the Ferris wheel. The secretary of tourism, stood in his chair, and grabbed them from the air.

"Get some for me," the archbishop shouted.

"Get your own," the president said. Standing on his chair he plucked money from the wind and stuffed his pockets full. On the next revolution he was prepared to jump onto the Señora's balcony. "Follow me," he shouted to his party. "We must stop her."

When the wheel was positioned high, and the president was leaning over the rigging, Señora Esperon ripped the documents she had just signed and threw the pieces to the president who reached for them with both hands. "Help me catch them," he shouted. "They can be pieced together."

And then he fell. And the Señora relaxed for the first time that day. And mother superior covered her eyes. And the parrots were silent.

The blue wheel turned and kept turning.
Another round of man-made stars exploded in the skies.
And the moon, which could not be seen,
*   rained torrents of blood.*

Wedged into the spokes of the Ferris wheel, the president was crushed against the platform, and his body was carried on many revolutions high above the crowd. Intestines hung from his lacerated stomach like bright garlands of flowers draped over the steel ribs and the inner workings of the blue wheel that turned and kept turning, sending a spray of blood, like a soft evening shower, falling onto the heads of the Independence Day celebrants who continued searching the street for another coin. Nothing had been seen and nothing felt. Nothing except a drop of warm blood on the back of a neck, on the back of a hand. One drop of something warm followed by another shower of gold coins falling from the balcony like confetti into open mouths and hands. And when there was nothing left on the floor to be swept into the street, Señora Esperon threw finger rings, earrings, necklaces, and bracelets into the crowd. "It is almost over," she said. "At last my hour has arrived."

The people fell upon their hands and knees,
But not in prayer.
And the wheel turned and kept turning.
The sky rained riches.
The yellow cloud descended upon the entire city.

And the survivor bore witness to all.

"Stop the wheel," mother superior cried. "Doesn't anyone see this horror? Am I the only one?"

As if she were following directions in a drama written especially for her, she limped her way to the table where Señora Esperon was folding papers into a large envelope. "We must cease this horror!" she cried. But the Señora did not respond. And neither did the parrots. Outside the poisonous cloud had fallen on the carnival and a golden fog was drifting through the house. On the Street of Merchants and Peddlers the oxygen tents were filled to capacity. Women and children were hurrying to find shelter, and the Señora's honored guests were holding hats and handkerchiefs to their faces.

"Help us," they cried.

"We cannot breathe."

"Stop the wheel," mother superior begged. "I don't care what they've done. Stop the wheel."

"If it's to be stopped only you will stop it," Señora Esperon replied.

She closed the French doors to the balcony and bolted them. She placed a chair in front of the doors and invited the Carmelite to sit down. "From here," Señora Esperon said, "you will have the best view."

The Carmelite watched the blue wheel churning the heavy air. "Will they live?" she asked.

"Their kind will always live."

"And what of us?"

"What of us?" the Señora asked in return. "My life is almost over. But yours, is only just beginning. Your life will be long, very, very long and your task most difficult, but that too is your fate."

"What is my task?"

"To understand everything that has been recorded; everything that has gone before and everything that is to come." Señora Esperon placed Fuerte's alphabet and the key to the tapestry in the Carmelite's lap. "It is all recorded here," she said. "Everything that Fuerte was allowed to know. Even the death of your dog-eared grandfather has been carefully set down. It was on this street that he shot my father, and I marked him by removing his ear, which I have kept as a reminder of everything that I must accomplish. But that is not all. In Fuerte's tapestry, which you will learn to read, you will see how the ruling members of your family demolished our most beautiful buildings, poisoned our air, our marshes, and our ocean, annihilated our poets. Villages were destroyed. Lives were lost. And today it is impossible to recognize the original inhabitants of this land. It is impossible to see a blouse or a dress and know instantly the history of the family as well as the village where the cloth was woven and embroidered. Today everyone speaks the same language, and it is not the language of the poets. You may say that our poets were murdered with clubs and knives, that your family was their greatest enemy, but I say their greatest enemy was mediocrity."

Mother superior bowed her head and wept. "I do not wish to be reminded of such horrible deeds."

"Our wishes are of no importance," Señora Esperon replied.

From somewhere within the folds of her black robes the Carmelite brought forth a small book bound in red leather. "Here's the rest of our story," she said. "This was found in the Hotel Carmina before it was destroyed. Many years later my mother bought it for a handsome price, and on the night she so mysteriously disappeared, she gave it to my father who was a family servant. On the night he was called into the courtyard and executed he left it in my bed. I was thirteen years old. We were living in the highlands. My uncles were plotting another revolution. My parents had been secretly working for the opposition, and the Forty Years of Peace was rapidly coming to an end."

"And you entered the convent."

"At the age of eighteen. As I have said, it was the only safe place for a poet. After all, I am my mother's daughter. And she was Carlota Montejo's only daughter. Unmistakably so."

Stunned by what she had just heard, Señora Esperon opened the journal to a marked page on which Carlota Montejo had listed the birthdays of her nine sons and one daughter. The first child had been conceived with a sea captain, the second with a Gypsy, the third with a monk, the fourth and fifth with Serrano and the sixth with the matador, José Maria de Vega. "My poet!" Señora Esperon said.

"Read on," mother superior insisted. "You cannot stop now."

After the birth of the matador's son, Carlota Montejo had listed three more children. Two of them were sons sired by the doctor. "My father!" Señora Esperon exclaimed. "Two of my poets may have been my brothers, but which two?" Of her tenth, and last, child, a daughter, Carlota had written: "My only girl. Her father, the mayor, a very ugly little man with moles. He made an impressive donation to my orphanage."

"Now you know," the Carmelite said. "That one night produced my mother, who was destroyed by her father's family." Hearing herself say this, she wept on her sleeve and into her hands. And when she finally stopped weeping and looked up again, the Señora was holding a tray with a silver chalice, a blue bowl, and a crust of bread.

"Now," she said, "we will celebrate communion."

"I am not worthy of the sacrament," mother superior confessed.

"Of this sacrament you are worthy," Señora Esperon replied. "You have earned it."

The Carmelite sank to her knees. The parrots flew to the floor and climbed the folds of her habit. They perched on her arms, shoulders, and head.

"The parrots are our witnesses," Señora Esperon said. "They are at the top of the tree in the animal kingdom because they have the ability to recognize the truth." Then she poured wine into the chalice and prepared the sacrament on a crust of bread.

"I give you food for body and spirit," she said. "May this feast renew your strength, purify your heart and mind, and preserve the memory of all that has passed before your eyes today and yesterday and all the days to come. Although your life will not be blessed with great happiness, you shall pass through the portals of honor and mercy and many thousands shall follow you. And your poems and the poems of my dead loves will be remembered, forever and evermore."

"Forever," said a parrot.

"Forever," said the Carmelite. She accepted into her mouth the crust of bread garnished with a sliver of meat. "It tastes of metal and unguents," she said. "Give me water!" The chalice was held to her lips and she drank as if parched, swallowing not only the wine but the Host as well.

"What have you given me," she asked, choking on the sacrament. "What have I eaten?"

"The sins of your grandfather and all who are like him," Señora Esperon replied. She placed the blue bowl in the Carmelite's lap and commanded her to eat. In the bowl, the remains of her grandfather's ear had been sliced and fitted together again like the pieces of a puzzle. "May this sacrament be a constant reminder of the evil that consumes us all. Eat so I may die in peace. So that I may die with the knowledge that you and everyone after you will forever remember what has been done."

The survivor consumed the sins of her mother's father,
And the family that bore him.
And when the bowl was empty,
It was filled with wine.
And the wine was drunk.
And the bowl was washed.
And in observing this celebration,
The survivor accepted the sins of the world.

After the sacrament had been consumed, Señora Esperon placed the envelope of legal documents into the Carmelite's hands. "You have inherited the parrots," she said. "And the parrots have inherited this house, and therefore the house is also yours. There

is a second deed to the property that clearly states this if anyone should question it, but I am quite certain that no one will."
The Carmelite received the envelope and held it against her heart.
"Everything is yours," Señora Esperon continued. "This house of
forty-three rooms, four balconies, two courtyards, and eight parrots. Yours. And everything inside this house is yours also. Within
these thick walls and in many small closets hidden all about, you
will find dozens of trunks; all of them overflowing with riches."

"I have taken the vow of poverty," the Carmelite said.

"And for that reason, you have wealth," Señora Esperon
replied.

Slowly, the Carmelite opened the envelope, and on seeing her
name Josefina Maria de la Paz Serrano y Montejo, inscribed on
the deed, her hands trembled and the papers fell to the floor. "I
have desired this for so long," she said, "and now that I have it, I
also fear it."

"From my mother," Señora Esperon said, "I learned that desires are often extravagant and needs modest. I also learned that
there is no reason to fear that which is beyond our control. It is
useless to argue with Fate."

"And what else?"

"From my mother I learned that Fate does not preclude
certain choices, therefore, it is possible to choose your day, but
not before your time. And now my time has come and my day
chosen; the pattern of this tangled life has been woven down to
the last thread."

"Don't leave me," mother superior begged. She stared into
the yellow night where the wheel was turning. "I cannot watch
this alone."

"You are not alone," Señora Esperon replied. "You have the
parrots. They chose you. And you also have the pilgrims."

"The parrots will always have a home here," she said touching each of them on the head. "And the pilgrims will always be
welcomed."

Beyond the balcony she could see only the bare outlines

of the wheel on which her uncle's body hung like an ornament. She forced herself to see him, and the others as well. They were slumped over in their chairs, their faces buried in their hands as if they had died of shame. Nothing moved except the wheel.

"I promise you this will be a humble house," said the Carmelite. "A dwelling place for the spirit, for all those who have lived here and died here; and for those who will go on living and dying behind these walls, let this house belong to them as well."

"Forever," Señora Esperon said.

"Forever and ever," the Carmelite replied. "For as long as this frail earth may exist."

"There is one thing more, that I request of you," Señora Esperon said. "Keep our blue bowls filled with water and flowers. Someone will do the same for you." She placed the lever in the nun's hands as if it were a scepter. "Only this will stop the wheel," she said. Then she removed the poet's dusty manuscript from a bookshelf. "This," she said, "is the poet's sixth poem, and it is not for you." She embraced the Carmelite and left the room.

On an easy breath, the easiest she had drawn that day, Señora Esperon descended the steps into the courtyard where Contenta was waiting.

"What have you done?" she asked, already afraid of the answer.

"You'll find out soon enough," Señora Esperon replied. In her hands she carried the poet's manuscript as if it was a serving tray, and resting on top of it was a bag of gold coins. "This is enough money to see you through your last days, but the manuscript is the true gift. It is a book of heart-rending sorrow."

"Will it make me weep again?" Contenta asked.

"That is the reason I give it to you. Now go, quickly."

Before Contenta could move, sirens sounded in every quarter of the city, and a squadron of policemen in gas masks arrived at the front entrance. "Open up," they shouted beating against the door with fists and clubs.

"They're coming for me now," she said. "I assume they wish

to ask me how to stop the wheel, and if not that, they wish to arrest me for inciting a riot. In either case, they are too late." She quickly rolled her father's chair into the shadows of the orange trees and sat down.

"Señora!" Contenta said. "What are we going to do?"

"You are going to leave by way of the side door," she calmly replied. "But I will stay. This is my final hour."

"And how will it end?" Contenta trembled at the thought of receiving the answer.

"It will end when I close my eyes," Señora Esperon said. "Do not mourn for me when I am dead, Contenta. This life has been a long voyage over a tempestuous sea, but the next one will surely be more peaceful. My companions are waiting for me. I can hear their restless sighs. I have kept them waiting too long."

"Who are your companions?" Contenta looked up to see if they might be waiting on the gallery.

"An angel, a doctor, and a saint accompanied by many poets," she said. "And very soon a weaver of poetry will join us."

Suddenly, there were more sirens; another squadron of policemen arrived, and the pounding at the front door became louder. "Leave now Contenta," Señora Esperon said. "Leave, and do not return. By the time they get in, I will no longer be here."

Unable to move, Contenta stood there embracing the poet's last poem.

"Leave!" Señora Esperon commanded. She rose from her chair and struck Contenta on the face. "Leave!" she said again. "You must not endanger yourself on my account."

Contenta fled through the narrow passage and across the small courtyard to the side entrance. Breathing through a damp cloth, which she held tightly to her face, she opened the door onto the avenue, and only after Señora Esperon heard the door slam and the ancient key turning in the lock, did she return to her father's chair and the fragrant shadows of her mother's trees. She admired Fuerte's tapestry for the final time and then she closed her eyes.

Before long the streets were blocked off, and the police

were knocking at both entrances. They pounded the thick doors with hammers and clubs. They shot their pistols into the air, and demanded to be let in. To their surprise the front door opened. The Carmelite stood in the portal and confronted them. "This house is mine," she said. "You may not enter. But you may have this lever. It will stop the wheel." A policeman took the lever, and the door was closed and bolted. Then the survivor returned to Eufemia's chapel. She removed her habit and put on Señora Esperon's kimono that smelled faintly of camphor. The parrots called to her from Eufemia's chapel. They had perched on the long table that the survivor had already appropriated as her desk. On the table were pens and paper on which the first lines of a poem had already been written. It would be the first of many poems she would compose in her house of forty-three rooms, two courtyards, and four balconies.

Drifting away in her father's chair, Señora Esperon heard everything as if from a great distance as if she had already passed on to the other side. Candle moths and fireflies swarmed around her, and a cool breeze caressed her face. All around her the wind chimes were announcing her victory, and off in another part of the house, servants she had never known were praying softly to an invalid saint. Somewhere there was music: a harp, a lute, and a piano. But what was the song? Somewhere there was poetry. But what was the poem, and who was the poet?

"The poet's name is of no importance," she said in answer to her own question. "Importance is never the poet but always the poem."

Suddenly her head drooped. Her arms relaxed and fell to her side, and the wheel stopped turning. Another round of fireworks exploded beyond the yellow clouds, and pistols were fired into the air in celebration of a new day. But Señora Esperon, who had already left her tired body behind, could not hear the explosions or the celebratory shouts of victory. She heard nothing except the wind trapped in the courtyards, the wind, the wind chimes, and Fuerte at her loom:

We only came to sleep.
We only came to dream.
It is not true,
It is not true,
That we came to live on the earth.

Edward Swift made his debut as a novelist in 1978 with Splendora, which The Houston Chronicle praised as one of the year's best comic novels. He has published six acclaimed novels as well as a memoir, My Grandfather's Finger. For many years Mr. Swift studied creative writing and literature with the legendary teacher and novelist, Marguerite Young. Also a visual artist, his sculpture and constructions have been exhibited in Miguel Herrera's 2/20 Gallery in New York City, the Museo de la Ciudad de Querétaro, the Museo Historico de la Sierra Gorda, and Fábrica la Aurora in San Miguel de Allende. He lives in Mexico.

www.edwardswiftartist.com

Acknowledgements;

I wish to thank Lulu Torbet whose comments and suggestions were invaluable to the final manuscript. I also express my deepest gratitude to Janet Byrne, Hope Swann and David Stanford Burr for superb editorial advice. A special thanks goes to Kelley Vandiver for the cover painting and to Zonagráfica for the cover design and layout. Finally, I thank my cousin Tracy Shopkorn for many years of encouragement and support on all fronts.

Book design by Zonagráfica
Cover design by Ernesto Herrera; layout by Paola Vera
The cover painting by Kelley Vandiver

What has been said about Edward Swift's Other Books

Splendora

Edward Swift has a particular gift for capturing the continuous low musical murmur of small-town gossip. He knows how stories seem to grow on their own, drifting almost unnoticeably toward the mythical. –Anne Tyler, The New York Times Book Review

Miss Spellbinder's Point of View:
A Biography of the Imagination

Much of Miss Spellbinder's Point of View is witty; some of it is gorgeous; some of it is disturbing; some of it is simply exhausting in its ingenuity. Over all it is like cotton candy spun of glass - glistening, insubstantial, and a deadly weapon. –Richard Dyer, The Boston Globe

A Place With Promise

A Place with Promise is a dignified, stately, intelligent book — everything a novel should be. – Carolyn See, Los Angeles Times

A Place with Promise has the surprising timeless particularity and inevitability of fable, and the clear-running stream of Swift's prose.–Richard Dyer, The Boston Globe

My Grandfather's Finger

From neighbors dwelling in bomb shelters to an island inhabited by albinos, and from atomic bombs to carnivals and amputated fingers kept in jars, Swift's portrayal of his childhood is not the usual nostalgic treatment. Instead, there is a darkness lurking about the edges of this town and about the edges of these stories, which lends strength to the author's memories and contributes to the success of this collection.–Booklist

Happily, the author manages to avoid the sentimentality of some other recent memoirs; though he shows great affection for his childhood friends and family, he harbors no illusions about them. Especially resonant are Swift's portraits of the women of his family, particularly his mother, who was widowed in WWII and became the anchor of his extended family. He provides a funny, mournful depiction of her as a woman who "was about transcending sadness with laughter." The mythic South at its most entertaining.–Kirkus Review of Books

Principia Martindale

Edward Swift has a sharp eye, a sharper ear and moral sense. In his new book (Principia Martindale) he leaves [Ronald] Firbank far behind – not without a nostalgic glance at Splendora— and rises to the *savae indignatios*, the savage indignation of another Swift, surely a distant relative, Jonathan by name.–Richard Dyer, The Boston Globe

Magically textured with an un-intrusive network of symbols, yet ripe and angry too: a funny/sad, acidulous scrutiny of folks whose arms are too short to box God in. –Kirkus Review of Books

The Christopher Park Regulars

Selected by the editors of the New York Times Book Review as a notable book of the year, 1989

...a rare and startling treasure. –Ellen Pall, The New York Times Book Review

www.ingramcontent.com/pod-product-compliance
Lightning Source LLC
Chambersburg PA
CBHW060947030726
47503CB00003B/767